I0565238

FIRE FINCH

WHEN TOMORROW CALLS

• SERIES •

1. Why You Were Taken (2015)

2. How We Found You (2017)

3. What Have We Done (2017)

ALSO BY JT LAWRENCE

The Memory of Water (2011)

Sticky Fingers (2016)

The Underachieving Ovary (2016)

Grey Magic (2016)

WHAT HAVE WE DONE

JT LAWRENCE

FIRE FINCH
www.firefinchpress.com

What Have We Done is a work of fiction.

Names, characters, places and incidents are the product of the author's imagination or are used fictitiously. Any resemblance to actual persons, living or dead, events, or locales is entirely coincidental.

2017 Paperback edition

ISBN-13: 978-0-9947234-1-3

1st Edition

Copyright © 2017 JT LAWRENCE

JT Lawrence has asserted her right to be identified as the author of this work. No part of this book may be reproduced or transmitted in any form or by any means, mechanical or electronic without written permission from the author.

All rights reserved.

Published in South Africa by Fire Finch Press, an imprint of Pulp Books.

www.jt-lawrence.com

Cover typography by Stuart Bache of Books Uncovered

Stock images by Shutterstock, NeoStock, Freepik and Unsplash.

Set in Bell MT

DEDICATION

This book is dedicated to the loyal readers of this series
who first encouraged me to write a sequel to
'Why You Were Taken'. It's been a ride! Thank you.

WHAT HAVE WE DONE

TEAL TRESPASSER

The Gordhan Hospital

Johannesburg, 2024

"I'm telling you again," comes Keke's terse whisper from behind one of the unisex restroom doors. "I'm telling you again to leave me alone."

Kate suspects Keke's talking on her phone, so she's shocked when she hears a reply. Bright nerves flash through her (Cadmium Current). She turns away from the smart mirror and forgets about the spilt mascara on her cheeks.

"Keke, please, just hear me out," says a man.

"No!" says Keke. "I'm not gonna do it. I can't."

"I'm not going to hurt her. I promise. All I need is—"

"Is that what you told the friends of your other victims?"

"Victims? Keke, what are you talking about?"

"The cops were here, Zack. They told me everything."

"You're going to believe the *police?* Really?"

"You killed Helena Nash."

"Helena Nash killed herself."

What the fuck? thinks Kate, adrenaline rising. She sneaks a little closer to the door.

"You helped her. And those others," says Keke. "I'm leaving."

There is a scuffle.

"Let me go. Let me go or I'll scream."

"Keke. Listen to me, please—"

"I'll pay you back, okay? I'll find a way."

Kate frowns. *Pay him back? What the hell is going on here?*

She tiptoes closer, her heart banging in her chest.

"You don't have to pay me back! This isn't about quid pro quo. It's about something far bigger than that. All I need you to do is—"

"No! Kate has been through enough. She can't deal with this. Let me go."

Kate feels a flare of anger. She slides open the door, and Keke and the man turn to look at her. His fingers are wrapped around her forearm.

"Let go of her arm," says Kate.

"Kate." He's good looking, dressed in a sharp dark suit and a silk tie. Teal Trespasser. "I have something I have to tell you."

"Then tell me." Kate can't remember ever meeting the man, but something about him is familiar. As if she's seen him before, on the homescreen, or in a dream.

"Not here," says Zack. "Not like this."

"I don't know who you are, and I'm not gonna play games with you," says Kate. "Tell me what's going on."

"It's complicated."

"Who sent you?"

"Now, that's an interesting question."

Kate glares at him.

He rubs his lips. "You wouldn't believe me if I told you."

There's a purple hammering behind Kate's eyes. It's exhaustion or frustration or, more likely, a debilitating blend of both. She has the inappropriate urge to slink down onto the hard cold floor and close her eyes for a long time.

Why does she attract the crazies? She's had enough crackers people in her life. From now on, she only wants conversations with sane people. Nice, non-crackers people who don't drag her into surreal, unpredictable worlds.

"You're wasting our time," says Kate, ready to leave. She wants to get back to Mally and Silver in the hospital ward. The purple hammering gets darker, starts tipping towards indigo.

Zack looks at the micro-camera in the corner of the ceiling, and whispers, "Is there somewhere we can meet?"

Kate scowls at the idea. "You really think I'd agree to that? What's next? Sweets from your trenchcoat pocket? No, there is not *somewhere we can meet.*"

Zack shows her his palms in surrender. He has beautiful hands, and Kate's annoyed at herself for noticing. Now is certainly not the time to appreciate them or the depth of his eyes (Stardust Surveillers). She needs to get out of here right now.

"Hurry up!" Keke fidgets, and Zack shoots her a look. What are they not telling her?

"Zack is a suicide agent," says Keke.

"A what-what? I don't know what that means."

The Suicide Contagion is pervasive, but what do the unlucky lemmings have to do with her?

"This will be difficult for you to understand, at first," he says, "but for the sake of your children I need you to have

4

an open mind—"

For the sake of my children? Kate takes a step away from him. He advances on her, gripping her arm. Firm, and thrilling.

"You're not threatening my kids."

"No! No. The opposite. I'm here to save them. To save you all. It's what I've been put here to do. It's the reason I—"

Kate is about to ask—*save us from what?* But there's a crash as a squad of men in black kevlarskin and exoscales break through the main door and flatten Zack against the sonic shower tiles. Kate cries out in alarm as she grabs Keke and they move away from the aggressive men, bumping into the basins behind them. Panic paints her insides a shrill shade of yellow. The men are shouting at Zack, jamming oiled gunmetal into his cheek. Telling him not to move, not to try anything stupid, not to breathe. Kate spots a glint of a police badge. They force his arms up against the wall and frisk him with gloved hands.

Detective Ramphele trails in and nods at a stone-eyed Keke, who nods back.

The men turn Zack around. "Girdler," the detective says, blinking, as if he doesn't quite believe what he's seeing. Zack is calm, his eyes unflecked by fear. Ramphele looks at Zack with something akin to admiration as he caresses the revolver in the harness strapped to his hip. "Zachary Girdler. I never thought I'd see the day."

"Zack. I'm sorry. I didn't have a choice." Keke's face

darkens, as if clouds have raced over the sun.

Unspoken words echo in the air: *You always have a choice.*

"They were going to arrest me for conspiring with you in Helena Nash's murder," says Keke. "They had me in cuffs and Marko was dying. The twins were missing. I was desperate. It was the only way they'd agree to—"

Zack clenches his jaw, says, "You did what you needed to do," but his eyes say *Jesus, Keke, what have you done?*

Kate's stomach percolates with dread. Her instinct tells her this shouldn't be happening, that this is not part of the plan.

But what plan? Whose plan?

Violence scents the air. Things are happening too quickly and Kate wants to stop and scroll backwards. The men snap smartcuffs on Zack and shove him forward.

"Don't take your eyes off him," says Detective Ramphele. "Not for a second, d'you hear me?"

"Yes, sir."

"He's a slippery motherfucker."

Zack doesn't take his eyes off Kate. It's as if a live wire connects them.

"Wait!" she shouts, but they don't.

Kate's desperate now to know what he needs to tell her, but the cops are all over him. She has the feeling that something vital is spooling away from her and if she doesn't grab on to it right now she'll regret it forever.

"Please, wait!" she shouts again.

"You have to come and find me," says Zack, "so that I can give you the message. You need to know. Your life depends on it."

The testosterone squad bustle Zack out of the restroom.

"I'll get you the best lawyer!" Keke yells after him. "I'll come see you!"

Ramphele shouts a laugh. "Where Girdler is going, you'll never see him again."

PART I

FUNERAL CAKE

1

TWELVE YEARS LATER

Seth's Apartment

Johannesburg, 2036

Kate takes another bite of the funeral cake. "What do you think?"

"Mm," Keke says, still chewing, "If this cake was a person I'd take him home and—"

Seth clears his throat, and she doesn't finish her sentence.

At forty-something, Keke still has that violet glint of mischief in her eyes. She winks at Seth, and he winks back.

"It's good." Keke clicks her tongue. "*Imnandi.* I'd go with this one. The other two were good, but … what's this one called again?"

Kate frowns. When her line of vision connects with the holotag, the name of the cake appears. "Death by Choxolate."

Keke snorts. "Ah, well, at least they have a sense of humour."

"Dark humour," says Kate.

"Perfect for the funeral business."

"They've got a lot to smile about," says Seth. "Have you seen how much they charge? I'm in the wrong business entirely."

"And what business is that, Mr Denicker?" Keke leans her leather-clad hip against the kitchen island's granite counter. "Last time I saw you, you were about to start at The Company That Shall Not Be Named."

"I'm still there."

Keke straightens her back. "Doing?"

"Advanced chemgineering. What else?"

"Home or away?"

"Sorry?"

"Are you working for them, or against them?"

"Ah, you know. The usual. A bit of both."

They snicker, but the truth is that if Bilchen even got a sniff of the fact that Seth was a biopunk hacktivist, he'd probably be thrown into some kind of (trademarked) dungeon.

"I keep expecting them to come to their senses and make me disappear."

Keke taps her chin. "Maybe they have a plan for you."

"Ja," says Kate. "One that involves luring you in and then chopping you up for iguana food."

Seth smiles. "With their reputation, it would hardly come as a surprise."

Keke licks some frosting off her fingertip. "Lucky iguanas."

"And with that sense of humour," says Kate, "you should be in the funeral biz."

Keke eyes what's left of the cake. "Don't tempt me."

"Who knew there'd be so much bank to be made in the urban death industry?"

"I love the way you say 'urban death industry'."

"Ha ha," says Kate, clearing away the confexionary boxes.

"But you guys seem to be coping well with your mom's

illness," says Keke. "How are you feeling about everything?"

Seth shrugs. "We're dealing, but it's weird, you know? Planning a funeral for someone who is still … alive."

She won't be for long. Kate blinks away the tears that sting her sinuses.

Funeral parties are trending this spring. Woke wakes are all the rage.

WHY WAIT TILL YOU ARE DEAD? is one of the less-subtle headlines Kate's seen on the forever-hovering city holoboards she wishes she could swat away. It costs more than a million blox to switch off the automatic ads that float into your neuroreality vision. Kate's always called it outright blackmail and refused to pay the ransom, but lately her resolve is sliding. She's tired of the constant laser-targeted marketing trying to scratch her eyes out. She imagines going for an old-fashioned walk along the purple-blossomed jacaranda streets with nothing crowding her vision—just breathing in the fresh air.

I mean, what's next? She'd demanded of Seth. *Are they going to make us pay to* breathe?

Seth had raised his eyebrows as if to say he wouldn't be surprised. As it is, inane people are buying up bags of Alpine Air as if their lives depend on it. Which in a way they will, if the SMOG score climbs much higher. Creeps are digging out their old Superbug masks and adding new bespoke touches: satin patches, copper rivets, intricate stitching, hand-sewn or thread-printed with their latest avatar and/or slogo.

The front door bangs closed. Bonechaser jumps up from her bed and runs to the front of the house. A flurry of happy pink barks peels into the air around Kate.

"Mally? Is that you?"

"We'll be in the cineroom!" shouts Mally, and a different door bangs shut.

What is it about teenagers slamming doors?

"If he breaks that Securodoor again, it's coming out of his allowance," says Seth.

"If a moody sixteen-year-old can break a hundred thousand rand security door, it deserves to be broken," says Keke. "I mean, what are you going to do in event of a Zombiepocalypse? You're going to *not* slam the door?"

"You're like them, you know," says Seth. "You have an answer for everything."

"I'll take that as a compliment!" Keke bats her eyelashes at him.

"No wonder you guys get on so well," says Kate.

There's something about Kekeletso that's always been youthful, quick curiosity and lithe limbs. She's always up for trying something new; just last week she was learning how to fly a Volanter. Her hot energy makes her skin glow.

On the other side of the scale, trauma and the sleep-dep that comes with parenthood has taken its toll on Kate, as she's reminded every morning when her swingbed mirror chime wakes her. She can feel she's growing older but is still surprised when she notices new textures on her skin: hashtags on the sides of her fingers; overnight crêpe on her wrists. Keke, on the other hand, gets work done regularly, after years of saying she'd never. She calls it 'saving face'.

I can't do lunch today. I'm at the spa, saving face.

But even on haggard days, Kate's not tempted to inject neurotoxic proteins and stem cells into her wrinkles. In a way, she's happy to grow older, finds herself less anxious, and more at ease with life, despite the constant challenges the kids throw her way. The vacuumbot glides in, seemingly happy for the opportunity to do some work, and inhales the sweet crumbs off the kitchen floor.

"Would it be wrong to go with the same cake for the twins' party on the weekend?"

"The funeral cake? Probably," says Keke. "But who cares? What have you planned for their birthday, anyway? Barcade? Light Jugglers? Mars Immersia? Drone ballet? None of them quite say *Sweet Sixteen*, do they?"

"Ha," says Seth.

"More like Not-So-Sweet." Kate calls up the twins' party-planning list and ticks off 'CAKE'. All the other boxes remain unchecked.

"*What* are you talking about?" asks Keke. "Your kids are the best. You *know* they're the best."

"Ha," says Seth again.

"Have you *met* other teenagers? They're vile. They're despicable. I cross the street when I see teenagers."

"Okay, so ours aren't that bad," says Kate, "but—"

"What's up? Is it Mally? His new girlfriend?"

Kate shudders.

"I wish you wouldn't do that," says Seth.

She shoots him a look: *sorry-not-sorry*. She can't help it that she gets chills when Vega walks in the door.

"It's just … weird, you know? It takes some getting used to."

First a robotic dog and then—

"And you just let them spend time in there, unchaperoned? That's very *avant-garde* of you."

"Their quality time is the least of our worries," says Seth. "It's Silver who's giving Kate grey hairs."

Kate touches the silver floss in her fringe. The streak of white has multiplied overnight.

"How very Marie Antoinette of you," says Keke, and smiles at the plates, empty of cake.

"I want to get her into some kind of rehab," says Kate.

Keke flinches. "What? Silver? Why?"

"You're overreacting," says Seth. "Silver's behaviour is totally normal."

"Her behaviour is not normal!" says Kate. "She's immersed *all the time.*"

"Normal," says Keke.

"Sometimes she doesn't speak to us for days. She forgets to eat, because she eats in the immersion, but then forgets that she has to eat in real life too."

"Normal."

"Have you seen how skinny she is? She fainted the other day, and couldn't figure out why. Then we realised she hadn't eaten in two days."

"So pack her some iso-protein bars and get her jackmate to set a reminder on her interface. And one of those smart sippycups that bump you to hydrate."

"Are you being serious?"

"What? It's a thing."

Kate holds a hand up to her forehead. "That's no way to live."

"It's the new way to live," says Seth.

"She wants to get meshed, and I don't know how to stop her. All her friends are doing it."

"You can't stop her, Kitty," says Keke. The words burn Kate's stomach. "I mean, once the tech gets a bit more sophisticated I'm going to do it too."

"You wouldn't!"

"Me too," says Seth. "It's scary now, but it'll seem completely normal to Silver's and Mally's kids."

Morgan has been nagging Kate to get meshed. He says an analogue brain is only capable of so much; that if they don't lace up soon then they'll be in danger of being on the same level as domestic cats to advanced AI, which is currently lapping them at every turn. Both scenarios fill Kate with a deep sense of foreboding. She doesn't want to be a house cat, and she doesn't want her brain to be upgraded. So where does that leave her?

"And it's normal for us to resist it, just like our parents resisted cell phones and ebooks. Besides, wouldn't it be great to ditch these lenses and mandibles?" Keke touches the translucent transmitter that runs from her ear to lips.

"I don't even feel mine anymore," says Seth.

"Just so that you guys know," Kate massages her temples. "I'm freaking the fuck out right now."

"You look calm to me."

"Years of parental practice."

What does Arronax always say? You can't stop progress. But that doesn't mean she has to like it.

"I just want you creeps to know that if you ever mesh, I'm

17

going to ... I don't know. Run away. Join the tribe of Disconnects. Escape to somewhere—"

Bonechaser starts barking.

"What's that sound?" Keke looks behind her, in the direction of the cineroom.

"It's the hound," says Seth.

"No, the *other* sound."

They all cock their heads. It's a siren, and it's getting louder. Bonechaser's barking rises a notch.

Something about the barking sounds off to Kate. It's the wrong note and there's an edge of ferocity to it. She's never heard him sound like that before. Is that siren ... coming from this apartment?

A loud snarling sound rushes at them. Mally starts yelling.

"Down, Chaser, down!" comes his muffled shouting. "Down!" and as Kate and Seth rush towards him, Mally begins to scream.

CHASER

2

Johannesburg, 2036

Kate, Seth and Keke run towards the rabid growling. The siren, with Mally's screaming, scores yellow lines in Kate's vision. As they tumble into the cineroom, there is a wet, meaty sound of teeth tearing into flesh. Mally shouts in shock and pain; his face is a mask of pure horror.

"Chaser!" shouts Seth. "Down!"

But the snarling dog continues to attack Mally. With another crushing bite to his upper thigh, the boy falls to the floor. When the dog goes for Mally's face, Kate shouts "No!" and there's a blast so loud it blinds her. She can't work out what's happening until she smells the gunpowder and hears Bonechaser whine. Her vision returns in spectral shapes: four people shifting and stirring around her, and a dying dog on the floor. Mally is holding his injured leg, watching his pants bloom with petals of crimson. Kate rushes to him, landing on her knees and throwing her arms around his shoulders.

"You're okay!" she says, as if she's shouting an order.

Mally's pale mouth trembles.

"Are you insane?" Kate yells at Seth, who's gazing down at his gun as if he can't remember what it is. "You could've shot Mally!"

Seth looks up at her. "You'd rather your son be mauled to death by a robotic dog?"

Keke doesn't move. They all look down at Bonechaser, whose whine has faded to a thin whimper, as she pants and follows her tail around and around in a circle, a great big hole blown into her skull.

Kate's shaking inside and out. "The fuck just happened?"

"Bonechaser is sick," says Vega, making Kate start. She'd completely forgotten Mally's girlfriend. Vega is, as always, perfectly unruffled. "We'll need to take him to the PeTTech vet."

Mally swipes away his tears. Bonechaser and he had been inseparable until Vega arrived on the scene.

Kate peers sadly at the dog. At first Chaser gave her the creeps, but over time they'd become attached. In fact, now more than ever—with the kids being teenagers—it seems that Chaser is the only one who's ever really happy to see her. The dog stumbles, and Kate automatically reaches out to help her, but Seth grabs her arm, shakes his head.

I just want to say goodbye, she thinks, as she watches the K9000 power down. One paw taps the floor in a death tic.

"Mally is in need of medical attention," says Vega.

Seth activates his Scribe. "I'll order an ambudrone."

"That is not necessary," says Vega.

"Of course it's bloody necessary," says Kate, with more venom than she intends. "He has a mangled leg. He's in shock."

"I have performed a thorough body scan," Mally's girlfriend says. "His wounds are superficial."

"Well, I'd still like to take him to a doctor."

"It is not necessary," says Vega. "I have the correct equipment to treat him right here."

She unbuttons her blouse, revealing perfect C-cups in a lacy push-up, and out of the top of her ribcage slides a neat compartment. Vega extricates the first aid kit from inside, and the drawer closes again, with hardly a hint of it on her skin. A headlamp snakes out of her temple, and when it turns on she smiles at them.

"May I use your kitchen table?"

Vega picks up Mally as if he weighs nothing, despite him being almost as tall as Seth, and carries him to the kitchen. She lays him gently on the table and opens her medikit. Kate hovers while Vega scissors his jeans open and sprays the wounds with disinfecting anaesthetic.

"Ah," he says with a sigh. "That's better already."

"Hold still," says Vega, "this will only hurt a bit." She holds the pieces of skin together and runs a surgical autostapler over the wound, leaving a miniature railway track of skin-coloured sutures. Kate finds herself uneasy, but fascinated. It's like Vega's just zipped him up.

"They'll dissolve in a few days," says Vega. "You'll be as good as new." She covers the smaller gashes with platelet plasters and packs the kit back into her ribcage, passing Mally an inhaler. "For the pain."

Seth puts a call in to Arronax. Her mermaid avatar spins open with a splash. "We've got a problem."

Kate walks out onto the balcony, and Keke follows. She holds onto the rail, then, with shaking hands, presses a button to roll open the invisi-screen, and they look out onto the hot city, grey embroidered with green, and breathe in the toxic air that smells of ozone and ash.

"You know that kind of defeats the object of the screen, right?" says Keke.

When the screen is employed, the air on the balcony is filtered and cooled. It's supposed to make you feel as if you're standing in the fresh air—*sans* pollen and pollution—*Protecting You without Sacrificing the View (TM)*, but it just makes Kate feel claustrophobic. Being shut in an invisible box is still being shut in a box.

"Seriously, what the fuck just happened?"

A drone speeds right past them. It's branded with a popular Chinese restaurant chain logo: three chopstix on a plate forming the 'A' symbol for anarchy, because who doesn't love rebellion *and* noodles?

"*Angaz'*. No idea. Robopup rabies?"

"Twelve years," says Kate. "Twelve years that robot's been Mally's best friend. The perfect pet. Loyal Labrador, they said. Programmed to be loyal. What's twelve human years in doggie years?"

Keke shrugs. "I don't know. But twelve human years is like twelve centuries in technology. Chaser's ancient. When's the last time you had him upgraded?"

"2029. They don't upgrade his model anymore."

"It makes you think."

"Of?"

"You know—" Keke gestures inside with a subtle flick of her eyebrows. "The Stepford girlfriend."

"Don't go there. I have enough to worry about."

JT LAWRENCE

"You must admit—she is kind of handy to have around."

"Yes."

"What else do you think she keeps in those compartments of hers?"

24

ELECTROSMOG & SUNLIGHT

3

Johannesburg, 2036

"Do you ever still think of the ... you know, the prophecy?" says Keke.

They're sitting down now, on the balcony floor, barefoot and stripped to their underwear, drinking whisky that looks like liquid gold in the last light of the sunset.

"Of course I do. Every day. Especially when I get frustrated with the kids. Then I feel guilty, because really we're all still here by the grace of ... what?"

"Lady Luck," says Keke. "Luck. And love."

An image of Lady Luck appears in Kate's mind, a hallucinogenic mash-up of the Statue of Liberty, Wonder Woman ReDux, and her memory of Solonne with her quiver of diamond-tipped arrows.

They clink their glasses and take a sip.

"You shouldn't feel guilty. You know you've got nothing to feel guilty about."

"It comes with the territory," says Kate. "Being a parent is a sentence to a lifetime of guilt."

They sit in companionable silence for a moment.

"Do you know that Solonne still sends the kids balloons every birthday?"

"Really?"

"White ones. I know she means well, but they spook the shit out of me. They float around for days reminding me of that stupid prophecy."

"I try not to think about it," says Keke, "but—"

"I know," says Kate. "Then another one of their predictions comes true and it's terrifying all over again."

"The Mars one! Shit."

One of the Celestial Prophecies is that the people stealing from the Red Planet would become a burnt offering to the multiverse to appease Celestia. The prophecies are mostly dismissed as charismatic cult claptrap, but people started to pay a bit more attention when the latest returning Mars ship disappeared in space, blipping the lives of fifty-two space miners, twelve tourists, and hundreds of trillions of dollars worth of equipment.

"Seth's always saying that anyone can write a 'prophecy' and then find some kind of data to support it. But it's just … It's uncanny, right?"

"Downright fucking terrifying," says Keke. The golden threads woven into her cornrows glint in the golden light. The whisky buzzes behind Kate's eyes. Amber Purr.

"Do you still remember the exact words?"

"Of course I do. I couldn't forget them if I tried. It's like they've been carved into my brain with a hot scalpel."

Sometimes she wakes up to Lumin whispering in her ear—

The last living Genesis Child will lead us to the Ledge.

—and she claps the lights on and she's alone, and his words slither away to hide somewhere in her bedroom, only to flicker in on her dreams another night.

"If the boy survives into his fourth summer then he'll live to be sixteen and that will be the end of days."

"And Mally turned sixteen a couple of months ago, right?"

"Right."

"And Silver's birthday is in…thirty-six hours."

"Yebo."

"Do you think the world will end before or after their birthday party?"

"It would save me some planning if it happened before. I still don't have a theme. All I have is some funeral cake."

"Well, that's easy, then," say Keke. "We'll have a rapture party."

Seth opens the balcony door to find the friends chuckling into their glasses. "You two had better come in."

"Nope, nope, nope," says Kate. "This is the most fun I've had since …"

Kate searches her recent memory and comes up blank.

"She needs some downtime, Seth," says Keke. "It's been a hell of a day."

Seth's eyes rest on Keke's exposed skin for a second too long. There is no time for desire.

"You have no idea," he says, spotting their discarded mandibles. "You're not connected?"

"We disconnected an hour ago. We needed some analogue time. Some electrosmog and sunlight, to feel human again."

"We have a problem," says Seth. "You need to see something."

Kate tips the rest of the whisky into her mouth. Birch and beeswax. "We'll sort out Bonechaser tomorrow."

What do you do with a broken pet, anyway? Is there some kind of memorial party planning service for them too? She wouldn't be surprised. Long gone are the days of choosing between being buried or cremated: humans can now pick from a menu of options including, among hundreds of others, vertical cemeteries, forest pods, essence amulets, and cryogenix. She wouldn't be surprised if the same options weren't available for beloved pets, although she guesses that robotic dogs have a different fate.

"Bonechaser is the least of it," Seth says. His face is pale despite the darkening sky. He throws their clothes at them. "You've got to connect right now."

RUNNING WITH THE RODENTS

4

Innercity

Johannesburg, 2036

Silver adjusts her vintage gas-mask and picks up her pace. Ironically, it makes it more difficult to breathe, not less, but she puts up with the discomfort because there's no way she's getting The Black Lung. She's seen the 4DHD VR animation at school, where they practically shove you right inside the diseased organ to show you what breathing raw city air can do to healthy tissue. *So* not gonna happen. Besides, the mask is, like, ancient, and totally original thread. Kate tells her that when she was young, like, a hundred years ago, everyone wanted new clothes all the time. They'd spend their weekends in malls spending money on new clothes, even though they had a full wardrobe at home. Even though they knew the shit was mostly FongKong, they wanted the shiny stuff. Bizarro. Imagine working all week for some evil corp and then spending your free time spending what you earned on things you didn't need, and then get into debt so that you can work some more. Suckers. And it's not like they didn't know it, either. They were always saying things like 'rat race' and 'hamster wheel' but what did they do? They kept on fucking running with the rodents, that's what. Running and running until they were all burned out and needed to retire at sixty-five. Sixty-five! That's like giving up on your life when you're only halfway through. Or die from a heart attack. What a joke. What a brainbleach. What a fucked-up way to live.

Her mandible chimes 19:14.

Shifuckfuck, I'm late.

Her appointment has been set for 19:00, and they said the procedure takes ninety minutes, all-in. Silver hopes it doesn't run over—she'll have to hurry if she wants to get home in time for her 21:00 curfew and not make the parental units suspicious.

Although, Silver sighs, Kate would always be suspicious. Can people be born with a paranoid gene? Kate certainly was. Or maybe she wasn't born with it … maybe it developed over time. Can't blame her, really. Kate gets that haunted look when Silver asks her about stuff, like why

Marko disappeared from their lives so suddenly and won't even beam or bullet them, or what happened to James. I mean, she's not dumb, she knows that her dad died before she was born, but why're they never allowed to ask questions about him? Talking, not talking, it hurts either way.

Silver turns a corner, as instructed by her mandible maps, and jogs down an alley wet with greasy puddles that shine in pearlescent colours. 64381, to be exact, if she were to describe it to Kate. She reaches a nondescript door and her dash pings. Silver raps on the painted metal, the same shade of grey as the smoggy dusk sky, and the speakeasy is slid open with a bang. Green eyes like dragon scales.

"Go home, little girl," says the owner of the scales. "This is no place for you."

FROM CHOP TO STAB

5

Seth's Apartment

Johannesburg, 2036

The women amble reluctantly inside, glowing from the drink and the heat. The air-conditioned apartment wakes them, turns their skin to instabraille. Kate buttons her asymmetrical hoodie right up to her neck. She sees a navy-cream ombré canvas bag on the floor and knows instinctively that Chaser's body is inside, and shivers.

Why is Seth so riled up? What can be worse than what just happened to Mally?

Kate and Keke put their mandibles back on.

"Kate connect," she says, and her dashboard appears, her Scribe blinks.

"Keke connect," says Keke.

They're both hit with a barrage of messages and alerts at the same time. It makes her temples throb and tastes of a scraped metal. She swipes them all away, but as soon as her vision clears, more messages stream in.

Prioritise.

The alerts freeze for a second then swirl around each other till the most important ones are at the top. Kate looks at the first one on the list, an Echo.news headline clip posted less than a minute ago, and opens it by thinking *Play.*

The video is amateurish, shaky, and not properly focused, but it's clearly the outside of The Bent Hotel, in Saxonwold, known for its interstellar prices and political dignitary guests. The giant motorised gate is opening and closing, as if someone is sitting on the remote. Then a commotion comes into view, just for a moment: Kate gasps when she sees a terrified woman slam into the wall of the entrance building, as if she's been thrown at it. Instead of sinking to the floor as Kate expects her to, she scrabbles around, trying to get purchase, trying to get out of the building, but then a hand clamps down on her leg and pulls her back inside. Her mouth is wide open, and Kate feels the woman's silent scream scrape her skin. She shudders again.

"What the fuck!" says Keke.

"Are you watching the same thing as I am?" asks Kate. "Bent?"

"What? No. The Loop."

"Connect to Keke," says Kate, and she watches on Keke's interface as the hyperloop speed train careens straight into a stationary cabin and explodes into a violent cloud of smoke and debris. A graphic at the top right of the screen is counting: a rainbow stopwatch as the numbers tick over. 489. 528. 540. Then Kate realises the units are the confirmed fatalities.

"Watch the Reality DroidChef one," says Seth.

Search. Reality DroidChef.

Hundreds of results come up. Kate chooses the one with the most confirmations. She wants to make sure what she is watching is real news, and not some cyberprankster who thinks it'll be cool to use his home SFX software and splice it into a major newstream's channel. The last time that happened, a fake clip of an actress being beheaded in Belarus made it around the globe more than a thousand times before it was outed as quack. The DroidChef clip has more than six hundred individual confirmation stamps on it.

Play.

Kate's already nervous of what she'll see. The image of

the woman being dragged back into the hotel is still jigging in her head. The video opens on the set of RDC; it was a live recording. The camera is trained on a chopping board, where a stamped silicone android's hand is making fast work of a no-tears onion. The knife is made of compressed carbonate. It's easy to see how sharp it is by how little resistance the genetically modified onion offers. Kate has seen the knife's ads: *Extremely sharp: Not recommended for human use.* The camera tilts up to show the chef: a smooth-faced femmebot with a toothy smile, who's not even looking down while the knife dices the onion at supersonic speed. The human host is looking at his watch and laughing as the bot tips the minced onion into a bowl and starts on a new one. He tells her to go faster, and beams some more. Usually Kate would snark at the brainlessness of it all, but for now her heart is pumping hot blood throughout her body. Her breath is shallow, and her fingertips tingle with adrenaline. The bot is smiling widely at the camera, her knifework a blur. The host grins and says something Kate can't hear over her nerves. She knows exactly what's going to happen. Does she have to watch it till the end if she already knows the conclusion? As she considers switching it off, the smiling android starts chopping her hand. The stamped silicone of her skin is lacerated to show titanium bones and latex tendons working underneath.

Keke hisses, an inhalation of cold breath through teeth.

The host's cheery face fades as he realises what's happening, and he blinks and automatically reaches to stop the robot from hurting herself further. Kate wraps her fingers over her eyes and peeps through. The chef tosses the knife a few inches into the air and catches it again at a different angle—so that she can change her grip from chop to stab—and without turning away from the camera or shrinking her smile, in a breathtakingly fluid motion, she drives the knife straight into the host's chest.

YOU SHOULD ALWAYS BE WORRIED

6

"I don't understand what's happening," says Kate. A moment ago she was on the balcony with her best friend, soaking up whisky and sunshine, and joking about Doomsday. Now they stand huddled in the cool apartment, hugging themselves and grasping for words as clip after clip flashes in on their vision. They were fire, and now they are ash.

Stop thinks Kate, and the news freezes. *Clear.*

She looks around the apartment as if she doesn't know where she is. Where the kids are. The real world punches her in the gut. "Where's Mally?"

"In his room. Resting," says Seth.

"With Vega?"

"Vega went out to replenish her medikit. Said she'd stay at her hostel tonight. Make sure Mally gets a good night's sleep."

"And Silver?"

"She's not answering my bullets."

"Well, that's normal."

"Should we be worried?" asks Kate.

Seth is deadpan. "We're parents. We should always be worried."

Keke chips in, "You're a human. You should always be worried."

Kate tries to stay calm. "At least we know where she is. Where she *always* is. It's the one upside of having a daughter addicted to immersia."

NOT KIDS LIKE YOU

7

SkinTech Clinic

Johannesburg, 2036

"There's a kid here," transmits the man with dragon scales for eyes. "Says she has a slot booked." He listens to the feedback then looks at Silver's hair. "Ja. Looks funny on a kid."

Despite the variety of artificial dyes and powders and shifting shades out there, creeps find her white hair unsettling.

"If you say so, Boss." Screeching metal on metal as the deadbolt is drawn aside; Silver is allowed access and the man locks the door behind her. They spend a moment eyeing each other. He's younger than he first appeared, head to toe in black, has a jaw-tattoo that incorporates his designer mandible, and kohl smudge on his eyes. He runs a metal detector over her shoulders, her back, her thighs. The machine beeps when it glides over her jacket, which is full of studs and steampunk corsetry. Hollow buttons and copper darts. They do it again without the jacket, and she's given the all clear.

He seems disconcerted by her, won't stop looking. She stands up to his gaze. "I take it you don't get a lot of kids coming around here."

"Oh, we get kids," he says. He means street urchins and child prostitutes, white lobster orphans. A city like this swallows kids whole. "But not kids like you."

Silver moves quickly through the lifi-lit passage, and when she gets to the end she turns into a large waiting room. The creeps sitting in their swingchairs instinctively look up at her. She's used to people staring. She glares back, and they look away. Keke says people stare because of the way Silver dresses. She means it in a good way. Silver's uniform of her bespoke steampunk hooded coat, rubber peelboots, fake-snake leggings—and of course her white hair and heritage gas-mask—is guaranteed to make even the most indifferent stranger take a second look.

Silver counts five patients in front of her. If they all take an hour each she'll never get home in time. It takes so long to get to this side of town, it'll be a shame to turn around and go back again. She's been saving for ages, and it's near damn impossible to get an appointment. Plus, she has her heart set on getting this done before Saturday.

A woman dressed like a Halloween nurse flutters into the room and nods wordlessly at Silver.

The painfully thin man next to her starts chewing his teeth, shaking his head in small, hard tics. A woman wearing a cybercap and cradling a fox in a shawl gazes blankly at the floor. Silver hesitates. Does she really want to go through with this? She follows the nurse.

The doctor stands up from behind his desk and opens his arms.

"Silver," he says warmly. His voice is exactly as she remembers it—a panther, a vibrating sports car engine.

"DarkDoc." She disappears into his arms for a moment. It feels good.

When they separate, the doctor lifts her hand as if to kiss it, but instead he raises it to his eye level and inspects her artificial finger.

"How is it? Giving you any trouble?"

Silver shakes her head. "No. No. Your craftsmanship has stood the test of time."

Morgan smiles and gestures for her to sit. The steel clips in his dreadlox glint in the light.

"Glad to hear it, but then to what do I owe this auspicious occasion?"

"It's my sixteenth birthday on Saturday."

"So it is! Happy birthday."

"I'm here to buy myself a birthday present."

"Well." He clasps his hands together. "You have my full attention."

"I'm stuck on the sixth level in Eden 7.0."

The techdoctor frowns at her. "You're not supposed to be anywhere near that game. It's for adults only."

"I know."

"How did you get in?"

"How do you think?"

"I'm assuming it would have involved hacking, and the best hacker in the country just happens to be your godfather."

"Exactly."

"He shouldn't have done that. There's a reason they don't let kids play that game."

Silver sighs. She's mature enough. The Net knows she's shrewder than most of the adults with whom she comes into contact. The rules aren't for everyone: The DarkDoc should know.

"Anyway," he says, "you can't access the seventh level. You know that. Not without—"

Silver blinks at him. "So then you know why I'm here."

Morgan laughs, and spins the brushed metal levitating sphere on his desk. "You know I can't do that for you."

"Why not?"

"You're underage, for one. You're only allowed neural lace when you turn eighteen."

"Sixteen, if you have your guardian's permission."

Since when does the DarkDoc care about the rule of law?

"And … do you have it? Kate's permission?"

"No," says Silver. "Obviously. But she's a technosaur. The law should make allowances for that."

He chuckles. "You do have a point."

"Please," Silver says. "Please, Doc. I have the Blox."

He doesn't need to know how she got the bank in the first place.

"How can I say no to my favourite kid in the world?"

A spear of excitement runs through her body. "You'll do it?"

"I'll do it."

"Oh, thank you!"

"Not so fast," he says. "I'll make you a deal."

"I'll do anything," Silver says. "Anything."

"Come back when you're sixteen."

"But I am practically sixteen!"

"And bring your mother."

"But we've already said—she'll never agree to it!"

"Then you have some convincing to do."

Disappointment flows through her veins like cold ink.

"Ah, to be so young," he panther-purrs. "So impatient."

Damn it. Damn him. Damn everything. Silver's so disappointed she feels like crying. She stands up, ready to leave, her gas-mask dangling by her side.

"Chin up, Silver. I'll chat to her tonight. I'll help you to get her on board. I'll even book the operating room for tomorrow morning."

It's no use, thinks Silver. *Kate will never sign the consent.*

Morgan pushes a button, and a few seconds later there's a knock at the door. It's the man who let her into the clinic.

"Boss?"

"I'd like you to put this young lady into a cabbie, please, as we discussed earlier."

"I can do that myself," says Silver.

And I'm no lady.

"My treat," the DarkDoc says. "And this way you'll have

company."

Silver looks at the time on her holodash. 20:00. She'll make it just in time for her curfew if she leaves now.

"You know where to take her?" asks Doctor Morgan.

"Yes, sir."

The door automatically closes behind Silver, and Morgan leans back against his swivel chair, puts his hands behind his head and thinks for a moment.

Beam Kate Lovell.

It rings three times, and then he hears her voice. Tense. The sound of her saying his name makes his thighs feel warm.

"Kate. Are you okay?"

"Define what you mean by 'okay'."

"We need to talk."

"I don't like the sound of that."

"Silver was just here."

A moment of shocked silence.

"What? Where?"

"Here, at the clinic."

"But ... she's supposed to be the at the Atrium. She's always at the Atrium."

"I've put her in a SkinTech cab with one of my most trusted assistants. You'll see her soon."

"Have you been watching the newstream?"

There's a knock at the door. The nurse points at her wrist.

"I've had back-to-back appointments. Speaking of which, I need to go."

"You'd better have a look." She says. "And thank you ... for sending Silver home."

"Sure. We still need to talk about her. About why she was here. I'll call you when I punch out."

"Thank you."

"Oh, and Kate—"

"Yes?"

"I don't know why I got this feeling ... but ... I think she knows about us."

MILK&SILK

8

Seth's Apartment

Johannesburg, 2036

"Silver's safe." Kate mutes her mandible. "She's on her way to us right now."

"Thank the Net," says Seth.

Keke sighs. "So what do we know about this shitshow that's happening outside right now?"

More and more it seems to Kate that her reality is spinning out of control. The rate of evolution of everything is just too fast. How can anyone keep up? Is she even meant to keep up? Or is that a recipe for insanity? She has a pervading sensation that she doesn't feel safe. An everyday sense of menace hovers, a constant vicious vertigo, and she finds it difficult to believe she's the only one who feels this way.

Seth puts his hands together in a quiet clap, as if he's about to start telling a really good story. "There've been some incidents over the last few days. Random. Seemingly random, anyway."

"Incidents? Like what?"

"Little quirks. Small glitches. At first they didn't seem too sinister."

"Like what happened at MegaMall?" asks Keke.

"Exactly."

On Tuesday a mannequinbot started screaming at a customer in Milk&Silk. The customer said he did nothing to set it off, but the security footage later revealed that he had sexually assaulted her. Except they don't call it sexual assault when it happens to a robot. Interference, they say. He had interfered with the skinbot: had shoved his hand into her designer brassiere in broad daylight. Or artificial mall light, anyway. It's not a criminal offence—not yet—so he'll get away with his story, Kate is sure. After all, what is he expected to do when the goods are flaunted to brazenly? Surely the skin was asking for it, wearing that seductive get-up? And conveniently avoiding the fact that the whole reason for her existence is in fact to model lingerie, and that a 5.0 robot is incapable of 'asking for it'.

"He got off lucky," says Keke, perhaps referring to the DroidChef incident.

"The mannequin didn't," says Kate, picturing her naked body being carted back to the factory if she was lucky, and the recycling yard if she wasn't.

"And then the JungleRumble thing," says Seth.

"Hey?"

"It's under the Blanket. I assume they paid handsomely for that."

"Nah. The CEO is Mashini Wam's daughter."

The president's real name is Mashigo Amahle, but she has the reputation of getting inconvenient people taken care of, hence the nickname. *Umshini Wami* is the one apartheid resistance song that stayed long after the struggle was over. Loosely translated, it means 'my machine': the song is about a fighter calling for his machine gun.

"But seriously, that amusement park was just an accident waiting to happen. I mean, hopped-up kids and robotic wild animals? What could possibly go wrong?"

Kate winces. She's seen the ads showing adults and children alike putting their heads into lion's mouths like old-school circus lion tamers. Riding crocodiles in the river. Winding boa constrictors around their necks. "There're always so many kids there. I don't actually want to know."

"I do!" says Keke.

"Then you need to hack the Blanket."

"Where's a talented hacktivist when you need him?" says Kate, but when she sees Keke roll her eyes, she regrets the joke. She hasn't even asked her how Marko is lately. Or where he is. Or if she thinks he'll ever come back.

Seth smooths over the awkward pause in conversation. "Well, they've closed it till further notice. Pending enquiry and all of that. I'm sure the government will assign a 'task team' to investigate."

"Ha."

"So … we're hoping that all these glitches are coincidence?" says Keke.

"There's no such thing as coincidence," Kate and Seth say, at the same time.

"When you look at the common denominators—" Seth fetches a glass from the kitchen cupboard and pours them all a whisky. "Then you'll see why this is a real problem."

"What are they? The common denominators?"

"Area, for one."

He projects a map of South Africa from his Scribe and red blisters emerge like a pox. Johannesburg is clearly the eye of the storm.

"Holy fuck," says Keke.

"And, more worryingly—"

"It's spreading," whispers Kate. More and more flags appear at the edges of the tornado. Fear is a yellow zip up her back.

"Yes, but that isn't what I was going to say."

"What's happening out there? What's causing it?"

"That woman who was killed at The Bent," says Seth, "that hand ... belonged to the hotel porterbot."

Kate sees it happen again: the woman's crazed eyes and open mouth as the thing clawed at her leg. Porterbots are known for their strength, they're manufactured that way to perform their jobs easily.

Keke's breath is a whisper of terror. "It's AI."

Experts have been warning us for decades.

Enslave AI before it enslaves us.

They'd been lectured about the danger of embracing artificial intelligence without restraint or respect for as long as they can remember. Not by dodgy fringe-dwellers or city disconnects but by the most respected people in the field. The graphic refreshes itself, and a surge of new flags pops up like a Mexican wave.

DRAGON SCALES

9

Innercity

Johannesburg, 2036

Silver is shown out the clinic. She puts her mask back on, and adjusts her breathing to the claustrophobic filter over her mouth. Her coat feels heavy on her shoulders. She should have known the DarkDoc wouldn't help her without Kate's consent. He's considered to be this renegade biotech specialist on the forefront of science, breaking rules all over the spectrum, but now Silver sees he's just like everyone else: a sheeple bleating the same tune as everybody fucking else. Why can't creeps think for themselves? She's so sick of it. Why can't she be eighteen already?

She's further enraged by the tears that spark her eyes.

Keep cool, Silver.

"Hey," says Dragon Scales.

He's hot in a bad-boy way.

She pulls her mask to the side again. "Hey yourself."

Sexy in a kind of grimy way that makes her feel a tingle of excitement in her pelvis.

He moves to open the cab's door, but stops as if something is just occurring to him.

"You wanna go somewhere?"

Danger strokes her neck.

"I shouldn't," she says.

"Why?" He laughs. "You have a curfew?" He opens the door.

"No," she fibs. "I just have to get back."

"I'll take you," he says, so she climbs in. "I'll take you anywhere you wanna go."

ON ICE

10

TWELVE YEARS PREVIOUSLY

ICE

Johannesburg, 2024

The security gate judders open and the navy van glides through, its tyres crackling on the tarmac. A guard acknowledges them with his palm as they pass. The sleek vehicle winds around the vast building and enters through a sliding turnstile at the back which elevates the van. They land up on the fifth floor. Once the ignition de-activates, Detective Ramphele turns his head to check on Zack.

"I'm still here," Zack says. "Did you expect me to have

vanished?"

Ramphele snorts. "I've seen the footage. I know what you're capable of—I don't understand it, but I've seen it—and I'm not letting you out of my sight."

Of course Ramphele doesn't understand it. He doesn't have the neural capability. He's still 100% bio, as far as Zack can tell. It's like expecting a goldfish to think out of the bowl.

Zack wipes the perspiration from his palms. This arrest is a risky development, and his anxiety is interfering with his regular cool reasoning. Ramphele's got a vice-like grip on him. A wild dog with a bone. Zack's anxiety taps him on the shoulder, insisting that he needs to escape. So much hinges on the successful completion of his mission; a mission he knows is now in jeopardy.

Zack stares forward through the superblack tinted windows, his mind racing. "Where are we?"

"You'll see soon enough."

"You're putting me on ice," Zack says. The Innercity Crim Establishment is the place you stay while you're awaiting trial.

"You'll be lucky," says the detective.

"Lucky to be on ice?"

"Lucky to get a trial."

"So Nash was right, then," says Zack, more to himself than to the cop.

"Helena Nash was a kid-killer."

"She wasn't, though, and you would have known that if you had done your job and hadn't had a complete fucking farce for a trial."

Ramphele grunts.

"It was the trial she deserved," says the detective. "And you—"

The doors unlock after their mandatory two-minute security quarantine. The cop holds up his Tile: Zack's mugshot is front and centre. Next to the picture are 3D icons for various folders. As far as he can see, there is an icon for every one of his deceased clients. Ramphele swipes up to show scores and scores of files. A hundred, two hundred? Dead.

"You'll get the trial you deserve, too."

AMPHIBIAN SUSPICION

11

Ramphele pushes Zack along by the small of his back; it is an intimate gesture. The entrance to the facility on this floor is modest, with just a hulking black gate that automatically opens after a dull buzzing sound comes from the adjacent security kiosk. Ramphele guides him through the hall and to the scabby timber reception desk that's pitted and tattooed with blue ink—a remnant from another era. No pens here anymore: A silicone stylus is less dangerous than a ball-point.

Never letting Zack out of his peripheral vision, the detective sigs a few holo-leaves and time-stamps them. The bored receptionist yawns them through.

The warden on admission duty is a woman taller than Zack and twice as built. The uniform is powder blue with an angular cut. Her eyes click into his and don't let go.

"So this is him," she says, curling the tip of her tongue over her bottom lip. Her tag reads WARDEN C BERNARD.

"Yebo," says Ramphele. "You ready for him?"

"Oh, yes." She slants her head as if to get a proper look at Zack. There's something cold in her eyes, something hard and shiny, as if her pupils are the point of something sharp: a kitchen knife or, more suitably given their surroundings, an ice-pick.

"Oh yes," Bernard says again, and he imagines her cracking her large knuckles, getting them punch-ready, even though her meaty hands are otherwise occupied. Her calves are solid; Zack guesses she's a walker. Bernard takes a plastic envelope from the detective then turns and pushes the pad of her finger up against the biometric access pad. An arrow lights up above the door.

"I'll call for details about the trial," says the detective.

"You do that," says Bernard. Ramphele looks on as the metal door and then a glass partition, slide open—a double mouth—and watches as the warden and Zack are swallowed up by the elevator.

Warden Bernard has a head of tight, wiry curls that she keeps gelled into submission. Her head is an army barracks of metal pins. She wears a choker with rivets that reminds Zack of a dog collar. Zack stares at the back of her neck as she turns away from him to select the relevant floor. Clammy. Her skin is too white. SPF100 junkie? Or because she spends her life in this prison. He guesses the latter. It lends her a slightly amphibian suspicion.

Zack breathes in deeply through his nose and sighs it out. How long will he be stuck here? Until a trial date is set. When will they decide that? Who knows.

The warden looks at him sharply. "Problem?"

He holds up his cuffed wrists. "More than one."

It's imperative to get on the warden's good side. Zack counts his lucky stars that he's reasonably good looking and that she's a woman. Never a guarantee, mind you, but it's a good start.

They get buzzed through the iron gate.

Christine Bernard collects Zack's ICE-branded prison clothes from a counter, and they walk down a corridor scraped by the thousands of reluctant heels before his. The door to his cell opens automatically, and Zack takes stock of where he'll be sleeping for the foreseeable future: iron bed, stained mattress, dog blankets, bare walls. He wonders off-hand if the absence of art and colour and natural light in prisons is a purposeful or accidental strategy to capture minds as well as bodies. Bernard further darkens the door.

Zack turns to her, and she tosses him his uniform; he

catches the orange overalls on his chest, and wonders how many creeps had worn this particular outfit before him.

"Get undressed," she says. He expects her to leave, but she stands there, watching him.

He starts with his tie: unknotting the teal silk and placing it over the back of a chair, then opens his white-collared shirt, button by button. Bernard swats her palm with her baton like a metronome. It has a textured handle for better grip and an expandable, telescopic rod; sixteen inches of solid steel for extra striking power.

Zack unclips his belt, drops his pants, and reaches for the overalls.

"Everything," the warden says. She eats him with her eyes.

Zack hesitates. He doesn't want to wear prison-issue jox, and he certainly doesn't want to be completely naked in front of Bernard. Not because he minds being naked—he's usually rather a fan of nudity—but because it will give her too much power, too quickly.

She sees his hesitation and it hardens her face. Her fingers wrap around the hard steel.

"Everything."

EVEN MY TOASTER IS INTELLIGENT

12

TWELVE YEARS LATER

Seth's Apartment

Johannesburg, 2036

Seth sets his Scribe to project the running news holo on the large white wall next to where they're standing. Echo.news is showing the hyperloop crash in slow motion.

"Speaker," he says, and the sound of the journalist's voice is amplified throughout the room.

"Mere hours ago we reported that these incidents were not linked. There was nothing to tie the Loop accident to The Bent Hotel murder. However, after consulting a panel of experts—"

"We approached you," says a man in a polka-dot bow-tie. His wiry hair and eccentric outfit make him look like an Andy Warhol-styled Einstein.

"Pardon me," says the journo, "I stand corrected. Dr Kirk called us to set up this piece."

Dr Kirk is sitting behind a desk, his fingers interlaced. His thumbs shoot up and he nods to acknowledge the journalist's apology. Kate gets the idea the doctor doesn't care who called whom, but it's his job to care about facts. His poker cap—a bright green visor with an open top—casts emerald light on his face, which makes Kate think of the Wizard of Oz, and the Tin Man who wanted a heart.

"Since chatting to Dr Kirk, we've changed our position."

The Echo.news ticker tape animates and winds around the room like the 1980s video game Snafu, an ever-extending pink snake flickering the death toll. The numbers keep changing colours.

CONFIRMED FATALITIES

HYPERLOOP: 612

BILCHEN SATELLITE DEPOT (SANDTON): 82

CARBON FACTORY: 39

PRINTADRINK: 14

JUNGLERUMBLE: 3

THE BENT HOTEL: 1

STREAM STUDIOS (DROIDCHEF): 1

MEGAMALL MILK&SILK: 0

When did the world get so utterly broken?

In 2028 more than half of the world's leaders were women. It seemed at the time more of a bitter, hard-won status rather than a triumph. And now it feels like a hollow victory, because really they were handed a poisoned chalice. It's as if the male leaders tossed them the keys to a car that broke down after having its engine fall out onto the highway during rush-hour traffic. The new strains of terrorism, the gummed-up rivers and noxious air. It's like inheriting a bomb that's about to explode and being expected to say thank you.

That's why seeing that old picture of the skinny polar bears is one of the saddest in history. Because at the time the picture was taken, it wasn't yet too late. So they can clone the bears now but where will they live? That's what happens when the polar ice melts and there are more plastic bottles than fish in the sea. That's what happens when humans think they're a superior life form.

And now this.

"Dr Kirk, can you tell us what your take is on these incidents? And what it could mean for the country? Are we facing a robot rebellion?"

Kirk's qualifications run along the bottom of his picture: Dr Kirk (Theoretical Physicist) CH, CBE, FRS, FRSA.

"We knew it would happen eventually, right?" says Keke. "A robot rebellion. The Singularity. I've watched enough sci-fi shorts to know the drill."

"Yes and no," says Seth. "This isn't either of those things, but that doesn't mean—"

"It's not a rebellion," says the scientist.

"Ha," says Kate. "Seth. How did you know?"

"How I know everything: maths."

Kate and Keke shrug at each other.

"Can you put my slide up?" says Kirk to the journalist, and he does so. It looks almost identical to Seth's map, but now has double the number of red flags.

"I've just come from an emergency meeting at NASP, and my associates and my hypothesis is that it's simply an update snag."

The journo pushes his blackrims up the bridge of his nose. "A snag?"

"Robots' codes are constantly updated. We're exploring new territory all the time. It's hardly surprising that the odd upgrade has some … unexpected consequences."

"Dire consequences, in this case," says the journalist. "Rebellion or not, artificial intelligence is … Well, it's killing human beings."

"Indeed. Just because the spur is at a micro level we shouldn't be fooled into thinking that it's an insignificant problem. If we don't fix this fast, we'll be facing a potential global catastrophe."

'Robot Rebellion' disappears from the ticker tape slugs and is replaced by 'AI Update Malfunction'. It hardly has the same ring to it, but the fatalities keep ticking over, flashing hue after hue.

"How do we fix it?" The journalist's forehead has developed a sheen. "I mean, there must be something we can do?"

"Even my toaster is intelligent," Kirk says with a wry smile. "I mean, I can't even unplug the thing because nothing has cables anymore. Everything just flies through the air."

The journo shifts uncomfortably in his seat.

"I apologise," Kirk says, when he registers the horror on the man's face. "It's just that … well, it's just that we've fully integrated ourselves in this neuroreality where AI is as much part of our lives as our own DNA. And now, well …"

He shrugs. Does he need to point out the obvious?

"What are you saying, Dr Kirk?"

"What am I saying? That's it's already too late. We've walked into the mouth of the monster, and we did it willingly, with our eyes wide open."

"There must be something we can do."

The scientist shrugs. "I guess you can switch off your toasters, but—"

The journalist completes his sentence, "—but they can turn themselves back on again."

REVENGE RETARGETING

13

"Your front door's not working," says a woman with a crisp British accent.

"Arronax." Seth envelopes her in an embrace that immediately makes it clear where she'll be sleeping tonight.

Keke's eye twitches.

"I thought you were in the Cape Republic?" says Kate.

Arronax always makes it clear that she doesn't like Joburg. She shakes her head and her hair changes colour from lavender to navy striped with black.

"I'm up for the *Biomimicry in Robotic Design* convention at the Lipworth Institute."

The Lipworth Institute is Johannesburg's answer to the Cape Republic's Nautilus. Founded and funded by an anonymous donor, it's the continent's premier robotics design outfit.

"I thought you already knew everything there was to know about biomimicry," says Keke.

"Arro's being humble. She's the whole reason for the convention. She was going to be the headline speaker."

"*Was* being the operative word." Arronax sighs. "Of course they'll cancel the whole thing now."

"Sorry you wasted a trip," says Keke.

Arronax casts a hungry look at Seth. "Not at all."

Seth fetches another glass and pours them all a generous shot.

"I need to be here, anyway, with what's going on. Attempt some damage control." Arronax takes a sip and pulls a face. She's not used to hard tack.

Seth motions for her to drink the rest. She's going to need it.

"This is probably the biggest setback I've ever encountered."

Kate laughs without mirth. "You're so English."

"What's that supposed to mean?"

"It's the fucking beginning of the apocalypse, and we'll all probably be dead tomorrow, but you call it a 'setback'."

"Oh." Her cheeks colour. "It's hardly that bad, is it? I was preparing for my talk while I was on the plane. I switched off my news alerts."

"It's bad," says Seth.

"A couple of isolated incidents?" Hope is liquid in her eyes.

"You'd better sit down."

They watch a news update together, which includes new frightening clips that have been sent in from all over the city. Arronax's body seems to wilt with every story, and her face is as grey as tap water. A man was killed at a gym in Lonehill by the orbital stepper he was inside. A pregnant woman was run over by a Turing cab. A patient at the Gordhan died when the nursebot administered a lethal dose of pexidine. The clip shows the surgeon robots being rounded up and locked in the disused hospital chapel, and the human nurses whipping premature newborns from their smart incubators.

"Oh no," says Arronax, pale hands flying up to her face. "Oh no, no, no."

"Those poor babies." Kate can't even think about what will happen to them. It hurts too much.

Arronax begins weeping. They're all taken aback. Kate's

never seen Arronax so much as tear up before. Now she's shaking and crying into her hands. Seth tries to comfort her, but she's so full of emotion she can't be touched.

"I'm sorry."

Still reeling from the picture of the newborns, Kate has tears in her eyes, too. "I'm sorry." What else can she say? Arronax's entire career—and her career is her life—wiped out in just a few hours. It's also a death of sorts.

"Can I see him?" she says to Kate, and for a second she thinks Arronax means Mally, but then her gaze skitters to the bag on the floor. Seth picks it up, lays in on the kitchen table, and Arronax tentatively zips it open. She runs her fingers over Bonechaser's damaged head. He smells like an electric storm.

"How is Mally?"

"Shaken up. Sad. He'll be okay."

He's been through worse.

Arronax starts crying again. She shakes her head, and her black highlights take over the rest of her hair (Raven Grief). Kate pours another round.

Arronax has spent the last ten years campaigning for #RoboRights, a charter to ensure that bots of any kind are afforded basic entitlements like the right to say 'no', and to protect themselves from harm. Her dogged determination ensured the Nancies' approval of a law that criminalised violence against robosapiens, and her latest project is pushing a bill that'll allow AI of any kind to refuse a human's instructions if it goes against their inherent moral code, and/or cause harm to any bot or living being.

It was her idea to add a circulatory system to the latest generation of robosapiens. Perhaps if they could bleed like humans, was her thinking, then they'd be treated more humanely. Unfortunately, it backfired.

Arronax came up against massive resistance. Creeps are scared by how very human-like the latest generation of automatons are, and giving them rights just seems to be a step too far. When Nautilus revealed that the new version of androids—7thGen like Vega—would have warm blood, it caused protests all over the country. Where do you draw the line, between humans and robots? Arronax says: Why does there need to be a line at all? The future could be a peaceful and mutually beneficial co-existence, with droids becoming more human, and humans absorbing more tech. Soon there wouldn't need to be a distinction at all. She covered this issue in her latest interview on ANDROID NATION which was widely disseminated on social media and taken out of context in various AI hate-groups. The alt-tech nazis just shared the *"why does there need to be a line at all?"* clip, making some people so riled up that they had beamed her death threats. One man in particular seems obsessed with Arronax and likes to leave poisoned easter eggs for her in all her favourite places. Revenge re-targeting. Not even augmented reality is safe anymore.

Arronax sniffs and pours herself another shot, and downs it. Pulls her seawater cardigan closed as if she is pulling herself together too.

"All right." She wipes aqua-glitter from her eyelids. "Best

we come up with a plan."

DEAD CITY SUNBEAMS

14

Innercity

Johannesburg, 2036

Dragon Scales starts the car. The headlights illuminate the narrow city street, sending the rats scampering. One rat stays perched on top of a dumpster, too hungry or old to care about the ignition of a hydrocar, or the shock of the bright light. He looks straight at them, eyes pinpricks of glow-in-the dark green, whiskers twitching as he nibbles whatever it is he's holding in his hands.

"Tell me about yourself," the man says.

He means, Silver is sure, what's a girl like her doing in a place like this.

They drive past more dumpsters, and more scattering rats, and then past the old sardine-tin security complexes overtaken by squatters and feral woodland creatures. Since the Seasian craze of Forest Critters lit up the local pet scene, the city has a wild animal problem. Foxes, raccoons and squirrels were brought in by unscrupulous animal dealers and sold as sterilised pets, and no one caught on until they were all expecting their first litters. To add to the population explosion (and confusion), sub-crazes streaked in: the sales of bio-identical robotic forest animals shot through the roof, and, more bizarrely, so too did the fad of dye-grooming your cat or dog to look like the original Critters. It's best to not look too closely while driving: Roadkill smears the city streets.

"You tell me first," says Silver.

"What do you want to know?"

"We could start with names. You could tell me your name," she says.

"Names are just a social construct to box people in. I don't believe in names."

Silver guffaws. "You don't believe in names?"

"Not ones that other people have given me."

"Okay ..."

"You don't think it's crazy that you live your whole life by the name someone else—who didn't even know you at the time—gave you?"

"It's just a name."

"It's never just a name."

"So what do I call you then?"

"You can call me whatever you like. What were you calling me in your head before we started this conversation?"

Silver hesitates.

"Come on, there must have been something."

"Dragon Scales."

Now it's his turn to laugh.

"Dragon scales. I love it. Do you see? Now we have something more than we had a minute ago. A connection. An agreement. It's so much better than just handing out a random tag that you'd probably forget by tomorrow."

"What will your name be for me?" asks Silver.

He narrows his eyes at her, as if sizing her up. "I haven't decided yet."

"But what were you calling me before?"

"I was calling you 'Kid'," he says. "But that's not right."

"I like it, though," says Silver.

"You like being called a kid?"

"I like it when *you* call me 'Kid'."

"I've got it." He looks at her hair. "Kid Silver."

"That's funny—" she says, about to tell him her real name.

"It was a brilliant band in the late nineties." He scrolls through his Scribe. "I'll play some for you."

"The nineties? Christ, how old *are* you?"

Music fills the car. Twisted rhythm, and subtle layers of drum loops and orchestration. Innocent and sophisticated at the same time.

"Dead City Sunbeams. Electric Sky. It's fucking perfect for you."

Silver can feel the music pulse through her body, a new beat of excitement swelling the inside of her chest.

"Yes," she says, relaxing into the sound. "It's perfect."

A few tracks in, they pass a stuttering solar-sign that says 'DISTRICT 12'. It used to be the meat-packing district, when creeps thought it was still okay to butcher animals for food. Silver shudders, thinking of the pictures she's seen of skinned cow carcasses hanging from hooks. The casual way the men worked on the corpses with heavy cleavers, as if they were cutting timber instead of previously sentient flesh and bone. Bodies traced with nerves, brains spiked with panic. On the heels of the vegan revolution the blood-stained concrete floors gave way to cotton and synthsilk: a bustling fashion district. Bustling, that is, until new clothes became unfashionable, and the industry caved in on itself. New businesses are hesitant to move into the area now, suspicious and/or superstitious, and the city doesn't want to change the sign again. Now it's just called District 12.

Silver's feeling drugged by the strange new music and the novelty of being in a car with a handsome man who keeps looking at her. It's almost like being in one of her RPGs. Why does he keep looking at her? There's something happening. Something he's not telling her. The car takes a right turn, which will drive them further into the CBD. They should have gone left.

"This isn't the way to my home," she says.

Dragon Scales keeps his eyes on her. "I know."

They park in the street, outside a warehouse. He opens the door and as Silver steps out she's assaulted by the stink of the city. She puts on her gas-mask then takes his proffered hand. It's warm. He leads her around the corner, looks both ways, then opens a door camouflaged by a realistic mural of the same smoky brix that make up the rest of the building. Sometimes she thinks of this city as an underground labyrinth: There is the day-time trade and pedestrian city, monochrome, with dots of colour where informal traders sell fruit and junk chips and grey tech, and then there is the underbelly, the mass of narrow alleys and secret doors and underground tunnels. A dark parallel universe. A shadow city.

Silver hesitates outside the door. She has a feeling that if she crosses the threshold there will be some kind of huge consequence, some point of no return. Her nerves light up her stomach and her face, so that she feels as if she's glowing. Not a pretty glow, but a radioactive shine. What is she doing here in this strange place with this strange man? Her clock ticks 21:12. Kate will be starting to worry now. She needs to get home. She needs to get back in the car and get home as soon as possible.

The dragon scales sparkle. His skin feels so good. He has this magnetic pull she's never felt before.

She needs to get home.

She needs to see where he's taking her.

She'll be sixteen in a few days. Silver's on a cusp, a precipice. If there is a time to turn your life upside down, surely it is now?

PRISONS NEVER SLEEP

15

TWELVE YEARS PREVIOUSLY

ICE

Johannesburg, 2024

Zack starts as he hears a shuffling sound at the door. It's pitch black. As his eyes adjust to the darkness, he can hear the groaning and thudding of the building's innards. Prisons never sleep.

The sound that woke him, real or imagined, pulled him from a dream of another life where he was free. He tries to grab on to the coattails of that dream, tries to make his way back to the light and colour and warmth of the parallel reality, but there's another sound at the door, and Zack knows it's Bernard again. The knowledge sets off a fizz of foreboding inside his stomach.

The door slides open and she floats inside. Stronger than her silhouette is her smell—perhaps a residue of bodywash—cucumber and mint, and something else that he can't name. Dog saliva. Yoghurt. Some kind of curdled dread, or is that his own body, reacting to hers?

She doesn't say anything. Bernard just stands there and watches him sleep.

PIRATE.
DESPOILER.
BANDIT.

16

Every morning there is a strict routine of exercise at the ICE. It doesn't matter if your muscles are cramping from lying on the nibbled rubber slab they call a mattress, or if you can hardly keep your sleep-deprived eyes open because of the yelling and snoring and swearing that is the 24/7 soundtrack in the hard, cold cells. It doesn't matter if you're healthy or ill, if you drink your three daily nutrishakes or if you're on a hunger strike. You do the exercise.

You strip down to your orange jox and climb into the Orb. The first time you do it, you worry about coming out alive. After that, it gets easier. The holistic fitness machine scans your body and your brain for the exercise that will most benefit you. It identifies Zack's weakest group of muscles—his lower back—and coaches him through various strength training exercises. The Orb knows the drills can get boring, so its additional features can exercise your mind too. Mini holo crossword puzzles and maths games. Slitherlinks. Memory contests. KenKen, Skyscrapers, Futoshiki, Hitori, Nurikabe. Unfortunately, the mental features are shut off for prisoners like him. They want his body to be strong, to complete the work they'll soon employ him to do in the penal labour camps, but they want his brain to be as dull as seaglass.

"Your lawyer's here," says Lovemore, the guard with the lazy eye.

Heady relief melts Zack's muscles. He gives his hands and face a quick shot of cold water, jumps into his overalls, then offers his wrists to the guard to cuff.

Thank fuck, thank fuck, thank fuck, is all he can think as he's led towards the admin wing. At last, someone who will be on his side. Someone who can get him out of this fuck-forsaken nightmare so that he can get on with his job.

The interview room is about as depressing as his cell, but it's a different kind of depressing, which he appreciates. As he sits down, a man arrives, and a new tension chills the room. Zack stares at the interloper's well-tailored suit with something close to envy. Of course, he knows the feeling is not about the suit at all, but a kind of nostalgic pang for the life he used to have—the life he'll never have again. The man approaches the table and offers Zack his palm. Zack doesn't take it. No one shakes hands anymore, especially not with a dangerous serial killer. Isn't that what he's supposed to be? Isn't that why he's in here?

The man retracts his hand and smiles to paper over the sudden awkwardness.

"Mpanghi," he says.

"Excuse me?"

"My name."

Mpanghi sits down, pretends to relax, and interlaces his fingers over the beginning of a potbelly.

"That couldn't have been easy," says Zack.

"What?"

"In school. Your name."

"Ha!" he says, and looks around. He wasn't expecting a laugh. His mirth surprises him. "You're right. It wasn't easy."

uMpanghi: Pirate. Despoiler. Bandit.

"Suits you, though," says Zack.

The man stops smiling.

Zack turns to the guard. "This isn't my lawyer."

Lovemore blinks at him.

"But I am," Mpanghi says. "I am your lawyer. Appointed

by the state."

Zack stands up. "There's been a misunderstanding."

"Sit down, Prisoner," says Lovemore.

"I don't need a state-appointed attorney. I have my own lawyer. Detective Ramphele said he would be called."

"Ramphele no longer works for the SAP."

"I don't care about Ramphele, I just want my lawyer. My real lawyer."

Lovemore breathes through his mouth, scratches his cheek with slender fingers. "I don't know anything about that."

"Well," says Zack, taking a step forward, "that's not a problem. Just let me contact him. All it'll take is one call."

"You don't have phone privileges," he says.

Zack swallows his frustration. "Can *you* call him for me?"

When Lovemore looks uncertain, he adds, "I'll pay you more than what you make here in a year."

"That won't be necessary," says Mpanghi.

"You're new here. You don't know what's necessary."

"You don't have banking privileges, either," says Lovemore.

"My lawyer will arrange that. My real lawyer."

Mphangi's eyes crinkle in a false smile. "I'm afraid that's not how it works."

There's something sinister about the man. Zack felt it immediately as he entered the room, thought it was maybe nerves from being cloistered for so long but, no, there's definitely something menacing about him.

"What the fuck does that mean?"

Lovemore says, "It means that just because you're rich, doesn't mean you get to call the shots. Doesn't mean you get special treatment."

"Used to be rich," says Mpanghi.

Zack looks at him. "What did you say?"

"Your accounts have been frozen, pending the outcome of the trial."

"They can't do that."

"They have, already. Don't worry, you'll get it all back … If you're innocent."

"And if they find me guilty?"

"Your money goes into the pot. You'll be paying for other criminals' trials. But don't worry, once they've enlisted you at one of the crim colonies, you'll be able to start earning bank again. Pray that you get into the space mining programme… I've heard that one pays the best."

It also has the highest fatality rate.

"It's against the constitution." Zack's chest blooms with anxiety. The money was going to be his ticket out of here. This isn't going according to plan.

Mpanghi and Lovemore look at each other and laugh without smiling.

"Haven't you heard? The Nancies keeps changing the constitution."

"Change it every day, like dirty underwear."

"Last week it was the *Amakwerekwere* ban. This week, well, your timing is very bad," says the lawyer. "The Criminal Asset Seizure Act was signed … last night. It was hardly contested in parly and I can't say I disagree with the tenets. I mean, why should wealthy people be able to get the best lawyers? Hardly seems fair. Now you'll all get equal treatment." He strokes his oiled beard; his eyes rest on Zack. "I mean, a murderer is a murderer, right?"

DOUBLE DECEPTION

17

TWELVE YEARS LATER

Innercity

Johannesburg, 2036

Silver is pulled along a dim passageway plastered with old-school bumper stickers, graffiti and chewing gum. Over and over again she sees the letters QE. QE. QE.

"QE?"

"Question Everything," says Dragon Scales.

At the very end she recognises a sticker of an image she

grew up with: a neon bunny. Seth would always point them out to her and Mally, when they'd spot them on a park hoverbench or a skateboard ramp.

That's Alba, he used to say, and tell them the story of the DNA-spliced rabbit in the lab. Silver named her cuddle bunny after him, and still secretly sleeps with the threadbare plush tucked into the angle of her elbow, her lips on his balding head.

"That's Alba," she says now, pointing to the sticker, and DS smiles.

They go further and deeper and Silver tries to remember the way but after the first few turns, her mind blanks, and her nerves start zinging again.

What the fuck am I doing?

As if reading her thoughts, he turns to her and says: "Almost there."

They reach another door, and he uses his fingerprint to unlock it. The fluorescent lights detect their motion and flicker on, overhead. It's a double volume room that looks like a disused operating theatre. Cheap white tiles everywhere, scratched and scuffed from years of scrubbing and harsh chemicals. Dusty now, smirched, with sinister black grouting. Pushed up against the walls are old OR spotlights and metallic trays; medical cabinets; IV hooks. Silver is sure she's still green. She starts to sweat.

Dragon Scales pulls a vintage dentist's chair into the centre, then shuttles the overhead spotlight next to it, switches it on, to test it. The bright light hurts Silver's eyes, and she looks away.

"This isn't what I was expecting."

Her voice comes out dull and flat: the room is soundproofed.

A tiny red light glows from the corner of the door, indicating that its locked.

"Don't worry, it's perfect for what we need to do."

Silver's insides have liquefied; at least, that's what it feels like.

"I can see you're nervous," says Dragon Scales. "I don't want you to worry."

Silver slowly steps backwards and knocks over a metal bowl. It clatters and rings on the tiles. "Let me out of here."

"Let me explain."

The hairs on her neck stand up. "I don't want you to explain. I want to get the fuck out of here."

"Why don't you sit down?" He motions at the chair and switches off the spotlight.

"I'll scream," she says, but they both know there is no point.

"There's no need—" he begins, but is interrupted by a shuffling sound at the door.

The small LED switches to green, and Silver breaks for it, but just before she gets there, another man comes in and she almost crashes into him.

"Whoa!" he says, catching her.

"Let me out!" Silver shouts, but the door swings on its hinges and closes softly, and the red light comes back on.

"Whoa!" he says, letting her go. "What the fuck, man?"

"Thank you for coming," says Dragon Scales. "We're almost ready for you. Kid Silver, this is Doctor Smith."

How stupid does he think I am?

Doctor Smith. A double deception, in just two words.

The man seems nervous. "She's just a little girl."

"She'll be sixteen soon."

"I don't know, man." He rubs his ear and then his neck.

"We have a deal," says DS. "Right?"

"I don't know," he says. "I mean, she's so young. Look at her. And I'm not even really a—"

DS interrupts him. "It's a simple procedure, you'll do fine."

'Smith' hunches over in his defeat, and pulls a roll of starched black fabric out of his shoulder bag. He loosens the tie and unrolls it onto a stainless steel tray, revealing surgical implements that glint in the harsh light.

Silver starts to scream. She runs for the door, pounding on it and shouting for help. From behind, Dragon Scales slaps a hot hand over her mouth and shoots a tranqtaser into her neck. The current travels down her limbs, a long, hot shock, and is followed by the warmth of the tranquilliser. It melts her. Silver's body wants to soften all the way to the floor, but Dragon Scales holds her up, carries her to the chair and secures her wrists and feet with the big brown leather straps and copper buckles. He switches the spotlight back on, momentarily blinding her, then angles the light so it's shining on her silver hair. She's woozy with the fear and the drugs; she wants to kick and fight, but her body is a warm, wet sponge.

DS holds something to her head, some buzzing thing, and with the vibration she feels her hair being shaven. A streak of white falls to the floor. She thinks he'll shave her whole head, but he stops at that one line just left of centre, where she used to part her hair. DS fastens a leather strap to her forehead now too. Silver tries to talk, to beg, but even her mouth is paralysed. DS spends a moment caressing her head, her cheek.

"There's nothing to be afraid of," he says, then holds her hopeless hand. "I know it seems scary, but this is the quickest and easiest way. We're not going to hurt you."

Silver's face is frozen; her tongue is numb. All she can manage is a throaty groan.

What has she done what has she done what has she done—

A tear runs down her temple.

Smith's face moves away, then pops up again, holding a mediquill.

"Anaesthetic," he warbles, then jams it into the tender crook of her arm. "Count down from ten."

The scalpel is out now and misted with antiseptic spray. The same spray is cool on her strip of bare scalp. Silver resists counting, but colour-numbers come to her anyway, and float before her. Rainbow sprinkles on soiled bandages. Spinning scalpel cupcakes. 10, 9, 8 ... and then they fade to black.

SHORN AND STITCHED

18

Dragon Scales watches as the med school drop-out applies the dressing to Silver's shorn and stitched scalp. He checks her vitals. Her body is twitching with stress, but she's alive. He touches her cheek, snaps his fingers in her face.

"Silver?" *snap, snap.* "Silver?"

She gasps as if drowning, her back arches and her eyes open and roll back.

"Can you hear me?"

A long, desperate gasp for air, then her body seems to relax. She lists backwards on the chair and her eyes close again.

"Is she okay?" DS asks Smith. "Is that normal?"

Smith shrugs. "What's normal? I told you I've never done this before."

Dragon Scales checks her pulse again, and it seems steady. He touches his mandible to place the call. "It's done."

A woman replies, "Good. Bring her in."

SKIN ZIP

19

Seth's Apartment

Johannesburg, 2036

Mally switches off his cinescreen and gingerly climbs out of bed. Standing makes his upper thigh throb like a motherfucker. He gives his worst injury a quick inspection—it's already healing, thanks to the stem-cell skin zip—and limps towards the kitchen. He stops short when he hears Kate's terse voice.

"Fuck," says his mother. She doesn't like it when *he* swears, but her mouth is one of the foulest he knows. So much for modelling the behaviour you expect from your kids. There's other stuff too, that she does. He doesn't blame her, though. No one said having a baby made you perfect. And in his case, well, she didn't even give birth to him, so all bets are off.

"What are we going to do?" That's Keke talking.

"Get out before the panic sets in," says Seth.

"Out?"

"Out of the city. Out of AI's reach."

What the hell are they talking about?

"Out of AI's reach? That doesn't even exist."

"The longer we stand here talking about it, the less chance we have of getting out alive."

Mally stares at a poster on his wall. It's a vintage one, a gift from Uncle Marko. It's a 2D cartoon of a Bender from Futurama, and the robot's saying: *Being a robot is great, but we don't have emotions, and sometimes that makes me very sad.*

"But where?" demands Kate. "And how will we live? What will we eat?"

"You know what I mean. Away from any kind of machine that can harm the kids. Besides, what will we eat if we stay here? It's not like the Bilchen Meal drones are going to keep delivering."

"Oh," says Kate, anxiety turning her voice to gravel.

"What's wrong? Kate? It looks like you're about to pass out."

"The kids. Silver. Silver's out there somewhere. Morgan put her in a cab, but that was over an hour ago."

Mally's never heard Seth so worried. "It's past her curfew. Silver never misses her curfew."

"What if she's—"

"She's still not answering her mandible."

"We have to go get her."

"What about Mally? We can't leave him here."

"There's no way he's going out there."

"Shit. What about Vega?"

"He's never seeing her again."

Mally starts tip-toeing backwards, away from the kitchen. He doesn't know what's going on—not yet—but there's no way he's not going to see Vega again. He'd rather die than never see her again. She is his soulmate, his best friend. Some people say that robots don't have souls—some even try to criminalise human/bot relationships—but Mally knows that's not true. Seventh-generation androids have got exactly the same proficiency for love as any bio person. Flesh and blood doesn't make you human, that's for sure. That's what he's seen over and over again in his sixteen years. It's what struck him into existence and what almost bashed him out of it again. Vega has as much vital force as any non-droid he knows. They love each other so much it hurts—well, it hurts him, anyway, deeply and achingly—

and there's no way Kate's paranoia is going to come between them.

Seth's Vektor is abandoned on the sideboard. Usually Seth's so careful with storing the gun: Mally's never seen it lying around before. He is obviously more upset with the Bonechaser incident than he lets on. He blinks back tears. He won't think about the dog now, he can't; there'll be time for him to mourn later.

He takes the availability of the Vektor as a sign, clips the weapon onto his utility belt and covers it with his shirt. He's reversed all the way to the front door now, which is still on the blink, allowing him a quick and soundless exit.

A NORMAL KIND OF MIDNIGHT

20

Mally's about to step into the elevator when he gets a bad feeling.

"Good evening," says the speaker inside the intelligent metal cube.

Best to stay away from anything with smarts, he decides, remembering his mother's tense conversation with the others. As he takes the stairs, he thinks of Silver, and his nerves gnaw at him. He should be trying to find her too, but he needs to keep his eye on the ball. He'll find Vega first, then they'll figure out the rest. Besides, his mother and Seth will probably go out to get Silver, that's what it sounded like. She's probably safe at the Atrium, anyway. Probably forgot to set the timer on her immersion and now she's missed curfew. Unusual for her, he reflects, as he gets a new lining of dread in his stomach. Silver knows that if she misses her curfew she'll be grounded for a week. She's so obsessed with gaming Eden 7.0 that a week without playing will kill her.

The other kids in their virtual class treat Silver differently. Well, they treat them both differently, but for different reasons. Mally because he's the only surviving Genesis kid, and also because of his controversial relationship with Vega. But they kind of revere Silver. It could be because of her eccentric appearance (beautiful, white-haired, bird-boned), her attachment to that grimy gas-mask, or her mad gaming skills. Or it could be because of her bionic finger, and the story that comes with it. The Net knows the kids like to tell that story. He's heard a thousand variations, each one more outlandish than the last, but Mally thinks people feel weird around her mostly due to the feeling you get when she walks into the room, even if it's a virtual room. It's like she has an air of electricity about her. Like there's static in the air. He used to think he was the only one to feel this way, thought maybe it's because they're twins (or kind-of twins) but now he sees it on other people's faces too. A kind of surprise, a curiosity, that she arouses wherever she goes.

She's always had it, her point of difference, whatever it is. He remembers people's reactions to her when she was a child, but with puberty it's been magnified. Intensified. The kids in class who are also into the Atrium Games say that the other players call Silver 'Ghost'.

Mally reaches the bottom of the stairs and his leg feels as if it's on fire. He roots in his pocket for the analgesic inhalant, sucks out a dose, and hobbles out of the front entrance, thankful that the biometric pad is still working, and stands on the hot pavement. It's almost midnight, but it's 36 degrees Celsius.

Coolvest.

His cooling shirt immediately temps him down. He puts on his facemask and swipes the ads out the way to check his newstream. Nothing cosmic seems to be happening in the headlines:

Shini Wam signs off New Nuke deal.

Mars shuttle still missing.

Have you got your flu sticker?

Roguebots vs Bot-Hunters: A Tipping Point.

The Orbital Space Junk Clean-Up Needs Your Help.

Crim Colonies profit up 17%.

Are your smart drugstax killing you?

Killer Porterbot; DroidChef; Hyperloop: What Really Happened?

Universal Basic Income is finally here!

So maybe whatever the parental units were panicking about isn't as serious as they think. Indeed, as people walk and airskate around him, it looks like any normal kind of midnight in Jozi. He stands for a second longer, wondering which tram to climb aboard. The Atrium is twelve blocks east. Vega's hostel is in the opposite direction. Is Silver really in danger? Probably not. Or at least that's what he tells himself, despite his nagging intuition, as he catches a westbound and heads into the smartificial sect of ChinaCity/Sandton.

MISTER GALAXY

21

TWELVE YEARS PREVIOUSLY

ICE

Johannesburg, 2024

Zack uses the mean bar of prison-issue soap to draw on the bag-washed brix of his cell. He uses the whole wall opposite his metal bunkbed as his canvas, and only manages to get the outlines done before running out of soap—a loose-lined sketch of a blooming lotus flower. He likes that it's almost invisible.

It's the best use of the soap he can think of: to add something pretty to look at. Something that embodies beauty and potential and hope because, the Net knows, there's none of that in here. More importantly, it's his daily reminder of The Truth, why he's here, and what he still needs to do. Zack stands there in his small grey cell and looks at the flower. Imagines it blooming and arching and then crumbling away to nothing.

I'm here to wake up the Lotus Eaters.

The arrest has temporarily derailed his plan, but there is always a way forward, and it's imperative that he keeps his nerve.

The small soap lozenge is one of those maddening details he's glad he's now rid of. They give you a pillow-case, but no pillow, a window with no view, and a piece of cheap soap with no water. He can't yet tell if it's lack of attention to detail or, in a more sinister vein: a welcome mat to the house of insanity. Sometimes he feels, psychologically speaking, as if they're giving him just enough rope to hang himself with.

He hears a whistle from outside. Lazy-eyed Lovemore. He knows without a doubt because Lovemore is the only guard who warns you before he enters. He's usually whistling a kind of musty gospel tune. Maybe he thinks prisoners deserve a modicum of privacy, or maybe the whistling is like his protective charm, to shield himself from walking in on cell mates doing things he doesn't want to see.

The door opens, and the guard motions for Zack to follow him.

Lovemore's not his favourite, but at least it's not Bernard.

The light hurts Zack's eyes; he blinks away the burn. "Where're we going?"

"Didn't they tell you?"

They walk down corridors and up stairs and on conveyor belts until Zack loses his sense of direction. It doesn't help that there are no windows and no natural light to gauge the scope of the sun. He wants to think that his lawyer, his real lawyer, has somehow managed to break through the red tape, or that the charges against him have been dropped, but he can't help but have a bad feeling. Everything about this place seems underhanded, opaque. Helena Nash told them so, said they had sped through her trial with one goal only, and that was to put her away forever.

They reach the courtroom, which is already populated by the jury and a sprinkling of press. He inspects the journalists' faces one by one, searching, hoping, for Keke. Surely she would attend? At best, to support him, at worst, to see him grilled and found guilty. But even that, he'd prefer over this: not one familiar face in the crowd.

"It's happening now?" he asks Lovemore. "The trial? Already?"

"You're never happy, you crims," he says, "nag, nag, nag for a speedy trial and then when you get one, you complain. We can't keep you on ICE forever, you know."

Yes, Zack knows. ICE costs the state cash, while the crim colonies pretty much print money. They don't want creeps to stay here for one day longer than absolutely necessary.

"But we don't even have a strategy, yet."

"You had the opportunity to liaise with Mr Mpanghi."

"You're kidding."

He's not kidding.

"That wasn't a meeting. That was an ambush."

Lovemore shrugs. "You weren't very co-operative for a man being offered free legal counsel."

"I haven't even shaved. I'm in prison overalls."

His bright orange suit screams 'dangerous criminal' and he has itchy, three-day stubble. His hair is greasy and his eyes are underlined by dark crescents.

"Don't worry about it, pretty boy, this isn't Mister Galaxy. You're not getting judged on your looks."

Zack knows very well that everyone, everywhere, is always pre-judged on their looks, and he knows for a fact that at the moment he looks exactly how they want him to look: like a degenerate serial killer.

Lovemore leads him to his seat in the front row of the gallery, next to Mpanghi, who nods to acknowledge his presence.

"Do you have a plan?" Zack whispers.

"Of course." He smiles: an ebony Cheshire cat.

Zack searches the gallery again for Keke.

The trio of judges trails in, and everybody stands. Zack doesn't recognise any of them.

His charge sheet is read aloud, and the corner-mounted cameras record the muted exclamations from the crowd behind him. The anchor reels off every victim's name, one by one, so that the jury can feel the mass accusation like a heavy stole on their shoulders. It's their job, is the clear, unspoken message, to secure justice for these people. The jurors take turns to cast suspicious glances at him, their minds perhaps already made up.

The anchor finally gets to the end of his list: 108 counts of premeditated murder. There's a hushed moment, an opportunity to let the gravitas of the charges against him sink in, and then the head judge claps his hands and says "Well! Let us begin."

BREAD & CIRCUSES

22

Every day when Zack is brought to the courthouse, he looks for Keke, and every day he's disappointed. Surely, surely one day she'll show? It starts to feel like an unrequited love affair of the criminal variety. Every day he slumps further into despair. He hasn't had a shower or a decent night's sleep in weeks. He's haunted every night by the looming silhouette of Bernard. He lies awake, waiting for her to arrive, and when she does—she always does—then he lies there listening to her breathe while adrenaline combs his nerves and keeps him awake long after she leaves.

Why does Bernard stalk him? Why does she watch him sleep? Does she know who he really is?

Impossible.

He's begged Lovemore for something, anything to read, to stop the slow atrophying of his brain. It's one of the most difficult things about being in here. He can deal with no showers, no company—and lately, no toothbrush—but with no sleep and nothing to read he will surely go insane. Every day in this place is a step closer to delirium.

Mphangi subtly sniffs the air, then moves an inch away from Zack. He doesn't blame him. He'd move away from himself if he could. Far away. Perhaps if he thinks about the metaphysical hangman's noose they're extending to him hard enough it will materialise. Something like Schrödinger's Cat. Schrödinger's Noose?

Stand up! Stand up! Observe!

Zachary Girdler is both alive and dead at the same time.

"When can I take the stand?" he asks Mphangi.

The pirate's eyebrows shoot up. "You're not taking the stand."

"Won't they want my testimony? Won't they need to ask me questions?"

He shakes his head.

"What if I want to say something?"

"What would you say?"

"I could prepare a speech. In my defence."

"This isn't *Law & Order*."

"Mpanghi. I need to get the hell out of here."

"Just let me do my job."

"But you're not doing your job! That's the problem. We just sit here all day watching the prosecutor paint me into a a corner."

"You need to trust in the judicial process."

Zack doesn't even know why he's arguing. It's not like he can tell the truth about what he does, anyway. Maybe he thinks that without any hard evidence—because he knows none exists—they won't be able to convict him. But no one seems to mind this minor detail. In fact, he gets the feeling that most of the time these people aren't even listening. He has his suspicions that one of the junior judges hasn't heard a word of the trial—Zack saw his earbuttons in, and his right foot is always tapping—and the day-dreaming jury don't seem to require any further convincing of his guilt. He can tell from their dagger glares that they were against him from day one.

The prosecutor comes to the end of his examination, and thanks the witness. The woman rises to leave the stand.

"Aren't you going to cross-examine?" Zack whispers.

Mpanghi shrugs, wrinkles his nose. *Nah*, his body language says. *Nah*. As if someone's offered him a tepid cup of tea.

"Next witness!" calls the head judge, and Zack can't help

but imagine that he's treading some Kafka-flavoured Möbius strip, a Lewis Carrol trial where everyone's crazy and no one seems to mind. "Next witness!" says judge, but he may as well be shouting "Off with his head!"

What was that quote about bread and circuses? Zack wishes he could remember it, because he thinks it might just sum up exactly what's happening here.

WHAT HAVE WE DONE

A FUCKING LUCKY PACKET

23

Lovemore is whistling outside Zack's cell again. Zack stops what he's doing—adding scratch detail to his lotus flower mural by using a small nail he pried from his prison-issue boots—and hides the tack inside a tiny slit inside his mattress.

The door opens, and Lovemore stops mid-tune and greets him in a celebratory manner.

"Prisoner!" Lovemore's never once called him by his name. Do they teach that in guard training, to keep the detainees at a distance? Will he get a number when he's taken to the crim colonies, concentration camp style? It should do a good job of further dehumanising him in the penal scouts' eyes. Maybe Zack is being paranoid. Maybe Lovemore's just not good with names.

Zack expects the guard to admonish him for drawing on the wall, or say something demoralising like, "They're just going to paint over that as soon as you're out of here, you know," or "Get scrubbing, Prisoner!" or maybe worse, but he acts as if he hasn't seen it at all. As if he hasn't seen it grow from a barely invisible soap sketch to a massive toothpaste and boot-polish shaded 3D-looking bloom.

"Jury's out!" says Lovemore, who is clearly having a good day.

"What?"

"Get your stuff, Prisoner. It's moving day!"

"But we didn't even conclude the trial. We haven't heard all the testimony. What kind of trial is over in three days?"

"A successful one," says Lovemore.

Zack almost chokes. "Successful for who?"

The guard shows him his big white teeth. "For everyone."

Mpanghi has a similar attitude. "Very good," he says, when he sees Zack. "A very good trial."

Zack's fuse is lit. "The fuck do you mean? It's been an absolute sham."

"The quicker the trial, the less expensive it is for the people. We all knew the outcome from the beginning, didn't we? There's really no point in dragging these things out."

The judges enter and everyone stands, then sits down again. Zack remains upright.

"Have you reached a verdict?" asks the head judge.

A juror with long white braids stands and says, "We have, your Honour." She clicks a button on the remote she's holding and their jury score is projected onto the evidence cinescreen.

Twelve red men. Twelve out of twelve. A dirty dozen.

"*Eish!*" Mpanghi looks impressed. "Full marks!".

Zack grits his teeth, curls his hand into a fist.

Do not punch your attorney. Do not punch your attorney. Not in front of the whole court, anyway.

The audience is pleased. They clap as if it's been a long but satisfying stage play. The head judge bangs his gavel and the people quieten down.

"Thank you for your service," he says to the jury, who look jolly for the first time. It's as if they've been holding their vote in for three days, and now they can finally relax. Now they're free to get back to their normal lives, spend whatever stipend they'll receive for their work here, root through their ICE-branded goodie bags for their Kool-aid flavoured jelly beans.

"Guilty as charged. We'll now proceed with sentencing."

"Sentencing?" says Zack. "That's not how it works."

The judge puts his gavel down. "Mister Girdler? You have an objection?"

Zack looks down at Mpanghi, who returns his glare with interest. *Is his client really stupid enough,* he seems to be thinking, *to piss off the judge who's about to sentence him?*

"You need time to consider the verdict, and then decide on the sentence."

"I don't need any more time," says the judge. "I've heard and seen enough."

"But—"

"Guilty of 108 charges of pre-meditated murder, Mister Girdler. I didn't need to think very long at all when it came to decide what we should do with you."

The jury has lost its cheer, now. They look on, fascinated. Zack realises then that none of this has been real, from the imposter lawyer to the actors on the jury bench. The head judge narrows his eyes at Zack. It's all been an elaborate ruse, a game, an expert choreography of power vs pawn.

"I'm not falling for this!" Zack shouts. "I can see what's happening here!"

The audience starts tittering. They weren't expecting an encore.

"This isn't a court of law. And you," he says to the judge. "A judge! I bet you don't even have a law degree. I bet you got your certificate out of a fucking lucky packet!"

Now the audience and press have their devices out,

recording Zack's outburst. Further proof, he imagines, that he's a madman, deluded and dangerous.

"Girdler," says Mpanghi, "sit down, man. You're making it worse."

"Fuck you!" shouts Zack, and uses all the willpower he possesses not to break the lawyer's nose.

"Where did they get you from?" Zack shouts at the gallery who are hiding behind their recording devices. They are all actors; he can see that now. Flashes from their cameras prick his already scratchy eyes.

The head judge bangs his gavel. "Mister Girdler!"

"Will the accused please sit down," pipes the prosecutor, enjoying the show.

This can't be happening. He can't go to a Penal Labour Colony. He has to get to Kate before it's too late.

"I will not sit down!"

A part of Zack is observing himself as part of the show. He knows the protestations before they leave his mouth. He sees himself wrecked by this insidious system: hungry, dirty, high on sleep-dep, and knows that it will be better for everybody if he just acts obsequious, because raving about the injustice won't solve a damn thing. No one cares about the rights of a person responsible for more than a hundred individually and immaculately orchestrated deaths. They just want to lock him up and throw away the key. This cannot happen. There's something at the very core of him that refuses to be deceived.

"I'm giving you one last chance to sit down!" shouts the head judge. The court security police start to pre-emptively make their way towards him: two navy uniforms in the corners of his vision.

"I can't believe you get away with this shit," says Zack.

Keep calm, now, keep quiet.

The security cops are right here. He prepares to fight them, but his cuffs keep his wrists bound.

"You get away from me!" he shouts at them. They both flinch, as if he's a rabid dog who's tried to bite.

"Come on, Prisoner," says one of the cops, one hand out towards him and the other tickling her thigh holster. "Take it easy."

"I have a name!" shouts Zack. His actions are spinning out of his control now.

"Take it easy and no one gets hurt." She has hazel eyes. Kind eyes. He's lulled into a second of letting his guard down when the other cop tries to grab him. Zack struggles, trying to get away while the creeps watch through their camera lenses. Flash, flash, flash.

He pulls back his arms, ready to right-hook the cop, but as he does so, his handcuffs bite him hard on his wrists. He looks down at them, at once shocked and unsurprised. He immediately feels the warm, comforting rush of TranX as it streamrolls over his adrenaline. It takes away his desire to fight, to run, to reason, and the floor rushes up to meet him.

No, no, no. This isn't part of the plan.

He hears snippets of conversation as his consciousness escapes like vapour out of his skull:

— unavoidable —

— Clearly a danger to himself and others —

— Maximum security is the only option —

— or psych ward? —

— sedation —

— paranoid —

— delusional —

— away for a long, long time —

It's a relief when the drug washes him away.

HOT TOKYO

24

TWELVE YEARS LATER

Innercity

Johannesburg, 2036

Mally's mandible buzzes. Vega calling.

Pick up, he thinks, and the call connects.

"Vega. I was just on my way to you."

"Mally," she says. "Mally." But something sounds wrong. Her tone is off.

His heart sprints.

"What's wrong? Where are you?"

"Mally," she warbles, sounding like a robot for the first time Mally can remember.

Find Vega. Find Vega!

His holomap spins out and shows him the destination pin. She's not at her hostel—she's closer than that—three blocks north, at the CBD Night Market. Mally instructs the tram to stop. Other vehicles hoot. He jumps off, and as he lands on the pavement a jolt of pain in his injured leg almost floors him. He can't see any northbound trams, and no cabbies are idling, so he starts to jog towards her location. Every step is a steel rivet in his flesh. He's running and murmuring now, he doesn't care what the people think as they stop to watch him hiss in pain. The teeth of the railway sutures are coming apart, opening his wound.

When he arrives at the market it's buzzing with vendors shouting and shoppers haggling. A mime dressed as a golden statue blows a kiss to a baby in a bubble-pram, and the baby starts to cry. Buskers in bowler hats sing a hundred-year-old song. Mally pushes his way through the crowd that smells of sherry popgrains and roasted nuts, body odour and barbecue sauce. Strawberry XugarSpray. He's fifty metres away from Vega now, and some of the market-goers step out of his way as he hyperventilates into his mask, sweating and bleeding, muttering to himself. It's a good tactic to part the crowds.

There's a booth at the outskirts of the Asian section called Hot Tokyo. It's a brightly lit mini-mart for the regular home staples not supplied by the fresh produce market: alt-dairy milks and cheeses, coconut water, hotwipes, detergents. His dash tells him Vega's in there.

"Vega!" Mally shouts as he stumbles through the wide entrance. The short woman at the till puts her hands up in fright, as if she's expecting to be robbed. Her eyes are magnified by the thick lenses in her old-tech frames.

"Vega!" Mally shouts at her, and the shop owner reverses into the shelves of blunt-vapes, snaffeine, and caramel condoms a decade past their sell-by date. Some of the products clatter to the ground. He shows her Vega's avatar, the ruby Alpha Lyrae star, and her eyes grow wider still. She shows him the panic button on the counter and speaks in Xiang. Mally's mandible insta-translates to English: "The man he took her," she says. "Called the cops. Called the cops."

"Which man?" he shouts, resisting the urge to shake the woman. Vega's location is moving slowly away from him. She babbles and shows him her old-school security screen, rewinds it two minutes by swiping a stubby finger, and Mally watches with horror as a man with a mohawk winds his arm back and punches Vega as hard as he can, smashing her cheek in and almost breaking her neck. There are other men surrounding the two, and Mally thinks they'll step in to help her but instead they laugh and cheer soundlessly.

"No go there. Wait for cops! No go there, he kill you!"

Hot saliva floods Mally's mouth, as if he's about to be sick, but he doesn't have time for that. The man staggers towards Vega and trails his hand over her hip, moves his crotch towards her in clumsy humping jerks while the others laugh. She is frozen; she doesn't have protocol for that. She tries to step away from the man, but slips on some spilled liquid on the floor where her groceries have been smashed. The man lunges at her.

"Where?" Mally shouts, but the woman shakes her head. She won't tell him, doesn't want him endangering his life for a robot. She doesn't understand. He scrubs through to the end of the attack where he sees the other men leave the grocery store, and the mohawk head-butts Vega then drags her by the hair out the back door. Mally tears his eyes away from the screen, looking for the door.

He races towards it, through it, and lands up in a crowded kitchen, then a steaming laundry room, then a black back alley, where the man has Vega's body spreadeagled over a dumpster, her skirt pushed up, her panties torn and hanging off a broken ankle.

"Stop!" Mally says, and the mohawk looks up at him with sour evil in his eyes. Muscles flexed, glaring at him as if he can't believe a kid is going to waste his time.

"Leave her alone," says Mally.

Vega's body is a mannequin.

The man takes his hand off Vega's knee and walks a few steps towards Mally. "Get outta here, boy. Mind your own business."

"I'm not leaving without her," says Mally. "And, anyway, the cops are coming."

The man laughs, then mocks Mally. "Ooh! The cops are

coming! The cops are coming!"

"They're on their way," says Mally. "The shop owner called them five minutes ago."

"You think I give a fuck about pigs?" He hawks and spits onto the littered ground. "You think the pigs care about what we do to fucking skins?"

Mally swallows hard.

The police force has had a fair amount of trouble with PR lately, with human cops abusing the new robo recruits.

It's to be expected, the Minister of Security said, *we presumed there would be a certain amount of resistance. Teething problems. Adjustment issues.*

Teething problems. Tell that to the recruit who had his head cut off with a bandsaw by his law enforcement partner.

"It's illegal, what you're doing. She's—" He hates to say the words, but they're true. "She's government property." He gulps the rising acid in his throat. "She's a 7thGen. You're d-damaging government property. And there's video evidence of you doing it."

The mohawk ambles back to Vega, a greasy stride of alpha male, ready to assert his power. He has a swastika scalp tat. He puts his hand back on her knee, starts to move it up her inner thigh, the thigh Mally knows so well. Vega's body shudders. The air is thick, foetid; Mally feels choked with haze and nerves.

The man unhooks the notch on his pants. He winds his

arms around Vega's calves and pulls her body towards himself. "You ready for me, robo-whore?" He slaps her caved-in cheek. "I'm going to fuck you till you bleed."

Something inside Mally explodes. Fresh adrenaline flushes through his heart and erupts in every cell of his body. What is it about creeps? What is it about these fucking toxic bastards that compels them to thrust poison into beauty? Why do they have to stain and maim? The fury fills his body, makes his bones vibrate. He unclips the Vektor from his utility belt and holds it up to the man with shaking arms.

"Whoa, cowboy!" he says, putting up his hands. "Where'd you get that?"

Now he's paying attention.

Now who's in charge, thinks Mally, but then there's a short melody of metallic clicks as the man returns Mally's Vektor's aim with his own, bigger weapons which he draws from behind him, one in each hand.

Where are the cops? Where are the fucking cops?

The mohawk advances. His comparative bulk makes Mally feel young, weak, takes him back to the childhood nightmare that still haunts him.

Vega's body jerks again.

He's close now, just a few metres away. Which bullet will reach him first? Panic evaporates what's left of Mally's thoughts. He pulls the trigger, but nothing happens. His brain is as blank as the weapon.

"I almost feel sorry for you," says the man. "You don't even know how to fire a gun."

Mally tries the trigger again. Nothing.

"You don't even know that Vektors can only be fired by their owners," says the man, "which, judging by your position, you are very clearly not."

Mally tries again, tries to force the thing to fire, but it remains stubbornly mute. The realisation slams into him. There's a biometric fingerprint pad on the trigger, of course, and no one but Seth can fire it.

"This is getting more and more interesting," says the mohawk. "A boy, with a stolen gun, rat-running the city streets to protect androids. I'm intrigued. I'm almost tempted to keep you alive—"

Finally, finally, the siren of a police drone wails overhead.

"—but, unfortunately for you, we've run out of time."

He raises his semi-automatic and aims it at Mally's forehead. His lips shrink as he looks through the weapon's sight and a deafening shot explodes the air.

WE'RE NOT SAFE ANYMORE

25

Mally thinks he's been shot. Thinks he can't feel the pain because of the shock, because of the blinding, eardrum-popping blast that's just happened in front of his eyes. He looks down at his chest, blinking away the bombshell, expecting to find a hole where his heart used to be, but his trembling fingers can't find any damage. If there's no damage, why can't he breathe? The police siren grows louder. Then he sees that the mohawk is sprawled on the ground, and the back half of his skull is missing. Mally can't understand what is happening until he sees Vega, who is now sitting up, her roscoe smoking.

"Vega!" Mally darts over to her. It feels like running on

air. His instinct is to ask if she's okay, but her face is conked in and her arm looks dislocated. Her ankle is definitely broken. He pulls her skirt down, unloops the shredded panties carefully from her feet and drops them into the dumpster, and helps her down from the garbage. She packs her radial gun back into the top of her arm.

"Come," Mally says gently. "Come, I'll take you home."

She makes an odd sound—a machine sound he's never heard from her before. A computer shutting down.

"Stay with me," he says, easing her forward. Vega stumbles as she tries to walk on her fractured bones. He'll take her home, to Arronax; Arro will know how to fix her. The two of them limp back through the laundry and the kitchen, then through the convenience store. The shop owner is nowhere to be seen. She's probably trying to flag down the drone. Those police drones are notoriously bad at following their heat seekers. The floor is still a battleground of dropped groceries.

Vega sees the spilt food and says, "I was gathering supplies."

Mally looks at the floor, confused. Dented tins of chickpeas, a box of protein cereal, an up-ended tub of soyghurt, a broken pink jar. Why would she need food?

"For your family," she says. "Something's changed. Something's happening. We're not safe anymore."

SINNER PLEASE

26

TWELVE YEARS PREVIOUSLY

ICE

Johannesburg, 2024

This time they're letting me use the mental gymnastics, too, thinks Zack, as he wakes up groggy and realises he's lying down inside the Orb. He feels the tightness of the band around his temple; his fingers trace the skin-warmed metal. It seems to be a regular jack-in cable, or, at least, the new, non-invasive, wireless version of the old port and cord. *They've decided I can keep my brain, after all.*

Zack wonders how to select the japuzzle of his choice. He

can't see a sidebar. Maybe it's because he's still half asleep. That tranquilizer hit him hard.

He senses movement in the room and then strong fingers lock his hands in place on either side of him. Click, click. The band flashes from opaque to transparent and Zack sees it's Bernard looming over him—who else would it be?— and she's got something in her hands. A black lozenge. Some kind of XDrive.

Bernard leans across him, yoghurt breath, and plugs it into the band squeezing his temple. She's sweating.

"What the ..." he begins, but Bernard shoves a rubber ball gag in his mouth.

"Shut up, Prisoner."

Zack's memories are like electric currents. Pictures in his head come alive and zap him with needle pricks and hot shocks, and they build until the whole band starts to burn him.

He groans.

Silver, Mally, Seth, Kate. The quills. The drawing of the lotus on the wall. The picture of Kate is the brightest. Not the haunted woman with mascara spilled down her cheeks he met in the bathroom of the hospital but the real Kate who devours him with her oceanic eyes, her skin like glowsilk.

"Don't fail me," she's saying.

I won't.

"It's the whole reason for your existence."

I know.

"Save her."

Zack tries to hold on to the picture but it burns up like a polaroid on fire. The memories sweep out of his head with a final burst of bright white and then there is peace and darkness. Someone approaches, whistling a gospel tune. Zack knows the song. Has heard it every day since he's been here.

Sinner Please.

Bernard whips the drive out of the band and slips it surreptitiously into her pocket.

"All set?" asks Lovemore as he enters the room.

"Affirmative." Her breathing is heavy.

Lovemore comes into view; he doesn't make eye contact.

"What are you going to do?" asks Zack, but his words leave his mouth as an unintelligible mumble.

Lovemore checks Zack's cuffs, then flicks a switch on the side of the Orb.

The currents fire up again but this time they're not small shocks, they're lightning bolts. There's a searing inside his skull: his brain in a hot pan.

Zack screams and bites down on the gag in his mouth. His whole body seizes.

He feels the blankness coming for him, rolling at him like a storm, ready to wipe out every part of who he is and what he was put here to do, and he knows there is no way he can stop it.

PART II

BLOOD AND A BRUTAL PAST

27

TWELVE YEARS LATER

Seth's Apartment

Johannesburg, 2036

"I'm going to find her," says Kate, her anxiety and anger billowing together, neon yellow and green, to create an urgent need to move.

Keke's eyes bulge. "You can't. It's already getting crazy out there. The Blanket's not going to keep this under wraps for much longer. I'm already getting alerts on my tickertape. Creeps are catching on."

"It's way past Silver's curfew now. Something's wrong. I can feel it."

It's not just an expression. Kate can literally feel a sick burning in her stomach. She knows this sensation: One of her kids is in danger. No second-guessing this time. No blaming it on PTSD-flavoured paranoia. Just trusting her instinct, and taking action.

"I need to find her."

"You go out there, you'll get caught in the full-blown panic."

"At least I'll be able to look after her."

"The thing about Silver," says Seth, "is that she can look after herself."

Kate can't believe he's being so blasé about it.

"Her martial arts in the games she plays do not count in the real world, Seth."

"We both know that's not true," he says.

Kate sees, in her mind's eye, the picture of Silver at four years old, bow and diamond-tipped arrow in hand as the lightning highlights her hair.

"That was different. She knew who the enemy was. She was armed."

"All I'm saying is, if someone has a chance of surviving

this, it's her."

"You're saying we should just abandon her to the wild city? Expect her to find her own way home? She doesn't know what's happening! A fucking waitbot could kill her! A traffic light! She doesn't know!"

"I'm not saying we should abandon her. I'm saying that if things are escalating out there then it'll take longer than usual to get home."

"That's exactly what I'm saying. She never misses her curfew. She's three hours late!"

"You're just going to go around in circles," says Arronax, looking up from her SnapTile.

"Well, that's helpful," snarks Keke. "We do hope we're not boring you."

Arronax ignores Keke's barbed tone. "All I'm saying is, if anyone's going to go out, they'd better stop standing around and talking about it."

"You think she should go?" says Seth.

"She's going, regardless of what I happen to think. All I'm saying is, the sooner the better."

Kate runs to her room, grabs her ancient revolver. She hasn't opened the secret shoebox for more than ten years, hasn't held the gun, never mind fired it, so she hopes it's still in working order. She takes out the leather thigh holster too, hard with age and neglect, and pulls it over her jeans. Kate jams the old-school revolver into its nook and then snicks closed the click-stud. How many boxes of ammo? She only has two. They'll have to do.

"I'm coming with you," says Seth, zipping up his hoodie.

Of course he's coming with her. They are joined in a way that other twins will never glimpse. They're two halves of the same person, really. Always have been. United by blood and a brutal past.

"I was hoping you'd say that."

Keke runs into the room, almost smashing into them. "Mally," she says. "Mally's gone."

Seth feels for his Vektor, then spins around to look at the table where he left it. "And he's taken my gun."

FOREHEAD TO NAPE

28

White Mezzanine, 2036

Silver wakes in a startling white room with a headache as bright as the walls. She rubs her wrists where the leather cuffs were, and there's no trace on her pale skin of being previously tied down. She's wearing a starched cotton shift and is naked underneath. Her mouth is dry, dry, dry, and her head is banging with a post-surgery spike hangover. Silver gets off the wheeled stretcher and finds a long mirror on the otherwise blank wall. She pulls off the spearmint gown and inspects her body. All her hair is still there, apart from the band that was shaved off from forehead to nape. The rest of her small body seems unharmed, her face clear and pale without her usual foundation powder and kohl makeup. She runs her hands over her ivory skin: her goose-pimpled stomach, her bony shoulders, her sub-rosa tattoo. Her fingers play on her ribs. When did she get so skinny?

Silver takes a breath then feels, gingerly, for the wound she knows is on the back of her head. When she finds it, her hand recoils at the puckered dressing. She guesses it's a platelet plaster, already mostly dissolved.

There's a simple closet in the room, camouflaged, white against white. Inside are her clothes and her gas-mask, that look filthy against the white walls. She dresses, drawing comfort from their familiar weft and warp. Her mandible is missing. She can't remember ever having been disconnected for this long. How long had she been unconscious? She feels sick when she thinks of how worried Kate must be. Wishes there was a way to tell her mom that she's okay.

Head pounding, she checks herself in the mirror again. *Is she okay?*

POWDER MUSK

29

Seth's Apartment

Johannesburg, 2036

Kate and Seth embrace on the pavement outside their apartment building. The midnight air is soupy: It makes her eyes water, and her own breath chokes her. Or maybe that's her nerves; maybe the electrosmog has nothing to do with it.

"Take care of yourselves," he says, looking into her eyes, then Keke's, as if he's memorising them.

"Don't say it like that," Keke's voice is deep with emotion. "Like it's the last time."

His shoulders move. A micro-shrug.

They watch as Seth hops on a westbound solartram towards Vega's hostel. They grab a tram heading east, and Kate says a quick prayer to the night sky.

Please let Silver be safe at the Atrium.

Of course she's at the Atrium. She's not home … where else would she be?

Augmented ads crowd their vision as they travel, hyper-targeted to their individual codes. Kate bought Blunt Kruffins last week from BAKED; now they urge her to try their new Hash Brownies. Athleisure Club wants her to update her jogger leggings with coolpatches; maybe that will encourage her to take up exercise again, as her last run, they note, was 249 days ago. She swipes them away, irritated. Blinks her burning eyes, tries to concentrate. Keke's face is bleak behind her mask too. What products are flashing in on her? Certainly something edgier than joggings. Or maybe she's ignoring the ads entirely. Maybe she's thinking of Marko, missing him. Wondering if she'll ever see him again.

They reach the Atrium. The Victorian structure is lit up spectacularly against the inky sky. Made up almost entirely of old glass framed with lead, the structure features interior lights that make the whole building glow. Long-established plants climb up the sides and curl into the windows, meeting the leaves of the inside plants that seem to want to escape. Some of the panes of glass are cracked or missing, some frosted with age. When the Nancies decreed that all buildings had to be made up of at least 20% living organic matter, most corps added plant pockets to the sides of their structures, and roof-top gardens. Herbsills and airplants. The Atrium let its regular garden grow wild into the building, so from the outside it looks like the plants are trying to consume it.

Kate and Keke walk right in without as much as a bell to announce their entrance. There are no security guards or swivelcams to side-eye them. Kate doesn't know why. Surely they're not immune to the White Lobster junkies looking to score?

She's been here before, of course. She brought Silver here for immersion parties when she was younger. At first it was a session a year, then ten, then all of a sudden Silver couldn't skip a day without feeling antsy. Kate doesn't know when or how it had gotten so out of hand. She wishes she had stopped it before it became such a driving force in her daughter's life. It hadn't been a problem until it was, well, a problem, and by then, it was too late. She walks past a party of jacked-in kids skiing on a mountain. The milieu is projected above the participants for the benefit of the gallery.

It's good exercise, Silver says, *it's completely interactive. I'm adopting skills. Working out. Problem solving. Defending myself. Designing worlds. It's about art and creation; it's not like I'm a crack addict.*

And it's true, but it's also taken her little girl away from her. How many other parents find themselves on this slippery slope, she thinks, as she walks past the guardian area, where parents are drinking coffeeberry shooters, one eye on the screen and the other on their own individual fixes. How many of these other parents had a sweet, strong, loving daughter (or son) and now see only a shell of that child? Kate's photographic memory means there's no lack of the pictures she's taken over the years of that young girl who used to crawl onto her lap with her glow-in-the-dark cuddle bunny. Her heart aches with the loss.

No one here seems particularly concerned about the AI malfunction. There's a hushed tone overall, and the feeling of inclusiveness whether the players are immersed in group experiences or going it alone. They're a tribe. Kate and Keke make their way past a group busy with a scuba diving simulation. Adults, this time. Either doing it to get certified for the real thing, or just happy to do it inside an inner-city building and not having to bother with heavy equipment, sea-sickness, dangerous currents, or the bends. A whale shark swims past them, and they all murmur a drugged-sounding "Who-o-oa."

It's not *real*, Kate would say to Silver, to which Silver would grunt, and spin her eyeballs.

It's as real as *this*, she'd say, gesturing to the apartment with its artificial sunrise and invisi-screen and synthetic ham sandwiches.

She has a point, Seth had chimed in from the couch, Bonechaser snoring on his lap.

What is REAL, anyway? Silver had asked. Mally had looked up from his flexiglass Tile, then, interested.

Kate did not have an answer.

Keke and Kate reach the stairs—the elevator has been out of order since Kate first visited, five years ago—and climb to the second floor. The second level is for recreational gaming: parties, training, team building, while the third is for hard-liners. The basement, well, it's the only place here that has restricted access, so who knows? Strictly 21+, and you have to know someone who knows someone to apply, like some secret underground New York swingers' nightclub. Kate wouldn't know where to start to gain entrance, although she's sure Keke, with all her contacts, would drift in like a breeze.

"What happens in the basement?"

Andy Warhol springs to mind, Studio 54 with a futuristic twist. Alcohash cocktails, cocaine shadowshots, deviant botsex.

Keke shrugs. "Never been."

"If you were to guess? From what you've heard?"

"Hardcore bot nooky. V-**XXX**-R. Kinky shit. I mean, it must be bizarro sex, right? Or why bother coming here?"

"Excuse the pun," jokes Kate.

Keke cackles her wild laugh, and people turn to look at her.

"Everywhere you look there's a novel neuroreality porn hub popping up."

"Adult Planet," says Kate. "Every time I see that flashing pink sign it makes me think of some kind of old-school cartoon. A pink animated planet. It tastes like those old lucky packet sweets. Powder Musk. Totally inappropriate."

"Now why ... " says Keke, giving Kate an eyeful, "is Adult Planet targeting *you* with their ads?"

Kate's cheeks warm. "I don't know," she mutters. "Their algorithms must be off."

Keke looks at her. "Right."

She clears her throat.

"Kate Lovell, you are not having *sex* are you? I thought you'd sworn it off forever."

Kate blushes some more. Why, she doesn't know. She's almost forty years old, for Net's sake.

"Don't take it the wrong way," says Keke.

"Is that supposed to be another pun?"

"Ha! You *are*! You wily slut. Who? How? Tell me everything."

But even if Kate wants to answer the question—which she doesn't—they've run out of time. They've reached Silver's regular jack-in console, and her pod is bare.

GRAVEYARD TREES

30

TWELVE YEARS PREVIOUSLY

Johannesburg, 2024

When Zack opens his bleary eyes, he sees a human shape sitting across from him. They're in a vehicle. He squints at the shape, tries to make out who it is. As he is rocked by the motion of the van he feels strangely at peace. The nagging feeling he's had for as long as he can remember is gone. There was something important he had to do, but it's faded now, and only cool relief remains.

In fact, he can't remember much of anything, anymore. He has vague recollections of life before his arrest, but it all seems so faraway.

He knows his name is Prisoner, and that the shape across from him is his warden, Bernard. She doesn't acknowledge his waking, but doesn't look away either. He knows he does not like Bernard.

Which crim colony are they taking him to? Lovermore told him that the space mining programme is the most dangerous, but also pays the most, and that the sky-scraping vertical farms are one of the easiest options: those aeroponic crops basically take care of themselves. Maybe they'll put him in a kitchen or a laundry. Maybe he'll have to clean toilets for the other crims. Or a hard labour option—they've probably put him down for that—laying trax for the first phase of the new smart Hyperloop.

The van slows and turns a corner. The windows are tinted the colour of tar. Zack tries to move, to get more comfortable, but when he looks down, he sees he's strapped into some kind of wheelchair.

"Where're we going?" he asks the warden. "How much longer?"

She doesn't reply. You would think she didn't know he existed if it weren't for her glare of cold steel.

They move at an unhurried pace, the speed of an extra-cautious cabbie, or a human driver with nothing better to do for the rest of the day, then they pull up and park. For a second there's a glint of paranoia: Will they even take him to a penal colony? Or will they just stop at an abandoned strip of veld and put a bullet in his brain? They'll tell the task team hired to investigate that he tried to get away, and what choice did they have? After all, they couldn't allow a serial murderer to escape.

The back of the van is opened, and the ramp folds itself down to the ground. Bernard kicks the brake off Zack's wheelchair and pushes him out. She brings a small black kitbag with her. The fresh blue of the sky is almost blinding. He tilts back his head and relishes the feeling of the sun on his face.

"Feels good?" Bernard casts her shadow over him.

Zack cracks open one eye to look at her. Could she not just allow him this one moment of bliss?

"Well, lap it up, Prisoner—"

I would if you let me.

"Because this is the last bit of sunshine you're ever gonna see."

Bernard drives Zack's chair roughly, swinging him away from the view of graveyard trees—tall, fragrant pines—to face the main building.

Zack is expecting some kind of ugly state structure—utilitarian concrete and chipstone and very little imagination—but the architecture he sees takes his breath away. It must be at least twelve storeys high, and is made from some kind of glossy white material. Its outline is irregular—like a shard planted in the earth—but it's made up of hundreds of hexagons. It looks like a giant piece of shiny white honeycomb. The grounds are carpeted in lush green grass, freshly mown, and perennials blooming and bursting with petal and seed, and there's a dense forest behind the shard.

Zack's confused. There's no branding outside, no state banner. Now that he thinks of it, there's not even a security wall around the place. What kind of crim colony is this? Bernard pushes him up the ramp to the entrance. Her breathing is ragged with anger and effort. The glass doors slide open to admit them, and a friendly security guard greets them as if they are day visitors, instead of a convict strapped into a prison-issue wheelchair and a huffing ham-cheeked warden.

"We've been expecting you," says the pretty receptionist, smiling warmly. "Welcome to SkyRest."

PUREST HUMAN

31

TWELVE YEARS LATER

Seth's Apartment

Johannesburg, 2036

Mally and Vega finally reach Seth's apartment building. A feeling has crept into the black city air that wasn't there an hour ago: slow, insidious, as if there is an undetected gas leak and all it'll take is an accidental spark to blow up the whole place. Maybe it's just them, the glances they're attracting. Vega is in pretty bad shape.

As they cross the road to get to the apartment, a cabbie speeds up, as if to mow them down. Mally launches them out of the way, onto the hard pavement, and the taxi just misses them. Pain burns a hole in his thigh. His wound is open again, his trousers are double-dyed by blood, old and new.

He gets up, helps Vega stand again, loops her arm over his shoulder. He knows he's supposed to report the malfunctioning cabbie, but now he's shaking again, and he just wants to get home and tend to his love. They eventually get inside and he breathes a sigh of relief as he feels the cool, conditioned air on his skin. The stairs are waiting.

"Almost there," Mally says, more to himself than to Vega.

Only Arronax is home.

"Mally!" she says "Where the hell were you?" but then she sees Vega, and she understands.

"You went to fetch her?" She starts weeping again.

Mally puts Seth's Vektor on the kitchen counter. "Don't worry, Arro, we're safe now. He's not sure why Arronax is crying.

"Safe?" she says, incredulous. "I need to let your parents know you're home." She wipes her tears on her shell-studded sleeves, sniffs, attempts to pull herself together. She tries to beam Seth and Kate three times each, but is met with a busy signal.

"The commstation must be down. We'll try again later. In

the mean time," she says to Vega, "let's see if we can fix you up."

"I'd really appreciate that," says Vega.

Arronax winces at the android's crushed face. She takes her gently by the hand and sits her down on a wingback. Then she grabs her utility bag and pulls up a stool next to her to survey the damage.

Does it hurt? Mally feels like asking, but realises it's a stupid question. She's been viciously attacked, humiliated, assaulted. Of course it fucking hurts.

Arronax sets to work. She fixes the ankle first, so that Vega can walk again. She is a nimble surgeon with her needle-nosed pliers and blowtorch. The room smells like burnt rubber and bitumen. Metal on metal. A car crash. Arronax moves on to Vega's fractured arm, her sprained hand.

"This part might be difficult to watch," she says to Mally. "Why don't you go get yourself a drink, or something?"

"No," says Mally. "I want to be here for her."

Just hours ago Vega was the one tending to his wounds. He holds her uninjured hand.

Arronax breathes deeply, and nods.

She peels off half of Vega's face. The stamped silicone gives way to a titanium skull—shiny, apart from the damaged cheek bone, which is like crumpled tinfoil. Arronax sculpts the structure back to its original shape and folds the silicone back over it, sealing it with some bright flashes of purple light.

"There," Arronax says, arranging some of Vega's lustrous long hair over the seam. "As good as new." She swallows hard.

Vega smiles. "Thank you."

Of course, it's not nearly as good as new, and Mally gets a twinge of sorrow every time he looks at Vega's face. It certainly looks a lot better than it did before.

"Thank you," Mally says to Arronax, eyes glistening with gratitude, and regret.

"What were you doing out there, anyway?"

"I went to gather supplies," says Vega.

"What supplies? You're almost 100% stocked, according to your meter. What did you need?"

"She went to buy groceries," says Mally. "For us."

He sees the floor of the convenience store again, littered with broken glass and spilled food. The owner of the shop, hugging herself and chattering in Xiang.

Arronax pauses, looks concerned. "That's not in your protocol."

"I am very fond of Mally," she says, "and he needs food to live. Things are happening out there. I knew it wouldn't be safe for Mally's family to go out for food. Mally's family are important to him. It will be best if they stay alive."

Arronax shakes her head, a shudder, and her hair turns a dark shade of purple. She packs up the rest of her tools. "Okay, kids. I'm going to try to reach Seth again. Promise me you'll stay here? Stay out of trouble?"

Once Arronax has moved back to her makeshift desk, Mally takes Vega's hand again. He wants to say something loving and profound, but the words don't come to him.

All he can manage is: "I love you."

"I know," says Vega.

"If you love me too, you can say it back."

"Okay," says Vega.

"I love you," he says again.

"I know," says Vega.

Mally laughs, strokes her abraded skin.

"You saved my life," she says.

"That's not true."

"You saved my life. I wouldn't be here now if it weren't for you. I'd be in the dumpster. You know that's true."

"But—"

"I owe you my life."

"No, you don't."

"I owe you my life, and you know what? I'm glad I do."

"Why?"

"Because you're the purest human."

"That's a weird thing to say."

"You have the cleanest heart in the city," says Vega.

"Again, a weird thing to say. But thank you."

"It's true. I can see it."

They look into each others' eyes.

"What else can you see?" asks Mally.

"I wish I could tell you."

"Tell me."

"I can't. It will fuck your mind."

Mally laughs. He's been trying to teach Vega to swear, but her code resists it, and muddles the words up.

"Do you mean, it will be a mind-fuck?" He laughs.

"Mind-fuck," she says. "Mind-fuck." As if she's a toddler learning a new word.

"It will blow your brain out," she says. This time he doesn't correct her; he just sighs and looks away.

"Your happiness score is low," Vega says. "Shall I make you some pancakes?"

He thinks of that mohawk man and how he punched Vega

with all his strength. Thinks of her body spreadeagled on the trash. Would he ever forget those visuals? Would *she?*

"Vega. I need you to help me understand something."

"Of course. What is it?"

He struggles with the words, looks down and clasps and unclasps his hands, still grimy from the altercation.

"When you were … when we were … when you were being attacked. By that man."

Vega looks at him, clear-eyed.

"You had your roscoe—your radial gun—the whole time. Why didn't you defend yourself?"

"Defending myself is not in my protocol," she says.

"You're not allowed to defend yourself?"

"Not against humans. Human life is more valuable than robosapien life."

Mally winces. "But then, later, you did shoot him."

"That's because he turned on you."

CURSED WHITE

32

White Mezzanine, 2036

"Let me out!" Silver screams, holding her humming head. "Let me out of here!"

She bangs on the walls, kicks the furniture. Tries to smash the glass of the tiny square window in her room, but it's reinforced flexiglass and she knows it's unbreakable. She thrashes around, shatters the plate of food that magically appears every time she wakes, upends the metal trolley, punches her stretcher.

The architecture of her prison is infuriating. The door to her room remains unlocked, but outside there is only a passage with walls as white as her ward. If she walks down the passage, she's forced to turn right four times and is then, of course, back at her door. The white membrane keeping her in is thin and elastic, like biolatex, but impossible to tear from the inside. It's like being trapped in a white soft-pop balloon.

Silver can't figure out if it's meant to be a unique kind of torture or a puzzle. Surely a puzzle would have some kind of clue? But this place is just a bleached rubber groundhog day.

Is someone keeping her captive? Or did she die in that grimy ex-abattoir and this is some kind of wretched middle earth? Some limbo? How long has she been here? It could be hours or days. Every time she wakes, she's back in her starched cotton shift, bathed and sweet-smelling.

Silver stops her tantrum and sits down on the floor, against one of the cursed white walls, and draws her legs up, hugs them, tries to comfort herself. Her bandwidth isn't coping with anything but the sincere desire to stop her headsplosion, which is a solid eight out of ten on her own personal Richter scale. The blue pain pills are there again, on their peach-coloured porcelain saucer. She crawls over to the tablets, holds them in her hand. The volume control of brainpain is on the rise, and she doesn't think she'll survive it if it gets any worse. It already feels as if it's scrambling her signals. Reluctantly, she puts the pills back on their plate.

The food lies spilled on the floor: transparent cubes of nutrijelly. She misses her mother with a keen sorrow she hasn't felt in a long time. Seth. Mally. If only there is a way to reach them, to let them know where she is. But how can she do that? She has no idea herself. Maybe Kate would retrace Silver's steps, figure something out.

Her gaze alights on her boots, which she hasn't bothered putting on this time, and travels up to her jacket, which is hanging on its lone ivory hanger. The back of the jacket is shaped with metal corsetry. Steel bones and five elegant darts of copper. Silver gets up and pulls the jacket off its hanger, starts chewing at the stitching.

With no tools at hand apart from her teeth and short nails, it takes two hours to release the first swatch of metal. She has stars in her vision as her headache reaches nine out of ten. She begins to unpick the next one.

MAYBE THIS IS THE FUTURE

33

TWELVE YEARS PREVIOUSLY

SkyRest

Johannesburg, 2024

The SkyRest receptionist picks up her Tile and comes around the sleek concierge counter, and is immediately replaced by an almost identical woman behind the desk. Same crisp snow uniform, sage-green silk scarf, claret lipstick, immaculate hair. Same automatic smile.

"I'll take Mister Girdler from here," the woman says.

Girdler? thinks Zack. He thought his name was 'Prisoner'.

The room is cavernous, light, and everything looks new and expensive. Tight-fisted Bernard doesn't relinquish the wheelchair.

"Didn't you get the transfer documents?" she asks.

The receptionist looks confused. "Yes, we did. We're all set up to receive Mister Girdler. Everything is in order."

"I'm not talking about his intake papers. I'm talking about my transfer papers." Bernard holds up her black bag.

"No," says Zack. *No, please no.*

"Shut up, Prisoner," she says to him through clenched, tea-coloured teeth.

The receptionist's perfect forehead creases into the beginnings of a frown. V-tox, Zack guesses, assuming that face-sculpting is part of the uniform. She looks back towards the new receptionist behind the counter, who swipes away a leaf and nods.

"I do apologise," she says, her face clear again. "I wasn't up to speed." Her name badge reads 'Gaelyn'.

Bernard wipes her hand-sweat onto her hips.

"There'll be someone along shortly to escort you to your new staff quarters," she says to Bernard.

"I won't be going to my quarters right now."

"But—"

"I'm staying with the prisoner."

"It's not necessary—"

"I'll let you know what is necessary and unnecessary," the warden growls. "You don't know this one, okay? You don't know what he's capable of."

The receptionist looks at Zack, adjusts her scarf. He gives her a friendly shrug.

"Can he walk?"

"Of course I can walk."

"We strapped him into the chair for the commute."

"Can you … un-strap him?"

Bernard doesn't answer her. Instead, she glares in Gaelyn's direction while she unbuckles Zack's straps with more force than necessary. Now he can stand, and walk, but he still has his smartcuffs on.

Yet another woman in the same mould (snow, sage, claret) appears out of nowhere and whisks the ugly wheelchair out of the building.

"Please, follow me," says Gaelyn, and clicks away in her silver-spiked stilettos.

They step onto a fast-track line, which is no small feat for someone in heels as high as hers. He feels a little in love with Gaelyn. Of course, he doesn't know her from a bar of soap, but she's just so different—the polar opposite, really—of Bernard. Neat, slim frame, beautifully styled hair and make-up. He can't remember the last time someone was nice to him; he craves more of her clear-eyed attention.

They hop off the line and walk towards an elevator. When they're inside and the doors close, Zack says, "You're very good with people."

Bernard sighs.

"Thank you!" says Gaelyn.

"You make people feel very welcome here."

"That's our warmth score," Gaelyn says, and chooses a floor on her Tile.

"Excuse me?" snarks the warden.

The elevator starts to rise.

"Our warmth score. All potential employees are measured according to certain traits. The points allocated then reveal which job will suit us best. There are one hundred categories. I scored highest in the warmth section. That's a combination of joy and empathy. Emotional intelligence."

"I can tell," says Zack, and in the background, Bernard rolls her eyes.

It's so nice to speak to someone relatively normal after all this time on ice. For now he'll overlook her Stepford aspect and appreciate her for what she's good at. You do, after all, have to have some serious talent to make a crim feel welcome at a penal colony.

The elevator climbs higher and higher, and when they

reach the top, Zack is relieved to see they're still in Johannesburg. Far in the distance, he can see the Ponte tower, best known for the number of residents who have hurtled to their deaths from its multicoloured windows.

When they reach the top floor, the metal doors open with a *ping*. The interior, as expected, reflects the exterior design: brutally minimalist, and empty. It's like some kind of exclusive VIP lounge. Zack moves to exit the lift but Gaelyn holds him back.

"We don't leave the elevator for this part of the tour."

The doors close, they drop a few floors, and they open again.

Now it's an open-plan office with young people working from their pods. Holo design pads are floating around with sketches and scribbled ideas on them. Some kind of brainstorming unit.

"We like to show the new intakes the whole building, so that you have a holistic idea of what happens here. So that you know how you can grow in the company if you're dedicated and you work hard."

Bernard snorts, but Gaelyn has the good grace to ignore her.

A few floors below that is a vast room buzzing with people speaking into small mics that are plastered near their mouths.

"Call centre."

There's also a smart canteen, where you can swipe a meal straight off a menu, a gym floor, a play centre, and a napping pad. Zack's hopes start climbing. He's never heard of a crim colony like this before, but maybe this is the future? Maybe the government has realised they can get the best out of their prisoners if they treat them well. This may be a prototype for future PLCs. Look at all these happy, productive workers! It's a far cry from the automatons in grey uniforms he has a vague recollection of seeing in what feels like a previous life. Are these people, these young, vital people … are they all criminals? It doesn't seem likely. Zack inspects Gaelyn. Is *she* a convict? Surely not. So how does this work?

She catches him staring at her and smiles. The elevator slides further down, till they reach the ground floor. Zack thinks they'll get out now but Gaelyn holds him back again. He likes the feel of her hand on his chest.

"You don't start here," she says.

Bernard smirks.

The elevator goes down past ground level, down, down, down, till Zack feels as if they are in the bowels of the earth, till the air is heavy and the only light is from the LEDs in the ceiling of the lift, giving both women disturbing white masks for faces.

Ping! goes the elevator, and the doors open for them one last time.

Gaelyn steps into darkness and smiles. "This is where you start."

They walk along a dark passage deep underground. Motion-sensitive LEDs flicker on to light their way. The walls are raw rock face and there's a hint of an odd smell— what is it? Damp? Mould? Old laundry detergent. Zack feels the weight of the earth all around him.

I should have known. I should have known I wouldn't be working up there in the light.

Gaelyn's heels provide a staccato soundtrack to his feelings of doom.

They reach a massive steel door. Gaelyn inserts her wafer key and looks, unblinking, into the retina scanner, and it beeps and unlocks. It becomes clear to Zack why the security outside the SkyRest building is light. They keep all the crims right here in this hulking subterranean lock-up, and there is no way to escape. A shroud of claustrophobia wraps around his head.

Once they're through the steel door, Gaelyn takes off her shoes and motions for them to do the same. Bernard's boots are bigger than his. They make their way into the Residence: decent looking recreation rooms, neat accommodation. Spick and span cafeteria that only stinks a little. There's even a ping pong table and a vintage jukebox in the corner. An air sanitiser spills a constant plume of humidified air into the space. It's not pleasant by any stretch of the imagination, but better than Zack expected after seeing that dungeon passage. Was that also done on purpose?

"Where is everyone?"

"They're working. We encourage a very strict work ethic here."

I'm sure you do.

She trains her cloudless eyes on him. "Keeps everyone out of trouble."

Gaelyn slides open the door to his room. It couldn't be any more different to the dirty, overcrowded South African prisons pre-crimcol days where you'd be in danger of being shivved for a cracked plastic dinner plate. Here there are no jail cell bars in sight, and the tiny room is Asian in style: a sleeping mat on the tatami floor, minimal, and spotless. A perfect cube of folded clothes sits on the corner of the mat.

Gaelyn asks Bernard to remove Zack's cuffs, and she does so. She then takes Zack's hands in hers, and before he knows what's happening she's clicked a single polished black band on his left wrist. It beeps.

"More comfortable?"

He runs his finger over its smooth surface, nods.

"Lewis?" Gaelyn calls down the passage. There's a muted sound of someone moving in the next room, then they hear that door slide open. Determined footsteps arrive, attached to what can only be described as an old Hipster Hell's Angel: seventy-something in the shade with a perfectly groomed grey beard, and hair to match; a cappuccino-skinned body that's seen a hundred pull-ups a day for decades; and a huge, elaborate tattoo that snakes its way out of his frayed vest—down his vein-mapped arms and up his neck. Hard scales and dangerous eyes. A dragon. He lifts his chin to acknowledge Zack.

"Mister Girdler, Lewis is one of our most experienced residents. If you have any questions, ask him. He'll show you around."

Lewis nods.

"You're going to be just fine, Zack," Gaelyn says.

Zack?

Is that my name? Yes, it feels right. Zack.

"All right!" Gaelyn says, hugging her Tile to her chest. "My job here is done."

Zack wants to say: *Don't leave me here.* For a moment, psychologically, he is reduced to a child hanging on to his mother's skirt, head buried in hard shins. *Don't leave me here.* He doesn't move, just watches as she turns and walks away from him. The only kind face he's seen in months. *Don't leave me here.* What have these people done to him? He forces his thoughts away from the retreating shape of the receptionist and looks Lewis directly in the eyes.

"Where do we start?"

A MAP
TO NOWHERE

34

TWELVE YEARS LATER

White Mezzanine, 2036

Once Silver's unpicked two pieces of copper, she uses the edge of one piece to sharpen the other. It already has a good shape—a long triangle—so all it needs is some friction to turn it into a more efficient weapon. She finishes it and is satisfied with her work, happy with what she's made despite the knowledge of what it will be used for.

Her head is still pounding off the scale. Even swallowing what little saliva she has sends lightning bolts of pain through her skull. Soon it will be over. She blows the metallic dust off the blade—copper glitter—and polishes it with her cotton shift.

Silver doesn't know why it's taken her so long to realise this is what is required of her. It should have been obvious from the start.

The bathtub is bright porcelain and so clean it's as if no one has ever looked at it, never mind bathed in it. Silver clicks the five-finger option and warm water rushes out of the tap. The water is as clear as drinking water. Silver's fascinated: She's never bathed in transparent water before. She adds another five fingers so that the tub is half-full. Over the top, vulgar luxury, she knows, but in her situation it's forgivable. She pulls her starched shift off over her head and slowly climbs in. It's like sliding into warm liquid glass. She lies back against the white slope, then slips under the water, feeling the warmth wash over her whole scalp and face and shoulders, and it feels so good—such a relief. She sighs out bubbles and stays under until her lungs protest.

When she surfaces, she's thinking of her family. Tears come. The warmth of the water tinges her usually ivory skin with pink, and the blue veins on her wrists are showing off. Beautifully sketched lines of navy. A map to nowhere.

Silver leans over the edge of the tub and picks up her hand-fashioned copper razor.

She cuts lengthways along the veins on both arms. Silver moans in pain as the skin parts. Doubt flickers in on her. Is she really doing this? Is this really the only way? But there's no going back now.

Of course she's expecting the blood. The more, the better. The quicker. But the starkness of the vermilion against the bath, the pulsing flow, startles her. She watches as the red spills down and creates underwater clouds, like upside-down atom bombs. Soon the porcelain is painted; the water is dyed.

Crimson Cascade, Kate would say.

Silver leans back again, resting her arms on the lip of the bath. She watches the last of her consciousness leak out of her wrists, and her eyelids swoon.

GHOST

35

The Atrium

Johannesburg, 2036

"Hey," Keke says to a passerby.

"Hey yourself," says the man, looking Keke up and down approvingly.

Jesus, does she never get sick of the attention? Kate's sure it would drive her mad—that constant gnawing of her body by every stranger she meets. Doesn't she ever feel that one day there'll be nothing left?

Instead, it has the opposite effect on Keke. Her back

straightens, showing off the perfect shape of her breasts, the flat board that is her stomach.

"We're looking for Silver. You seen her?"

"Silver?"

"She usually jacks in here." Kate motions at the empty pod. At least, she thinks she does. The initials 'GK' are scratched into the smooth shell, making Kate second-guess herself. She hasn't been here with Silver for a long time. It's one of the ways she's let her drift away. Again: the ache.

"Teenage girl, long white hair."

On the wall there's a slogan splashed in violet: *As we design, so, perhaps, we were designed.*

"Small," says Kate. "She's quite small for her age."

The man's eyes widen. "You mean, 'Ghost'?"

"What?" snaps Kate. For some reason, the name unsettles her. Her hair stands on end.

"Ghost?" says Keke. "That could be her."

The man looks impressed. "She's a legend around here, you know. She's, like, the best player in the whole place."

Kate remembers when Silver was a toddler and used to put a white serviette over her head at dinnertime.

I'm a gho-o-ost, she used to say. *I'm a gho-o-ost.*

What do they know? What's going on? Paranoia, as

familiar and shocking as cold water, splashes her in the face. "Why do you call her that?"

The man looks puzzled at her reaction. "It's her avatar," he says, frowning. What he means is: *You don't know your own daughter's avatar?*

"And ..."

"And what?"

"And it fits her perfectly."

"What's that supposed to mean?"

His eyes meet Kate's. "She's impossible to kill."

"When's the last time you saw her?" Keke slips easily into her investigative journo cloak.

"She was here earlier." The man's wearing a perfumed shirt and the fragrance comes off him in feathers of invisible smoke. Amber, pepperwood, juniper berry. Kate tried out a perfumed bra when the trend hit, but her kids kept on sniffing the air around her and saying *Can you smell that? Can you smell that?* as if someone had stepped in dog shit instead of what it was supposed to be: Citrus Burn.

"When?" asks Keke. "And where did she go?"

"I don't know. Time gets a bit foggy in here." The lights are always set to daylight-bright and there are no clocks on the walls. "I'd guess at late afternoon? I don't know where she went, but she did say something."

This gets Kate's attention. "Yes?"

"Well, Nova was teasing her, saying she'd beat Silver to the win."

"Win the game?"

"Ja. All in good fun, because everyone knows that when Silver turns sixteen she's going to dominate Eden 7.0. I mean, we don't stand a chance. The only reason we're ahead of her at the moment is because we're meshed and she's not."

"You need to be meshed to win?"

"You need to be meshed to access 7.0."

"And she said she was going to get meshed when she turned sixteen?"

"It goes without saying. She's a fucking prodigy. Have you *seen* the worlds she's designed? She's like a freaking space architect. And her colonies are brilliant. Even her bio systems—"

"So," Kate interrupts, "Nova was goading her—"

"Not goading," he says, "not really. We're always just stinging each other. We're all close friends and we look out for one another. Nova loves Silver like a little sister."

Along with the warm fragrance coming off him there are other scents: tea, and timber. It's difficult to see his face when there are so many shapes in the air between them.

"And then?"

"And then Silver said she was leaving early, which she

never does, so we asked her why, and she said that she was going to get her sixteenth birthday present."

The bright bulbs start hurting Kate's head, as if somehow the light is seeping into her brain and dehydrating her thoughts.

"Which is?"

The man smiles, showing the distinctive grey, ground-down teeth of a hard-line gamer.

"Well, she didn't say, but ... isn't it obvious?"

"She wouldn't," says Kate as they jog out of the Atrium.

Keke glances at her, purses her lips.

"Silver wouldn't do that. Go out on her own and get it done against my wishes. Would she?"

"Get meshed?" says Keke. "Of course she would. She's been talking about it for two years. You just haven't been listening."

"I thought it was a phase. Everything's a phase, with kids, you know?"

"Not this."

"And I *was* listening. Just because I didn't want her to get it, doesn't mean I wasn't listening."

"What I mean is ... and don't take this the wrong way ... that you weren't *listening*-listening."

"What the fuck is that supposed to mean?"

"You heard Silver asking if she could get the neural lace. She wasn't really asking. What she was saying was that she was going to get it with or without you."

"Well, then, in that case, there's nothing I could have done to stop her, right?"

"No, but you could have gone with her. You could have made sure she got it done safely."

Kate's face burns: anger swirls with regret. A whirlpool on fire.

"Wow, Keke, look at you. All the answers. Why don't *you* try to parent fifteen-year-old twins and see how you do with that?"

Keke grabs Kate's arm, makes her stop walking, arrests her with her ice-blue biolenses.

"KittyKat. I'd never be able to do what you do. It's terrifying."

"You're not helping."

"I wouldn't even like to *try* to be a mother. Not for a day. I'd rather shoot myself."

"Again, not helping."

"Sorry. I don't know what to say."

"They always tell you everything," says Kate.

"Well, they wouldn't if I was their parent!"

They hurry out of the Atrium and stop on the pavement outside, not sure where to go next.

Kate's mandible begins to ring.

"Kate," purrs the DarkDoc. "I've been trying to reach you."

The combination of the static and his gruff voice blows silver streamers into her vision.

"The commlines are a mess," she says. "It'll get worse."

She doesn't hear the next few words.

"…I need you to come here as soon as you can."

"I can't," says Kate.

"I need to see you before—"

"Before the world ends?"

There's a pause. More shimmering static.

"Something like that."

Usually when he says those words—*I need to see you*—Kate feels an immediate rush of warmth to her pelvis, but today the yellow adrenaline is splattering over all her other emotions.

"I can't."

"Things are getting dangerous out there. Please come to

me."

"I can take care of myself."

"I know. It doesn't change how I feel."

"I want to be with you too," says Kate, and Keke makes googly eyes at her. She turns away. "But I can't. Silver is missing."

"No, she's not," says Morgan. "That's what I'm calling to tell you."

"She is," says Kate. "She's not at home. We're at the Atrium. She's not here, either."

"I know. That's because she's here, with us."

IS THIS THE REAL WORLD?

36

"You're fucking the DarkDoc?" asks Keke.

"Language," scolds Kate, not because she minds the word—god knows it's one of her favourites—but because it's become a habit to try to keep things clean with the twins around.

Keke is genuinely shocked. "I did not see that coming!"

"Stop with the sex puns already."

"How? Where? When?"

They pass a mean posse of men with automatic rifles, clubs, and hunting knives. It says *Fuck Robots* on one of the men's wide chests. Another man wears a face mask emblazoned with a pixellated swastika and an anthrobot's severed arm around his neck like a mantle. Badly drawn prison tattoos scribble their skin.

Bot Hunters. Science deniers. Alt-tech nazis.

The hate group gathered momentum last year when a few of the older generation of anthrobots started spontaneously activating their self-destruct buttons in crowded places. There were six bomb blasts and more than twenty fatalities before they were all seized and taken off the market.

TERRORBOTS! the newstream tickertape had screamed, whipping people into a frenzy of panic and suspicion of all things AI, but then when the terror attacks had been properly investigated, it turned out that an unidentified human had hacked the switches, so it hadn't really been a robot rebellion at all. Of course, the alt-tech nazis didn't let the truth get in the way of their mission to 'enslave the enemy' and drive other violent propaganda. And, while the new anthrobots still have baked-in self-destruct switches, the only way to deploy them now is for both the bot and a human to activate it at the same time. Unlike humans, 7thGen robosapiens are untouched by the Suicide Contagion, which in theory ensures that the detonator will only be deployed in true emergencies.

One of the men glares at Kate. She feels for her gun and is relieved when it's still there in its holster, thigh-warmed.

"I want to know everything," says Keke. "Spill!"

"It's not important. We've got bigger things to worry about."

"Oh no, you're not going to get away with that. I want details."

Kate motions for a northbound tram to stop and they hop on, relieved to put space between themselves and the creeps.

Keke's still looking at her. "This is a mindfuck on so many levels."

"So the world has gone completely mad and we're practically in the midst of a civil war but you think that my sex life is a mindfuck."

"It is!"

"Why?" asks Kate. "Am I that out of the game?"

"You're as hot-damn sexy as ever, and you know that," says Keke. "But—"

"Yes? Get it all out of your system. We're on our way to see him, and I don't want you acting crackers around him."

"The DarkDoc!"

"He has a name, you know. Morgan. I don't call him the DarkDoc in bed."

"You should," says Keke. "That's hot."

"No," Kate shakes her head, laughing. "No. It's not."

"That voice," says Keke, pretending to be enraptured.

"I know," says Kate. "It's the voice that did it."

"I thought you hated doctors."

"I do. I did. It's complicated."

They ride past 4D street art. Animations of characters and slogans. Japanimé. Logos and tags and avatar stamps. Two-dimensional bumper stickers read 'QE'; 'Wake Up' and 'Is this the Real World?'

"You're gonna tell me where we're going?" asks Keke.

"You haven't given me a chance!"

There's a screeching on the other side of the street. A cabbie drives off the road and straight into a Mexican food truck. A big bang and smoke and yelling, but no one seems too badly hurt. Pedestrians hurry past the tacos and salsa on tar. The wall in the background says 'The Internet is God', and it animates so that the words 'The Internet' and 'God' swap places every few seconds.

The Internet is God. God is the Internet. The Internet is God.

"Holy shit," says Keke. "What the fuck. This is so surreal."

"Morgan's with Silver. That's why we're going there."

"She's safe?"

"He didn't say that."

"What did he say?"

"That we need to get there as soon as possible."

"That doesn't sound good."

"He wouldn't say more than that. Said he didn't want me to worry. He'll tell us everything when we get there."

"Get where?"

"The Lipworth Institute."

SMUDGED WITH ASH AND HEARTACHE

37

The Android Pod

Johannesburg, 2036

Any hope of finding Mally at Vega's hostel evaporates as soon as Seth arrives. The front door has been blown wide open, and now the entrance to the building is a gaping, smoking maw. Looters stream out with chips and roscoe bullets they'll never be able to use. Seth hears shouting and mad laughter. Broken glass crunches underfoot as he makes his way inside. Whoops of victory ring out as people kick cabinet locks in and smash the expensive tech with baseball bats. *Fuck Robots* is emblazoned on more than one of the fire-smoked walls.

Some robosapien bodies lie in pieces on the floor, completely human-looking at a glance. Human from the outside, anyway: stamped silicone, padded by flesh-coloured sponge—it's just the colour of their blood that gives them away. That, and, if you look closely enough, the white titanium bones.

A man in a camouflaged exo-suit walks with purpose through the trashed hall, finger on the trigger of a large automatic weapon: a metal-melter. Instead of bullets, it's specifically designed to fry a robot's circuitry. Seth recognises the type. These people are usually underground, but it seems that the AI uprising has coaxed them out of their secret bunkers.

This is not good news, he thinks as he stops and looks around at the chaos.

The Bot Hunter sidles past Seth, bumping him just hard enough to send a message. Seth automatically feels for his Vektor, but remembers it's not there just before his hand comes away empty. He turns to look at the man, and they exchange hard looks before letting go.

There's another small explosion a few rooms away. The looters jump, but recover quickly, then seem energised by the destruction. They remind Seth of grinning hyenas, come to steal the scraps from the Grim Reaper's table.

Seth grabs one of the young men running past.

"Where are they?" Seth asks. "The robots?"

The man shakes himself loose from Seth, shrugs, then takes off.

A woman's shaking voice sounds from behind him. "They took them."

Seth turns around to see a woman smudged with ash and heartache. Was she there all along? She's so grey he didn't even noticed her when he walked in.

"They took them," she says. Her shoulder is bleeding: some kind of black shrapnel is poking out, pointing towards Seth.

"Are you all right?" he says. "Can I help you? Take you somewhere? Hospital?"

"What's the point." It's not a question.

Seth leaves the exploding building with the feeling that it will devour itself before dawn. He sees a NASP policeman—code for Roguebot Cop—handcuffing an anthrobot.

"I don't understand," the bot is saying. She looks like a fourth-generation model, quite obviously not human, so an easy target for brutes like this. "There is no reason for my arrest. I didn't break protocol."

The cop swipes perspiration from his eyebrow. "It's for your own safety."

"I don't understand," she says.

A distraught woman in a faded yellow dress is arguing with the cop. She has a wailing toddler on her hip. A small patch of blood and dirt is visible where the kid's knee is bleeding onto her.

"She was helping us!" the mother keeps saying. "Don't you understand? She was helping!"

"It doesn't matter," says the cop.

The toddler cries and cries.

"My child fell in the street. This robot helped her. Why are you handcuffing her?"

The cop's lips shrink; he doesn't have time for this. He's got a whole city to clean up.

"I don't understand," the bot says.

"You don't need to understand, buttercup." He finally clicks the cuffs in place. A van with the NASP insignia rolls up and he walks her over, helps her up into the pen, which Seth sees is crowded with all kinds of anthrobots.

"Where are you taking them?" asks Seth.

The cop ignores him.

"Hey!" shouts Seth. "Where are you taking them?"

They slam shut the back door and the vehicle speeds away.

YOU USED TO BE ABLE TO SEE THE STARS

38

The Lipworth Institute

Johannesburg, 2036

When Kate and Keke arrive at the Lipworth Institute they are scanned and frisked and interviewed and snapped. Their DNA code is verified by the bottle of water they are offered on arrival.

"Someone's paranoid," mumbles Keke.

"Not paranoid," says Kate. "Safe."

"Now they've got our numbers," says Keke. "They could print a copy of you right now. They could clone your ass and keep you in a cage in the basement and no one would be any the wiser."

"Jesus. Now who's being paranoid?"

"I'm just saying. Stranger things have happened."

"I'd like to think that my family would know the difference between me and a facsimile."

"Ha," says Keke.

"What's that supposed to mean?"

Keke shrugs. "This place just gives me the creeps. It's so … clean. White."

"Really."

"It doesn't bother you?"

"It doesn't bother me. In fact, I like it. It gives me a break from my synaesthesia. It's like a palate cleanser for my brain."

"What did you say about me being crackers earlier? For the record, I am not the one who is crackers."

A smooth white robot cycles up to them. "Good morning."

Is it morning already?

"Good morning," says Kate. "Doctor Morgan said I should meet him here."

"Of course, Miss Denicker, please follow me."

After a few steps the droid stops and addresses Keke, "I'm sorry, but your access has been denied."

"Excuse me?"

"Your code has not been pre-approved."

"What the fuck does that mean?"

"Your record," says Kate.

"My record?"

"Your criminal record," says the bot, helpfully.

"My record is clean!"

"Not according to the SACRKS. I'm sorry."

"If you're talking about what happened in 2024, they dropped the charges."

"Hmm," says the droid.

Keke stands her ground.

"And the 2021 charge was also dropped."

Sensing Keke's persistence, the droid shifts into peace-making mode. "Please feel free to wait for Miss Denicker in our Metro Revolvorant."

Keke's mandible beeps.

"Please accept this credit to treat yourself to a complimentary beverage of your choice."

Keke acquiesces with a sigh. "Fine. Whatever. I'll wait for you at their crap-o-rant. Keep me posted!"

Keke zooms up in their external elevator that only has one stop: The Metro Revolvorant. It's empty apart from a bored waitbot vacuuming the glass floor with its skirt. The vertiginous view reminds her of that old club they used to go to in the 20s. *What was it called?* She met many a contact there.

The restaurant is superglass from floor to ceiling, and, as the name suggests, it slowly revolves to offer the patrons a view of the whole city, which would be magnificent if it wasn't for the electrosmog that covers Johannesburg like a static dirty dog blanket.

You used to be able to see the stars.

When did the air become unbreathable? Slowly, slowly, then all at once.

How things can change so much in a decade. Now the outside sky is grey-black, with only the slightest hint of dawn. Keke grabs a seat and punches in her order for an iced coffeeberry. Despite her melancholia, it's not the worst place to watch a sunrise.

"Welcome to the Metro Revolvo!" says an electronic voice, and Keke almost jumps out of her leathers. The waitbot's LED eyes regard her with a neutral expression. It puts her drink on the table, and Keke thanks it, despite always making fun of Kate for doing the same thing.

It's a fucking droid, Kate, she would say.

Manners are manners, Kate would fire back, especially if the kids were with them.

The bot goes back to vacuuming the already spotless floor. Keke thinks it might be the loneliest thing she's ever seen. Without warning, she feels a heaviness on her chest, as if the whole sad empty restaurant is itself a vacuum, and it's crushing her.

This is not the time for an existential crisis. Pull yourself together.

She knows what she needs to do.

BALLS IN A BEAR TRAP

39

TWELVE YEARS PREVIOUSLY

SkyRest

Johannesburg, 2024

Lewis takes Zack around the residence. He's a man of few words, and of those words at least half are swearwords, but Zack gets the general gist of how the system operates. The three separate wings are all identical to this one. They work eight-hour shifts then replace one another, like a relay team. Work, leisure, sleep. Work, leisure, sleep. Work, leisure, sleep. Cogs in a machine.

Zack expects the rooms to be cold, but a warmth emanates from the walls. Their residence will still be vacant for another half hour.

"Let's grab a sandwich before the mob gets back," says Lewis as they pass by the cafeteria. He skims two subs off a tray and hands one to Zack, who doesn't have an appetite—hasn't had an appetite in days—but accepts it anyway. They sit at a plastic table.

"It's your day off?" asks Zack.

Lewis laughs, wipes invisible crumbs from his beard. "No. No such thing in here." He takes another bite. "They always get me to do the babysitting."

Zack's never been the ingénue before; he's used to being the mentor. He's used to being the one with the silk tie and all the answers.

"No offence," Lewis adds.

"None taken," says Zack. "I'm just … adjusting."

"You'll get used to it soon enough," says the old hippie. "Things are simple in here, which is more than I can say for the outside world. You work hard, you get Rewards. You keep working hard, you level up."

Level up? thinks Zack. Something about the phrase ignites a flame of anxiety in his chest. An important thought is hovering, just out of his reach.

"You level up all the way," continues Lewis, "and you get out of the dungeon. Up to where all the pretty white space is with entertainment rooms and cinescreens and virtual gyms and office pods. And decent food," he says, crumpling up his serviette and shooting it into the corner bin. "Not this cardboard panini shit. Or so I've heard."

Zack notices for the first time the lapel on Lewis's vest.

"These are my stages," he says, tapping the five colours on his chest. They're like military stripes. "Two more to go before I get elevated."

"Elevated?"

"Promoted. To up there," he points to the ceiling.

"How long have you been here?"

"Jesus. I don't know. How'm I supposed to know? You see a fucking calendar in here?"

"Longer than the rest?"

"Most of them."

"Are we talking years? Or decades? How long does it take to get up there?"

Lewis shrugs. "It depends how hard you work." He looks at Zack's sandwich, untouched. "Good decision," he says.

In the remaining time before the work shift is over, Zack learns how to slam the side of the jukebox in exactly the right position to get it to play 'A Little Less Conversation' (which kicks him in the gut with nostalgia for a nameless woman with burnt caramel skin), how to hack the sonic shower so that it gives you an extra thirty seconds of spray (*believe me, on some days you'll need it*), and what you have to do to get Rewards.

"Rewards? Like treats? Like, for a dog," says Zack.

"Sure, you can think of it that way."

"What's the best way to think of it?"

"Ways to make your life here more comfortable."

Lewis shows Zack his own room. It's pimped out with body-building equipment, a long mirror, a comfortable looking bed, and a beard-grooming kit.

"Some inmates use Rewards for snax. Chocolate and nutnut cookies and shit. Not me. I want to look my best when I get up to civilisation."

Zack eyes out the SkyRest-branded shaving foam canister and cut-throat razor. It looks well used. "They're not worried that you use that as a weapon?"

"Ah, no," says Lewis. "No bad behaviour in here. It's not worth it. They'll strip you of all your stages. It's a fate worse than death."

Lewis points at the corner of the ceiling. Zack assumes a microcam is there.

"Every room. They watch everything we do. Real time. No one gets away with anything. It's a clean way to live, you know. Transparent. Puts you on your best behaviour. In the real world if someone pissed me off, I'd probably fuck them up. That's one of the reasons I'm in here. Now I let shit slide. All actions have consequences. I meditate the anger away. It's a lot fucking healthier."

"What happens to you in here if you break the rules?"

"No one breaks the rules."

"That can't be true."

"Listen," says Lewis, looking up at the camera again, then back to Zack. "I'm only going to say this once."

Zack looks at him.

"Do not break the rules in here. Do not break the fucking rules. Got it?"

He nods.

"Do not start trouble. Show up for work. Don't wander off. Don't cause fights. Okay?"

"Okay," says Zack.

"You do not want to be thrown in solcon. Not in this place."

Lewis looks away now, and there's something in his eyes that wasn't there before. What has he seen?

Zack tries to lighten the atmosphere. "So there're never any punch-ups?"

"Well, I wouldn't say that. Put a bunch of men in a dungeon and there are going to be skirmishes. But they're rare. There's just too much at stake. Plus—"

"Plus?"

He taps his black bracelet. "They can stop a brawl before it escalates. They've got eyes on you, right? Plus they monitor your heart rate, your blood sugar, your adrenaline, and this thing packs a hell of a current. Someone up there gets antsy, and they can floor every single one of us with a push of a button."

"They can taser us all? All at once?"

"Taser, monitor, drug…" he polishes the cuff with his sleeve. "Basically, they've got our fucking balls in a bear trap. So my best advice is to act accordingly."

MIDNIGHT ELVES

40

"You ready for your first shift, Girdler?"

Lewis stands at Zack's sliding door. The bell rings.

"I think so." Zack doesn't mind the idea of hard work today. It might help with his nerves. Lewis gestures for him to follow, and they join the rest of the crims as they stream out of the residence and into the adjacent factory. Zack calls it a factory, but to be honest he still doesn't know what products SkyRest makes. He receives a few mildly interested looks from the others, but most of them ignore him. Soldier ants, worker bees: all in the same grey soft-cotton kit.

"What is the actual work?" asks Zack.

"That's not an easy one to answer."

Zack laughs without humour. "What do you mean?"

"It's not like we're working on an assembly line, right? We're not manufacturing shit. This isn't fucking Bilchen."

"Then ... what?"

"They identify what needs doing and they funnel us accordingly."

"But what? What work?"

Why is Lewis being so evasive?

"Anything. Anything that requires labour as long as—"

"Yes?"

"As long as we're not seen."

"By who?"

"By the clients. By the pretty people in the honeycomb. We're like ... the midnight elves. You know, the little crims who steal inside and do all the work. Like an invisible workforce, you know? The ghost in the machine. No one wants to see the elves. It breaks the spell."

They keep walking.

"So, give me some examples, so that I know what to expect."

Lewis sighs. Zack can see him thinking: *I'm too old for this shit.*

"Okay, so … the day before yesterday we were chopping wood for the incinerator. The day before that, we were creating seed eggs. Before that: chopping fucking onions. Before that: re-potting saplings. Birch, I think they were. Silver birch."

"What are seed eggs?"

Lewis holds up a hand to stop him from asking more questions.

"You're not ready to know that shit yet. You're going to be in here a long time. You're gonna need to learn some fucking patience."

"Sorry," says Zack.

"I'm not mad. I'm just telling you like it is."

They trot into an artificial greenhouse. There are no windows, because it's deep underground, but the ceiling is covered in thousands of lo-glo bulbs, and the plants— thousands upon thousands of plants—reach up to their fake suns like disciples who don't yet know they've been swindled.

They line up along the rows of aeroponic vegetation. How many are there of them? Zack does a quick headcount. Two hundred? Each row seems to contain a different plant. Theirs has a purple flower.

"Slow and steady," says Lewis, tapping his stages. "Slow

and steady wins the race."

Zack looks at Lewis's lapel. "Hey. You got another stripe."

Lewis's eyes twinkle. "Close now," he says, "real close. I think you had something to do with it."

"I doubt it," says Zack.

"You filled in the satisfaction report, right?"

"Well, there was a form. It asked how I would rate my initiation experience."

"Right," says Lewis. "I think that's what tipped the scales. I mean, I knew I was close."

"What's the first thing you're going to do?" asks Zack. "You know, when you're up there?"

"I'm gonna go for a swim. Did you see that swimming pool?"

"No," says Zack. "I thought pools were illegal."

"Not in state institutions. Not when they service a community like this."

"You saw it?"

"Oh yeah. Oh man, that pool. As blue as the fucking Atlantic. I haven't been for a swim since 2009."

"That does sound pretty good."

"And then, then…I'm going to have a meal. A proper

meal. And a CinnaCola, with ice. Real ice. Not fake ice."

"I don't think they make that anymore. CinnaCola, I mean."

"Ah." Lewis looks disappointed.

"Listen up, residents," says a familiar voice from the front of the greenhouse.

A medium close-up of Bernard's toad-skinned face is beamed into a hexagonal-framed hologram above them.

"We're going to be spraying the plants today. It's important that you spray them hard enough to dislodge any insects—"

Insects? Down here? And: *So they've given her a job to do.*

"—but not so hard that you damage the leaves or uproot the organism."

Bernard nods at the creep holding the holocam and they track down to her hands, where she demonstrates the correct procedure. Zack can't help cringing when there's a close-up of her hands and her broad, flat fingernails. She was in his room again last night. He heard the door slide open and something inside him shriveled up like it would never be the same again. And now she's here to stay.

"What are these plants, anyway?" he whispers to Lewis.

"It's fucking alfalfa," says Lewis. "Can't you tell?"

HOLLOW BUTTONS

41

TWELVE YEARS LATER

White Mezzanine, 2036

Silver wakes in the same white room, in the same spearmint shift. At first she's confused, and then disappointed. She pulls the linen off her body and inspects her wrists. No wounds, no scars, as if her suicide didn't happen at all.

"Fuck," she says.

Her disappointment grows bigger inside her, out of control—a veld fire—and changes quickly to a hot white fury. She takes it out on the furniture again: the side table, the chair, the plate of breakfast nutrijelly. Silver tries to smash the small square of reinforced flexiglass that should be her portal to the outside world but all she manages to do is hurt her hand. She stops shouting when the tears come, not because she's no longer angry but because she can't yell and cry and breathe at the same time without hyperventilating. Silver cries until her eyes are swollen and her head pounds with its terrible ache, and she has to lie with her cheek and temple on the cool floor for relief.

She stares at the two cobalt-coloured tablets lying on the tiles. Slowly, slowly, she crawls towards them and picks them up. She knows that if she swallows them they'll take away her pain. Her unremitting headache, her glowing hand, her heartbreak. They'd make this hell-flavoured purgatory easier to handle. She wants to take them so badly, but instead she stands up and walks to the cupboard and finds her jacket, and pushes the pills into the hollow buttons of her coat. She checks on the other buttons, feeling them with the tips of her fingers, as if her eyes are not to be trusted. Twenty-four have now been filled. Twelve to go. That should be enough to escape.

UNDER THE SURFACE

42

TWELVE YEARS PREVIOUSLY

SkyRest

Johannesburg, 2024

Once the plants are sprayed and inspected for any kind of malformations or disease, the workers move on to other things. Some go to help in the kitchen, some, the laundry. Zack and Lewis are enlisted to saw and chip wood, along with another ten men. What surprises Zack most is how much space there is down here. The outside building—that white honeycomb shard planted into the earth—is the tip of an iceberg. An anthill that is rooted deeply and widely under the surface.

"Be careful," warns Lewis, looking at the humming machine. "These are industrial chippers. They'll chew your fucking arm off if you daydream."

They start feeding the appliance with the hunks of wood supplied. It makes short work of even the hardest wedges of timber. They both grunt and sweat with the effort of hauling the heavy pieces.

"No offence, but … aren't you too old for this kind of work?" Zack is only half joking.

"Fuck off," says Lewis. They both know he is the stronger of the two.

It's gratifying labour, and the air is filled with a dusty forest fragrance that penetrates their paper masks. They bag all the wood chips, and pack them into trolley cages which are wheeled away by another team. They sweep the floor till it's spotless; so that no one would be able to say there were twelve men in here making whole trees disappear.

After an exhausting eight hours, the bell rings, and they amble back to their residence, stretching sore muscles and rubbing dirt off their skin. Bernard follows them from behind. Zack ruffles his hair and sawdust falls onto his shoulders. His cuff beeps green.

"Hey," says Lewis. "The gods approve!"

Zack looks at him, and Lewis slaps him on the back.

"You got your first Reward. What are you going to choose?"

"I don't know."

"You don't know?" Lewis wipes his arms and hands with a damp rag.

"I guess I'll look through the catalogue."

"You need to set up your wishlist, man. Most of us have lists a mile long. You don't even have an idea?"

Zack still doesn't have an appetite, and there's nothing he's seen in Lewis's room that he wants to replicate, but then he gets it.

"A book," says Zack. It's exactly what his atrophying brain requires. "I'll request a book."

Lewis shakes his head. "Sorry, man. Down here? No books allowed."

GOOD ANGEL, BAD ANGEL.

43

TWELVE YEARS LATER

The Lipworth Institute

Johannesburg, 2036

"Morgan!" Kate runs up to the DarkDoc and hugs him. He's standing outside a private ward in the medical wing of the Lipworth Institute. Why Africa's premier robotics lab needs a medical wing is not clear to Kate, but more pressing questions are crowding her head.

"Kate." His arms and his voice envelop her, and she allows

herself to be held for a minute before she breaks away. Morgan's solid frame is always a comfort. She feels grounded when they're together: When he's touching her there's no danger of flying off into space. He holds her by her upper arms now, as if to inspect her. His warm skin is cedar leaves and cardamom: a fresh winter fire. She doesn't see her shapes when he talks, despite his voice's dark resonance. Instead it goes deep inside her.

Kate swallows hard. "Silver?"

"Before you see her …" the DarkDoc says, "let's talk."

"Let me see her first. Is she in there?" She moves towards the closed door.

"Kate. Please. I don't want you to—"

But it's too late. Kate leans against the door and rushes in, and when she sees Silver, she's so shocked that the blood drains away from her head.

"Whoa," says Morgan as her knees give way, and he grabs her.

"What happened to her?" Kate tries to blink away the dizziness. "What the fuck happened to her?"

Silver is bone-white. She's in a spherical oxygen tent, unconscious. IV bags hang on steel arms above her shoulders. One white, one red. Good Angel, Bad Angel. Her head is bandaged, her wrists shackled to the bed with velcro strips. Silver looks so small and defenceless on the hospital bed it makes her want to cry.

Kate approaches the transparent plastic dome and unzips it just enough to hold her daughter's cold, sleeping hand. She looks so young. Too thin and too fragile. A bird with a smashed wing. The skin on her inner arms has bright red welts, a few platelet plasters dress where the skin is broken.

"It's her sixteenth birthday tomorrow." Kate doesn't know why she says it.

"I know," says Morgan.

"How did you find her? How did you know she was here?"

"I got a med-alert from the institute. They must have scanned her dynap code. I'm still listed as her primary physician."

"Why didn't they call me?"

"The commlines have been unstable. I couldn't get hold of you either, but I kept trying until I did."

Kate re-sets her mandible.

You have three hundred and eight missed calls, it says.

"You called me three hundred times?" she asks Morgan.

A half-smile. "That sounds about right."

Kate blinks at him. "Thank you."

"It's nothing. Besides, it's the good samaritan who brought her in here you should thank. And the Institute. She couldn't be in better hands."

"Why are her arms strapped down?"

"She was harming herself. Scratching. She almost hit a vein before we realised what was she was doing."

"What happened to her?"

The DarkDoc pulls her to the visitors' couch where they sit down. He hands her a paper cup of some kind of lukewarm flower tea. Chamomile? No. The shape of chamomile is oval and rough-edged. This is soft. Palest yellow on white (Pee Snow). She puts it down on the ledge beside her.

"I want to know everything. Don't leave anything out."

"I don't know much, yet, but as far as I can see, Silver's had a bad reaction."

"A bad reaction? To what?"

"I've examined the wound on her head. She got laced. I don't know where or how—"

"Oh no," says Kate. "Oh no. It's my fault."

Liquid guilt spreads inside her, blackening and embittering her organs. Cold Tar.

"It's not your fault."

"I should have done it with her. Gone with her. Given her permission. Then *you* could have done it. Instead of … instead of *this*."

They both look over at Silver's still body. Morgan

squeezes her hands.

"You were trying to protect her. Besides, I should have known when she came to see me that she wasn't going to take no for an answer. Silver's stubborn ... like someone else I know."

He's trying to lighten the mood, but it doesn't work.

"I'm sorry," Morgan says. "I should have accompanied her home."

"I should have gone with her in the first place!"

"You did what you thought was best."

"Did I?"

"Kitty. Of course you did."

"Did I do what I thought was best, or what suited me best?"

Kate's so angry with herself, she feels like bashing her head on the wall. "I've just been ... trying to stop her from drifting away, you know?"

"I know."

"It's like immersion just takes her further and further away from me. And now look at her!"

"She's catatonic."

"Is she in a coma?"

"No. Her vitals are there. Shallow, but all there. She's just not … conscious."

"I don't understand."

Morgan steeples his fingers. "It's like she's … somewhere else. Like she's slipped away from us and left her body behind."

Kate buries her face in her hands for a moment then looks at him. "Can you fix her?"

His immediate expression tells her all she needs to know.

"There are so many ways to mesh," he says, "so many different laces on the market. And on the grey market. It's impossible to regulate any of it, never mind creating proper peer-reviewed studies of how it affects different people in different ways. The tech evolves every single day … it's just spinning away from us."

Kate's hopes drag. The DarkDoc is the southern hemisphere's pre-eminent biotech doctor. If he can't fix her, who can?

"You'll try, though? You'll do what you can?"

Kate can see he's already rehearsed his answer.

"It's too risky."

"You have to try!"

"I'd be going in blind. The chance of causing irreversible damage is just too high. I wouldn't take the risk with a patient I didn't know, never mind with Silver."

Kate blinks at him, waiting for the information to sink in.

"So. There's nothing we can do?"

The DarkDoc smooths his black beard. "I didn't say that."

TRUMPET OF DEATH

44

TWELVE YEARS PREVIOUSLY

SkyRest

Johannesburg, 2024

This time when they are led into the hall to work they are given special protective gear. Thin plastic overalls that crunch when you walk, wide face masks, and biolatex gloves. The air is less stale than usual.

The guard with grey hair and a voice like dusk stands in front of them. The younger guard—a blond, fresh-faced assistant—films him so that his face is broadcast in the hexagonal holoframe above the residents.

"Good morning," he says, and the men mutter their replies. Zack picks up that the guard's name is Xoli. He seems to enjoy the attention. "You'll be wondering why you've been given extra kit. It's because we're dealing with a new substance today. It's part of our experimentation in a new, cutting-edge technology, and we need your help. It's not without risk, though, so please be careful and keep your prophylactix on at all times."

There's a murmur of interest. Virgin tasks are few and far between, from what Zack's seen, so getting to do new work seems like something to look forward to. The men are instructed to move towards the trestle tables, and the day leaders peel away the covers to reveal large tubs of dark brown organic matter.

"Now for those of you with foraging experience," says Xoli, and there are a few laughs, "You'll know that this—" He holds up a large lily-shaped, charcoal-coloured mushroom. "—is called a Black Trumpet. Cornucopioides. Also known as black chanterelle, and … Trumpet of Death."

Zack studies the tub in front of him. He can see the fungi between the humus and brittle leaves.

"Now, mycologists would usually tell you that there's nothing to fear from a black chanterelle, and they'd be right. In fact, these mushrooms, in the wild, are really quite delicious and will do you no harm."

Xoli holds up his specimen, and the camera zooms in.

"However, this batch of fungi has been adapted by our

bioburial scientists, who spliced its helix with Dermestid."

The room is quiet.

"Anyone?"

A few frowns and head-shakes.

"Derme-stid. Skin Beetle. A Dermestid is a flesh-eating beetle."

Zack's skin crawls with imaginary insect legs.

"So, I introduce to you ... *Carnacraterellus cornucopioides.*"

"A man-eating mushroom," says someone at the front.

Xoli looks pleased. "Correct."

The men murmur. Xoli talks them through the process: find the mushrooms, identify the mycelia, harvest the spores, store them safely in the envelopes or soil trays provided.

"Please work carefully," he says. "And, whatever you do, don't breathe the spores in. As you can imagine, you don't want these suckers seeding your lungs."

Later, in his room, Zack lies on his mat and swipes through the Reward catalogue. What he really wants now is sleeping pills. He hasn't had a good night's sleep since he was arrested. Although, even if he has the pills, he probably won't take them. Only one thing is worse than Bernard watching him sleep, and that's not even knowing she's watching him sleep.

He might request a bed or a decent mattress at least, but those cost a lot more than one Reward. He'd have to save up if he wants a big purchase like that. A small mirror, perhaps, for above the sink? He doesn't know what he looks like anymore. Maybe it's best to keep it that way. Prison pyjamas and artificial light, atrophying brain. Thinking about looking at himself every day in these conditions make him decide against it. He imagines himself as hollow-eyed and hollow-boned. That's what it feels like, anyway.

He scrolls and scrolls until he eventually finds something to buy. The app congratulates him on his redemption (if only it was that easy) and informs him to expect delivery in the next open chute.

The dinner bell rings, and Zack silently congratulates himself for getting through most of the day.

Zack joins Lewis's table in the cafeteria. Lewis points at him and says "Girdler" for the benefit of the other diners. The men shoot him cursory glances. One or two mumble *hello*.

"You're not eating?" asks Lewis.

Zack shakes his head. "Not hungry."

"You gotta eat."

"What is it?" asks Zack.

"Who fucking knows," says Lewis, and some of the other

men laugh.

Zack grabs a tray and chooses the least unattractive option at the counter. Some kind of tofurkey with grey sauce and matching mash. Some pretty leaves on the side that makes the food look slightly less dire.

Back at the table, he takes a bite of mashed potato. Or, at least, he thinks it's mashed potato. It's difficult to swallow.

"You'll get used to it," says Lewis.

I doubt it.

"Soon you'll be eating decent food," says a shiny-scalped man to Lewis. He lifts his eyebrows at Lewis's lapel and points his fork up to the ceiling.

"Ah," says Lewis, relishing the thought.

"I heard they've got an artisanal ice cream shop up there," says a man who looks like a professional wrestler. "There are, like, a hundred different flavours. And if they don't have the flavour you want, you can make a request and they'll make it for you."

"Ah," says Lewis again.

"I'd ask for salted butterscotch," says the wrestler. "In a cinnamon cone."

"Black Choxolate," says the bald man, but there's not much hope in his voice. He only has two stages on his lapel.

"Eighties Bubblegum," says Lewis. "Remember that? Summers at the South Coast. Blue ice-cream dripping down your chin."

For a moment they all look lost in their memories of childhood treats and open skies.

"And you'll forget all about us," says baldy.

"I fucking won't," says Lewis.

"Yes, you will," says the wrestler. "And you should."

"I'm ready," says Zack to Lewis as they finish their game of table tennis.

"Hmm?"

Lewis is buoyed by the dinner conversation about his inevitable elevation, and Zack wants to take advantage of his good mood. "You said you'd tell me what SkyRest does when I was ready."

Lewis scoffs. "You're not ready."

"Lewis. Please."

He puts his bat down and takes a long, hard look at Zack. The ball vibrates on the table, then comes to a stop. Eventually Lewis capitulates with a shrug. "All right," he says, and Zack follows him to the cineroom.

MENACING HALO

45

TWELVE YEARS LATER

Metro Revolvorant

Johannesburg, 2036

Keke projects her contact list and hesitates before tapping on Marko's avatar, a saffron silhouette of a man meditating with a giant ball of fire behind him. She knows she's not supposed to call him, but this is an emergency. Besides, the chance of the call actually going through, all the way to an out-of-the-way ashram in India, when there's chaos on the ground here, is infinitesimal.

She's surprised when, on the third attempt, the phone buzzes. It's ringing on his side. Her pulse quickens. There's a click. All of a sudden Marko's face is right there in the restaurant, projected over Keke's empty glass. His eyepatch remains an accusation—will always be an accusation, whether he ends up forgiving her or not.

"Keke." He smiles.

He looks like a different person.

"You've lost weight," she says, past the tears.

"Have I? I suppose I have. That's what a fruitarian diet does. And fasting. We do a lot of fasting here."

"I know we agreed I wouldn't contact you," says Keke. "I'm sorry."

"Don't be. It's absolutely lovely to see your face."

Don't get emotional. Don't say anything tender.

"I miss you." The tears spill down her cheeks. "Sorry. Sorry. I promised myself I wouldn't cry."

"It's okay," says Marko. "It's okay."

She sniffs and angrily swipes away the tears. Clears her throat. This isn't why she called him.

"How's your mom?"

"I don't know, actually," Marko says. "She's still travelling. The last time we chatted she was feeding orphans in Udaipur."

The line is bad. Marko's face keeps snowing over.

"I'm surprised you answered. You're still unplugged?"

"Yes. This is the first time this old Tile has rung in ... months."

"When will you ... Do you know yet, when you'll come home?"

"This is my home now, Keke."

Keke swallows more tears, tries to un-crumple her face.

"It's not."

"You're right. There's no such thing as 'home'. Not really. It's just an emotional attachment to a place, which serves no one."

Keke feels her heart harden against him. If she's honest with herself, really honest, she can't stand this version of Marko. This bean-eating, meditating, philosophising, asexual silhouette. Yes, he's probably a 'better' man, but not for her. The essence of him is gone. What makes it more difficult, of course, is that she's the one who caused this emergence, this evolution, and she still hates herself for it, even though she felt at the time, and still feels, that she had no other choice. Her decision to sacrifice Marko's eye saved Silver's life. How could he resent her for that? Of course he's never admitted it: He didn't want to cause any further pain. But it became too difficult for them to live together. When he first came home after being discharged from The Gordhan, he found it hard to talk to her, to look her in the eye. As he grew stronger, Keke tried to initiate sex—

nothing too strenuous—but he wouldn't (couldn't?) get it up. Then, before she could get a handle on the situation, he was off to visit his mother in Goa, and suddenly an ashram had swallowed him whole. He hadn't been connected since.

"You're not going to like this," she says, "but I need your help."

What he used to say: *Anything for you, M'lady*.

What he says now: "Keke … you know I can't."

"You don't understand."

As if the emotional static isn't bad enough, the phone connection is crackling too.

"We're all in danger, Marko. There's something going on here."

"What?" Marko snaps to attention. His dreamy look is replaced by worry. "What's going on?"

"There's some kind of … artificial intelligence malfunction, they're calling it. A robot rebellion. An uprising. There've been over a hundred fatalities—and those are only the ones that we know of—and it's spreading."

Marko stares at her. "Wait. What?"

"Did you hear me? People are being killed by AI."

"AI doesn't rebel. Their code prohibits it."

"I told you, they're malfunctioning."

"Impossible."

The line is dropped. Keke calls him back, fifth time lucky.

"That's why we need your help."

"That is totally out of my area of expertise."

"Bullshit."

"It's not! I don't know the first thing about defective droids, and even if I did, how would I do anything from here?"

"You've got that Tile."

"This Tile is ancient. The tech is, like, eight years old. That's, like, ninety-six in tech years. And the signal here is terrible."

"I feel like you haven't yet grasped what is going on here."

"I—"

"Forget about our problems. Forget about being disconnected. We're in danger, Marko. Kate, Seth, the kids." She thinks of Mally and Vega. Wonders about Silver. "Especially the kids."

Marko bunches his hair up in his fists.

"I'll get on a plane. I'll get on the first plane."

"Jesus, Marko. Aren't you listening? AI wants to kill us."

Keke side-eyes the waitbot who is still vacuuming the

restaurant floor. No wonder they've gone postal. Imagine that is your entire existence.

"What are you saying? That they've closed the airports?"

"Of course they've fucking closed the airports!"

Everyone knows how much damage can be done when a plane is used as a weapon. Finally something clicks in Marko's brain. Keke can see a sudden clarity in his expression.

"You say it's spreading?"

"The Nancies are trying to keep it under the blanket. The danger of mass hysteria, blah. But yes, it's spreading. Twenty-four hours ago there were a couple of seemingly isolated incidents reported. Since then it's just exploded."

"It doesn't make any sense. AI is specifically programmed to never harm humans or animals."

"Something's changed."

"Marko scratches his head again. "Those initial incidents. Were they spread out? Or did they come from a common point of origin?"

"As far as we could tell, a common point, but none of the reports were official. Just first-hand accounts posted on SMstreams by civilians."

She brings up a sub-screen showing red pins on the map. There's a definite concentration over Sandton. Within a few seconds it updates, adding hundreds of new pins in a menacing halo.

"Holy Hedy Lemarr," says Marko.

For a second Keke glimpses the old Marko, and it twists her heart. *Not that it matters anymore.*

"This isn't a malfunction, Keke."

His face flickers in the static. She loses him for a while then he comes back.

"Keke?" he says. "I've lost you. Keke?"

"I'm here," she says, "Marko. I'm here."

"Listen to me. If you can hear me. This isn't a malfunction."

And just as Keke's about to ask what it is, and what they can do, they get cut off, and she doesn't get through to him again.

CRAVING

KEKE

46

Ashram Ramanana

Panchagiri Hills, India, 2036

Marko smacks his Tile in frustration. The signal here is worse than the itch on a neckbeard. No wonder these mountain yogis preach unplugging. It's like being back in the dark ages for Net's sake.

"Sorry," he whispers to the device. "It's not your fault that quantum tech hasn't reached us yet."

He needs to be nice to the Tile. He polishes it with his

sleeve. It might be the only way to keep Keke safe.

There's a faint knock on the door. A swami sweeps in, and stops in his tracks when he sees Marko with an electronic device in his hands. There's confusion in his frown, and disappointment, even though he tries to not show it.

"Marko, it's time for the retreat to begin."

They've planned a three-day silence retreat, which they'll finish off with a *yajna*. Suddenly Marko thinks if he has to scrub one more stone floor he'll turf himself out of a window.

"I can't," says Marko. "Sorry. I have an emergency."

"An emergency is a manmade concept." The sage's voice is a calm, clear pond. "Look around you. There are no emergencies here."

Marko's hand shoots up to his eye-patch. He traces the edges with clammy fingertips.

"It's my friend. In South Africa. She's in trouble."

"It's not up to you to fix her situation. Do not take that power from her."

"It's important. I just need some time. Half an hour. I'll join you as soon as I can." The fib flushes his cheeks.

"As you wish," says the swami, and starts to leave. He puts his hand on the door. "I hope that you will not undo all we have accomplished in dealing with your technology addiction."

If Marko could push the man out of the room he would.

"Yes," says Marko. Yes. Whatever it takes to get rid of the guy.

Knowing that Keke and the others are in danger has burst the incense-fragrant bubble in which Marko's been living. He's been trying his best to sort out his head, to fix himself before he can try to repair his relationship with Keke, but knowing that she's in trouble now and he can't go to her feels like someone is punching his lungs. Will he ever see her again? He thinks of all the time he's wasted, being here, when he could have been with her.

To be frank, his stay here has been pretty lame. He realises now that he was after some kind of eighties Hollywood spiritual training, some kind of Karate Kid/Sensei shit. Wax on, wax off. But really he's been playing along. Hoping that if he drinks the Ashram Kool-Aid for long enough he really will find peace and forgiveness. Pretending that he can be happy in this analogue world of mindful physical chores and meditation when really he's been jonesing for his online life: being completely in the flow when he's doing what he's best at. Most of all, of course, he's been missing Keke, although 'missing' is too weak a word. Images of her hold his sleep hostage: the warm fingers of his memories keep him wide awake. The feel of her, the scent. 'Craving' is more accurate a word. It could pretty much sum up the past few months. Years? Whether he admits it to himself or not, he's been craving Keke.

He restarts the Tile, hoping a new connection will be cleaner, but the call to Keke won't go through. He wants to tell her he might be able to help, after all. It's true he has no experience in defective droids, but he suspects something else is going on: something more sinister. Yes, he's a conspiracy theorist, and yes, he's naturally paranoid, but something about this 'rebellion' feels dirty, and he has an idea what it is.

He tries to call her again, without luck, so instead he concentrates on finding out what he can about the attacks. He thinks it'll take a while to get back into the saddle, hacking-wise—especially on this troglodyte of a Tile—that maybe he'll be a bit rusty and need time to adjust, but he's wrong. As soon as he's in, it's as if he's a bullet in a greased chamber, and within twelve minutes he's scraped enough darkdata to prove his theory correct. It feels good. He doesn't want it to, but damn, it feels fucking fantastic. His synth-heart is pounding. The footage of the Bent Hotel murder plays over and over in his head.

The bad news is that he was right about the so-called rebellion not being a code malfunction. As soon as he saw those red pins multiplying he knew. He recognised the pattern immediately. It's not a coincidence, or an uprising, or a defect. It has all the hallmarks of an infective agent that multiplies within the host.

It's a virus, and it's the scariest thing he's ever seen.

CORPORATE VIDEO OF DEATH

47

TWELVE YEARS PREVIOUSLY

SkyRest

Johannesburg, 2036

Lewis and Zack enter the dim cineroom, and Lewis dials up the lights, interrupting the crims watching an old nature documentary.

"Hey!" some of them say, before realising who it is.

"Sorry to interrupt, gents," Lewis says, pausing the film. "We need the room."

The men complain under their breath, but no one dares confront Lewis. They stand up and amble out.

"Scram!" he says to a laggard then closes the door behind him. "It's not like they haven't seen that grizzly documentary a hundred times before."

Zack flips through the available titles on DVD. The titles are milquetoast. No new releases, no sex or violence. Just old wildlife shows, clean sitcoms, and vintage feel-good films. He picks one out, cracks open the cover and inspects it. 'Eternal Sunshine of the Spotless Mind'.

Lewis laughs at the old tech. "When's the last time you saw one of those?"

Even the dusty DVD player looks a hundred years old.

Lewis changes the amp source then types in a code to unlock a SkyRest-branded video. When prompted to confirm, he looks at Zack. "You sure you want to know this shit?"

Zack nods.

"It's like bad porn," he says.

"What?"

"I mean, it's not something you can un-see."

Zack nods again, and Lewis shrugs and clicks play.

They grab a seat in the front row, and the film begins. The introductory shot is drone-footage of the architecture: we see some flattering angles of the white honeycomb shard among the deep green of the surrounding forest, and a woman's honey-tongued voice-over begins.

"Welcome," she says, "to SkyRest."

Is that Gaelyn's voice? Or do they all just sound the same?

An ultra realistic animation of a tree falling in a forest occurs. The tree soon greys and shrinks as it breaks down, and new growth—bright green saplings—shoots up from the nurse log.

"It's easy to become disconnected from nature when you're living a high-speed urban life. Part of this disconnect is thinking of death as an inherently negative experience."

Something about the death industry feels familiar to him, but he's not sure why.

Is this why I was sent to this particular crim colony?

"But what makes SkyRest different from other urban vertical cemeteries?"

Unseen things click into place one after another in Zack's mind, like someone shuffling a deck of cards.

"SkyRest offers clients a variety of burial options—"

Hexagonal frames appear on the screen to illustrate the available alternatives, and the first frame is enlarged: Inside is a tombstone.

"Our traditional burial contains all the hallmarks of a conventional burial, except that it takes place on one of our sky storeys. You are welcome to visit the resting place of your loved one any time of day or night."

The next frame is an urn on a mantelpiece. "If you end up selecting customary cremation, we have a variety of options to deal with the ashes. These include, amongst others: having them mixed with oil paint, and commissioning an artist to create a unique work for you. Having them distilled and turned into jewellery, or having them buried under the rootball of a sapling that you can take home and plant in your garden."

Seems sensible. Zack doesn't see what the big deal is so far.

"If you don't want to keep the remains, we also offer water cremation."

Okay, that's a new one, but still, hardly controversial.

"These are all popular burial solutions," says the speaker, "but none of them is environmentally friendly, and at SkyRest we strive for a carbon-double-negative footprint. If it's also important to you to leave the world with causing minimal damage, you may consider our earth-friendly options."

Zack's ears prick up; the SkyRest logo animates on screen.

"SkyRest introduces ... Recomposition™. Your Doorway to Immortality."

Immediately Zack thinks of zombies. Does this place

bring dead bodies back to life? A shameful amount of bank has been spent on immortality tech, but as he thinks it, he knows this isn't that kind of place. Everything he's seen has been deep green and eco-devoted—and he's petty sure zombies don't fit into that equation.

"For most people, the suddenness and permanence of death is difficult to accept, especially when it's a loved one. With SkyRest's trademarked Recomposition™ technology, your spirit can live on by nurturing the earth that sustained you during your lifetime."

Seth hardly blinks.

"Traditional burials are anything but natural. Bodies are preserved with the known carcinogen, formaldehyde, and then sealed in caskets that further embalm them, taking up valuable land and leaching poison into the ground. Even cremations are not without environmental damage: a single cremation pumps a toxic cocktail of chemicals into the air. In fact, our legal team here at SkyRest predicts that both of these options will be banned by 2040. Recomposition™ offers a positive solution to those looking for an earth-friendly burial."

The animation of the nurse log returns.

"Recomposition™ interlaces the cycles of life into the meaning-hungry, time-starved urban fabric and reminds us that, as humans, we're deeply connected to the natural ebb and flow of Mother Earth."

A young woman is lying on a forest floor, asleep. Dead? Naked, apart from some strategically placed autumn leaves.

Her long blonde hair is styled against the dark ground. More and more dead leaves cover her pale skin until she is no longer visible. The earth has swallowed her up.

"There you go." Lewis pauses the video. "Happy now?"

"Yes," says Zack. "No. I don't understand what the big deal is. Why the secrecy?"

"What can I say? It's death. People get cagey."

"How does it work?"

"You want me to draw you a fucking picture?"

"Can we watch to the end?" Zack already knows the answer and is frustrated. He's not sleeping, not eating, and he just wants answers. Is it too much to ask?

Lewis turns off the screen. "You're not ready for the end."

The video has jogged Zack's degraded memory. Pictures of dead people flash in on him: Face after face of obliteration.

Ramphele's file.

Then in a dreamlike scenario he sees himself injecting a young girl, and she collapses and dies in his arms. The disjointed memory fills Zack with bewilderment and fury.

"Do you know why I'm in here, Lewis? Do you know what I was convicted of?"

"Don't know. Don't wanna know."

"I was found guilty of killing over a hundred people."

Lewis's hand freezes on his beard.

"So don't tell me that I can't handle the end of a fucking video. Don't tell me I can't handle a sanitised corporate video of death. I am Death's friend, okay? I'm the Grim Fucking Reaper."

COSMIC CHESS GAME

48

TWELVE YEARS LATER

The Lipworth Institute

Johannesburg, 2036

Kate finds Keke at a booth in the dawn-lit Revolvo. Bathed in an orange glow, she's staring out the window with tears streaming down her cheeks. Her face is still: There's no sniffing or fussing, the tears just flow. It's as if she's one of those cinegraphs that used to be in fashion where only one element of the picture moves. Kate approaches Keke slowly, not wanting to wreck her reverie.

"What's happened?" she asks. "Keke?"

"It's beautiful, isn't it?"

Kate looks at the view. The daybreak colours are insane. It's as if someone has painted the regular sunrise with liquid LSD.

Keke has a faraway look in her eyes. "I mean, I hate that air pollution 99.9 percent of the time. But, hot damn! This is not one of those times."

They spend a moment absorbing the magnificence.

"The last sunrise will be the prettiest," says Keke.

"Who said that? Confucius? The Dalai Lama?"

"Nope," says Keke, draining her third drink. "Yours truly."

"Don't. It's not our last sunrise."

"I've got a bad feeling, Kitty. A very bad feeling."

"Silver's really sick," says Kate.

This shakes Keke out of her daydream. "Shit! I've been so deep into the Doomsday and Marko shit that I completely forgot why we were here."

"You were right. She got meshed. Some backstreet job that Morgan doesn't know how to treat."

"Brain damage?"

"We're not sure yet."

"Fuck! I'm so sorry. I don't know what to say."

"There's nothing to say, really."

Keke climbs out of the booth, knocking over her empty glass as she does so, and hugs Kate. They kiss each other's cheeks, then sit down again. Kate tastes Keke's salt on her lips.

"Wait," says Kate. "Did you say you spoke to Marko? Seriously? He took your call?"

"Reluctantly."

"It's been, what? How many years?"

"I don't know," fibs Keke. "I've lost count."

"Motherfucker. How is he?"

"Skinny."

"And he just answered? Like, 'Hi Keke'?"

"Pretty much."

"Did you tell him you've been waiting for him?"

"No. It wasn't that kind of conversation. I asked him for help. To hack the roguebots."

"And?"

"And … not his speciality."

"I guess not."

"Ja, well. He could have fucking tried."

"Morgan said much the same when I asked him to treat Silver. Hands off. Said it's too dangerous."

"He probably knows best."

"Yes."

"Well," says Keke, rubbing the tear-marks off her face. "Looks like we'll have to do it our-own-fucking-selves."

"Looks like it," says Kate, and they smile at each other.

There is some kind of reckoning in the air, as if they've reached the end of something. Kate senses a new kind of nostalgia—a wistful pre-remembering. Would this really be their last day together?

Keke takes a deep breath, as if she's ready to rush off and save the world. "Doomsday or not, we'll make it count."

The servbot cycles over and picks Keke's glass up off the floor.

"Welcome to the Metro Revolvorant!" it says to Kate. They wait for it to leave before speaking again.

"I do have a favour to ask," says Kate.

"Anything."

"Well, if I'm honest it's a shitload more than a 'favour'."

"You know I'll do anything for you," says Keke.

"This is different."

"Spit it out, woman!"

"Morgan told me something about Silver. He didn't think it was important, but—"

"But?"

"I think it might be. Something is telling me it is, or I swear I wouldn't ask you."

"For Net's sake. Do I need to wrestle it out of you?"

"Okay. So Silver's in this, like, dream state? And she's been mumbling things. Urgent things. So I was trying to listen to her and she wasn't making sense, but then she said very clearly …she said 'Zack'."

Keke's eyes flare. "Zack?"

"Yes. As clear as day. Zack, Zack, and then she said 'Get Zack'."

"I don't understand the connection."

"Nor do I! But remember that day at The Gordhan when he said he needed to tell me something important? But then he was arrested before he had the chance to say anything else and then—I'm sure I told you—it kept bothering me, not knowing. So I tried to track him down. I wanted to visit him in prison and talk to him. But when I started asking questions …the police closed ranks."

"I know," says Keke.

"You know? You know what?"

"They wouldn't tell me where he was, either. They said it was a special case because he was so dangerous. Didn't want the press sniffing around. Didn't want anything to be reported above the Blanket. I tried to get details about his trial but no one I spoke to could tell me anything."

"Exactly. It was like the system just swallowed him whole."

"It happens," says Keke. "Remember that politician who challenged Shini Wam in parly? She also disappeared with no trace. And that journo—Mpumi—remember him? You always said that he looked like a *Drum* magazine cover model."

Mpumi had a balling retrosexual Sophiatown afro-vintage chic look going on when they met. Now Kate imagines him as a little older: just as immaculate as before, but perhaps with a little grey salting his hair.

"Oh shit! He helped me on the Betty/Barbara story."

"Gone. One day he was promoted to chief editor at Echo.news. The next day his boyfriend reported him missing. Like they've just been plucked from reality. Like some kind of cosmic chess game."

"That's terrible. Why would they snatch *him*? Was he reporting on corruption?"

"Nah. Nothing as innocent as that. According to the rumours on the ground, he was some kind of double agent. He was pretty ruthless. He'd do anything for a story. He made a lot of deals with a lot of dangerous people."

Kate sighs, taps the table. "Oh, well then. Never mind about the favour."

"You wanted me to find Zack?"

"Yes. I realise this is a serious leap of logic, but ... something is telling me that he might be our only chance to break Silver out of her state."

"Well, I have reasonably good news for you then."

"Hey? But you've just said—"

"I said the police wouldn't tell me where he was. I didn't say I stopped looking."

BLOOMS OF YOUR BELOVED

49

TWELVE YEARS PREVIOUSLY

SkyRest

Johannesburg, 2024

"I'm sorry about last night," says Zack to Lewis over breakfast. Lewis raises his white eyebrows at him and motions for him to sit.

"No worries. I expected it. It's always difficult for initiates to process the work they do here. But," he says, pushing his plate away, "after what you told me, I think you'll have no problem fitting in."

Zack sits and looks at the abandoned food. No-egg omelette? Dutch baby pancake? He can't stand the idea of eating food he can't identify.

"What I said … isn't really the truth," says Zack. "Not the whole truth, anyway."

"I don't need to know, man. I'm not your priest. I'm not your lawyer."

"But I want you to know that it's not what it sounded like. It's not what I made it sound like."

"All right."

"I'm not a serial killer," says Zack.

Lewis looks at him over his coffee mug. "Really."

"It's complicated."

"Okay," says Lewis.

"Okay?"

"No one's perfect, right? We've all done wrong. Inside of here and out."

Has Lewis accepted his apology?

"But there is one thing." Lewis traces a scar on the table. "And I don't mean to offend."

Zack looks at him.

"Have you looked in the mirror, lately?"

"What?"

"You look like shit, man."

Zack finger-combs his hair, rubs his eyes. "I haven't been sleeping."

"I can see that. Your eyes have more baggage than a supermodel."

"I actually think I feel worse than I look."

"Not fucking possible," says Lewis, and throws his head back, laughing. A few residents stop eating their omelette/pancake to look at him, and Zack laughs too.

"Any advice?" he asks.

"Advice? Sure. Get a fucking mirror."

Zack laughs.

"No, seriously," says Lewis. "You'd better start sleeping. And start eating! The way you're looking ... well ..." He gestures at the building above them. "If you're not careful, they'll be using you in their next video."

The now-familiar siren sounds, letting them know that their work shift is beginning. The men sigh, bin what's left on their plates, and lope out of the cafeteria. This time they're led to a hall Zack has not yet seen. A warden shows them how to re-pot plants that have grown out of their containers. Roses, hydrangeas, maples, trailing Boston ivy, Virginia creeper. Considering yesterday's video, he reckons taking a thriving Boston ivy plant home instead of ashes is a good thing. You could have this urn of ashes in your house that you don't know what do do with, or you could have this plant that can cover a whole wall—a whole building—and flicker from season to season between green and red. An everyday reminder that the person you've lost is not really lost at all. Or a rose bush: you can forever have the blooms of your beloved.

They tap the plants' containers to release the roots, then ease them into the soft new soil. It's therapeutic work, and Zack starts relaxing for the first time since being here. They play classical music over the sound system. His shoulders unknot; his brain untangles. After the re-potting, they have to shift some soil in wheelbarrows, then they're instructed to sweep up and bag the sawdust and kindling in the wood-chipping room. The exercise feels good. The work is easy and monotonous and becomes like meditation. He keeps checking his cuff for his next Reward, and wonders how long it will be till he gets the first stage on his lapel.

This place isn't so bad. Then he corrects himself: *It could be worse.*

When their shift is over and they've showered, and they're waiting for dinner, they hang out in Lewis's room. Lewis is still in good spirits, doing arm-lifts and eating protein pretzels. His bare chest ripples with muscles a man half his age would be proud to have, and his tattoo seems darker than usual, the colours richer. The illustration seems to pulse on his skin, as if the dragon is alive.

"Getting ready for that swim?" Zack asks.

"I can taste that water, you know. I can feel it streaming through my hair in that first dive. Cooling my scalp."

"Going to be a good feeling," says Zack. "After all this time."

"Oh, yes." He drops from the bar then downs half a bottle of water. "Oh, yes."

Lewis offers him the SkyRest-branded packet of pretzels. Zack hesitates.

"Go on," says Lewis. "They're not going to bite you."

Zack reaches his hand inside the bag, grabs a few then sprinkles them on his other palm. Tentatively puts one in his mouth. It's not too bad.

"Will you tell me the rest of it?" asks Zack.

"The rest of what?"

"The rest of the video. Tell me how they do it?"

"All right," he says, sitting down. "Sure. Why the fuck not?"

Zack eats another pretzel. They're quite good, actually.

"What do you want to know?"

"Everything."

NITROGEN-RICH MATERIAL

50

"Ever heard of Ouroboros?" asks Lewis.

"Your tattoo," says Zack. "The serpent that devours its own tail."

Zack knows the ancient Egyptian circular symbol of eternal return that has been re-used and recycled by philosophical trains from Greek magic to alchemy to Kundalini health goths.

"Right. So they have this system going here. It's completely self-sustaining. Everything you eat, wear, or touch in this place comes from this place. *It is its own* immortality."

"Recomposition."

"Recomp's the main technology, yes. There are others on the menu, and even more that they're experimenting with."

"How does the recomp work?"

"Recomp is when they take the ... nitrogen-rich material—"

"The what?"

"The nitrogen-rich material. That's what they call it."

"Do you mean, the bodies? The dead bodies?"

"Yes, that's what it means."

"So they take the nitrogen-rich—the bodies—and place it inside a mound of carbon-rich material ... so that's the sawdust, and the wood chips. They add a bit of moisture, some extra nitro on top to get it going. Maybe some alfalfa."

Zack remembers the pretty purple alfalfa blooms they had worked on during a previous shift. What had Lewis said about them? That they're a feminine herb, element of the earth, and especially good on sandwiches.

"Then the microbes do their thing. The microbial activity gets the pile cooking. Their heat kills the bad shit. The pathogens. That's what you can feel."

"What do you mean?"

"We call it our underfloor heating. The warmth, from the

middle of the building? That's the core. That's where it all happens. Bodies in the top. Compost out the bottom."

Human compost.

Saliva rushes into Zack's mouth. He tries to swallow his revulsion.

"Then they cure the compost. Sometimes the clients want to take the compost home. They plant a fucking tree or whatever. Or they let someone here do it for them. They plant one of those saplings in the forest at the back. Put a tag on the tree, or a bench with a silver plaque underneath it. But most of the compost goes unclaimed. That's the stuff we use for the aeroponics. It's what we use to grow everything in here."

Zack spits out the pretzel he had in his mouth.

Lewis laughs. "Ja, that's pretty much the standard reaction."

Zack looks around the room. His uniform, the linen, Lewis's snax, the soap, the toothpaste, all emblazoned with the SkyRest logo.

"Yes," says Lewis. "Even the toiletries. Hemp oil and Miswak and Homosapien. So best get used to it."

Zack reaches for his water and rinses his mouth out, spits the water into Lewis's basin.

"Once you've had time to process it, you'll see that it makes complete sense. It's the full circle, you know? None of that embalming shit. No poisoning the well. None of that hanging onto dead bodies. If you think about it, being attached to a dead body is way weirder than letting it go back to the earth, you know? No waste, no harm, just energy doing its thing. Going round and round like it should. The process is actually a fucking beautiful thing."

"Does everyone in here ... Do the rest of the residents know?"

"Most of them. Some have been red-flagged. Admin decided it's best to not tell them. The truth doesn't serve everybody."

Zack feels ill.

The bell rings for dinner time.

NO ONE LIKES TO KEEP A SECRET

51

TWELVE YEARS LATER

The Lipworth Institute

Johannesburg, 2036

"You know where Zack is?" Kate asks Keke.

"Of course I know where he is."

"You found him?"

"It wasn't easy, but when I couldn't find any kind of record for him, or anything about his trial or sentencing, I tracked down that cop."

"The cop that—"

"Yes. Ramphele. The guy who cuffed me while I was with Marko in hospital. Aiding and abetting a serial killer, he said. Bullshit."

"I can't believe you've known all this time. Why didn't you tell me?"

"You had enough to deal with. Lumin. The Resurrectors. Mally's surgery and recuperation. I'd already unwillingly unleashed his crazy on you that day at The Gordhan. I thought you'd sooner forget."

"I still dream about him," says Kate. "It's crackers, because, really, I don't know him. I mean I met him for a few seconds but when I dream about him, his face is as clear as day. It was like we had this weird, intense connection."

"I know. I think about him every day," says Keke, "but for a different reason."

"Why?"

"Isn't it obvious? Because I'm the reason he's in there."

"You're not."

"I am. I'm the one who made the deal with Ramphele. Zack trusted me, and I set him up."

"You're not the one who killed people. He's in there because he killed people."

Keke shakes her head. "Zack's not a killer."

"Twelve years," Kate says, shaking her head in disbelief. "Feels like yesterday we were in that hospital. Can you imagine being in prison for that long? Especially when you're innocent. Can you imagine what that does to you?"

"I tried to tell the detective that, but he wasn't interested. He'd been chasing Zack for years."

"You must have made him so happy by agreeing to help him."

"It was weird because he was so desperate to arrest Zack, right? It was like his life depended on it. But then when I saw him afterwards he was ... upset."

"Upset?"

"Like ... properly depressed. We met at a hole in Randburg. The place was disgusting. Faux-flagstones that smelt like week-old beer. Broken glass on the floor. The autoloos were broken. They were literally serving cockroaches at the bar." Keke shudders. "I could tell he was a regular there. The beer was cheap; I know because I kept buying him round after round. It's like he had an uncontrollable thirst, like no amount of booze would ever slake it."

"You've always been so good at your grind."

"Yes, well. It's easy, actually. No one likes to keep a secret. That's what I've learnt. A secret has too much power. It builds up ... it makes people feel uncomfortable. Most people are just waiting for an excuse to spill."

"It's a relief," says Kate, "it diffuses the power."

"Exactly."

"So what did the depressed detective have to confess?"

"Ramphele wouldn't confess. He wouldn't tell me anything about the case—but there was definitely something dodgy going on—I could feel it ... I could see that it was eating him up on the inside. And then after our meeting? Guess what?"

"What?"

"He went missing. The station I called said he'd retired, but there were no documents to prove it. His file just blipped out of existence. Someone else I spoke to said that he just stopped coming to work one day."

"What the fuck?"

"So I figure, either he did something that he couldn't live with—like putting an innocent man away—and pretty much erased himself ... or someone didn't like what he told me. Considered him too much of a liability."

"The cosmic chess game."

"The fucking cosmic chess game. But I did manage to find out where they were keeping Zack."

"Where is he?"

"SkyRest."

Kate's quiet for a moment. She feels her cheeks warm. "SkyRest. Seriously? That's in Fourways. That's, like, twenty minutes away in a tuk-tuk. Zack's been living less than half an hour away from us for twelve years and you've never fucking said anything?"

"What would be the point?"

"To ask him what he was going to tell me!"

"Just because it's close, it doesn't mean that you can just pop in for tea and scones. SkyRest has the highest security out of all the PLCs. It where they send only the dangerous crims. There is a strict no-visitor, no-contact policy. And there are, like, three layers of biometric security. Besides, knowing he's so close … it would've just made you more frustrated."

"How do we know he's still alive?"

"Because if he was dead they'd have to report it. That's true for any crim colony. Remember the vertical mine shaft colony in Phokeng? The crims lived in the shaft?"

"They were shut down. Not profitable enough."

"Yes, they were shut down, but not because of the business. That was the Nancies spinning their usual bullshit our way. The business was going well—well enough, anyway—they were shut down because their crim death rate was above the acceptable threshold."

"But can't they just *jook* the numbers?"

"They would if they could. No doubt. But the UN Human Rights Council audit them, so they have to add up or they're in for a world of pain. If there's even a hint of creative accounting with bodycount the HRC will shut them down before you can say penal labour camp."

"And that would bite our economy."

"In a big way. Last numbers I saw said that the colonies made up thirty-eight percent of our GDP."

"Holy shit."

"Imagine closing them down and going back to the prison system that costs the country money instead of making it money. Now you see the motivation to keep their operations clean. Or at least clean enough to stay out of trouble."

They spend a moment just looking at each other.

"So Zack is alive. At SkyRest," says Kate.

"All facts point to that conclusion, yes."

"We need to break him out," says Kate, cool as TranX.

Keke chokes. "Have you not heard what I've been saying? It's impossible."

"It's the only way to save Silver."

"You don't know that."

"It's my best guess. Why else would she be asking for him? She's never even met him. Never heard his name."

"I can't explain that. I mean—"

"She hasn't said one other word. Not one. Not 'help me' or 'Mom' or 'Mally' or anything. 'Zack', she said. 'Get Zack'."

"How?" says Keke. "On a normal day it would be impossible. Now we're dealing with the roguebots and the Bot Hunters too. Have you seen the reports? They're killing each other in the streets. Civilians too. It's only going to get worse."

They both look at the servbot, who has stopped vacuuming. Its eyes are closed, as if it's powered down for a nano-nap. The overhead lights flicker, then stabilise again.

HER MOUTH IS LEMON PITH

52

Seth's Apartment

Johannesburg, 2036

Keke stands and gathers her things.

"Where are you going?"

"Where do you think?" says Keke. "To SkyRest. To get Zack."

"No," says Kate. "It's too dangerous."

"Ah, well," says Keke. "It'll be exciting, if nothing else."

"Don't fuck around, Keke."

"I'm not."

"When I asked you the favour ... to find out where Zack is ... I didn't mean I wanted you to go out and find him. I'd never ask you to risk your life for me."

"I'm not doing it for you. I'm doing it for Silver."

A lilac rush of sad gratitude spirals in Kate's peripheral vision. "You can't. You're right, it's impossible. You won't even be able to get in."

"What kind of fairy godmother would I be if I wasn't willing to duel with a few roguebots and break into a maximum security crim colony to find a character in Silver's dream?"

Kate smiles. "No ways. *I'll* go after Zack. You stay here and be with Silver."

"I'm not welcome here," says Keke.

"This place is safe."

"No place is safe. If artificial intelligence is really trying to kill us, then ... no place is safe. I may as well go out with all guns blazing."

Then what's the point of anything? What's the point of finding Zack and saving Silver if they're all going to die, anyway? But Kate knows she has to do something. She thinks of Silver's body lying in that white room, so close to living and so close to dying. She has to try, despite the odds, because that is what having children does to your heart. It cleaves it in two—or in her case, three—and it feels as if you have your heart beating outside your body, just out of your reach, pulsing along and weathering the elements.

"I'm doing it no matter what you say," says Keke, "so you can wipe that look of desolation off your face."

"Don't," says Kate, but she only half means it, and hates herself for it. She's already asked so much of Keke.

Keke is halfway out of the restaurant when she turns and says: "I'm sticking you with the bill!"

"Ha ha," says Kate. "The drink was complimentary!"

"Ha ha!" shouts Keke. "I had ten!" and then she's gone, and there is a blue watercolour wash all over, and Kate has the very real feeling that she'll never see her best friend again.

All of a sudden her mandible beeps with an outgoing call response. When she couldn't get hold of Seth earlier she had set her device to perpetual silent dialling. It's taken more than two hours to place the call.

"Seth!" she yells.

"No need to shout."

"I've been trying to … Never mind. Have you found Mally?"

"Not yet. I've been to Vega's hostel. It's not good."

"What?"

"It's like civil war here. It's like the fucking apocalypse. Looting. Explosions. Bot Hunters in full force, taking out anything without a pulse."

"Oh no."

"Now that the light's coming up I can see the full extent of it. It's ... terrible, Kate. It's terrible."

Kate's body tenses with anxiety; her mouth is lemon pith.

Seth clears his throat. "They're rounding up anthrobots. The AI Security Branch."

"And doing what with them?"

Usually this news wouldn't dye her insides yellow but she knows Mally is out there and would do anything to protect Vega.

"I don't know," says Seth. "They're saying it's for their own protection, but I doubt it."

Kate remembers the revolver strapped to her thigh.

"Oh, shit." There's a bright green spike in her anxiety. She runs after Keke, calling her name, but she's already gone. She breathes hard into the mandible. "Shit!"

"What's wrong?" says Seth, still on the line.

"Keke. I forgot to give her my gun. If it's as bad as you say it is out there, then—"

"She's going out into the city? Unarmed? That's insane. Stop her!"

"It's too late. She's gone."

"Where?"

"She's going to SkyRest. For me. For Silver."

"What?"

"I'll explain later. I need to go after her."

"I'll meet you there."

BONE BARK

53

TWELVE YEARS PREVIOUSLY

SkyRest

Johannesburg, 2024

Zack is in the forest. Dark as dread. He's running from something. Someone? The leaves hit his face, the thin black branches whipping his cheeks and arms as he races away from the danger. Where is he? This must be the forest that surrounds the crim colony. Has he escaped? He runs despite the dark, despite not being able to see more than a metre in front of him, despite the soft mounds of earth that threaten to swallow his feet and twist his ankles. He runs and runs despite not having any energy left in his limbs. Panic pushes him forward; makes his legs feel weightless.

He's wearing his suit and tie. He doesn't know how. He doesn't know in which direction he's running. He'll just keep going until he reaches the edge then strategise when he gets there. He needs to leave the threat behind.

But there's a problem with his plan or, rather, a problem with the forest. Because he keeps running but he's not getting anywhere. He can sense that despite his frantic pace, he hasn't moved an inch—an enchanted forest, a cursed forest. All of a sudden, he's flying through the air and lands in a shallow ditch full of leaves. The air is knocked out of him. He touches the soil on the banks that surround him and realises it's not a ditch at all. It's way too deep. It's a rectangular hole, six feet down. A grave. The realisation doesn't help to get the oxygen he needs into his lungs. The air is thick with the aroma of humus and clay. Leaf mould. Too thick to breathe. He scrabbles to climb out of the hole; he can't find a foothold.

He makes it halfway up the bank of soil when a rock gives way and he falls back down. He collapses hard, onto his back, and the shock of it keeps him lying like that until his head stops buzzing. But in the place of the buzzing is another sound: a whispering, rustling, an animal ticking, hundreds of insect legs. There's a pin prick on his ankle, then on his hand. He jumps up and shakes off the things. One is trying to get inside his ear and he swipes at it with a yell. Another sharp pain, on his leg, and then there are stings all over as the beetles swarm over him. Zack screams as he tries to sweep them off. As if sensing his panic they bite down. They want to get their feed before their dinner disappears. He starts to feel the wetness of the trails of blood mixing together. His fingers frantically scrape at the walls of black soil, and one of his nails tears off. Eventually he finds a root to grab onto and uses all the strength the adrenaline gives him to haul himself up and out of the death cube.

Zack pulls off what's left of the flesh-eating beetles and crunches them underfoot. He's dripping blood. Once he's sure he's free of the bugs, he puts his hands on his knees and waits for his lungs to catch up with him. The danger is still present, some unseen evil in the forest, but there's also the danger of him passing out and then there'll be no way he gets out of here alive. How did he get here? All he can remember is—

There's a sound behind him, a dead branch snapping. He spins around, his heart already trying to judder out of his body. Zack tries to make out what—who?—made the noise. He starts reversing and backs into a wide tree trunk. He puts his hands out to steady himself against the bark, but as his palms touch it, he recoils. It doesn't feel right. He turns towards it and yells in fright. Bits of bone are embedded in the bark. Bone bark. The branches further up are cartilage and sinew. There is some hair, some cheekbone. Teeth. Fragments of the pale woman from the video are part of this tree. An eyeball swivels to look at him, and he yells again, wants to run but his horror keeps him rooted to the spot. A shaft of moonlight casts the softest light on the tree, and Zack realises it's not the woman from the video. It's him.

Zack is yelling into the dark. A large hand is covering his mouth. Spongey, cold skin over his fevered jaw. His eyes click open. It's Bernard trying to suffocate him. He tries to fight her but she has the advantage of being above him, and uses all her heft to pin him down, knee on shoulder. He struggles and struggles, but is made weak by the starvation, the sleep-dep, the forest nightmare. Zack tries to call for Lewis, but her hand cancels out any trace of his voice. Gradually he stops struggling, thinking she will kill him now, she'll kill him and would that be that bad? But as he stops fighting her, she eases off too, until there is just one soft hand on his mouth the other goes to her own, an index finger crosses her lips telling him to be quiet.

"Shhh," Bernard says.

ELEVATION

54

The day's chute delivery arrives with a neatly wrapped Rewards parcel for Zack. The bald resident—Spud, they call him—hands it over.

"Congratulations!" Spud says, slapping Zack on the shoulder. Zack thinks he means for the Reward but then he looks down at what Spud is eyeing: he has a colour stripe on his lapel. His first Stage.

Zack swings by Lewis's room and is shocked when it's empty—not only of Lewis but also all his things. It's completely stripped down to the basics, with just a sleeping mat on the floor.

"Isn't it great?" says a voice in his ear.

Zack spins around, holding his Reward parcel against his chest. It was meant to be a gift for Lewis. Spud is grinning.

Zack's mind is furry with last night's events. "What?"

"Isn't it great?" Spud says again. "He's gone! Promoted!"

Zack shakes his head. Of course. Lewis has been Elevated. That's good news. That's really good news, but why does it make his stomach simmer with dread? He looks down at the gift. His nails are lined with dirt, and one of his fingernails is torn.

STAINED FOR SLAUGHTER

55

TWELVE YEARS LATER

Fourways

Johannesburg, 2036

Keke hops off the northbound solartram and stands still for a second, adjusting to her new reality. On her way to Fourways she's seen things she'd never believe if someone else had told her about them. It's as if the city has begun to eat itself.

Right now, right in front of her, a school smokes in the early morning light. A teenager in a blackened, frayed school uniform stumbles towards her, and Keke catches her. Ash floats like grey snow in the air.

"Hey," says Keke. "Are you all right?"

The injured girl's having problems talking. Too traumatised? But then Keke sees she's having trouble with her mouth. It looks as if her bottom jaw is stuck.

Jesus.

"Are you okay? What happened?" but the girl still can't talk. She's just leaning into Keke and drilling into her with wide eyes. Suddenly Keke realises none of the girl's wounds are bleeding, and she jumps backwards, causing the schoolgirl to fall onto the pocked pavement and skin her knee. No blood.

Keke shows the girl her palm. "Sorry. I got a fright."

The anthrobot keeps trying to talk through her closed jaw. She's becoming more frantic now. She stumbles towards Keke, who reverses, not wanting to be touched again.

"I didn't mean for you to fall. I just didn't realise—"

The non-bleeding girl keeps coming; Keke almost trips over a blown-out tyre.

"Stay where you are," says Keke. "We'll get you some help."

Her promise rings hollow in the hazy air. All around her she sees broken tarmac, maroon soil, sharp rocks.

276

The schoolbot starts crying. She's terrified.

Of what?

Then the answer becomes clear as a dozen other schoolgirls come out from behind the redberry pines adjacent to the slowly burning building.

Like a cackle of hyenas the girls prowl round them. They're armed with various make-shift weapons: a fragment of glass, a hammer, a rock. A palm of stones. The anthrobot is crying: a long, shrill wail that is almost human. Keke pulls the bot towards her. Her burnt uniform dusts Keke's hands with black.

"It's okay," Keke tells her. "You'll be okay." It's only then she sees the blue circle spray-painted on the back of the bot's uniform. Marked as non-human: stained for slaughter.

They're surrounded. The girls kick up red dust and inch forward, tightening the circle.

"What's going on here?" demands Keke with an authority she doesn't feel.

"What's going on here," mocks the bobbed girl with the hammer. She wears her school dress's collar pointing up and has a illustration of a lobotomised chimp on her face mask.

Keke has read about the bullying of teenbots in schools. Her first reaction was that they should not put anthrobots in school—what is the point?—but apparently there are many advantages to doing so. It's important that the human kids get used to having AI around, and the machine-teens help the kids with extra lessons. They're also well stocked, so you could always ask them for an extra stylus, a needle and thread, a platelet plaster or a protein bar. The bots' presence makes the kids more competitive, which is great for the schools' academic and sports performance, but it's a double-edged sword: The most competitive take exception to the over-performing bots and abuse them.

"Hand her over," says the blonde girl holding the shard of glass. She has blue paint on her fingers.

"Why?" says Keke. "Why are you trying to hurt her?"

"*Her?* It's not a *her*. It's an *it*. It's a *robot*."

Keke flicks her eyes over to the bot's uniform. XARINA, the holotag says.

"Her name's Xarina," says Keke.

"We don't call her that."

Keke takes a step backwards. "Robots are here to help us."

The girls snort and snarl.

"Looks like we've got a robo-sympathiser," says the blue-fingered girl, angling her head. "They're even worse than the robots."

The kids step closer and there is more dust, like red smoke in the air. Their practised movements send ice water down Keke's spine. Choreographed cruelty.

"What did she do to you?" demands Keke.

"She's not *real*, don't you get it?"

A swarm of Special Task drones buzz in the sky above them. They're in a hurry.

"But why hurt her?"

"Where have you been?" demands the freckled one. "The machines have gone mad. They're killing people. We need to protect ourselves."

Xarina whimpers and shakes. Strangers walk past their sinister huddle, turning their eyes away, seeing, but not seeing.

Fuckers. Who are the robots, now?

"This android isn't violent. Look at her. Look at her!"

"We can't take that chance," says the blonde. "Terry's aunt was killed by a supermall escalator."

The plain girl Keke assumes is Terry nods.

"And Mrs Nduli was attacked by her Elfbot."

When Keke looks confused, the girl adds, "Her home security bot. The one that's supposed to *protect* you."

Glass shard says, "They'll kill us all, if we don't stop them."

"I'll take her with me," says Keke. "I'll make sure that she doesn't hurt anyone."

"*You!*" The brunette laughs. "What are *you* going to do?"

"I can take care of myself."

"Whatever," says Freckles.

"Let's see, then," says the schoolgirl with the hammer. "Let's see how well you can protect yourself."

COLD-BUTTER BODIES

56

TWELVE YEARS PREVIOUSLY

SkyRest

Johannesburg, 2024

There is a jovial atmosphere in the cafeteria at breakfast time. Word has spread that Lewis has finally been elevated and the other residents are exuberant. Part of it is for Lewis, and part is the stoking of their hopes that they, too, will one day be promoted. Two men at an adjacent table each have only one more Stage to go. They laugh over their salty French toast at the inmates who joke around them about the clear blue pool and the craft ice cream and the all-you-can-watch film suites.

Zack's stomach is still roiling when it's time to start the work shift. He's left Lewis's gift in his room—still wrapped—even though he's sure he'll never see him again. They walk over to a hall where trestle tables are set out with old-school sewing machines, and the men are divided into those who can sew and those who can't. Zack is in the latter group, so he is tasked with unrolling and cutting fabric according to overhead projector templates. They set to work as the machines hum in the background. Usually the white noise would be calming, but today it's as if the buzzing is inside his head. His new shift-partner is a slimy man with nervous eyes, and adds to Zack's feeling of unease.

After two hours of work, a bell rings and the men sigh and stretch their arms and backs before they're shepherded to the next task. Zack trails behind the group, trying to avoid his new partner. There will be a five-minute toilet break before the next grind begins. Without really thinking, without even meaning to, Zack peels off from the crowd and slips into a dark room. He knows they're constantly monitored—knows they're watching his every move—so he doesn't understand why he's doing it. If he gets caught, he'll get docked any Rewards due to him. He may even get stripped of his first Stage. But there is an instinct stronger than fear, stronger than the desire to climb the ladder that leads him away from the others.

Zack slips in quietly, and waits for his eyes to adjust to the low light. The space has an earthy smell—is it one of the potting rooms?—but he doesn't see any plants or soil. He blinks, trying to make out what it is in front of him. He inches forward, towards a large dark shape. When he's closer, he sees it's a dozen make-shift platforms built from old building palettes, and they each hold up a large burlap bag with hand-sewn, re-purposed zips.

Wood chips? Sawdust?

But the shape of the bag is wrong. It's too long. It's horizontal. That, and the zip, makes it look like a—

He moves towards the bag closest to him. As he touches it, the bell rings for the next shift to start, and he jolts. Time to go, but he stays there, his body and brain frozen.

They'll miss him soon. He'll be in trouble. His hand travels back to the zip. The smell is stronger now, the dark humus scent reminding him of his nightmare last night. Damp soil and something else. What is it? He pulls down the handle of the zip.

Inside the bag is more brown burlap, wrapped around a sphere, like a dressing. Zack keeps unzipping the rest of it and flinches when he sees that the round bandaged thing is attached to a neck, and a torso. There's a noise in his ears, a humming. It's the adrenaline telling him to run.

So it's a dead body. So what? It's to be expected, isn't it, in a place like this?

The body is ivory, veined with blue. Zack zips it up again. He really needs to go. They've probably noticed he's missing. If he goes now he can still use the excuse of an extended toilet break or—less convincingly—that he got lost. If he doesn't get back now there'll be someone in here to drag him away. He moves to the next bag and opens it. An ash marble torso, waiting to be recycled. One more, he tells himself, he doesn't know why. The Net knows he doesn't want to see another one of these cold-butter bodies. But the next body isn't pale. The skin of the strong neck is loam-coloured and wrinkled, and as the zip moves, tooth by tooth, opening the bag, something in Zack knows what's inside before his brain clicks. He sees the top of the tattoo that he knows so well: Ouroboros.

It's Lewis. It's Lewis.

Lewis, who is supposed to be ten storeys above him, swimming laps in a crystal pool.

Zack stares at the rest of the tattoo: the dragon's head, its circular body, eating its own tail. He draws away, realises he's close to hyperventilating. Then he opens the bag further, and there's a strong ribbon of that soil smell—and now Zack identifies it—mushrooms. Forest mushrooms. And he sees openings in Lewis's skin—his stomach and thighs—like a sea-sponge, dark holes stretched by and embroidered with thriving funghi where they have rolled spikes over his skin and sprinkled in the shroomspores of the fungi that is eating his flesh. Dark meat with mushroom gills.

Zack turns his head away from the body bag and sprays vomit onto the black concrete floor. Water and bile splashes out of him. He wants to run, but his body heaves and heaves. When he straightens up, there is a silhouette at the door.

THE COOLER

57

Two guards come running, almost falling over Bernard in their hurry to get to Zack. They stumble, and shine their powerful flashlights into his eyes.

"Don't do anything stupid," she says.

It's a bit late for that.

The guards—Xoli and Samuel—move forward and Zack puts his arms up in surrender, wonders distractedly why they didn't just drop him with a current from the cuff. In his blinded state he has a flashback of Lewis's myco-ravaged flesh and almost vomits again. He covers his mouth with the back of his hand. He feels arms around him as the men guide him away from Lewis and the other body bags in the room.

"Where to?" asks Samuel.

"Solitary, for now," says Xoli. "Till they tell us otherwise."

What had Lewis said about solitary confinement? To avoid it at all costs. You go in the Cooler, you'll never be the same. That's if you're lucky enough to come out. Lewis said that 'luck' and 'solitary' do not often go hand in hand. Zack's head is spinning. He just can't get around the fact that Lewis is dead.

The young guard blinks. He seems surprised at the harshness of the punishment, but sets his jaw and moves Zack along.

"Stop," says Bernard, as they get to the door. "I'll deal with him." She looks smug. A cat that finally has the canary in her claws.

"But—"

"Girdler has been a menace from the start. There's only one way to deal with him and I know how." She runs her fingers up and down her baton, moistens her lips.

The guards look uncertain, but hand him over anyway. She pushes Zack in front of her.

"Start walking, Prisoner," she says. "The Cooler's got nothing on me."

Zack expects to be taken somewhere dark and beaten to

within an inch his life, so when he figures out where they're going he slows down and waits for his brain to catch up. Bernard pushes him forward.

"Stop dawdling, Prisoner."

His mind is a spiderweb of questions and pictures that won't fade. Bernard grabs two chairs from the common room and marches him to his room, makes him sit in one; she takes the other for herself. The residence is empty: Everyone else is still working. He should be used to her observance by now, but can still feel her ugly dishwater eyes washing all over him. Should he be grateful that she saved him from solcon? Or does she have something worse planned?

Heeled footsteps approach. Gaelyn. She arrives and beams at Zack.

"Mister Girdler!" she says, as if they're meeting by coincidence somewhere light and sunny—on a cruise ship, maybe, Cinnacola cocktails in hand—instead of in an underground penal colony cell.

"I do hope you're settling in nicely?"

Zack just blinks at her.

"I heard we had an incident," Gaelyn says, but Zack doesn't answer. "Now, I don't want you to worry too much about that. It's natural that you are curious as to how SkyRest functions. I only wish that you had come to me instead of exploring on your own."

"I was just—"

"I know, I know. There's no need to explain yourself." She squeezes his arm. The contact, the human touch, is a surge of warmth. "Now, I see that we need to start taking better care of you."

Bernard snorts.

"You're half the size you were when you arrived a week ago. Is anything the matter?"

What a strange question to ask.

"Tell me what I can do to help you," says Gaelyn. "It's my job to take care of you."

He finds himself gradually defrosting. "I've been battling to eat."

"I can see that!" Gaelyn says. "Your cuff is reporting very low blood sugar. Don't worry, I know just the thing." She makes a note on her Tile. "We'll have you sorted out in no time. I don't want you to worry about anything. Are we all okay?"

She searches his face for agreement. Zack wants to agree. He wants to stay on her good side.

"What happened to Lewis?" he asks.

Gaelyn's eyes flicker for a moment, then return to their friendly shine. Her smile is wide. "Oh, we're so thrilled to have him upstairs with us!"

Zack frowns at her.

"If anyone deserved a promotion, it was Lewis! Always

such a pleasure to have around. And the way he embraced our philosophy, well, we couldn't be happier to have him with us. We hope that, after this hiccup, you'll work hard to join us too."

"But he's not up there," says Zack, and Bernard's eyes flare.

Shut up, she's saying. *Shut the hell up, Prisoner.*

"What do you mean?"

"Lewis isn't upstairs. He's in a body bag."

"What?"

"Lewis wasn't elevated. He's dead. You can deny it as much as you want, but I saw his dead body in that room."

Gaelyn looks concerned. "No wonder you're not yourself! If you think you saw Lewis's body you must have had quite a shock."

"I know what I saw."

She frowns again, and feigned worry pouts her lips. "Hmm. This is unfortunate. Maybe the others were right."

"What do you mean? Who are the others?"

"The Residents' Care Team. Your history … during the trial. They predicted you'd need some pharmaceutical assistance."

"I don't."

Gaelyn makes another note on her Tile.

"Just for a while. Till you adjust. Moving here can be a traumatic experience! We need you to be able to cope with your new environment. We can't have people making waves, upsetting the others."

"Maybe the others need upsetting," whispers Zack.

"Excuse me?" says Gaelyn.

Bernard stomps on his foot. *Shut up!* she's saying.

"I said maybe the other residents need upsetting."

"If I were you," says Gaelyn, "I'd be very careful of what you say next."

Zack wants to shout at her, yell in their faces. He holds himself back. Getting thrown in solitary isn't going to help his cause.

"I'm going to let you off with a friendly warning. You can even keep your first Stage. I think you'll find that life is a lot easier down here if you co-operate."

Gaelyn tucks her Tile into her utility harness, and turns to leave.

"What's the first thing he did?" says Zack to her retreating back.

She turns around. "Excuse me?"

"What's the first thing Lewis did when he got up there?"

Gaelyn turns on her most winning smile. "He stripped off the new clothes we gave him and jumped in the pool!"

TINTED MIRROR

58

TWELVE YEARS LATER

Fourways

Johannesburg, 2036

"Stay away from me!" Keke shouts as the schoolgirls close in on her. "You just stay the fuck away."

The injured anthrobot keeps up her high whine.

"Judas," someone hisses.

Judas? What have these kids been reading? Anyway, they

have the story the wrong way around.

"You're a traitor," says the blue-fingered girl. "Taking a robot's side."

"I'm not taking anyone's side, but I'm not going to let you hunt someone down."

She's about to add, *What would your parents say?* But then thinks better of it. Where did they learn to hate so easily in the first place? Who taught them to be so vicious? She guesses it started at home.

The girl with the hammer strikes a blow on Xarina's shoulder. The pitch of the whining goes up a notch.

"You stop that right now," says Keke. *You little bitch!*

Freckles throws a stone at the anthrobot, and it glances off her chest.

"Harder!" says the girl with mirror braids.

The next stone hits Keke on her cheekbone and temporarily replaces her vision with sparkling stars and pops.

Keke touches her cheek where the stone has drawn blood.

Motherfucker! It hurts.

She needs to run. She wasn't convinced the kids were going to go through with the attack. She should have bolted as soon as she saw them sauntering up like pack animals. Why did she hesitate? Now it's too late.

The hammer strikes the bot again. The blonde girl with the blue fingers and sharp piece of glass eyes Keke nervously. Is this really how it's going to end? At the clammy hands of these schoolyard jackals?

The combination of Xarina's high-pitched whine and Keke's glowing cheekbone makes her feel out of control. Suddenly the rock slams into the bot's chest, and something in Keke snaps. She takes the blood from the cut under her eye and with two fingers, paints lines on her face with it: across her forehead, down her cheeks, over her nose and chin. Then she starts screaming as loudly as she can. She launches herself at the hammer-wielder, wrestles it from her, then starts swinging it and shouting at the others like a madwoman, hoping to scare them off. She smacks the stones out of Freckles' palm, breaking a knuckle in the process. Freckles cries out and cradles her hand.

The girl grasps to retrieve her hammer, but Keke shouts "Away! Away!" and when she doesn't move, Keke hits her on her shoulder with it, exactly as she had done to Xarina. The girl squeals and shrinks away.

From behind Keke comes the unmistakable buzz of a taser, and Keke feels it bite into her hip: an electric cobra. She shouts in surprise and pain, but really it's no more than a short shock: nothing like the usual debilitating current— and she sees that's because Xarina had moved to shield her, and the jolt she'd felt was just the residual current from where she's in contact with the bot's body. Keke smashes the taser out of the girl's hand so that it lands on the littered ground, right in front of Xarina, who picks it up.

"You don't scare us," says the girl with venomous eyes.

She goes for the taser, but Xarina gets to the trigger first, and the bot sends a perfectly aimed clean shot of cobalt electricity right into the girl's chest. The current is so strong it flings the schoolgirl's vibrating body onto the pavement, knocking her out. She's still shivering on the ground when Freckles makes exactly the same mistake and gets the same treatment. The other girls yelp and shout, but they don't help their friends. Xarina shows the taser around, as if asking them who wants to be next. Three members of the gang step down from the fray and slowly reverse out of the circle. Keke feints at the timid one— Terry?—with her upraised hammer, and she backs away too. A girl with a neon pink face-mask high-kicks Xarina in the chest. It does no damage—except perhaps to the girl's ankle—but it sets off the others to attack too, and soon there are four of them kicking the anthrobot. The bot drops the taser as they begin tearing into her with their fists and nails and teeth. They strip her singed clothes and stamped silicone skin. Her hair comes out in clumps. They kick her in her most vulnerable joints and she falls to her knees, then just as she looks like she's about to succumb, the bot looks up at Keke with bright eyes, as if something has clicked in her processing and she realises that she is much stronger than them.

Xarina's shrill screaming now transforms into a deeper bray as she roars and flings the attackers off her body as if they're nothing more than dolls. She forces her fingers into her own mouth and pulls off her lower jaw, then uses the disembodied titanium to slam one of the girls on the side of the head, and she spins away from them. Xarina's still shouting when she picks up a saucer-eyed girl and throws her twenty metres away, into a dirty bricked wall. Bones break. Xarina turns on the next girl; there are still three left, including the blonde with the glass, a girl with mirror braids, and a mean-looking blunt-cut brunette. Keke looks around at the injured girls' bodies with horror, keeps hearing the sound of those young bones breaking, and feels as if she's caught in a dream.

The brunette drops her rock. Mirror braids holds up her hands in surrender.

"Stop," Keke says to the anthrobot. "Don't hurt them." She can't bear to see any more violence.

Xarina turns to look at Keke. Half of the anthrobot's face is peeled off, most of her hair is gone.

"We're out of danger," says Keke, "you don't need to fight anymore."

The skinned bot blinks. She lowers her arms and stops shouting; she's still for a moment, processing the information. Her body seems to relax and, seemingly exhausted, she drops her metal jaw to the ground.

Without hesitating, the brunette slams Xarina from behind, causing the schoolbot to fall face forward into the red sand. The girl with mirror braids picks up the taser and jams her finger down on the trigger, sending fifty thousand volts into Xarina's body, paralysing her. She keeps going, sending pulse after pulse into the synthetic schoolgirl's body, until they can smell burning rubber and metal, and still she doesn't stop. Braids has this spooky look on her face, a cold indifference. The wrecked face of the robot, turned sideways out of the dirt, watches Keke as it jerks:

desperate, beseeching: an image Keke knows she'll never forget. Some pedestrians have slowed to watch, now that the opportunity to help has passed. Multi-coloured face-masks seem to flow past in a weird stop-animation in Keke's peripheral vision.

"Enough," Keke says, putting her hand out, even though she knows it's too late, but the girl ignores her and keeps melting Xarina.

"Enough now," Keke says, moving to take the taser away, and then she feels a hot, sharp stinging in her lower back, and the stinging turns to a searing pain, as if someone has stabbed her with a hot knife, and she turns around and sees the blonde girl looking up at her with a shocked expression, as if she had never really expected the glass to penetrate Keke's skin. As if it was too easy to slide the transparent dagger into sinew and organ. For that moment, connected by weapon and flesh, it's as if Keke can hear the blue-fingered girl's thoughts, and it's like she's wondering how something so simple and quick can have such dire consequences.

They stare at each other with matching shocked expressions, a tinted mirror of panic.

Is this what most violence is like? thinks Keke as the stars come back to reclaim her vision. *Ordinary people shocked by their own and others' swift actions?*

It feels as if the blood in her head drains out all at once through the new wound, her life flowing out of her. Keke's mind is as light as the sky above; her consciousness is floating upwards to join the grey clouds. She never expected death to be so welcoming, or so brisk.

Then there's no more time for philosophizing as she swoons to the ground.

Keke collapses next to Xarina, two cut-down bodies on the rough rusted soil. Creeps begin to gather around them, snapping footage for their Flitter feeds. Keke's vibrant blood puddles around them. The anthrobot tries to say something but without the modulator in her jaw-part the words just stream out as a sad sigh. Keke matches the sound with her own. Xarina moves her palm towards Keke, and they hold hands and look into each other's eyes as they both power down.

RETCH

59

TWELVE YEARS PREVIOUSLY

SkyRest

Johannesburg, 2024

Xoli and Samuel arrive at Zack's door. Xoli is carrying a SkyRest-branded suitcase.

"Mister Girdler," Xoli says, gravel for a voice.

Zack looks from them to Bernard and back again.

"Where do you want him?" asks Samuel.

Xoli glances up from opening the silver catches on the

case. "That chair he's in will do."

Zack frowns. "What are you going to do to me?"

The older man coughs and says, "Nothing to worry about, brother. We're just going to fix you up."

"I don't need fixing up."

The guard shrugs, points to the ceiling. "Orders from above."

Samuel ties Zack to his chair with some kind of wide elastic strap that he fastens at the back. He pulls another one over his arms. Zack struggles against the restraints but knows it's no use. The older guard pulls a transparent silicone bag from the suitcase—it's filled with a creamy liquid—then a thin plastic pipe. He tears the packaging open with his teeth and connects the two.

"Ready?"

"Ready," says Sam, holding Zack's head still. Xoli pushes the pipe up Zack's nose and threads it through down into his throat, causing him to retch. He struggles and some of the white stuff splatters on the floor.

"Take it easy," Xoli says, re-threading the pipe. "Just take it easy." He casts hard eyes at Bernard. "Can we have some help here?"

Bernard approaches and wraps her meaty forearms around Zack's head, holding it still.

Zack shouts and retches some more, and then he can feel the cool liquid running down his throat.

His vision becomes blurred before Gaelyn comes in. It takes twelve minutes for the bag to drain, and by the thirteenth minute he is lying, untethered and asleep, on his mat.

When Zack wakes, he's alone. There is a cool mist of relief. His tongue is swollen, his throat dry and scratched from when they force-fed him. Force-fed him what? Some kind of triple-strength nutrishake. Spiked, no doubt. He knows a sedation headache when he feels one.

What else did they give him? Some kind of psychotropic: an antipsychotic would be his guess.

"Something to control your hallucinations," Gaelyn had said. "Something to help you get some rest." What happened after that is a blur.

Zack tries to stand, but he falls back down again. His brain is slushed ice.

They wouldn't have to resort to feeding him if he just ate his meals, they said. The drugs they can administer via his cuff, but, unfortunately, nutrition still requires a manual approach. Zack crawls to his basin, splashes his face. Swigs half a bottle of water. The cool liquid balms his bruised throat; his thoughts are scudding clouds.

What did he do to get into trouble? He can't remember. There's a constant niggle of foreboding you get when you know you've done something wrong. Vague memories come to him: a circular dragon tattoo. A clear blue pool: empty. A beautiful biker with burnt caramel for skin. He can't think of her name, or how they met. Then a more urgent thought about a woman with long red hair. Kirsten? Katherine? He needs to see her. Has to tell her something really important but he can't put his finger on what. It's there in his head, right there, and just as he thinks he can grab onto it, it disappears behind the pharma fog.

HONEYED HALLUCINATION

60

TWELVE YEARS LATER

Fourways

Johannesburg, 2036

"Move out of my way!" shouts Kate as she elbows the voyeurs. "Keke!"

Keke opens her eyes. She looks drunk, as if she's seeing some kind of vision, some incandescent daybreak honeyed hallucination. Kate almost stumbles over in her hurry to reach her friend.

"Keke!" she shouts, without meaning to, because the crimson spill scares her. She kneels down in it, anyway, and examines Kekeletso for injuries. A large fragment of glass in embedded in her lower back. Where did it come from? Some kind of explosion? Or an accident? Kate can't tell. She shields her eyes and looks up at the flashing mandibles surrounding them.

"Has someone called an ambudrone?" she asks, and someone answers "They're offline."

They're offline?

"Is anyone here a doctor?"

Heads shake.

"A nurse?"

A small man steps forward, hand half-raised. He sheepishly turns his camera function off. "I did a first aid course once."

Kate holds Keke's face; she's still conscious. Good.

James had told her once when they were watching a film about a man who had an axle perforate his chest that you shouldn't remove the foreign object, because you could make it worse. The object could be holding the body together, in a way, and/or staunching the bleeding. Depending on the shape, removing it could cause more harm than the initial penetration. Think of a ninja star, James said. But this isn't a barbed object, and that advice is fifteen years old, before skin zips and platelet sprays. Does the same advice apply? *Leave it up to the trauma team at the hospital,* she can hear him say, but right now the hospital ERs are overflowing, and even the closest one is a too-risky cab drive away.

Kate doesn't know what to do. She shakes her hands out as she thinks, then feels for Keke's pulse. It's weak. Or is that just the pulsing of blood in her own nervous fingers making Keke's seem faint?

"Don't worry, Kex," she says, trying to smooth her worried face into something more comforting. "It's not as bad as it looks." The last sentence is for her own benefit.

Kate reaches over to Xarina's metal corpse and levers open her chest cavity with the back of a hammer she finds. She retrieves the medikit and rifles through it. It's well stocked. Maybe she will be able to help, after all. She hauls it over to Keke, shakes her hands again, and gets to work. First is the hand sanitiser for herself, and the disinfecting anaesthetic spray for Keke's wound, which she uses liberally. The camera flashes from the crowd are little tinfoil shimmers in her head, and make her teeth hurt.

"I'm going to take care of you," says Kate. "You'll be fine."

"Ha," says Keke, attempting a smile. "You forget that I know you don't have any kind of medical training whatsoever."

"True," says Kate, "But what I lack in expertise I will make up for in charm and extra anaesthetic."

"That's a deal I can live with."

Keke's bravery makes Kate falter.

What if—

She'd never be able to live with herself. The shard glitters in the rising sun.

"Now," says Kate. "Do you think I should take the glass out?"

Keke's eyes open a little wider. "What do you mean, do I think you should take the glass out? Of course you need to take the fucking glass out. What kind of fake doctor are you?"

"It might make you bleed more."

"I have a glass dagger in my back for fuck's sake. What other option is there? Jesus Christ, can you at least pretend to know what you're doing?"

All right, thinks Kate. *All right.* A spray of relief. If there's a consensus it takes the pressure off her. She'll take it out. She prepares by laying out her instruments on the medikit white apron on the ground: PainStop Pen; pliers; saline wash; gauze, stemcell gel, skin zip. As an afterthought, she pulls on the biolatex gloves that smell like young tree sap and talcum. Seeing the surgical setup, Kate's boldness returns. She can do this. A Special Task volanter arrives in the sky, chops the air above them, kicking up the dry red sand, then moves on.

Nothing to see here. Just your regular Doomsday hustle.

Kate uses the painkiller injection pen to blast six shots of lidocaine into Keke's lower back. She also squirts the painkiller inhalant up her nose.

"Ahhhh." Keke sighs. "Thank you."

"I haven't done anything yet."

"Oh, yes you have," Keke says. "You're a fucking goddess."

Kate laughs out loud.

"Seriously. Has no one ever told you that?" says Keke.

"Go home, Keke, you're drunk."

"Ha! Wishful thinking."

Kate picks up the pliers and steels herself. "Ready?"

"Ready," says Keke, and Kate secures the teeth of the tool around the glass shard, prepares to use some muscle, and pulls it smoothly out. They both gasp: Keke in pain, and Kate in sympathy. At first the wound hardly bleeds, and for a second Kate is so relieved she feels as if she can fly, but then it starts pouring out, like a pump has been turned on, and Kate grabs clumsily for the saline wash. She works as quickly as she can, gritting her teeth as she washes the gaping wound that makes her want to faint, drying it with the gauze, filling it with the gel and tearing the paper off the back of the skin zip with her shaking fingers. Finally she places the zip, closes up the gash and covers it with a large platelet plaster which is probably unnecessary, but makes her feel better.

"Done." Kate snaps off her gloves.

Keke open her eyes. "Seriously?"

The voyeur creeps begin to leave.

"I know. I surprise even myself with my superior surgical skills."

"When I stand up am I going to find my ass sewed to my elbow?"

"No." Kate laughs. The feeling of relief is back. "But you've lost a lot of blood, and I don't know how much internal damage there is, so ..."

"Don't worry. I'm not going to sue you for malpractice."

"Seriously. Your kidney may be sliced in half, for all I know."

"Ah, well, luckily I have another one."

"You're still drunk."

"I like it this way. What's in that inhalant, anyway?"

Kate checks the bottle. "Pexidine."

"It's a thing of wonder and beauty."

Kate hands it over. "It's all yours."

Keke struggles to get up.

"Whoah!" says Kate. "Whoah. I don't think you should be standing."

"Nonsense," says Keke, "I'm as good as new." She lets out

a sharp exhalation, screws up her face, and lies back down again.

Kate looks around at the dead robot and discarded weapons. "What the fuck happened?"

"I'll tell you later. What are you doing here, anyway?" asks Keke. "You're supposed to be with Silver."

"I couldn't let you do it on your own, and I forgot to give you this." Kate points at her gun.

"That would have come in handy," says Keke.

"Besides, I thought I could help Silver more by getting Zack instead of sitting in a hospital ward holding her hand."

"I guess that in my condition, breaking into a crim colony is now out of the question?"

"You guess correctly. Ten minutes ago I wasn't even sure if you were going to live."

"Yay?"

"The only place you're going is the Lipworth Foundation."

"They won't let me in," says Keke.

"Not as a visitor, but as a patient they're obliged to."

One last question hangs in the air. Who will accompany Keke? She's not well enough to make it there on her own on a solartram, and the mutinous cabbies are too dangerous. But if Kate takes her, she'll be too late to get Zack and save

Silver. They huddle there at an unspoken impasse with everything at stake—Keke not asking, Kate not wanting to refuse.

SHELL

61

TWELVE YEARS PREVIOUSLY

SkyRest

Johannesburg, 2024

Zack completes his grind—making hemp oil soap—and shuffles back to the residence with the rest of the men. How many shifts has he done now? They all seem to blur into one. They automatically move from one thing to another: work, shower, rest, eat. Butternut wedges for dinner, spongey reconstituted peaches with soywhip for dessert. Zack's learnt to eat the food now. No matter how unappetising, it's the better option. He's regaining some muscle mass. He never wants to be as weak as he was when

Bernard held him down to force feed him. He needs to be able to work.

Zack has two stripes on his lapel now, and he's working hard to win his third. He needs to fast-track up that ladder. He doesn't know why his need is urgent, but it is. Every time he finds himself exhausted, he thinks of the Stages he needs to earn to get up, to get out, and it keeps him going.

Despite the sedative effects of the psychotropics, he still wakes every night to Bernard in the room. He needs to be strong. He needs to be able to defend himself.

The wrestler resident has also been elevated. It came about suddenly. He still had two Stages to go before promotion but on Tuesday last week he was gone and his room was stripped bare. It caused some excitement. What did the man do to level up so quickly? What was his secret? Could anyone remember what he was saying or doing differently? Everyone had worked doubly hard that day, thinking of the ex-resident relishing his longed-for salted butterscotch ice cream.

Elevation through Hard Work.

The residents are happy for the wrestler, but Zack feels uneasy. Is it envy, or something more? For some reason he just can't imagine the wrestler up there, among the savvy-looking worker bees. Something about it just doesn't feel right to him.

Zack climbs on top of his new bed and holds the unopened gift on his chest. He can't remember what it is or who he'd bought it for, but every time he's tempted to open it, a deep sense of foreboding stops him. He's been able to save up enough Rewards for a new mattress and a few other home comforts. He's requested books a few times but his requests disappear into thin air. "What do you need books for?" Zack can imagine Gaelyn saying. "You've got everything you need right here."

Because I need waking up, he would tell her.

Because I've lost myself.

Because I feel like I'm stuck in a shell.

TWELVE YEARS LATER

62

SkyRest

Johannesburg, 2036

Zack hears Gaelyn call his name. He finishes up-combing his salt-and-pepper hair and runs a bit of styling clay through it. Uses a SkyRest soluble steri-wipe to clean his hands before heading down the residency passage. When he reaches the open door of the blank room, Gaelyn greets him with a wide smile, and motions towards the new resident.

"Zack," she says, "this is David."

Zack nods at the man.

"David, Zachary is one of our most experienced residents."

"If you have any questions, ask him. He'll show you around."

The men size each other up.

"Right!" says Gaelyn, who hasn't seemed to have aged at all since the day Zack first arrived. "My job here is done. Call me if you need anything."

Zack lifts his chin to the newbie. "Let's grab a sandwich before the rest of the mob gets back."

David watches Zack eat his shamwich with an expression that can only be described as revolted.

"Go on," says Zack. "Eat something. You'll need your strength. There's a lot of work to do."

"What kind of work?" asks the man.

"All kinds," says Zack, wiping his mouth with a rice-paper serviette. "To keep it interesting. You do your Quota, you get your Rewards."

"And then you get promoted?" he says.

"Elevated. Yes."

"You get to go up there?"

"Yip," says Zack. "You work hard, you climb the ladder."

"How long does it take? How long have you been here?"

He looks at Zack's lapel which is fully striped apart from one last Stage.

Zack shrugs. These whippersnappers are always so damn nervy.

"Twelve years," says Spud.

"What?" David looks around. The other residents are sauntering in: dirty, sweat-soaked. They shuffle towards the showers. Spud wipes perspiration off his forehead with his arm.

"Zack's been here twelve years."

"Really?" says Zack. It feels so strange to put a number on the time he's been down here.

"I've been here sixteen. I started a calendar when I first arrived. Not that the years matter. The only things that matter are these babies," he taps his lapel.

David looks at Spud's shirt and blinks away the start of tears. After sixteen years, Spud only has eight Stages out of twelve.

"Cheer up, Snapper," says Zack, scrunching up his serviette and launching it into the corner bin. "You'll be okay."

THE INVERSE
OF
PANDORA'S BOX

29

SkyRest

Johannesburg, 2036

Zack's dreaming again. It's a similar variation every night, as if his subconscious is trying to pull him into some kind of realisation—characters from a previous life trying to get through to him. A man with a dragon tattoo is telling him something but his voice is so distorted Zack can't make out any of the words. Sometimes the dream takes a sinister turn and he lands up in a forest under dead leaves. Sometimes worse: sometimes he's buried alive. The real nightmares are when he's covered in beetles that bite his back and his legs and leave small trails of dark blood.

There's no evil in the dream tonight. Tonight it's the biker woman who, in slow-motion, kisses his cheek and whispers something into his ear. Her vitality radiates off her. He wants to hold her, wants to climb inside her, would do anything to feel her vibrance against his lonely skin.

Then a miracle happens. She breaks out of the dream and is right there in his room with him. He can feel her hand on his face. How is this happening? He's wanted this moment for …has it really been twelve years?

But something feels wrong. He ignores it at first, so desperate for the dream to be true, but the skin feels wrong. And the smell. It's not nutmeg, like it should be, but yoghurt.

Zack flinches, his eyes click open, and he knows who it is before his eyes adjust. Of course it's Bernard. It's always Bernard. But she's never woken him like this before, her toady palm on his cheek. Her too-white face is a sinister moon. He hears a gasp, realises it must have come from him. Zack scrambles backwards into his pillow, away from her.

"What do you want?" he asks. "What the ever-loving fuck do you want?"

He hates her. Hates every part of her, even the way she breathes. He wishes she would stop breathing. She doesn't answer him.

He can't do this anymore, can't stand it one night longer. One way or another, this will stop tonight.

"Why do you do it?" Zack asks.

He's surprised when she finally speaks. "What?"

"Why do you watch me sleep?"

"Isn't it obvious?" Bernard asks.

Twelve years. Twelve years! Something about that makes Zack want to blow this place up, with Bernard in it. Without any warning, he's reached his tipping point. Something is twisting inside him, coiling, ready to strike.

One Stage to go. Just one more Stage and you'll be elevated. DON'T DO ANYTHING STUPID.

"It's not obvious," says Zack.

"Then I've done my job."

"Is it over?" asks Zack. "Your job? Are you going somewhere?"

"You're the one who's going somewhere. It's time."

A warm breeze of hope.

"Do you mean … I'm being elevated?"

His heart lifts in his chest.

"Is that why you woke me? Are we going now?"

"You're due to get your last Stage tomorrow night."

Zack's besieged by conflicting emotions. He covers his face with his hands.

Twelve years.

He should be feeling a clean hit of joy, shouldn't he? Instead, his stomach is a cement mixer of longing and dread and something else he can't identify.

"That's good news. That's really good news." His voice is flat.

Bernard screws up her face. Her contempt is almost palpable; it's like the room is crowded with her scorn.

"Good news?" she snarls. "Don't you understand anything?"

"You're upset that I'll be gone," says Zack. "You'll have no one to harass."

She snorts in disbelief. "Harass?"

"What would you call it? You've worn me down so much that I don't even know who I am anymore."

"Well, I'll remind you who you are. You are Zachary Girdler. And you had better start acting like it, before it's too late."

Zack is taken aback. She's never called him by his name before.

"What's that … What's that supposed to mean?"

"It means you need to wake the fuck up."

He's never heard her swear before, either. Never seen her so riled up.

"Wake *up*!" she says, and he senses she wants to shake him, but holds herself back. "Remember *why you exist*."

"I—"

"Do you really believe that Lewis was promoted? After what you saw?"

Lewis?

He has a vague recollection of the man.

Lewis? What is she talking about? What did he see?

"Lewis was elevated," Zack says, as if hypnotised. The words don't seem to come from him.

"What about Mulalo? Steven? Azwi? You think they're all up there?" She skewers the air with her finger. "Playing fucking foosball?"

Suddenly it seems unlikely, but where else would they be? Out on parole?

"I thought you were smarter than that!" Bernard punches the bed.

"What do you mean?"

"You of all people should know the truth about this place."

Bernard's words echo in Zack's head. Something is resonating through the smog that is his brain.

He knows. He knows. He knows. But why isn't he seeing it? Because he's been worn down by this place. Worn down, beaten down, dumbed down. They've drugged the memory out of him. Zack doesn't know anything anymore. He gave up a long time ago. He lost the plan.

"On the first day here I saw the upstairs levels," Zack says. "I saw the different floors. The VR room, the restaurant, the open-plan offices."

"You saw what you wanted to see," says Bernard. "Lewis saw a pool. Steven saw an ice cream shop. That initiation tour is a fucking hologram. Why do you think we didn't get out of the elevator?"

As he hears it, he knows it's true.

"But then where do the promoted men go?"

"You know the answer to that. You saw the body bags."

"What?"

"Karōshi," says Bernard.

"No," Zack shakes his head. Thinks of the friends he's lost.

"Karōshi," she says again. "They monitor your declining health as you work yourself to death. And then, one day, the circle is complete."

Zack sees the dragon tattoo clearly now. Ourobos. Lewis.

The circle is complete.

Bernard is agitated. Her fingers keep flying up to her hard-gelled curls. "You want to know why I'm in here every night? Why I watch you sleep?"

Of course he does. He does and he doesn't.

"I'm protecting you."

"What?"

"Don't you understand anything? I've been protecting you all along."

Zack's head is spinning. Bernard grabs his leg, forces him back into the moment.

"You need to focus," she says. "We don't have much time."

"Focus on what?"

"On your end game."

"I don't know what that is anymore."

"Think, Zack. *Think*. I don't know the details. It's up to you to remember them."

Bernard places a band over his temple, and plugs the black lozenge XDrive into it. There's a flicker of light in his head and hot sparks in his skull as his backed-up memories are restored. He remembers the cardboard cut-out trial, the Orb, the first of the zombie drugs. Other concepts come to him, too, but he doesn't understand them yet.

"I've been able to access your cuff. Over the past forty-eight hours I've been weaning you off your SkyRest medication. You should be seeing things more clearly now."

That's why he had the dream. The reaching for the truth. Pictures, moments, names are coming to him, slowly at first. It's as if his mind is opening up and is in danger of absorbing every starless concept around: the inverse of Pandora's Box. The zombie spike is wearing off and exposing what he's always known, deep down. It gains layers and scope and force and speed and he feels like it's going to bowl him over and leave him for dead.

A lotus flower blooms in Zack's head. "I need to get out of here."

Bernard's eyes glint. "I can help you."

PART III

REDPEPPER PROXIES

64

Ashram Ramanana

Panchagiri Hills, India, 2036

Marko's done what he can to warn the Nancies about the V1R1S, and sent them his recommended shutdown procedure. He made it clear that it's imperative to cut the power to the entire country, and the neighbouring countries, to stop it from spreading. If the contagion beats the shutdown they'll have to use the Kill Switch, and no one wants to resort to that; if it comes to that they may as well nuke the whole country. He doesn't know yet if they've taken his advice.

Now Marko fistpumps as he finally finds the IPX of the person responsible for creating the V1R1S. He's been working for fifteen hours solid. He's been knee-deep in darkweb dungeons and redpepper proxies. He's sweated through his scratchy roughcotton robe. There's a plate of congealed dhal on his side-table. The swami urged him to eat, but he doesn't have time. He hasn't been able to get hold of Keke, and he has a terrible twisting feeling in his gut that is telling him she's in real danger.

Marko's longed-for epiphany finally arrives, and it's nothing to do with sun salutations or silent retreats. It's all about Keke.

He's been such a fool. Once this disaster is over he's going to kick himself like no man in history has ever kicked himself before. And then he's going to rush back to South Africa and give every remaining second to Keke. Keke! Love of his life; fuel for his fire. What a damned fool stupid bastard he has been. What had he been thinking? He loves her like fire loves wood. If he is the bird then she is the join between his breast and wing. He was nothing before he met her and he's nothing now. Keke is his creator. She makes him into the best version of himself. He'll worship her the way she loves to be worshipped. The way she deserves to be worshipped. Gradually, with his tongue, in slow circles. Until she shouts out and squeezes him between her godly and glorious thighs. Marko feels himself get hard. He adjusts himself, and a notification pops up on screen.

The image of Keke fades slightly as he discovers the IPX.

"Come to Papa," he whispers, squirming in his seat. When he licks his dry lips, his tongue comes away salty. He needs electrolytes. He needs hydration. He doesn't care; he's so close to the answer he can feel nipping at his fingertips.

"Yes, yes, yes." It's the right place. An unmistakable server signature. Now it's as simple as finding out who it belongs to and shutting the motherfucker down. He sends a dummy NASP email to the address he finds. If the owner of the address opens it, it'll escalate Marko's privileges and he'll be able to identify and destroy the Root. He automates a SMPR flash where the fucker's identity and physical address will be broadcast to every South African with a mandible. He smacks the 'send' key and then stares at the screen, waiting. He's going to catch the ratbastard who put Keke in danger if it's the last thing he ever does.

Marko plays an invisible piano on the table top. He hums a made-up tune. He searches for his secret stash of nutnut cookies, and he waits.

He starts when there's a knock on the door. Damn it, is he going to have to wrestle the swami to get out of *yajna*? But when he looks up there's a young local boy holding out a white courier satchel to him. More kids hop on their bare feet and giggle from the doorway. They're excited about something. Marko takes the bag and looks at the waybill, dated last week. He gives the kids all a cookie and tells them to scram.

It's a drone delivery from Johannesburg, but the sender's address is blank.

HAPPY HOUR

65

Fourways

Johannesburg, 2036

When Kate hears the annoying buzz of the Volanter again she feels like swatting it out of the toxic sky. She can't stand the hovering, hovering, hovering. Can't they just land or fly away? Anything but this supremely irritating humming giant mosquito that feels as if it's inside her head. Then, as if by magic, it does start to descend, whipping up the red smoke and litter as it does so, and they both have to cover their eyes to prevent them being sandblasted.

It's not a Special Task sunchopper. It's a handsome metallic navy affair with a pinstriped belly and bling on the blades. It lands, and as the dust begins to settle, Seth steps out.

"How?" is all Kate can manage to say. Relief, certainly, and also perhaps the after-effects of the trauma of finding Keke bleeding—what she at first thought was dying—on the ground. She blinks away the tears.

"How?" The answer is not important. What is important is that Seth is here in a Volanter—a Volanter!—and she knows the Lipworth Foundation has a dronepad.

"She's hurt!" Kate yells at Seth, who nods and tenderly picks up Keke and carries her to the aircraft, helps her up into the bucketseat, straps her in. Keke winces, then puts on the headset and clicks the ignition button. She switches off the smartpilot; she knows she has to fly it manually. The blades start whirring above them.

"You okay?" shouts Seth, and Keke nods. Gives them a thumbs-up. He leans into her, kisses her cheek, stays there a moment longer than expected.

"See you on the other side!" she shouts, and pulls the stick backwards. The Volanter begins to rise, and within seconds it's humming high in the sky, then it's gone.

Seth watches the sky.

They start walking towards SkyRest, two blocks away. Questions crowd Kate's head.

"Mally?"

Seth's lips turn down. "I didn't find him."

Her heart contracts. She can't think about that now. Unknowingly, she's stopped in her tracks.

"Come on." Seth pulls her gently along. "One thing at a time."

"Did you steal that Volanter?"

"I don't like to use the word *steal*. It has negative connotations."

"Who does it belong to?"

"I don't know. Some billionaire? I found it at the golf course."

"The golf course."

Kate thought that golf had gone the way of cigarettes and swimming pools. She hasn't even heard the word for over a decade.

"That AstroGolf place."

"You stole a sunchopper from a billionaire at a fake golf course."

"It was happy hour."

Kate looks at her digital clock display.

"It's 9AM."

Seth shrugs. "Billionaires don't care."

Kate laughs. It feels good. How life can be so dire and so stupid all at once makes her feel slightly human again. She still has Keke's blood on her knees.

"I pulled a giant piece of glass out of Keke's back."

Seth glances at her, perhaps to see if she's joking.

"Forgive me if I find that difficult to believe."

"I swear."

"You can't even look at a needle without passing out."

"That's not true. Not anymore."

Having kids has toughened Kate. She's dealt with smashed faces, broken bones, even … an image of Meadon flashes in on her vision. A dark night, the long ribbon scent of roses, Lumin's swift hands, and a crunching sound she'll never forget as long as she lives. No, she's not going to think about that. Not now. She has to focus on getting Zack.

"What's your plan?" asks Seth as they get to the SkyRest building.

"I don't have one," says Kate. "Don't look at me like that."

"You think we'll just be able to walk right in and collect him? A serial killer. From the PLC with the highest security in South Africa."

"When the situation is so impossible I tend to not overthink things."

"Or not think at all."

"Shut it. I'm in survival mode. I'm moving on instinct alone. It's the best I can do."

It's always been like that between them. Seth for thinking, Kate for feeling. Maths and colour.

She's tempted to add *Just trust me*, but Seth has a rule that you should never trust people who say that.

The receptionist at the entrance greets them with a wide smile. Kate's auto-targeting adstream had delivered a few of SkyRest's marketing messages to her while she was researching the funeral party.

Was it really just yesterday that they were eating those funeral cake samples?

SkyRest is the leading innovator in the urban death industry. The last ad she saw informed her that she could have the ashes printed into anything she likes: a flashdisk brimmed with downloaded memories; a decorative ceramic fruit bowl; a knock-off of a designer garden chair.

The guard cheerfully relieves them of their weapons.

"Welcome to SkyRest!" The receptionist points to her holotag. "I'm Gaelyn." Despite the situation outside, her make-up is perfect, her forehead uncreased.

In fact, the whole place looks remarkably orderly, given the chaos on the streets. Maybe they're even happy about the apocalypse. It is, after all, what they specialise in. More bodies to turn into soap and FongKong trinkets. Gaelyn doesn't bat an eyelid at Kate's dirty and blood-stained clothes.

"I'd like a tour of your products and services, please," says Kate.

"Forgive me being so bold," says Gaelyn. "But when you walked in, the system scanned your dynap codes."

Kate flushes. "Is there a problem?"

"Not at all. I just wanted to offer you both my sincere condolences about your mother."

"Thank you," says Kate.

"Has she been ill long?"

"Not too long."

Anne has stage four uterine cancer. It spread to her lymph nodes before she agreed to see a doctor, so although there are many different and effective cures for cancer, it's too late for her. The disease has already ravaged her insides. Her senior smartwatch SOS suffer-score is a solid eight out of ten. Rather than languish in hospital, she's chosen elective death. The living funeral is scheduled for next week, and the plan is for her to be surrounded by her loved ones, say goodbye, and take the pentobarbital.

"We hope that here at SkyRest you'll come to understand a more positive experience when it comes to death. In ancient times it was regarded as a passage and celebrated accordingly. It's only the modern western way that has shrouded it in fear. Soon your mother will no longer be suffering, and we'll take care of the rest. I hope you take comfort in that."

Gaelyn sticks a small green dot on each of them, then takes them past the front desk, past a watercooler, the door to the emergency fire stairwell, and through the exhibition hall. The second she steps away from the reception desk, a carbon copy replaces her.

Suddenly a deafening siren rings through the air. It fills the space with red zigzags. Kate and Seth both flinch at the sudden noise, but Gaelyn remains completely unperturbed. There is chatter at the front entrance. Men in kevlarskin onesies appear, holding long, smooth weapons with two handles that look like they're straight out of a space opera film. Where did they come from? It's like they jumped out of the walls.

"Stay where you are," says the SkyRest announcer. "Stay where you are."

Two of the guards jog towards Kate and Seth. Apart from the bulletproof suits, they wear graphene face armour with moving parts that agitate when they talk.

"Come with us," they say.

KILL SWITCH

66

"No," says Kate.

The SkyRest guard looks at her. "It's for your own safety."

"I've heard that before," says Seth.

"What is the situation?" Gaelyn's smile is as wide as ever.

"We have a TX599. All visitors are to come with us."

Seth looks around. As expected, there are no other visitors.

Gaelyn takes a step forward. "I'm afraid we'll have to continue this tour another time. We have an unusual situation."

"What's happening?"

"We've never had a situation like this before, but don't worry. If we all just follow the protocol, everything will be fine."

Kate doesn't know what to do. There's no way she's going with the thugs. No way she's being trawled into another dark van, not without kicking and screaming.

Gaelyn shakes her head in what looks like a nervous tic. "Will be fine," she says. "Will be fine."

"Reset," says one of the guards.

"Reset," says Gaelyn. "Affirmative." She cocks her head and looks at Kate. "If we all just follow the protocol everything will be fine." The receptionist tries to take a step forward, but her body arrests in that awkward position, and she can't seem to get out of it. "Will be fine."

The guard picks her up and throws her over his shoulder. The other motions with a nod to take her away.

"Come with me," says the remaining guard.

The twins stand their ground.

"I'm not offering you a choice," he says. "You have to come with me right now. We're about to have a serious security breach, and it's not safe to be in here."

"What do you mean," says Seth, "that you're *about* to have a security breach. What does that mean?"

"You don't need to know the details. You need to—"

"We do if you want us to move," says Kate.

The guard looks at the green sticker with annoyance. He would have carried them away just like Gaelyn if he was allowed to. Something about the sticker is putting him off.

"Due to a situation that is out of our control, we need to shut down the building."

"What situation?" asks Kate. "Do you mean the rebellion?"

"Shut it down? What?" says Seth, "The whole building? You can't."

That would be a disaster. Or would it?

The guard bites down and his jaw muscles ripple. He's clearly annoyed to be wasting time with stubborn civilians, but he can't touch them, and he can't leave them here. The siren is ringing and the red zigzags are still scraping Kate's eyeballs. Seth checks his newstream.

International Texpert in India Confirms 'Malfunction' is a Virus

V1R1S Spreading with Deadly Consequences

Switch Off, Unplug, You Can Stop the V1R1S

V1R1S Reaches Cape Republic, Thousands Dead

Prepare for National Shutdown

Call for the KILL SWITCH Now

Roguebots Not Rebels: Meet the V1R1S that's spreading at the speed of light

"They've confirmed it's a virus," says Seth. "They're going to be shutting down the city one band at a time."

"Shutting down?"

"Cutting the power."

"The government? They can't do that. This place is solar."

"It's not the government. It's everyone, everywhere. Doesn't matter if they're on the grid or not. Doesn't matter where the power comes from. Everyone's responsible for shutting their own power off over the next few hours by staggered deadlines, north to south, or face the consequences of the V1R1S spreading."

"Why *staggered?*"

"I don't know. To give them time to loot the national treasury before it goes offline forever?"

"But don't the roguebots have back-up battery packs?"

"They won't last forever. And, combined with the Kill Switch, it'll stop most of the AI from icing any more people."

"They're going to trigger the Kill Switch?"

"It looks like it."

It's a three-signature government decision. Not only will the Kill Switch terminate all robot consciousness, including surgeons and nurses and teachers, it'll kill every iteration of artificial intelligence in the country, from smart fridges to traffic lights to artificial hearts. Activating the Switch will cause planes to drop out of the sky. It'll break the country in half, wipe out trillions on the Cryptox Exchange, and take out thousands of civilians. Would Mashini Wam really have the ovaries to do that? Do they want her to? Kate pictures the premature babies in their smart incubators and wants to cry. Then she thinks of her own baby, Silver, and can feel the blood drain out of her face.

"Silver," she says. "She won't be able to get back."

Seth's mouth is a hard line. In a low voice he says "We need to get Zack and get back to her before the Lipworth shuts down."

Kate looks around for evidence of the blackout, and, as if by magical thinking, things start fading. First it's the display LEDs lighting up the products at the back of the exhibition hall, then the darkness bangs towards them and mechanisms all around are frozen in time. Seth and Kate stand in the dark, momentarily lost in space.

"How long do we have?" she asks.

"Not long enough."

GHOST CUTLASSES

67

If the mission to find Zack seemed difficult before, it seems impossible now. Yes, Kate had wished for SkyRest's power to be cut to disable the security system, but she hadn't thought further than that. She hadn't thought of standing here in the dark, in a building that goes up eleven storeys and down—who knows how many?—She hadn't thought of being marooned here surrounded by thick black unfiltered air with no clue how to find Zack. She also hadn't thought of how the disabled security system wouldn't just let Zack out, but the rest of the dangerous crims too. Without wanting to, she imagines being stuck down in the bowels of this building, being stuck with murderers and rapists and never getting out again. Silver fading away in her hospital bed, Mally being killed in his sleep by his Stepford girlfriend. Sudden bright yellow panic squeezes her lungs, imaginary voices shout at her, and Seth hears her breathing become ragged and holds her arm.

"Don't panic," he says, as if it's that easy to avoid a panic attack.

Kate tries to keep her heart from climbing into her throat. She thinks of other situations more dangerous than this that she's survived, and not only survived, but dominated, and slowly this thought, the memories, take the fright out of her adrenaline, and replace it with energy. Her chest is still galloping, but her mind is clear.

One by one, individual torches come on, like white sabres in the dark (Ghost Cutlasses). They're coming from the guards' heads; their face armour has some kind of built-in headlamp.

"We don't have much time," says the guard. "Come with me."

"Give us your head lamp," says Kate.

He hesitates.

"Give us your headlamp, and we'll go with you."

The guard shakes his head then unbuttons something on his utility belt. He swivels the head to turn it on, and hands it to Kate. She's never been so happy to see a penlight in her life. It's the new tech one, the glow-worm, that you can break in half. She does so, and hands the other half to Seth. As agreed, they follow the guard out of the product display room, and as they get near the front entrance, Kate grabs Seth's arm, and they peel away into the emergency stairwell.

They run down the stairs as fast as they can without falling. Kate has that familiar burnt-orange feeling again, *deja vu*, and remembers being in The Office stairway with Seth on the day they found each other again, discussing The Genesis Project and Non-Lizards. They climb down, down, down, and the air gets cooler. Space opens up around them: the stairs are designed in a wentletrap. Winding green, bruise-blue, iced magenta, dry khaki, lemon zest, until they hit fresh pomegranate and can hear voices. They leave the spiral stairwell and run along a stone hewn passage, pushing open a disabled securodoor. This darkness is different: it's redolent of yeasty dough and hand sanitiser and sore throats. Despite the lack of light, Kate's vision is shot through with soft, wobbling blox of colour: Jailhouse Nutrijelly.

"Who's there?" says a man, making Kate almost drop her torch in fright. She shines it in the direction of the voice. A monochrome face appears. He shields his eyes and squints, trying to see who's holding the light.

"What's going on?" asks someone else. "Why are the lights off?"

"Has something happened?"

"Are we being punished?"

Kate surveys the room. There must be fifty of them. Why are they gathered here? Why haven't they bolted for the open door, to escape?

"When will it come back on?"

"The water dispenser isn't working."

"It's getting difficult to breathe."

The men, faces shining, begin squirming in agitation. Sweat slick.

Seth tests the waters. "Gaelyn sent us."

"Ah," some of them say. There is audible relief. Gaelyn knows about their situation. It will be fixed soon.

"You're not being punished," says Kate.

The mood changes; everything is going to be okay.

"It's a scheduled break in supply for maintenance reasons. Gaelyn apologises for not warning you in advance."

"Ah," they say. Gaelyn's the best. Everyone loves Gaelyn.

The door is standing wide open. Kate knows the lights are off, but ... surely with no guards in the immediate vicinity at least a few of them would have tried to escape?

Irrationally, the fact that the men are so meek in the face of what is probably their one and only chance of ever escaping, makes Kate more uncomfortable than the fact that she's surrounded by dangerous crims. Something about this setup feels very wrong.

Seth grabs her arm and it jolts her out of her anxious thoughtloop. "Listen," he says.

Far above them there is the sound of metallic thunder, and it's getting louder.

"Where is Zack?" Kate says.

"Zack?" they say. *Zack zack zack? What has this to do with Zack?*

"He's gone," says a man towards the front of the group. The light hits his shiny scalp.

"What do you mean, 'gone'?"

"He's been elevated," says the man. The others murmur.

"Elevated?" asks Kate. Seth is pulling Kate away.

"Promoted!" he shouts. "He was promoted last night."

Seth pulls Kate away from the clammy residence, out into the stone passage where the emergency staircase is, and a breath of cooler air. They race down the steps, but only get down one flight when they hear the thunder coming towards them again, hard boots on metal stairs, and see the urgent beams of torches above them, and have to jump off the iron spiral and crouch in the dark corner behind it.

Seconds later the kevlar-skinned guards smash past them and stream into the passage and whatever room is on the other side of it. Kate waits a moment, then they go for the stairs again. Seth is first up, and just as Kate puts her foot on the first step, a large body grabs her from behind and smacks a meaty hand over her mouth. Kate shouts, but Seth doesn't hear her, and keeps going. Kate struggles and tries to throw the person off, but all she manages to do is drop her torch, and it goes skittering off the edge of the step and falls down into the black vortex, smashing on the stone floor far below.

ROCKY RABBIT HOLE

68

Kate elbows the attacker in the kevlar-padded ribs and yells for Seth, but the hand over her mouth is firm and hardly a sound escapes.

"Sh-sh-sh-sh-sh," is the hissing, too close to her ear, and the sensation makes her shout louder. She imagines a giant hissing cockroach scuttling next to her head, and she wants to faint with the creepiness, the crackliness of it. She half expects the insect's scratchy leg to brush her face but the thing that caresses her ear is not carapace but soft cheek skin, female, and smells of *tsatsiki*.

The woman slams Kate sideways, and in the dark Kate

expects her head to be smashed against the rocky wall. She's surprised when the wall is missing and she falls into a room, hard, cracking her elbow on the stone floor. She gasps in pain, but keeps quiet when she hears the guards running again.

"Don't make a sound," whispers the woman. Is it a Gaelyn? No, she's far too substantial for that. Too strong. Her white sabre cuts through the air, illuminating another door on the opposite side of the narrow room—or is it a passage?—they're in. She offers Kate a hand up.

"Who are you?"

The woman doesn't answer. Kate gets up on her own.

Kate holds her elbow while the electric blue current buzzes inside the bone. "What do you want from me?"

"Come," she says.

"No," says Kate, and starts walking back towards the staircase, towards Seth.

"We've been waiting for you for twelve years," the woman says, and Kate's legs stop working.

"What?"

"We don't have much time."

The torch is again throwing light on the doorway where the woman wants her to go.

I'd be mad to trust this woman, Kate thinks, but then she remembers Betty/Barbara in the basement with the warning and the key, and the message that had led her back to Seth and saved her life. She'd also thought B/B was crackers, with her barbecue sauce BO and dog-hair jersey, spouting about assassins and Doomsday, but she'd been right, and Kate wouldn't be here without her.

With a deep breath to steady her nerves, Kate follows the woman through the doorway, and they hurry down a hall then another passage that snakes its way around one way and then another so that Kate loses her sense of direction. Just as she starts second-guessing her decision to follow the woman, they reach a door with an antique padlock which the woman unlocks with a small silver key attached to a lanyard around her neck. Seeing the key makes Kate's thoughts tumble down around her—*is she dreaming? When the lights come back on will this woman have Betty/Barbara's face and start babbling about hit lists and seed banks?* But it's just Kate's panic murmuring. She knows that B/B is dead, has been dead for almost two decades, and that this woman is another brand of insanity altogether, and she is just as crazy for having followed her so deep into this godforsaken rocky rabbit hole.

The woman opens the door and pushes Kate inside. The sound of the lock clicking closed behind her sends ice into her veins. No more passages, no more doors, just a small blank room crowded with claustrophobia. The cell is just concrete and dripping water, and a thin, dirty mattress, grey and blue stripes, and Kate's sudden panic makes her want to fling her whole body at the door, break through it, fractured elbow be damned, and run away as fast as she can. She'll die down here if she doesn't fight her way back up to the light and the air. Kate feels the weight of all the people who have beaten her to it, leaden on her chest. Who knew souls could be so heavy?

Kate turns to the woman and braces herself, ready to fight with everything she's got, when a familiar voice comes from the corner behind her. Kate spins around.

There is a grey mask at the end of the beam of light.

"You've come," says Zack, and there is a look of wonder on his face.

DEAD MEN DON'T CARE

69

Seth ascends the stairs, boots hitting the metal steps, but something immediately feels wrong. He stops and turns around, and Kate is gone.

"Kate?" he whispers urgently. "Kate?"

Now the panic claws at him. He doesn't want to go back down. He doesn't want to die down here. It shouldn't make a difference, really. Dead men don't care, but he can't help feeling that he'd rather die somewhere in the open, where he can see the sky or the faces of the people he loves, instead of having this great hulking weight over him.

"Kate?"

Dread and terror roil in his stomach. His body is warning him to get out while he can. Each step down ramps his anxiety higher. When he reaches the platform it feels as if the coolness of the rock face is seeping into the marrow of his bones. Where could she have gone?

Seth moves as quietly as he can, back towards the warm core of the building. How would he possibly be able to find Kate in this lightless labyrinth? Already he's made his way through passages and openings that all look identical. Empty black barns and doorways to nowhere. His foreboding sits high in his chest.

Eventually there's a room that's not empty. There's no one in it, as far as he can see, but there are pallets in the centre, with some kind of high-tech cooler boxes stacked on top. What could be on those pallets? He shouldn't look. He really shouldn't look. He has to find Kate and get out of this sour netherworld as soon as he can.

But, really, what could it be? It will drive him crazy not knowing. He'd be thinking of this room for the rest of his days, wondering what is inside the bloody coolers. Anyway, it'll only take a couple of seconds to check it out.

There is a row of brown boxes and a row of red. He walks up to the first row and flicks his flashlight beam over the lids.

Extremely hazardous, it says. *Biohazard*. It has a 3D tag of a man in a hazmat suit. *Danger. Ingozi. Don't touch.*

That old trick.

Seth's seen that gimmick a hundred times in the black clinics and evil corps he's exposed. They slap a couple of 'biohazard' stickers on anything they don't want nosy staffers knowing about. Put a half-convincing 'radioactive' label on a safe door and you'll never have to worry about anyone ever breaking in.

Fucking amateurs, he thinks, as he snaps open the catches of the first lid.

Inside the box are neatly filed flexiglass envelopes, all labelled with a numeric code. He lifts a random one out and shines his penlight at its centre. It looks like some kind of print. A round stamp the size of his palm made up of pinpricks of black material with a blank circle inside. Geometric, but certainly organic, like the iris of an eye. He think he recognises the pattern, but he can't think what it is. There's something about the network architecture of the thing: the Fibonacci fractals are clear, but why a stamp, and why here, in this box, in this subterranean cavern? He lifts another, then another. They're almost identical.

Seth peels one of the envelopes apart to get a closer look. The radiating lines and dots are indeed some kind of organic matter. Mycelium? He brings it even closer to his face, and when he does, he knows for sure. He sniffs a bit closer. There's no mistaking that earthy scent, like rainforest soil, truffle shavings. The circular designs makes sense now: the gills. These are mushroom spore stamps.

Seth doesn't bother to close the box, just moves on to the next one. Again, similar designs, but slight—evolving— differences in size and density, as if they are working on crisping the subspecies. He figures all the brown boxes contain mushroom spores, so he moves to the other side of the pallets where the red cooler boxes are. They have the same biohazard warnings, and the lids are secured with matching yellow-and-black chevron tape. The lid itself is slightly different too. It has a pattern of tiny holes. Whatever's inside needs air, and he hesitates to open it. He really shouldn't do it. He shouldn't even be in here. He needs to find Kate, but it will only take another ten seconds and then he'll be out.

He puts his ear to the breathing holes. There's a faint crackling from inside, a susurration. There's definitely something alive in there. Seth begins peeling the tape off the sides as quickly as he can without making too much noise. He snicks open the catches and lifts the top tentatively, his heart thumping, half expecting something to jump out at him. The rustling is louder now and it smells like old leaves and decay and something else that makes his stomach lurch. The light from his torch illuminates the contents, and Seth flinches and almost drops the lid. Hundreds of beetles scuttle and swarm over each other, their nutty carapaces vibrating, frantic with hunger. Seth is about to close the box when he sees something else in there: a large round shape at the bottom that they're all flitting over. He wants to look closer but can't stand putting his face any nearer to the insects. What is it? What has got them so excited? He puts his hands on either side of the container and gives it a good shake, dislodging the beetles from the object, and then immediately wishes he hadn't. The cooler box is suspended half on, half off the pallet. A severed head stares back at him. Half of the skin has been eaten away, revealing large patches of clean white skullbone. Both eye sockets gape with black vacuums for eyes—tea-coloured teeth grimace.

Seth's fright makes him fumble with the container and he half-falls, and the box falls with him, spilling the colony on to the concrete screed floor. Sensing a long-awaited freedom, the beetles scatter, and the decomposing skull rolls and knocks into the wall.

Fuck. Shit. And then, totally inappropriately: *Own goal.*

A beetle bites his hand and Seth shakes it off, stands, and crunches it underfoot. He brushes his body with his fingers, pulling the hungry beetles off his clothes; finds one in his hair and throws it across the room.

Seth has seen enough, and he moves to leave the room. He tries to close the door behind him to keep the bugs contained, but the smartlock isn't working. When he hears footsteps coming in his direction, he pushes himself up against a wall, out of sight. It's a trio of prison guards; they must have heard the box hitting the floor. He holds his breath as they rush past him, torches blazing, into the *biohazard* room. Their boots crush the early insect escapees.

"The fuck?" says one.

"We're not supposed to be in here," says the other.

"Holy shit. This is not good."

Seth folds around the corner they've just rushed past. He breathes as quietly as he can.

The first guard talks into his mandible: "We need a clean-up in the bio section."

There is static.

"Hello?"

"Jesus, Samuel. You really think they care about some bugs right now?"

"I can't get through to Gaelyn."

"There's no one at the desk, you idiot. We have two hundred convicted murderers and paedos and no way to keep them down here. Do you think they're gonna send a fucking janitor? Wake the fuck up!"

"I just ..." Samuel says, "The signs, you know. The hazard warnings. I just think we have to contain this somehow or there'll be trouble."

"You're as thick as pig shit, Sam. You know that?"

"Sam's got a point," says the third man. "Remember when we lived in the barracks for training?"

"Not you too. What the fuck are you two on about? We've got a catastrophic security breach here. We're probably going to be lynched by the mob before cereal time and you two are worried about some fucking bugs."

"I just mean, remember the roaches there? One day there was one and the next day there were a hundred. These things know how to breed."

He's got a point. Seth's pretty sure the flesh-eating insects are laying eggs in invisible crevices as they speak. He shudders. *Samuel's right. This does not bode well.*

"You two are un-fucking-believable. Hurry up, we need to get to the convicts."

"Yes, sir."

The man shakes his head and he walks towards the residence, away from Seth, muttering under his breath. "Trust my luck to get stuck with these morons on fucking D-Day. Tweedle-dee and Tweedle-fucking-dumb."

"I just really think, Sir—" says Samuel.

"Oh for Christ's sake!" the man explodes. "Fine! Fine, Pig Shit! You stay here and clean up this mess, and when you're done you can join the grown-ups in the residence, okay?"

"Yes, Sir."

The two guards march off, and the man in charge smacks the wall for good measure, in case his yelling did not adequately convey his frustration.

Samuel takes his automatic rifle off his back and plants it down against the wall. Maybe Seth has overestimated his intelligence after all. The man steps back inside the *biohazard* room and by the sounds of things, begins to swat the bugs with an unseen tool.

As soon as the two guards are far enough gone, Seth sneaks towards the gun and nabs it, then steals away. Kate is close; he can feel her through the warm walls. Seth clasps the weapon to his torso.

Thank you, Pig Shit.

GREY SKULL

70

Zack's appearance is so shocking that Kate has to look twice to make sure it's him. His body is strong, firm with the kind of muscle you get from hard labour, not like the bicep-kissers in coolvests you see all over your adstream. But his face … is a grey skull. Bone ash. What have they done to him? The years in here have stripped him of his spark.

"Zack?" She's still uncertain.

"You've come," he says, as if in a trance.

"I told you she'd come," says Bernard. "Even though she took her sweet time."

"What now?" says Zack.

"Don't look at me." Bernard motions at Kate. "She's the one who's supposed to be setting you free."

"I don't know how to get out of here," says Kate.

"Yes, but you have that," says Bernard, gesturing at the green pixel on her chest. "And that's our ticket. Guards can't touch customers, and that means if you protect Zack, they can't stop us from leaving."

Kate looks down at the green dot. "That's all it'll take? A pixel?"

Well, a pixel and an apocalypse.

"There's no way to escape without it. Zack would be shot on his first step out of here. They would have put a bullet in me, too. The order was to wait for you, and we did."

Bernard gestures that they should follow her.

Kate sees through the guard's brusqueness. She can see by the way the woman looks at Zack—what is left of Zack—that she very much cares if he stays alive. They follow her out the door and turn right into the passage.

"This isn't the way we came in," says Kate.

"We're going out the back," says Bernard.

They hurry along what seems like a Möbius strip, and Kate feels as lost as ever, but then she hears people, faint at first, then louder. Excited gabble, like bubbles in the air.

Kate grabs Bernard's arm. "We can't go that way. There're people there."

"It's the only way." Bernard pulls her baton off her utility belt.

They get closer to the clamour. Kate's adrenaline is now flashing neon yellow at her, and her instinct is to run in the opposite direction. The image of the small damp cell drives her forward.

"Watch out," says Bernard. "The other pods aren't as well behaved as the one you've seen."

"Not as heavily medicated, you mean," says Kate.

Bernard looks at her. "Yes."

They all slow down as they approach the residence.

"Be as quiet as you can." Bernard switches off her torch and Kate follows suit. They slip into the dark common room where a crowd of excited men are chattering like monkeys. They have two flashlights between them—*where did they get them?*—and they're hopping and kicking something in the middle of the room. Cursing. It's a guard. No, two guards, curled up on the floor in an attempt to protect themselves from the blows.

Kate tries to ignore the terror that slams into her chest. The darkness takes on a sinister quality and the air curdles around her. She tries not to breathe too hard but her anxiety is crushing her lungs.

They flatten themselves against the wall as much as they are able, and slowly move around the room to get to the door on the other side. Smoothly and quickly they go, averting their faces, hoping the men will be too distracted by the guards to notice them sliding along the walls in the dark. Kate can't help but glance at the men, shadow rubbernecking, horrified by the naked violence in stuttering monochrome. An action scene in an old movie—an avant-garde stage play.

Kate, Zack and Bernard are just a few footsteps from the door when there is a loud "Hey!" and a man with a bulging face is looking right at Kate, caught in the scattered light.

"Run!" shouts Bernard.

They launch forward, but stumble in the dark. Kate falls hard on the concrete floor. A hand reaches out and grabs her leg.

Kate screams and kicks at him. Her adrenaline is like a current zipping up inside her body.

"Help us!" yells one of the prisoners. "Get us out of here! We'll die if you leave us here!"

She kicks the man in the face but he just shouts, firms his grip, and pulls her along the floor towards the centre of the room. She lashes out, but he's much stronger than her. Bernard appears and strikes him on the head with her baton and he lets go and rolls away, but then another prisoner takes his place and grabs Kate around the hips. She yells and punches him in the face, struggling against him while

Bernard lands as many blows as she can on the other approaching men and their greedy hands. Kate's fear is smothering her; she chokes on bile as she kicks and screams and is dragged further into the mob. Zack is fumbling with something in his uniform pocket while men shove and punch him. He's not even fighting back. It's as if he's gone inside himself, some protective measure to block what is happening.

Fight! Kate wants to yell at him. *Fight!* But all he does is look down and fumble.

Kate screams and scrabbles, trying to get away. Her elbow fizzes with bright blue pain as she flails against them. Her voice is fading, her muscles trembling from fear and fatigue.

This is not how I die.

She lands a well-placed kick to a man's jaw, and he lets her go. Another grabs her, an insane leer on his pale face. She tries to kick him, too, but he catches her foot and twists it, and she yells as the pain jolts up her leg.

Bernard is using her strong arms to hand off attackers and strike down anyone in her way. She whacks the man whose hands are wrapped around Kate's pelvis, whacks him so hard on the temple Kate hears a crack, and he falls away without further resistance, leaving a comet of red on her chest.

"Help us!" they keep saying. "Get us out of here!" they shout as they attack.

Kate's able to get to her knees but is pulled back by her

hair, and she roars as she turns to elbow the man in the groin, and he sinks to the floor. Another man climbs on top of Kate, then another, and she's flattened against the hard ground, smacking the side of her head on the way down. She can't find the oxygen she needs to stay conscious. Static blows into her brain and threatens to close her eyes. Her whole body throbs navy. Despite the close moaning and babbling, Kate hears Bernard yelling and whipping the prisoners with her baton. Kate's eyes are closed now but she imagines the woman as twice her normal size, roaring and smashing the men in her way like Godzilla. Kate's consciousness is streaming out of her but if she passes out now she's dead. Not only dead, but worse: because she can feel the men's hands all over her, grabbing for her breasts, her stomach, between her legs, pulling her hair and fingers and lips as if they mean to dismember her. They are wild dogs ready to carry off parts of her, and when one prisoner digs his nails in behind her ear and tries to peel it off, it gives Kate the furious energy to buck and shove the heel of her hand hard up into his nose. The cartilage gives way with a crunch and he hoses her with his hot, sick blood.

Her terror feeds her energy.

"This is not how I die!" she shouts, and jumps up and kicks the next man high in the chest, sending him lurching backwards, then knees the next attacker in the groin. Another man, about to jump on her, is side-swiped by Bernard's baton, as is the next, and then there is finally some space to make an escape out of the room.

"Zack!" shouts Kate.

Still Zack fumbles.

For fuck's sake!

Bernard moves to grab his arm, to yank him out of the room, when a convict shocks her with a punch to her jawbone, then wrestles the baton out of her hand and cracks Bernard on the back of the head with it. Her body hits the floor with a hefty smack.

The man is about to kick Bernard's bleeding head when Kate punches him as hard as she can in his stomach, cracking her knuckles. He exhales hard, but doesn't move. He sets his sights on Kate. Shaking out her stinging hand, she steadies her stance, ready to defend herself, but her confidence drains out of her as more men come, and more men, and Kate gets the idea that no matter how hard she fights, they'll just keep coming at her. Multiplying like Agent Smiths over and over again until there are hundreds of them and nothing left of her.

DARKMEAT VENUS FLYTRAP

71

Kate's heart is wild. She manages to floor one of the men with a well-timed kick to the groin, and smashes another convict's nose, temporarily blinding him. She has to keep on fighting, but there's just one of her and seemingly dozens of them. The prisoners move together now as one, wanting to swallow her up: a darkmeat venus fly trap. Kate's muscles are burnt out, she has no more energy to fight them off. She loses a sleeve to the mob, then feels them tugging at the naked arm as if to pop it from its socket. They descend on her. Kate's voice is hoarse but she screams anyway, a ragged moan that is lost in the chaos of bodies. Bernard bleeds black on black.

Kate trains her eyes on flashes of Zack, who finally stops fidgeting with his uniform pocket and pulls out a piece of sharp glinting metal. He starts swiping at the men and they cry out in surprise and pain as he slashes their throats and arms and anything else he can reach. They spin away from him, spraying blood, and he cuts and cuts as if he is mowing down a field of weeds. The floor is slippery with the warm artery oil. The men over Kate disappear one by one. Finally, the stragglers, not fancying their odds of survival, back away and leak into adjacent rooms. Kate is coughing up vomit. Her face is wet with tears, although she doesn't remember crying.

Zack puts the cut-throat razor back in his pocket, and levers Kate off the ground. He's shiny with sweat and other fluids. Bernard has surfaced, shaking her head, dizzy, unsure on her feet. She finds her steel baton and hugs it to her stomach. They run out of the residents' room and along a passage, turn left and then right. As they run, Bernard trails her hand along the wall, inspecting it as she goes. Suddenly she stops and her hand wraps around the edge of a camouflaged door.

"Here." Bernard unhooks the catch and slides it open, revealing a doorway to a dark tunnel. The air flowing out is cool and scented with soil. They climb through, and Bernard slides the door closed after them. Despite the steep slope they quicken their pace and leave the heat of the silo core behind. The secret subway has rails on the ground, like a makeshift mining shaft.

"What is this?" asks Kate.

"The best way to shuttle bodies out of here without being

seen," says Bernard.

"Bodies?" says Kate.

"Corpses."

Kate shivers. She's seen enough dead bodies for the day. Her wrecked state of mind spills over into her imagination, and she daydreams of the tunnel interior being studded with eyeballs and teeth, and whips her hand away from the sandy wall.

"We're almost there," Bernard says, mostly for Zack's benefit, who seems to be flagging. As Kate gets her hopes up that they'll be in the fresh air soon, Bernard curses and Kate almost walks into her back. The flashlight illuminates a huge heap of soil where the shaft has collapsed, blocking the tunnel. Bernard issues a string of expletives so coarse even Kate is surprised. Sounds are coming from behind them now.

Guards? Criminals?

"They'll find us in here," says Zack. "They'll follow our trail."

Kate and Bernard look at the ground where fresh crimson drops shine. Betrayed by their own blood.

Bernard uses her baton to tap the ceiling. Clods of sand rain down on them. It's loose: loose enough to move. Bernard dislodges more of the soil. It's their only option.

"Dig," she says.

They dig and dig the hard soil above them. It coats them

in dust and mud and the grains on the ground becomes their step up so that they can dig some more. The baton is especially helpful, and they take turns with it. Zack dislodges a small, sharp rock and uses it as a hammer to speed up the work. When Bernard has the baton Kate uses her hands, scraping the skin off her fingers and palms and tearing her nails off while she frantically claws to get to the fresh air and light. Whenever they hear a sound from silo-side they stop to listen.

"Hurry, hurry," says Kate, more to herself than the others. They all know what the stakes are. Zack gives Kate his cut-throat razor. Perhaps he'll use his digging rock as a weapon if the stragglers decide to take another chance with them. It's hard work digging upwards because you lose circulation in your arms if you hold them up for too long, never mind trying to move stubborn soil. And there is just so much of the stuff. It's everywhere, including Kate's mouth and eyes. Eventually they hit something, some kind of weak strata, and there is a rumbling sound above them.

"Watch out!" shouts Bernard, just before the landslide buries all of them and they have to fight to breathe, and crawl and kick so they don't drown in it, have to swim upwards through the silt, but they all do it and when their heads are above the mound that's just almost swallowed them they whoop and smile with their soil-covered faces— just white eyes and grins—because the outside air has rushed to meet them: dappled light and cool forest air and the smell of decomposing leaves. They've made it. It was like digging her way out of her grave, as if she'd been buried alive, but here she is, here they are, alive, with the worst behind them.

They struggle to wrench their limbs free from the heavy soil, and once they're all above ground level they look at each other again with stupid grins. Kate laughs, ridiculously, frantically, because of course there's nothing to laugh about. Yet here she is, with two virtual strangers, and they've just escaped a certain death not once but twice. Now they're standing in a godforsaken forest and she has what—or, rather, who—she came for.

For a moment it seems like time stops, and her urgent issues seem far away: Silver unspooling in a hospital bed, Mally staring into Vega's dangerous eyes. Keke butchered by a schoolgirl. For now she just breathes in the chlorophyll-rich air and rubs the sand off her cheeks, reminded as she does so that her elbow is probably broken—at the very least fractured—and of course it's the same arm she broke in 2021, and damaged again in 2024, and she thinks: perfect. Because she's alive.

And then the clock starts ticking again, and she remembers that she needs to get to Silver before the Lipworth powers down. And this makes her think of Seth, and her heart turns grey.

CORPSE COMPOST

72

The three of them hurry along in the brindled light of the forest. It's the first time Zack has been outside in twelve years. It's utterly peaceful, a block away from the SkyRest building and its subterranean cells, and further still from the jagged Jozi skyline and all the mayhem contained therein.

Kate trips over what feels like a root of a tree but as her body pitches forward, and she softens the fall with her good arm, her face comes close enough to the ground to see the slipping-off skin of a marbled arm escaping the ground. She yells in alarm and backs away, reverse crawling, but then her elbow sinks into the soft soil and there's another limb— a short leg—and a half-decomposed face with teeth bared in a death snarl. She shoots up, stumbles again, and suddenly

Zack is right there, catching her hand.

"Don't panic," he says, and she looks at him as if he is crazy. "They can't hurt us."

They're ankle-deep in decaying flesh and bone, soil and leaf mould (Corpse Compost). The idea is sickening to Kate, but the truth Zack speaks evaporates her fright. These skeletons are harmless. The men trying to tear her apart underground were the real danger. Roguebots and Bot Hunters and the V1R1S are a real danger. Anyway, there's no time for fear.

With her mind on her kids, Kate's able to half-ignore the bones she feels cracking under her boots, and the squelching of putrefied flesh she hears.

"This is one of their experimentation fields," says Bernard, slightly breathless with the effort of walking through the soft matter.

"I've dreamed of this forest," says Zack. "Dreamed of it enough times to know that it can't hurt us."

Kate steps on a particularly slimy part and slides a little, then gags.

"Keep your focus on the trees," he says.

Kate looks up, and Zack's right, the trees are shimmering with health and energy and fresh new leaves. The new life that is nourished by the death below. She realises they're all breathing easily without their face-masks on, as if they're in a bubble of oxygen.

Kate wants to call Seth, but realises that her mandible is gone; ripped off by the crims. She says a quick nonsense-prayer to the multiverse, hoping he's making his way back to the Lipworth Foundation. She has a bad feeling.

Kate shudders. "I need to find Seth. What if he went back down to find me?"

"He wouldn't want you going back," says Zack. "He'd want you to save Silver."

ANTHROBOT ACADEMY

73

Seth's Apartment

Johannesburg, 2036

Mally and Vega sit on Mally's bed, facing each other and holding hands. He leans forward and kisses her on the mouth, tentatively, tenderly. Her body warms and arches. She runs her fingers through his hair, and his scalp comes alive under her touch. Other parts of his body, too. She knows exactly what sets him on fire.

Vega starts pulling at his cargo pants. He stops her with

gentle hands.

"Don't," he says. "Not today. Not after what you've been through."

"I want to," says Vega. "I am very fond of you."

"I love you," Mally says, "but we don't have to have sex to prove it."

"I want to," says Vega. "Things are happening in this world. What if this is our last chance?"

Vega opens her shirt to Mally. He traces the perfect outline of her breasts over her smooth brassiere, feels her pulse through her warm silicone skin. Spends a moment with his hand covering her heart pocket which contains her living hard drive, her Soul Shard. Vega slips her fingers under the waistband of his pants and pulls them down. His desire is clear. She kisses him, and he melts under her, sinking into his pillow. She moves her lips and tongue down his body.

"This isn't why—" Mally starts saying, but then his yearning overcomes him and the sentence turns into a groan.

Vega knows, anyway.

She knows this isn't the reason he dates her. Other men do it, of course, commissioning girlfriends from the anthrobot academy to use as house-cleaning sex slaves, but not him. He thinks he fell in love with Vega the first time he saw her in virtual class. His feelings were so strong that first meeting he lost his usual shyness and asked her if he could meet her IRL. Since then they've been practically inseparable, but he's turned down every sexual advance of hers—apart from kissing and some light fondling—because he doesn't want to treat her like an object. He loves her superintelligence, her skewed humour, her spirit. He loves the spark in her eyes, the way they learn from each other all the time, and the way they just get each other in every way.

Net, he loves her, Mally thinks, as she starts to pull down his cooljox.

And she's right. Who knows what's happening out there, or what's going to happen tomorrow? *Will there even be a tomorrow?*

He doesn't know, but what he does know, now, and the knowledge surges inside of him, feeding his desire, is that it *is* time. They've waited long enough; it's the perfect time to consummate their relationship. He sits up and starts to tug off Vega's shirt, and she one-handedly snaps her bra off behind her back. The sight of her naked breasts makes his heart swoop, and he's light-headed for a second as he moves his mouth down to kiss them.

The doorbell rings, and they both jump. His parents, perhaps, or an errant Silver. Would Kate ring the doorbell instead of using the biopad? Possibly. The front door has been giving problems. Either way they sigh, smiling, and pull their clothes back on.

"Purest human," Vega whispers, buttoning up her shirt as Mally leaves to answer the door.

Arronax has beaten him to it.

"… here as a representative from the National Android Safety…" a stranger is saying.

Arronax senses Mally behind her and turns to include him in the conversation.

The man looks at Mally, as if sizing him up. Beady eyes. Twitching fingers. He's wearing a cheap blue suit so new it makes Mally immediately suspicious. How does he not get egged in the street wearing that? He could at least fray the edges a little.

"Good morning." His holotag flashes with the NASP logo. Govender is his name. "I was just saying … that I'm here to interview Miss Alpha Lyrae about the incident last night."

"Why?" asks Mally.

"It's regulation," says Arronax. "All anthrobot assaults need to be reported."

"Well, it doesn't matter anymore," says Mally.

The man nervously adjusts his mandible. "Why do you say that?"

"Let's just say … the creep responsible for the attack won't be doing it again."

"We know," says Govender. "A man is dead and Miss Lyrae's roscoe bullets were found at the scene. I'm sure you can appreciate how this needs to be investigated."

Arronax frowns. "What are you saying?"

"Vega's in trouble?" Mally can feel his cheeks colour. "For defending herself? For saving my life?"

"Not in trouble," says the man. "Not unless she did something off-protocol."

"Well, she didn't," says Mally, and tries to close the door, but Govender jams his foot in the way.

"I'm going to have to interview her," he says.

"She's been through enough," says Mally.

"It won't take long."

"Then you'll leave?"

"Then I'll leave."

They set up in the open plan kitchen. The 'interview' comprises Govender downloading Vega's memory of the assault. Arronax is busy on her SnapTile while they complete the transaction. The rep watches Vega's version of the attack and flinches with every shot fired. Once he has a copy of the video, he inserts his diagnostic key into the back of her neck and it flashes red.

"This is bad," Govender says. "This is worse that I thought."

"What's that supposed to mean?"

"It means we're going to have to take her in."

Vega stands up, dusts the creases in her outfit, ready to go.

"Hell no," says Mally. "You're not taking Vega anywhere."

"I'm afraid it's not up to you, Mister Lovell," says the man. "Alpha Lyrae has undergone significant damage, both on a hard- and software level. She needs to be tended to."

"Tended to?"

"She's not safe as she is, but don't worry, we'll be able to help her."

"No," says Mally. "No way."

He's seen the news. Seen how the Special Task Police are rounding up bots of all kinds and keeping them in electric wire-festooned concentration camps.

"We'll fix her up. Reboot her. She'll be as good as new."

"I'm not going to let you do that," says Mally.

"With all due respect," says Govender, "it's not up to you. Under section 17C of the NASP act we're to claim all damaged bots and—"

"Don't speak about her like that. Like she's someone's property."

"But … she is," he says. "I realise you're young and—"

"It's got nothing to do with age," Mally says. "It's about being decent."

"Alpha Lyrae is government property." Govender starts to approach Vega, puts a hand out to take her arm. "And as such, she's—"

"You leave her alone!"

"It's okay, Mally," says Vega. "It's protocol."

"I don't give a fuck about protocol," Mally says. "I'm sick of hearing about fucking protocol. He's not taking you anywhere."

"I'm going to have to arrest you for obstructing reclamation," says Govender.

"No," says Vega, giving the NASP representative her best smile. "There's no need for arrests. I'll come with you."

Mally blocks the man's way. "There's no way I'm going to let that happen."

Arronax looks up from her device, and Mally watches as her face drains of colour. She flashes her eyes at him and grabs Seth's Vektor gun from behind the instakettle. It won't fire without his bioprint, but Govender won't know that.

"Get out," Arronax flicks the weapon in the direction of the door.

Govender shoots up with his hands in the air. "What are you doing?"

"Get out," Arronax growls. Her hair changes from silver-lilac to deep purple edged with black.

Vega looks confused. "What is happening?"

"Now is your last chance to walk out of here," says Arronax.

The man keeps his hands in the air and stumbles backwards, towards the front door.

As he crosses the threshold he says "She'll kill you too, you know. There's no such thing as a good robot."

"Bullshit," says Mally. "You don't know who you're talking to. You should show some respect."

This catches Govender off guard. He looks from Mally, to Arronax, to Mally again.

"Keep quiet, Mally," says Arronax.

Mally ignores her. "This is Doctor Arronax."

"Shut up, Mally!" says Arronax, but Mally can't help himself.

"She's lead engineer on 7thGen robosapiens and the founder of the RoboRights movement."

Govender's eyes widen, and he stumbles as he backs into a cabinet. "Well, then," he says, when he's regained some composure, "Doctor Arronax. Maybe you deserve to die at the hands of one of the monsters you've created."

Mally moves to punch him in the face, but Vega holds him back. Govender doesn't need any more encouragement to get out. As he leaves, he narrows his eyes and says, "My advice is to kill the robot. Kill her before she kills you."

"So much for NASP being around to protect anthrobots," says Mally.

"That man wasn't from NASP." Arronax shows Mally her screen. She's deep in the NASP intersite, and there's no such staff member.

Now it's Mally's turn to be confused. "Then who was he?"

"I don't know, but his agenda's clear. And by now he would have broadcast this address and our identities to all his Bot Hunter mates."

"Oh, shit," says Mally. "I wasn't thinking. I'm so sorry."

"Don't worry. You didn't know. The important thing is to get out of here as soon as possible."

Arronax is packing her cardigan and Tile as she talks. She opens a few kitchen cupboards and grabs crackling packets of food: mango biltong, butter popgrains, and protein pretzel stix, and shoves them into her backpack. The Vektor goes into her lab coat pocket.

"Where will we go?"

"I have a safe room. In the city. We can stay there till—"

Till what? Till the danger's passed? Probably not going to happen. Till we run out of food? Till we die?

He can't see a positive outcome. He doesn't even know if he'll ever see his family again. There's a hand on his back and he turns to look at Vega. Her eyes are electric. "Let's go," she says.

YOU ARE EXCUSED FROM YOUR DAILY GRIND

74

ChinaCity/Sandton

Johannesburg, 2036

Kate, Zack and Bernard rush through the city, tram-hopping and skirting the worst of the flash civil war zones. Kate's head is still bleeding from the hit she took at SkyRest. As they hurry they grab a pack of hotwipes from a vandalized vending machine so they can at least clean their faces of the blood and dirt that covers them. Kate's arm is glowing with pain. She can't help but stare at Zack's grey face.

What did they do to you? she wants to ask, but it's not the time.

On the southbound solartram they zip past pedestrians: shell-shocked, angry, bewildered. Some people look as if they're on their way to work, but they're not quite convinced they need to go in. It's not like there's a Doomsday memo, thinks Kate. An apocalyptic announcement.

DEAR CIVILIANS. TODAY IS THE END OF THE WORLD. YOU ARE EXCUSED FROM YOUR REGULAR DAILY GRIND. ENJOY THE DAY.

"Keke will be so damn happy to see you."

Zack's face animates. "Keke?"

"She tried to go to your trial."

"There was no trial."

"That's what she was worried about."

"They hired some actors and a cardboard court. And just like that ..."

"Are you angry with her?" asks Kate.

"Angry with Keke? No. Never."

"But—"

"She's not the reason I went to the crim colony. My job is the reason I was arrested in the first place. Because creeps don't understand the big picture."

"What is that? What is your job?" asks Kate.

"Do you know the allegory of Plato's Cave?"

Kate shakes her head. She's heard of if before, but has no idea what it means, and she's certainly not in the mood for riddles.

"What about the Lotus Eaters?" asks Zack.

"No," says Kate. "So can you please just tell me what the hell is going on?"

They pass a giant bonfire spewing acrid smoke. People are tossing pavement detritus into the flames. Broken furniture, boxes, anthrobot limbs. Some of the people are bare-chested and they've stained themselves with some kind of war paint: blood? Ash and spit? They've got wild eyes and shout randomly as they feed the fire.

"Yes," says Zack, taking her hand. They arrive at their destination and jump off the tram. "It's almost time."

There's no way the Lipworth Foundation's security system will let an escaped convict in. Bernard senses Kate's hesitation and says, "Leave it to me."

She has a word with the guardbot and there's a call to

someone else, and with a ping of green their entry is authorised. Bernard is clearly more influential than Kate imagined. The receptionist advises them that the power will be cut by 14:00. They hurry through the shiny, brightly lit white corridors, avoiding the elevator. "It's 12:39," says Kate, looking at her bare wrist: a habit she's never been able to kick.

They arrive at Silver's private ward. Kate pushes open the door and sees her daughter in the oxygen tent, in the same position and state, and it's as if she'd just left a moment ago.

The DarkDoc stands up, relief splashing his face. "Kate."

He takes her by the shoulders and holds her an arm's length away, inspecting her.

"Jesus Christ. What happened? Are you okay?"

Kate squeezes her elbow and winces. "I could do with some painkillers."

"I'm afraid we're all out," Morgan says.

"You're kidding," says Kate. "You're kidding, right?"

"They've put all the narcotics on double lockdown. It's to stop the looters from coming in here."

"How's Keke?" Kate asks.

Doctor Morgan replies in his vintage-engine purr: "She's fine. I checked in on her half an hour ago. She's a tough cookie. She wanted to be discharged ... wanted to go looking for you. I told her to hang tight, that you'd be back."

"Surgery?"

"No. The surgery bots have been powered down."

"What about human? Human surgeons?"

"Not here. This isn't a hospital. My bet is they're all working their third or fourth shifts in a row in ERs all over the city."

More people who didn't get the memo. Or maybe they want to spend their last day helping strangers. That kind of generosity of spirit doesn't come naturally to Kate. Her first instinct has always been selfish: to protect her own before anyone else.

"I'm so glad you're back," says Morgan. "I was worried."

Zack walks up to the oxygen tent, unzips it, sticks his head in and scans the back of Silver's head. He looks worried.

"So you're Zack," says Morgan. "Silver's been saying your name over and over. She seems to think that you're the one who knows how to save her."

Kate thinks of the mob at SkyRest. "She'd better be right."

"It's not going to be easy." Zack's face remains the shade of overcooked oatmeal.

"What do we do? How do we wake her up?"

Zack blinks, deep in thought. "It's not so much about waking her up. She's actually awake, even though she doesn't look it."

"Then?"

"You're really not going to want to hear this."

"Tell me," says Kate.

"It's going to be an extremely … difficult thing for you to do."

Jesus, this man with his non-answers. If he hadn't just saved her life she'd want to throttle him. He is just not capable of a straight answer. Her face heats up: anger, desperation (Fraught French Rose). "I'll do anything."

This seems to snap him out of his trance. "Silver's mesh …"

"I know," Kate says. "It's like some backstreet … I can't believe—"

"No," Zack says. "Not backstreet. The opposite is actually true. It's a highly sophisticated piece of—"

DarkDoc jumps in, "I've never seen neural lace like that before. It looks to me like some biopunk put it together with what he could get drone-delivered to his basement. And the way it was implanted, well, it's a quack-job at best."

"I agree that the surgery itself was badly done," says Zack, "but—"

"Doctor Morgan is the leading techdoctor on the continent," says Kate. "If anyone knows about mesh, it's him."

"Look," says Zack. "The reason you don't recognise the

lace is because …"

Zack has the doctor's full attention.

"It's because this technology hasn't been invented yet."

SLATE SORROW

75

"Um…" says the DarkDoc, scratching his scalp, perhaps thinking Zack is delusional. "Hasn't been invented yet?"

"I know," says Zack, "it's not easy to understand."

"Help me."

Kate's brain is also whirring. *Not been invented yet?*

"Aliens?" she ventures, and it does a good job of breaking the tension. They all cough out a single laugh, apart from Bernard, who seems to be the victim of a permanent humour failure. Kate pictures Bernard suddenly as a chubby baby in a vintage highchair, with a cooing young mother pulling faces and playing peekaboo in an attempt to make her ever-serious baby laugh. In Kate's imagination, baby Bernard ignores her mother and just stares ahead.

"Not quite." Zack finally has some colour in his face. He's looking more vital, more like the Zack Kate met that day at the Gordhan when her twins were toddlers. It's as if his sense of purpose, being here, helping her, is making him age backwards.

"Then?" asks Doctor Morgan.

Kate says, "Why you? Why would she ask for *you* of all people?"

Words drift unsaid in the sanitised air like white balloons.

"I promise you I'll answer all your questions," says Zack.

As his eyes find Kate's, she realises they still have a connection—a strange, electric, impossible connection—after all this time.

"I'll answer every single one of them, but right now we need to get you meshed as soon as possible if you want to save Silver before they cut the power to this part of the grid."

Kate blanches. "What?"

"According to my calculations," says Zack, "This power will be on for another..." He checks the clock on the wall. "Seventy-three minutes. That's barely enough time to implant the lace, get you immersed, and for you to bring

Silver out."

"It's too risky," says Doctor Morgan. "It's way too risky. And even if it weren't, we'd need more time than that."

"I need to get meshed?" asks Kate, still shocked at the turn of the conversation.

"Honestly: the risk is substantial," says Zack.

"It's more than substantial," says Morgan. "We don't know what we're dealing with here."

Zack stands his ground. "It's the only way."

"You can't do it," the DarkDoc turns to Kate. "You'll end up...you'll end up like Silver."

They all look at the bone-white body inside the oxygen tent.

Kate drags her gaze back to Morgan. *Don't you see?* Her eyes say, *I can't not do it.*

"It's a simple procedure," Zack says to the DarkDoc.

"Don't look at me!" says Morgan. "There's no way I'm going to perform that surgery."

"You've performed tech surgeries that are way more grey market than this," says Kate. It was, funnily enough, how they had met. Morgan had agreed to perform a surgery that was dangerous and illegal—one that had at the same time cost Marko's eye and saved Silver's life—and here they are again. "You've never let red tape stand in the way."

"It's not about red tape."

It's about you, his eyes say, but she turns away so she doesn't have to see his plea.

"Those were patients," Morgan says. "Virtual strangers."

Kate paces as they talk. They're running out of time. Her nervous energy is making her feel as though she's walking on air. "It doesn't matter."

"Of course it matters!"

"This thing, right now, saving Silver," says Kate. "That's all that matters."

"I can't be responsible for sending you into catatonia. Because that's exactly what I'd be doing."

"You'll be doing what I'm asking you to do. It's my decision."

"Look at the clock," says Zack. "We don't have time to argue."

It's twelve forty-nine. The ChinaCity/Sandton band will be shut down at fourteen hundred.

"Please," says Kate. They've been in this position before. It was Keke who had finally convinced him to go through with it. Keke is uniquely persuasive when it comes to people of the opposite sex. Or any sex, really. "Please, Morgan. Please. It's our only chance."

He turns inwards, steps closer to her, and says in his low voice, "I don't want to lose you." When she can't think of a reply, he continues, "But something tells me I already have."

They start moving to the operating room. Bernard pushes Silver's bed along so they can all stay together. They get Kate settled in what looks like an operating chair. Zack pulls a hospital gown over her head and adds another layer of linen while Morgan washes his hands and collects the implements he needs. The tools clatter in the silver tray, and the cold metallic sound sends slush down Kate's spine. Zack and Bernard throw on cotton gowns and scrub their hands, too.

Why are they helping her?

The DarkDoc has a cold, hard edge of desolation around him (Slate Sorrow). He's holding his freshly sanitised hands up like surgeons do in old films. He automatically looks around for his team, expecting them to know what to do, but it's only the escaped criminal and his warden.

The DarkDoc shakes his head, closes his eyes and is quiet for a moment. He fills a syringe with an orange liquid, fits a needle, then takes Kate's arm in his tender, gloved hands.

"What's that?" asks Zack.

"Anaesthetic," says Morgan, and brings the needle to the crook of Kate's arm.

"Stop," says Zack. The doctor frowns at him.

"You can't use general anaesthetic for this. Kate has to be fully conscious in the immersion. We can't afford any downtime."

"The local anaesthetic is on lockdown," says the DarkDoc. "I can't do this without anaesthetic."

"Yes, you can," says Kate. Her knuckles are white.

GALAXY OF BRIGHT ROLLING PAIN

76

"Jesus, Kate. Do you even know what you're saying?"

"Get on with it," says Zack. "We don't have a second to lose. I'll brief her. I'll talk her through the difficult parts."

"The 'difficult parts'?" says the DarkDoc. "We're about to perform brain surgery without any kind of anaesthetic. We don't even have painkillers, for Net's sake."

They all look at Morgan, waiting. The flash of anger passes, and his face clears. "Fine," he says. "We need a laser blade. The surgical ones are locked away."

Zack thinks of Lewis and pulls out the old cutthroat razor, bought with his first SkyRest Reward twelve years ago. A gift that was never given. "Will this do?"

It's patterned with dried blood. A landscape of dark brown blooms and grasses on a flashing silver background.

"Is it sharp?" asks the DarkDoc.

"Yes."

"Then it'll do."

Zack quickly washes it at the sterile station while Bernard parts Kate's hair and uses scissors to cut away the long strands. Zack brings the soap spray with him on the way back, spritzes the area of her scalp that needs shaving, then picks up the razor and puts a hand on Kate's shoulder.

"Hold still."

As Zack shaves the back of her head, Kate's practically blinded by the burnt orange of *deja vu*. Of course, she knows why. She's done this before, except last time she was cutting a chip out of her own scalp to save her life. The orange throbs in her temples; she's never felt it as intensely as this before.

"We'll need to secure her," the DarkDoc says. "If she moves during a sensitive time in the surgery it will be catastrophic."

Bernard finds large surgical bands and they tie Kate down. Every part of her body is fixed to the operating chair. In a strange way the restriction is comforting, but when she hears Morgan picking up a scalpel, the terror comes running at her. A ferocious dog of fear.

"I need to score through your lambdoid suture to insert the mesh properly."

Kate tries to nod, but she can't move. Zack comes into view.

"Okay, talk to me," says Kate, her teeth buzzing with nerves.

Zack takes a seat in front of her and levers it right down so that they can look each other in the eyes.

"This whole procedure will only take ten minutes," says Zack.

"Eight," says Morgan.

"Eight minutes, Kate. Okay? It's gonna be hell, but then it'll be over."

"Okay."

"I'm going to talk you through the whole thing. Focus on what I'm saying, not what you can feel happening."

"Okay."

"Eight minutes."

"Okay."

Zack nods at the DarkDoc, and he makes the first

incision.

Kate draws in a sharp breath through her teeth. The pain is acute, but it's manageable.

"First I'm going to brief you on what you need to do to bring Silver back. Then, when the pain gets unbearable, you must find a place in your mind, in your memory, where you can go, and leave this room behind. Think of a place you want to go. Get it ready in your mind. You'll need to disassociate. Got it?"

"Got it." Kate knows which memory she'll use. She can feel the scalpel make two more incisions, and the small flap of skin is folded back. She clenches her jaws. It's a low blue flame of pain.

"All right," says Zack. "Once you're meshed, you'll be able to become totally immersed."

"How?"

"You'll just see it. It'll be all around you. Like a projection, but deeper. More real."

"Like my synaesthesia?"

"Like your synaesthesia on MDMA."

"Where will I find Silver?"

"Let your subconscious do the work. You two are connected in a way that's difficult to explain. You know where she is, you just need to find her, and you need to do it quickly, and get out."

"I'm worried I won't be good at this. That I won't be able to find her."

There's a sharp stinging at the back of Kate's head and she cries out.

"Just remember that the immersion isn't a foreign thing. It's not someone else's design. It's all yours. It uses your thoughts to create itself. The lace is just the connector. You are the operating system."

"Yes." Kate remembers that from the VXR therapy she had for her PTSD. The experiences were so vivid because they came directly from her brain. It was like living and breathing in the actual downloaded memory.

"So you go, follow your instinct, and find Silver as fast as you can. She'll be close."

There's another sharp pain, as if someone has stabbed her in her brain stem, and stars explode in her head. Zack keeps talking but she can't hear him over the pain. All she manages is a low groan. Blue fireworks, silver stars, hissing agony—it's as if there's no space for her brain anymore, it's all being crowded out by the galaxy of bright, rolling pain.

"Can you hear me, Kate?" says Zack, but she can't talk and she can't move her head. She's desperate to know what else Zack is saying, needs to know what he's telling her, but all she can hear is the groan she can't keep inside.

Bernard hands Morgan the bonesaw beam.

"It's almost over," says Zack. "This is going to be the worst part, now. And then it's over."

Kate feels water on her face. Is she crying? Sweating? Clear liquid drips onto the expensive tiles below her. She can't imagine how the pain can get any worse.

"Get ready to leave the room," coaches Zack. "Visit your memory now."

Morgan begins to score through her lambdoid suture. The laser makes a crackling sound as it cuts through the fissure in Kate's skull. It's so intense her body begins to shake. Saliva splashes out of her mouth.

"Two minutes," says the DarkDoc.

Kate wants them to stop, would do anything to make them stop. She struggles and tries to tell them she can't survive this pain.

"Leave the room," says Zack, but she can't. The pain is so overbearing it holds her right there in its terrible vice: It's like being frozen but burning hot at the same time. She wants to scream but her voice is no longer working.

The buzzing continues, and it feels as if her brain is exploding in slow motion. Kate vomits. The bile splatters the floor with bitter green. Zack wipes her mouth for her, her nose, and cleans the floor. "Leave the room," he says in a hard whisper, and Kate closes her eyes and swims away from the operating room. Swims through the ceiling and out of the building till she's way above it and it's not smoggy anymore: It's 2022 and the sky is a brilliant clear cold blue.

A DIFFERENT KIND OF FAMILY

77

Kate's flying through the sky, away from the city and towards the South Coast, back in time, back to a memory that's so dear it feels as if she's climbing back into a warm bed. She's ripping through the air, over towns and cities, and slows almost to a stop when she reaches Westville, KZN, where she was born.

From above, Kate recognises her hired electric car, idling by the river embroidered by weeping willows and rushes and reeds. She sees her mother, her real biological mother, walking towards the river, and all of a sudden she's pulled out of the sky as if caught in a giant vacuum, sucked down with a force, and she finds herself shunted into her younger body that's sitting in the car. The rearview mirror tells her she's in her late twenties again, and when Kate looks down at her belly it's stretched and round. She runs her hand over it. Silver.

Kate breathes and lets go; she allows herself to relax fully into the memory.

Westville, KZN, 2022

Kate sits in her hired car, parked a little way away from the river, under the glittering dappled shade of willow trees. She takes off her safety belt, adjusts her tender back in the chair. Her left arm is slightly paler and thinner than her right, still recovering from being in the exoskeletal cast she had to wear for months.

She breathes in the muddy green smell of the river (Wilted Waterlily): a smooth, undulating smell. Balmy Verdant. Rolling Hills.

God, Kate has missed driving, the freedom of the open road to the thrumming soundtrack of your choice. Stopping for a hydrogen refuel—not as pungent a memory as petrol—and greasy toasted cheese in a wax paper envelope. Flimsy paper serviette. Vanilla whipped Soy-Ice in a hard chocolate coating that you get to crack open with your teeth. Noticing, inside the store, that all the Fontus fridges are gone. Kate imagines them yawning in recycle tips, stripped of any valuable metal, or re-purposed as beds or dining-room tables in townships.

Kate winds down her window further, allowing more of the clear air into the car. After tossing out the air-freshener at the car rental agency (Retching Pink) she drove the first hour with all the windows open to try to flush out the fragrance. Artificial roses: the too-sweet scent painted thick vertical lines in her vision. Her sense of smell seems to be in overdrive lately, and the shapes more vivid than ever.

It's a superb day: warm, the humidity mitigated by a cool breeze, and the sky brighter than she's ever remembered seeing it. The branches of the weeping willows stroke the ground, whispering, as if to soothe it. She can smell a hundred different shades of green in the motion of leaves.

A woman pops up in the distance, walking towards the river. She has handsome silver hair, a thick mass of it, twisted up and fixed in place with a clip and a fresh flower. A stained wicker picnic basket in her hand. She is tall and moves in elegant strides: not rushing, nor dawdling, her sense of purpose clear. She doesn't look around for a good spot; she knows exactly where the good spot is.

The woman sets down her basket, lays out a picnic blanket, smoothes it down in a practised movement. Once she's removed her shoes, she sits with her legs out in front of her, crossed at the ankles, leaning back on her hands with her eyes closed and her face to the sky.

The woman takes out her clip and lets her hair tumble down like mercury. Kate unthinkingly touches her own short hair, rakes her fingers though the awkward length of re-growth. The woman relaxes like that for a while, then sits up and opens her basket, bringing out a plastic plate and knife, a packet of crackers, cheese triangles. A small yellow juicebox.

Kate snaps a photo of her with her LocketCam, then retrieves the cooler-box from the back seat that she packed that morning. She takes out a dripping bottle of iced tea, a packet of Blacksalt crisps, and a CaraCrunch chocolate bar. Watching the woman by the river, she opens the foil packet and starts to eat; then she remembers the bright green apple in her bag—Granny Smith— and eats that too.

So this is what her real mother looks like. Not just her non-abductor mother, more than just her biological mother, but her real mother. She can feel it. She sees Seth/Sam in her body language, her straight nose. But the hair and the eyes are hers.

She looks again at her reflection in the rear-view mirror, touches the new streak of grey at her temple (Silver Floss). Kate feels a welling up in her chest, an inflating of her ribcage, and breathes deeply to stay calm. Warm tears rush down her face; she is used to the feeling now, even welcomes the release. During the past few months she has made up for a lifetime of not crying.

The woman looks so peaceful, so at ease with the world, a trait Kate hasn't been lucky enough to inherit, but she hasn't always been like this; she has also had her dark days. They never moved house—they still live at 22 Hibiscus Road—as if they thought if they moved, they would lose all hope of the twins finding their way home.

Anne Chapman visits the river almost every day, the spot where she used to sit in the shade while the twins splashed around, and then later, their subsequent children: another son and daughter, born five years after Kate and Sam, spaced three years apart. The children, now grown, visit often, and the family looks like any normal, happy, loving family. It would be difficult, seeing them laughing and joking at family dinners, to guess at their sad, fragmented past.

Kate's yearning crowds the car. How she would love to meet her mother, grasp her hand, taste her cooking, ask her about the years before the kidnapping, and after. But looking at her, seeing how content she is, how restful her spirit seems, she knows she can't do it. It would be like smashing a shattered mirror that has taken decades to put together. Its hold is tenuous, gossamer, and she won't be the one to re-splinter it.

No fresh heartbreak.

She has a new life, *thinks Kate,* like I do now. *She thinks of Seth at home in Illovo with Baby Marmalade: how good he is with him, how gentle. Seth who wants to keep his Genesis name, instead of 'Sam,' says it doesn't suit him, and he's right.*

He has a new life too, despite not changing his name. She pictures what she guesses they are doing now, sitting on the couch in front of the homescreen, Baby Marmalade asleep in his arms, Betty/Barbara the Beagle snoring in her usual spot, her snout on Seth's lap. The wooden floor littered with nappies and wipes and teething rings and toys.

A different kind of family, *James said.*

An unusual family, but a family nonetheless: waiting for her to return home, and anticipating its new addition.

She thinks of her Black Hole, which is still there but has been sewn up to the size of her skin-warm silver locket. It's the smallest she can ever remember it being, but it yawns when she thinks of James.

Kate watches her mother pack up, shake the blanket, fold it and put it away, then start walking back in the direction from which she came. Kate reaches for the door handle, then stops herself.

No. No. *But when that feels too harsh, she allows herself a concession, thinks,* at least: not today. Maybe tomorrow, but not today.

After a few steps, her mother turns and looks directly at the car in the distance. Kate can't see her expression. A moment goes by, and Anne turns back and continues her walk home.

Kate takes a few breaths with her head back and her eyes closed, then snicks her safety belt in and starts the car, swinging it into reverse. Her back is aching again, her ankles puffy. She adjusts her position, rubs her swollen belly.

"Time to get you back home, little one."

Born seven months apart, her babies will be almost like twins. A different kind of twin.

Kate begins to drive away and gets as far as the stop sign at the top of the road when she changes her mind. She turns the car around and races back to the parking lot at the river. Her mother is gone.

GLASS MERCURY

78

Westville, KZN, 2022

Kate clambers out of the car, fighting with her safety belt with dumb fingers, almost tripping in her rush to catch her mother. She leaves the door open, not caring, and runs as fast as she can, hands on her pregnant stomach, down the peppermint slope and shouting, "Anne! Anne!"

A small, faraway thought occurs to her: that she must look completely crackers with her strange, short haircut, her mismatched arms hugging her round belly, running and shouting after a woman who she thinks might be her real mother—the mother she was taken from so long ago. She doesn't care. She's near the river now, can hear it gurgling, and looks frantically for the woman who was just here. Shields her eyes from the sunshine and squints up in the direction she was walking. There's just an empty path.

Her desperation flashes monochrome. It cat-claws at her: needles in her skin.

"Anne!" she shouts as loudly as she can. "Anne Chapman!" but there's not a soul in sight. Just the river and the green-flavoured breeze and the birds.

Kate stops running, and rests her hands on her knees. Her lungs are hard elastic. When she straightens up again, the woman has stepped out from behind the willows, a look of unabashed wonder on her face, still grasping her picnic things.

"Anne Chapman?" asks Kate, whispering now, also stung by the quiet hope in the moment. They're only a few metres away from each other.

The woman blinks, drops the basket with a grassy thud. Her hands go up to her face and she touches her nose, her mouth, as if to test if the moment is real, or a dream.

"Sorry," says Kate. "I know it's a lot to take in. I wasn't going to—" She stumbles over her words. "I was going to wait and—"

"It can't be," the woman says, hope now like flames in her cheeks. "Can it?"

Kate's heart is sprinting; she puts her palm over her chest as if to tell it to slow down.

Calm. Calm. Stress is not good for the baby.

They stand marvelling at each other. Silver floss for hair, and eyes the colour of the sound of the sea. It's like looking into a time-travelling mirror (Glass Mercury). Then Anne reaches out through the mirror and touches Kate's chin, and it's so tender that Kate just wants to melt under her touch and the poignancy of the moment. The sense of her immense loss—thirty years of tender, unconditional love she missed out on—almost bowls her over. A life stolen. The overwhelming feeling of her own personal tragedy splashes her world purple.

The abducted two-year-old in Kate wants to yell Mom! *and fling her arms around her mother, but the moment is strange and disjointed and not the Hallmark scene she imagined it could be. Yes, they're bound by warm flesh and blood—always would be—but their relationship is eternally eroded by deprivation. The heart-bending truth is that they are virtual strangers, and this realisation, coupled with the rolling feeling of squandered time she feels, punches Kate in the stomach, and it hurts so much she winces, and holds on to her belly.*

"Oh!" says Anne, stepping towards her, taking her by a shoulder, "Are you okay?"

There's another jab, and Kate exclaims with a sharp intake of breath. Anne lays the blanket out and, holding her good arm, helps Kate to sit down.

"I think," says Kate, recovering, "I think the baby just kicked for the first time."

Immediately the pane of cold glass that's between them shatters and falls away, and they both start weeping. They hug and hold hands and cry and cry. Their salty cheeks touch, their tears run together. Sniffing, they both search for tissues but come up empty-handed. Kate uses her sleeve to wipe her face.

"Kate. My darling Kate. After all this time. Is it really you?"
but Kate doesn't need to answer.

BRAIN ON FIRE

79

The Lipworth Foundation

Johannesburg, 2036

As the memory comes to its end, Kate is pulled back into the operating room. The back of her head is still sizzling with pain, but it's not the overbearing, black-hammer kind that knocks you into oblivion.

The DarkDoc smoothes a thin platelet plaster over the wound. "Done."

"Kate?" says Zack. "Are you with us?"

Kate lets out a low groan. "Fu-u-u-uck. That was—" But she doesn't have a word to describe it.

"It'll take you a while to adjust to the mesh," says the doctor.

"I don't have time."

They unwrap her limbs so she can move freely again. Morgan shines a pen-light into her eyes. "How do you feel?"

Woozy, she's going to say. *Brain on fire*. But there's something else. She looks around the room, looks at the people's faces. It's like there's an extra dimension.

"Intense," is all she manages to say. The pain is fading.

There's the ordinary world, real life, which is how regular creeps experience reality—Kate calls it 'monochrome'—without the extra shapes and sounds and colours that she sees, then on top of that is her synaesthesia. But now, now there's an additional layer, and it's rich and beautiful. Enhanced. Like you've only ever seen black-and-white films but then you turn on a switch and all of a sudden it's 4DHD hypercolour with textures that come right out at you, as if you can feel them with your eyes.

"Kate?" says Zack, moving into her field of vision.

My god *he's beautiful*. He is the most beautiful thing she's ever seen. She wants to touch him.

"It feels like," says Kate, "it feels like my eyeballs are drunk."

"It's not your eyeballs," says the DarkDoc, coming into view.

He's a magnificent man too. So strong, so gruff and handsome. Is he really her lover? It suddenly seems unlikely.

"It's your brain." The doctor emanates deep red energy. It's as if his chakras are glowing in short bursts. Kate thinks she can see his heart beating, as if she has some kind of new real-time X-ray heat-sensing ability. She wants to touch him, too. She was wrong to say it felt as if her eyeballs are drunk. It's more accurate to say that every neuron and nerve ending in her whole body is tripping on some kind of futuristic neat-tech rainbow crack version of LSD.

"I understand now," Kate says. "I understand why Silver wanted to get this."

"This is just the beginning," says Zack.

"How much time do we have left?"

Kate has forgotten about the warden. She looks at her, takes in her stocky frame, her firm muscles. *How strong she is, like an Amazon warrior! But more royal than that, with her silver baton. A military queen.*

"Forty-eight minutes," says Zack, bringing Kate to attention. "That's if they shut off the power at fourteen hundred exactly."

"It's not enough time," says Morgan.

"It's all we have."

Kate stares over at Silver inside the dome of the transparent tent. It looks like a bubble to her now, as if they are all underwater and the sleeping Silver is protected by her own special pocket of air. It's like a fairytale.

"Tell me what I need to do."

BRIGHTCANDY CANAL

80

"All right," says Zack. "Doctor Morgan's and my theory is that Silver got stuck in between reality and her RPG immersion."

Kate splutters. "Theory? That's all you have?"

"That's all we have."

Jesus Christ on a cracker.

Kate's mind is racing, and her thoughts feel as if they leave heat trails in their path. Words tumble out of her mouth. "RPG? How do you get stuck? I've never heard of that before. Is it because it was a backstreet mesh? It wasn't done properly … it didn't work well enough?"

"We think it's because it worked *too* well," says Morgan. "That particular lace is so advanced … and Silver so adept at immersion that we think she went too deep, too quickly, and …yes, she got stuck."

"Usually when you have trouble immersing, you just come out and restart. But for some reason Silver's not doing that. We know she's not in Eden 7.0, and we know she's not here with us, so our theory is that she's somewhere in between."

"Eden 7.0?"

"It's the updated version of the role-playing game she's always in. It's so advanced now that you can only play if you're meshed."

"How do you know she's not in the game?"

"Doctor Morgan has patients at the Atrium. They haven't seen Silver since she left the building yesterday. Not in the game or in real life."

Kate remembers her earlier trip to the Atrium, but now in her memory it has a glow to it, a promise, irresistible potential.

"They were on high alert there, when I called," says Morgan. "Rushing to fetch everyone out before the grid goes down. Do you understand the implications, Kate, if you're immersed when the power is cut?"

"Yes," says Kate. "No power, no Net. No Net, no way out."

Morgan nods at her, slow and sad.

"Forty-six minutes," says Bernard.

"All right," says Zack, "You've gotta go."

Kate's blood rushes through her veins; there's a lightness in her head. "But I don't know what I'm doing!"

"I'm going to dial you in." Morgan clicks something on his mandible and talks softly to it. "Going through."

Kate grabs Zack's hand.

"You've got the greatest chance of finding her. She came from you."

"But I don't even know how to—"

And just like that, Kate's body goes limp. Her consciousness is sucked out of her flesh and bone and transported through a rushing-light fibre-optic tunnel (BrightCandy Canal) and the ether goes cold and dark around her.

MEZZANINE PUZZLE

81

Kate's consciousness is rushing and rushing as if she is being teleported through space and time and her heart is going mad in her chest—even though, looking down, she doesn't have a chest (or a heart, for that matter)—until she reaches some kind of plateau where it feels as if she's standing on top of a skyscraper, and then she tumbles—her soul tumbles—back down and into her body. It's a soft landing, and it smells of rosemary blooms and bright moss.

A version of her body, anyway, where neither of her arms is broken and her scalp is untouched. She stands up, dusts herself off. She can feel it's not her real body: can feel that she's not really standing. It's like being in a super-realistic dream. How long has it taken her to get here? There's no way to tell. All she can do is find Silver and get her out as soon as she can.

Kate's standing in an overgrown garden, rampant with new buds and tangled vines. Warm, humid air streams into her shocked lungs. No roses in sight, thank the Net. She's never felt comfortable with them since what happened at the Luminary. The thorns always remind her of Bongi's betrayal, of Mally's almost-fatal injury at the hands of Lumin, and it paints her heart cold black. The plants here have the opposite effect: the promise and innocence of bursting blooms; the scent of citrus leaf and Penny Royal and apple blossoms form a soft invisible lattice, lifting Kate's spirit. As she is lifted, she sees where she is.

The Atrium looms large, glowing in the fading light. Kate makes her way through the creeping jungle, almost expecting the tendrils to snake up and around an ankle, keeping her back, not to consume her, but to protect her from the danger ahead.

Kate's relieved. She had pictured being delivered into some low-oxygen cosmos where she'd have no idea how to find Silver, but this is easy; she knows exactly where to go.

Kate runs towards the Atrium. She rushes through the entrance, expecting to see the regulars jacked in at their pods, but the place is deserted. The whole floor looks disused, as if everyone left in a hurry and a dust-storm has swirled through. Kate climbs the stairs to Silver's level, but before she gets there she knows it will be barren too. And indeed, Silver's spot is as empty as the others'.

'Ghost' it says on the outside of her booth, 'GK', and Kate shudders.

"Hello?" Kate's voice bounces off the glass walls.

Silver must be close. Why else would Kate be here? She trawls through the abandoned building, thinking, looking for a clue. She remembers being here earlier and talking about the basement. Wonders how Keke is. Kate's loath to go down there—still spooked by what happened at SkyRest—but she doesn't have a choice. Once she's decided, it's easier, and she makes her way past the stained mugs, half-eaten fauxburgers and forgotten lockets of snaffeine. She pockets a red lanyard she finds with an Atrium chipcard attached to it. The 4D mugshot is of the man she met here previously. She doesn't remember his name, just the scent of his perfumed shirt: amber, pepperwood, juniper berry.

As Kate descends to the basement the levels get darker. The dust is so thick here it's like sand. Where does it all come from? She looks at the cracked windows and the vines that wind themselves around them and anything else in their path. Left to their own devices Kate is sure the jungle would consume the Atrium altogether. She follows the darkness down.

"Hello?" Kate calls. No answer, and no echo this time, either.

She reaches the basement door with the 'off limits' sign, holds up the chipcard and it clicks from red to green, just like she knew it would. This isn't real life. Not a game, not quite, but somewhere in between: a mezzanine puzzle. She'll take advantage of her virgin clover while it lasts. The heavy door swings open.

HOT IN HER POCKET

82

In the Atrium underground, the only light is the warm buzzing coming from the occasional levitating lightbulb Kate passes. There are doors everywhere. How will she know which one is right? She walks along, minding her step, trying not to stumble on the mounds of sand that cover the ground. The sand is her reminder that this is not real, that her real body is passed out in the OR under the watchful eye of Morgan and Zack. Where is Seth? Being underground again makes her nerves fizz with the recent trauma of the SkyRest crim colony. Deep breaths of the musty, cool air keep her calm, or calm enough. It'll take her hours, days, to check out all these private immersion rooms; hopefully she'll strike it lucky.

The first door Kate opens leads to a dark, sound-proofed room, with a VXR shell in the centre. One of many identical spaces, she guesses. She steps inside the capsule and reaches for her mandible but remembers now that she's meshed, she doesn't need one anymore. Kate brings up the interface just by thinking about it, and blinks 'go'.

She's immediately transported to a dim, overcrowded, high-ceilinged hall of shouting creeps, mostly brawny men with popping veins, but some women too. Their skin is slick with sweat and oil, and the sour smell of body odour and liquor hovers like a low cloud. The woman next to Kate is shouting and pumping her fist in the air. Her dark lipstick is smudged; perspiration glints from her eyebrows. The navy scent of danger perfumes the air. Kate moves forward a little, trying to glimpse what they're all shouting about, and then she sees the boxing ring in the centre. Batcam drones flap and squeal above the elevated stage, recording the action.

Two men are up on the platform, but they're not boxers. The man with a peroxided box-cut and emerald silk shorts slams his opponent—a man in red with a metal mouth—against the corner pillar then smashes his fist into his jaw with such force that it riles the crowd up even more. Metal teeth scatter like spent bullets onto the platform and into the crowd, and they cheer.

"Finish him!"

Kate tries to turn around so she can leave, but heaving bodies are pressed against her now, and they're not letting her through.

It's a simulation, Kate tells herself, *it's a simulation. Keep calm.*

These are all real people. They may not physically be in the room with her but they're all real somewhere, just like she is. The thought makes her feel sick.

The box-cut drives his fist into the man's stomach now, causing him to double over, and when he does so, the attacker knees him hard in the face, forcing him back again. He pins his opponent against the pillar and lays into him so viciously his eyes close and he slides to the floor.

This isn't an ordinary fight club. It's some kind of death match. The audience screams and spits and gesticulates. "Kill him!"

The man in the green shorts starts yelling and kicking his opponent's unconscious body. He kicks him as hard as he can, shouting for the coward to get up and fight. The crowd boos the half-dead man for not rising to the occasion. Kate tries to leave, but the crowd's noise and the flashing of the batcams interfere with her vision, and she can't call up her interface to escape. Finally the fighter's eyes open and he gets up on one elbow, and the box-cut jumps on him, smashing his head onto the stage's white tarp.

"Finish him!"

Someone throws a knife into the ring. Without hesitating, the man in green grabs the knife and drives it with both hands into the neck of his opponent, and the crowd goes mental. There's a jet of blood, a slow-motion arc of red mist that spray-paints the tarp. The killer stabs him again and again to the cheering, and just when Kate thinks the fight is over, the man who seems to be lying dead on the floor reaches up and grabs the box-cut and throws him a metre into the air. He roars and pulls the knife out and uses it to hack at the box-cut, who is now screaming and slipping in the crimson spill. The graphic violence shocks Kate, but it's the colour of the box-cut's blood that spins her head. The fluid that dribbles out of his fresh gashes is apple green. It forms its own splashes and smears on the tarp, which is beginning to look like a Jackson Pollock canvas. Kate tries to look away but the shrieking batdrone footage is projected everywhere. It's impossible to not look.

Red shorts hacks at the box-cut until his arm comes away from his torso and he throws the limb into the hungry crowd, then he starts sawing the man's neck. The green-blooded man gasps and gurgles as the tendons in his neck spring apart.

Knowing that they are robots doesn't make it any easier to watch. Kate's been pushed to the front now, and she doesn't know how to get back to the Atrium. The box-cut is dismembered, bit by bit, and fed to the baying crowd. Once there is nothing left of him, the remaining fighter throws up his arms and yells in manic victory, and the noise in the hall becomes deafening. In his excited state, the man drops the knife and it goes scudding across the platform with just enough momentum to drop off the stage, right in front of Kate. Without hesitating—without thinking, really—she quickly picks it up and slips it into her coat pocket. Her hand comes away sticky with green blood (Robo Sap).

The winner is carried away while some feral-looking young kids—rat hunters—loosen the tarp at its corners, taking care to not step on the still-wet artwork, and clip one side of it to a rod, which is then lifted on a pulley system, displaying the painting for everyone to see. The creeps cheer and cheer, and then the auction begins. The street urchins disappear into the crowd: they move along by crawling along the floor, where there is more space to manoeuvre, and no doubt pick a few pockets on their way. Kate won't judge them, her own plunder glowing hot in her pocket. Copying them, she goes down on her hands and knees and pushes her way out. Glass shards lacerate her palms, and some careless boots and heels find her head and back, but she just puts her head down and moves as fast as she can. Eventually Kate reaches the edge of the room and cooler air, and she covers her ears and calls up her dashboard. This time it works, and she blinks 'escape'. When her eyes open again she's sitting, with tight lungs, in the VXR shell. She leans back for a moment to appreciate the solitary cool, dim room, and when she opens her white fists they are clean and injury free.

DOOMSDAY DEBRIS

83

Fourways

Johannesburg, 2036

Seth is on his way to the Lipworth Foundation. Despite the clusterfuck that is the current satellite situation he somehow manages to receive the occasional bullet from Arronax. Mally is safe, they're together, and they're heading to the Lipworth. More than that: He knows exactly where in the building they'll be, and he has the code to get in. There's a specific room he and Arronax use there for their meetings. She hates hotels and feels uncomfortable in his apartment, so the safe room at the Lipworth is perfect for what Arronax has taken to calling her 'layovers'.

There's the tastefully decorated office she gets to use when she's in Jozi to consult, and the safe room is *en suite*. That's where they usually end up, on the floor or up against the wall. Sex with Arronax never disappoints.

Seth walks along the city street, dodging broken bottles, burning cars and litter bunting. There's a feeling of wildness, of savagery. Seth reaches back and his fingers play on the automatic rifle he snatched from SkyRest. Jozi isn't the prettiest or the safest place to be right now, but it's better than being in that surreal, subterranean prison with the building weighing down on your every pore. He is still creeped out by it, as if he needs a sonic shower and memory detox to get those damn scuttling, biting beetles out of his head. Seth had searched and searched for Kate, but had just become more lost. Eventually he'd found the staircase again, and couldn't resist climbing up and out, into the open air. He had to trust Kate found her way out too. His intuition was telling him she was no longer underground, and he had to trust it. They've always had an eerie sense of connection: those first milk years in Durban, followed by the gaping absence of each other, growing up. And now that they've been living together for sixteen years it's as if they're joined at the hip, telepathically speaking. This doesn't mean they always agree. They drive each other insane sometimes. Seth knows his twin sister better than he knows himself, knows how strong she is. She would have found her way out. All he can do is hope he's not wrong.

Even the solartrams have stopped working now, despite their promise of 24/7/365. It's always a problem, thinks

Seth absent-mindedly, when companies use numbers as slogans. Numbers are steady, stable, incontrovertible. There are no terms and conditions attached; they are not punctuated by spinning asterisks. Not that it matters now. Not that anything matters anymore.

A naked woman streaked with dirt ambles along the pavement towards him. Blood on her cheek, non-seeing eyes. Seth can't tell if she's human or droid. He skips out of her path. He's five minutes away from the Lipworth, and he needs to keep going.

Seth coughs into his face-mask. He blames the toxic-smelling smoke in the air. He's had this irritating niggle in his chest since leaving SkyRest, like an itch in his lungs he can't scratch.

There's a wolf-whistle from across the road. A flaming car passes in slow motion. The wolf-whistle again, this time louder. Despite his instinct telling him to keep walking, he looks around. He can't help it. Monochrome cityscape and interactive street art. The rolling, burning car. Then he sees the man, a barbarian with a tank for a body, and he's not alone. It's a group of them—five? Six apoca-pirates—and they're leering and passing around a bottle. The whistler holds a dirty timber baseball bat over his massive shoulders. It's studded with nails and shards of glass. Doomsday Debris.

The gang begins to cross the road, clearly headed in the direction of the naked woman. They whistle and catcall and call her a 'pretty bitch'.

Keep walking, Seth tells himself. *Keep fucking walking.*

"What you doin'?" asks the biggest man, adjusting his pace to walk alongside her. He has rocky shoulders and a black vest that says 'Fuck Robots'. The woman doesn't answer him. Seth doesn't even think she hears him, considering the state she's in. Seth forces himself to ignore the situation and keep walking. He's almost there.

"Hey!" shouts the barbarian right into the woman's face. "Answer me when I speak to you, bitch!"

Seth slows down, his shoulders sag. He was so close to getting to safety.

"Larry asked you a fucking question," says one of the men, slapping her on her back. "Have some fucking respect."

Another man throws a crushed can at her, and it glances off her temple, opening up a dribble of new blood. Seth's fury heats his stomach; his veins pulse. He is so goddamned sick of these entitled sadobastards.

"You know what I think, Larry?" says a woman—there's a woman in the gang too. "I think she wants to suck your cock."

The men laugh and make animal sounds: grunting; licking; laughing. Dirty tongues wagging. Seth's hands turn into fists.

"Slow down now, missus. Where are you going in such a hurry?"

The barbarian with the baseball bat takes her hand. If Seth didn't know better it would look like a loving gesture, but when she resists, tries to keep walking, he yanks her arm so hard it swipes her whole body sideways.

"I said slow down!" Larry shouts, and now that Seth is closer, he sees the man's saliva fleck her face, and she betrays her consciousness by flinching.

Seth still can't tell if she's human. Does it even matter? He used to think it did.

"Leave her alone," says Seth, but the gang is so busy heckling and taunting the woman they don't even notice him. He pulls the automatic rifle up and out of the makeshift holster on his back.

"Leave her alone!" he shouts.

The rifle is a powerhouse. Branded—appropriately—with the SkyRest logo, loaded with frangible bullets designed for maximum surface damage. That's code for maximum pain. Designed to injure instantly, intensely, without the lethality of hollow points. Perfect for keeping prisoners on their best behaviour—perfect for trigger-happy guards who aren't allowed to kill their charges but who like the feel of a large automatic weapon in their hands.

"Who the fuck are you?" says Larry, twirling his bespoke bat.

"Get lost," says one of his henchmen. "Does she belong to you?"

"She doesn't belong to anyone. She doesn't have to. Step

away from her right now," says Seth, the weapon thrumming with potential in his hands.

"The fuck is that thing?"

The naked woman tries to slip away, but Larry catches her wrist.

"You don't want to find out," says Seth. "Leave now and you won't have to."

The barbarian smiles. "Is that right?" He hands the woman to the pack and addresses Seth squarely, runs his hand over the nail- and glass-studded bat and squeezes, puncturing his own palm, and the blood begins to run. If he feels pain, it doesn't register on his face. He's even bigger than he looked before.

Seth feels strangely calm. This might be the end, but, looking around at the air, thick with pollution, the immutable damage, the quick-breeding fires, the sorry excuses for humankind right in front of him, he feels at peace with the idea of dying. This world is broken. It's been broken for a long time. Sure, he was used to some kind of privileged existence, binge-watching series streams in his air-filtered, temperature-regulated, drone-delivered-processed-food-on-demand apartment, but that is no way to live. It's not really living, at all.

His survival instinct is still strong, but his fear of death swirls up and away into the electrosmog that surrounds him.

"I'm going to ask you one more time to keep walking," says Seth, lifting the gun so he can look through the sight.

He softens his shoulder where he's expecting the impact from the butt. There's that annoying tickle in his lungs, so he coughs hard to try clear it before taking aim. It's changing from a tickle to a sharp prickling sensation: more pain that itch.

One of the men starts touching the woman. His filthy, callused hands trail over the distressed woman's stomach, then over her hip to squeeze her butt. His nails are outlined in grime. Another man begins to approach Seth, and he trains the rifle on him. The man gets closer. Deciding against a second warning, Seth pulls the trigger.

Three frangibles rocket out of the weapon, and all of them connect with the greasy man: face, chest, thigh. Designed to come apart as soon as they leave the barrel, the bullets separate into a spiralling core and three sharp petals. The lead alloy blooms in the air, as if breathing, then embeds itself in the flesh of the target.

The man roars, confused as to why there is so much pain, like a rolling flame over his body, and tries to pull out the strange bullet that has bitten into his cheek. This causes more damage and he shouts again. His other wounds bleed oily black through his dark clothes. Angry, he wants to swipe at Seth, but his limbs are contracting with the pain, and he lands on the tar. While watching him writhe, Larry advances, lifting his bat, preparing to swing. The woman with the denim-dyed hair flanks him, her spiked knuckleduster glinting in the afternoon light. Seth fires at the barbarian and gets him in the chest and stomach. Larry doesn't acknowledge the bullets at all; he just keeps coming.

Seth realises the man doesn't feel pain, and he has to rely on his agility alone as the bat comes rushing for his head. He sidesteps Larry and manages to shoot two of the others as they advance. They roll away in pain. The bat comes for Seth again, and he gets out of its way just in time. There's a sudden sharp pain in his lower back, and a wet sensation. Seth turns around to see that the woman has slashed him with her spikes. Before he can respond, she punches him in the stomach with them. It's like being stabbed four times at once, and he shouts in surprise, looking into her dilated irises as the consequences sink in. Satisfied, she pulls them out, and it feels as if she's taking his organs with her. Then there's a loud thump and all the air is knocked out of Seth's lungs. The tarmac scrapes his face. He can feel the bleeding where he's been struck across the back with the bat, and where he's been stabbed in front. A pair of boots walks up, and before he can raise his arms to protect himself, they kick him in the face. It's the loudest thing he's ever heard.

The naked woman stares at him, as if she's thinking.

The bat comes for him again, and takes out his left knee. Seth rocks and shouts in pain, coughs up some blood. There are five of them now, surrounding him—a circle of tormentors. They're all in the sky, and he's eating dirt. They discuss among themselves what they should do with him, if there's any more fun to be had before he flatlines.

"You know what?" says the barbarian. "I feel like watching a show."

BRAIN BLEACH

84

Kate stumbles out into the corridor with its gentle, stuttering light and examines the doors. She's already seen too much violence in her life, too much pain. She's going to have to summon up all the courage she has to open another door, never mind the number of doors needed to find Silver. And, when all of this is over, she promises herself, she'll go in to a nice padded room somewhere in the mountains. One of those places that remove unwanted memories and lets you download happy ones in their place. Brain Bleach, the dubsters call it.

There must be more than twenty identical doors here. Kate walks down the passage, trying to get a feel for which one could be the right one. She calls up her interface again, and now that it's on, when she looks at a door, a green holotag comes up.

DNA CASINO WITH TOPLESS BARSTAFF, says the one she's standing near. She keeps moving down the passage.

PLASTIC SURGERY PRACTICE IN VIVO XXX-HOT MODELS

ROMAN FEAST (WITH LIVE ORTOLAN) AND SODO-ORGY

BDSMXV SEX DUNGEON X-GRAPHIC DUBCON & OFF-LABEL BE WARNED 21+

Kate steps back, to see which one she's already visited.

ROBO DEATH MATCH ART CIRCUIT AUCTION

She keeps walking, reading the green tags on the doors as she goes. When she finds a red holotag, she stops. Does that mean the room is not vacant? It doesn't say what the immersion's theme is. She puts her hand on the doorknob.

Metallic, cold. Canary-coloured adrenaline kicks her in the head. Kate takes a deep breath and opens the door.

HANSEL & GRETEL

85

White Mezzanine, 2036

It's not a door but some kind of portal to another place altogether, because now she's standing in a white passage and it's clean and beautiful and there's light everywhere.

Yes! I've reached the next level. But then she's immediately worried. Has she really reached the next level? Is she closer to finding Silver now? Or has she done something wrong and she's back at the Lipworth Foundation?

It's all the white that's bothering her. This is what the Lipworth looks like, but then she interrogates the setting further: She kicks a wall and it doesn't hurt. She runs down the corridor and she's so full of energy and stamina she feels as if she can run all day. Indeed, she'd have to, because it looks like an infinity corridor with no beginning and no end. There are strips of mirrors, too, silver reflecting white. She stops in front of one, inspects herself.

Kate has her mane of red hair, slick-styled and shiny, and her scalp is uncut. There's no more pain. Her wrinkles are gone, her eyes have a cosmic sparkle. She lifts her damaged arm to see she has full mobility, and it no longer hurts at all. Not only that, but she's wearing some kind of body-hugging superhero catsuit in ombre orange. The colour pops against the white and it's as if it's feeding her body energy, like when you lace up your runners tightly and it makes you want to sprint. She can't stand still; she needs to move. Needs to hurry. She moves away from the mirror, sees entrances to more passages, all identical.

"Silver?" Kate knows she has to find some way to step up. What is she missing? "Silver?"

The dark orange. Her brain is trying to tell her something, but she's removed from her clear, real-life thinking. It's like there's a filter on her thoughts down here—up here?—wherever she is, and she can't grab on to the nagging idea that's trying to present itself.

Think!

The burnt orange is *deja vu*, right? So what is familiar about this moment? It's the white corridor.

Lipworth. We've been through this already.

But, no, it's not that. The memory isn't of the Lipworth Foundation. It's a lot deeper than that. Further away, but more entrenched.

Of course, when she's got it. Of course. It's so obvious. It's the white interior of the Genesis Project headquarters—also subterranean, also bright white. But what does it mean? Then she thinks of fairytales: of Silver stuck in her sleeping body like Snow White. Of the thorny rose maze of the Luminary. Of the one she knows best, the one she lived through, herself, and still has the book James gave her: Hansel and Gretel. Kate and Sam. Toaster waffle roof tiles. She thinks of the breadcrumb trail of scuffmarks that had led her out of Genesis and saved her life, and looks down at the floor. Kate doesn't notice anything but white, but then she squats and sees them. Tiny multicoloured dots. It's weird because they're not part of the floor, not really. It's like her neural lace is projecting her synaesthesia onto the floor, as if she feels lost but something in her brain knows the way.

Kate follows the pixels for a while and, just as she begins to second-guess her fairytale theory, the breadcrumbs veer left, and after a while they lead her sharp right, and then something tells her she's close and she calls: "Silver?"

Kate hears someone's voice and stops in her tracks. Someone is there.

Silver?

"Mom?"

"Silver! I'm coming!" Kate runs towards the voice but there's just white mist everywhere, and she can't see where she's going. She trips on air, somersaults and falls, but it doesn't hurt. She doesn't feel anything but relief as she scrambles up again to follow the sound of her daughter's voice.

"Mom!" shouts Silver, and there she is, on the other side of some kind of thin white membrane, a biolatex film. Kate can see the outline of her hands and elbows as she pushes through the screen. She starts pushing too, tries to tear the elastic with her nails, her teeth. It tastes like the rubber of soft-pop balloons. Kate thinks of the Gordhan, of Mally in a body cast, of Solonne.

"Can you cut it?" asks Silver.

"Cut it? With what?"

"Don't you have anything?"

"What do you mean? No."

"Look at your weapons."

"Silver," Kate says, touching her forehead against the screen. She wants to say: *my silly girl. I didn't bring any weapons.*

"Look down, Mom. Look at your utility belt."

And she's going to say *I don't have a utility belt,* but then she looks down and she does have one. It's the knife she picked up at the death match, which she pulls out of its sheath and stares at. A thought nags at her: *this is all too easy*. Finding the Atrium, finding the chipcard, then the knife, the portal, the breadcrumbs, and now, finding her daughter. But she doesn't have time to waste so she ignores the idea and goes with her good fortune. Maybe it's her virgin clover. Maybe it's something else.

"Stand back," Kate says as she slices through the white.

CAR CARCASS

86

Innercity

Johannesburg, 2036

The gang hauls Seth up and strips his clothes off with a hunting knife.

"You're going to do it," says the barbarian with the bat.

"Do what?" asks Seth, but he already knows the answer.

Two of the gang members push the naked woman face forward over the bonnet of a burnt-out car carcass and spread her legs with coarse hands. The front of her body is stamped with the dark residue of the vehicle: white and black; negative, positive. She doesn't resist, and they step back, dust their hands, and put away their weapons. The nunchux are clipped away, the hunting knife goes back into its sheath. One of the men makes lewd gestures over his own junk while another pushes Seth's broken body towards the woman.

"I can't," Seth says, coughing and gesturing at his dripping wounds.

The woman licks Seth's blood off her spiked knuckleduster. "I can help you with that."

The men snigger. One of them has picked up the automatic rifle Seth dropped. He aims it at Seth and motions with its nose for him to obey the instruction. Larry looks on, amused, bat hanging at his side. Seth limps as slowly as possible towards the splayed woman, trying to buy time to think. Every step on his shattered knee sends an arrow of pain up his body, and he's coughing up what looks like bits of raw kidney. When he gets to the woman, he gingerly levers himself over her. She recoils beneath him.

"I won't hurt you," Seth whispers.

His blood trickles on her. One of the men throws a broken bottle at him. "That isn't how you do it!" and the rest of the gang laughs.

"Hurry up, you cunt," says the denim-haired knuckleduster. "We're waiting for our show."

Seth's earlier thought, before he was stabbed, was to run; he was sure he could outrun them. Now every step is agony, and they're bristling with weapons, including his.

I was so close. He thinks of his family, and of Keke. Always of Keke. He knows he should have told her years ago how he felt about her, but it was never the right time. She's in love with Marko, despite his insane decision to leave her.

He pictures Kate, his better half, his puzzle piece. The kids. God! To see them one more time.

The woman beneath him shifts slightly, bringing him back. She's saying something under her breath. He can't hear her.

"What?" he whispers into her neck, hiding his lips from the enemy.

"That's more like it," says the barbarian. "Let's see some action."

Another piece of debris comes flying at them. It bounces off Seth's shoulder.

"What did you say?"

The man with the SkyRest gun aims it at Seth.

The woman whispers, "I said get ready to get down."

"What?"

"On the count of three."

Seth couldn't be more confused.

"One," she says. "Two. Three."

Seth hits the deck, and the woman spins around and releases her roscoe. The smart steel barrel of the gun pops out of her forearm and she fires round after round into the yelling gang members, flattening them with its firepower. They're all cut down apart from the barbarian, who seems indestructible. He must have ten bullets in him now, but he keeps advancing. The naked woman keeps firing. Seth can taste the gunpowder. He leopard crawls to where the freshly dead bodies lie and wrenches the hunting knife from the man's holster. Larry reaches the woman and starts to throttle her. She's out of bullets. Seth crawls quickly towards the savage and slices through both of his heel's tendons. He may not be able to feel pain, but he won't be able to walk without his achilles. Seth expects to see yellow cartilage and bone, but instead is shocked by a flash of silver titanium before the blood washes over it.

The robot barbarian falls down, slamming the woman down with him, and Seth lurches in his direction, knife raised, ready to slit his throat.

The woman tries to stop him. "He can't hurt us now," she says.

"I don't care," says Seth, severing the head from the barrel-chested body.

They pick a few garments off the still-warm dead bodies. The clothes have an evil stink. The femmebot pulls on a pair of dark jeans. Her carbon-dusted breasts are still bare. Seth retrieves his gun, and gives the bat to her.

"Bye," he says, and starts limping away. He can only shuffle along, anything quicker and the pain stops him in his tracks. He's still bleeding from the spike-holes in his stomach.

"Let me help you," she says. Her ribcage drawer slides open.

"I don't have time. I need to go." He coughs up more clots and spits them out on to the hot tarmac.

"You won't get anywhere in that state."

"I will, or I'll die trying."

"Wait," she says, touching his arm. "Take this. I don't have anything else left in my medikit." She hands him an inhaler. Pexidine. Seth unscrews it and gives himself a large dose of the painkiller in each nostril, then pockets the bottle.

"Thanks."

"I can't do anything about your knee," she says. "My scanner surmises that your tibia is shattered and the patellar tendon is shredded, presumably by the splintered bone. You'll need surgery."

"That sounds about right," he says, grimacing from the jolting pain he feels every time he puts his weight on it.

"But that's not your biggest concern," she says.

Seth looks at her.

"You have severe internal bleeding in your lungs. As

things stand, I can't tell if you'll die from the blood loss or the oxygen deprivation. Both seem just as likely."

"Wow," says Seth, lungs gurgling. "Don't sugarcoat it."

"I'm sorry," she says. "Is there a way to sugarcoat death?"

"Ha," he says. "Good point."

The bot closes her drawer, and skin there is almost seamless. She props him up with a steel shoulder and helps him walk.

"I'll help you to where you're going," she says. "But I can't stay. I have something I need to do."

"Thank you," Seth says. "Do you want to put a shirt on?"

"Do you want me to put a shirt on?"

Seth shrugs, and they stagger together towards the Lipworth Foundation.

FORCE QUIT

87

White Mezzanine, 2036

Kate and Silver fall into each other with yelps of relief. Silver's body is bird-boned and brittle, and it makes Kate want to keep holding her. It feels so real Kate can even smell Silver's signature scent: white apple flesh, rum and sage. She wonders how long it's been since they hugged like this. Not since Silver was small, she's sure. As a toddler, Silver would steal into her room at night and slip into her bed. Mally would do it too, of course. Sometimes they'd even climb into each other's beds and she'd find them snoring sweetly together in their twin pyjamasuits. She had read something about how you shouldn't let your small kids come to your bed at night, how becoming dependent on a parent to fall back to sleep would give them insomnia issues for life.

They need to learn to self-soothe, Kate used to tell herself as she carried the small bodies back to their KidKocoons. A stab of guilt when they'd cry in their sleep that they wanted their mama, and there she was, alone and lonely in her own bed; and a stab of guilt when she'd let them stay cuddled up to her, their imagined future insomnia fuelling hers.

Of course, after Lumin she couldn't give a toss who wrote what in which parenting stream. If the twins padded through to her bed during the night, she'd pull their little bodies as close to hers as they'd let her and they'd sleep with tangled limbs, breathing each other in all night.

Silver's the first to let go, and this breaks Kate's reverie. What is this place? It looks like an executive hospital room, but the periphery is wavy, as if the VXR designer didn't finish the full render. Kate picks up the plate of nutrijelly cubes for a closer look when Silver smacks the dish out of her hand. It clatters and vibrates on the tiles, the jelly-like blocks of soft lego on the floor, reminding Kate again of a simpler time. She moves to clean it up.

"Don't!" Silver's eyes are wide.

"I was just going to ask you what it was."

"Don't even touch it, and don't eat or drink anything while you're here."

"What is this place?" asks Kate.

"I don't know."

"We need to get out right now," says Kate. "They're shutting down the grid."

"I'm ready," says Silver. Pale, brave.

"How do we do it?"

Silver bites her lip. "You really don't know?"

"No."

"Zack didn't tell you?"

"For Net's sake, Silver—"

"He didn't tell you what we need to do?"

"All he said was, it would be good practice."

"What?"

"It would be good practice. I don't know what that means. We were rushing—*are rushing*—to get you out in time."

"I don't think you would have agreed to come if you knew—"

"Of course I would have!" Kate takes her shoulders. "I'd do anything for you. Don't you know that?" Her sinuses sting with new tears.

"But—"

"Just tell me."

Silver blinks away her own tears. "This isn't going to work."

"We'll make it work!"

Kate feels the time ticking away, and her mind is awash with blue watercolour: aquamarine exasperation. "You kept asking for Zack. How do you know him?"

"He comes to me in my dreams."

"You have dreams in here?"

"Only of him."

"He came to you in your dreams and told you how to get out of here?"

"I've always known how to get out. It's the same as my games."

Kate frowns. "Then why are you still here?"

"Because it's not working. It's like this place is some weird limbo that you can't—"

Silver's lost for words. Anxiety climbing, Kate motions for her to continue.

"—but then Zack told me that you'd be able to do it. That it would work if *you* did it. That he'd send you. And he did."

Kate feels like shaking some of the urgency she feels into Silver. It's time to go.

"In order to leave a game or an immersion when you're still alive, you usually just say 'escape', right? Or blink the 'quit' button," says Silver.

Kate nods. She thinks she may have known that.

"But sometimes it doesn't work. Not often, but sometimes. Like, if the software hangs or there's some kind of update blitz or whatever."

"Right."

"Then you have to force quit."

"Right."

"But this place ... blocks your interface, blocks the voice commands. So you can't force quit the regular way. You need to ... action it."

"Okay," says Kate. "How do you action it?"

Silver looks at her. Electric eyes. Then Kate understands.

"Oh."

"It gets a little more complicated," says Silver.

"Tell me."

"Ever since I started playing RPG with Seth when I was little ..."

"You've always been so good at the games. He was always saying so."

"But it's more than that. It's more than my skill set. It's that ... I realised that I couldn't die."

The understanding begins to snow down on Kate in large indigo flakes.

"No matter what. No matter which war I fight in, which bridge I jump off, I stay alive."

"That's why they call you 'Ghost'," says Kate. "Because you never die."

"It's always been a gift," says Silver. "My secret weapon."

"Until now."

"I tried to force quit here. I cut my wrists in the bath."

Silver shows her pale arms to Kate. The skin is flawless.

"When I woke up I was washed clean and back in bed."

Kate's heart swells in empathy. "I'm sorry you had to go through that. Especially on your own."

"I'm starving myself—" She plucks at her loose gown. "—but it's not working."

Silver seems manic now. She opens a cupboard door and grabs her jacket, throws it on the bed, starts pulling at the copper buttons.

"What are you doing?"

Silver extricates a pill from inside the hollow button at the collar, then moves down to the next one, and the next, till she has a pile of capsules.

"I've been saving up pain pills. Hiding them. I have over fifty, now."

"You were planning to take them all at once?"

"But it won't work. I realised after the bath. It won't work."

"What I don't understand is how I can help. If you can't die, then what can I do?"

Silver picks up the dagger Kate dropped when they first embraced, and hands it to her, handle first. She closes Kate's confused fingers over it. Kate looks down at it. The knife is brassy and intricate; a dragon with pearlescent eyes has been engraved into the metal. Its tail whips out the end of the handle and back to its mouth, forming a scaled loop.

"You know what Uncle Marko always used to say."

"What?"

"That there's always a hack for everything."

"That's probably true."

"Mom," says Silver. "You're my hack."

SMOKE & SHIMMER

88

The Lipworth Foundation

Johannesburg, 2036

"Come on, Kate," says Zack, searching her face for clues. "Come on. You're running out of time."

Mally bursts through the operating room swing-doors and sees both his sister and his mother lying unconscious on the clinic beds. He freezes.

"What the fuck are you doing to them?"

"Take it easy, Mally," says the DarkDoc, his palm pleading patience. "We're helping them."

Arronax and Vega enter the room too, then Keke limps in.

"Zack!" Keke says, eyes sparkling despite her obvious pain.

Zack looks up and smiles at her. "Keke."

Arronax looks at the bodies. "We've got to move them."

"We can't," says Morgan. "Not till they emerge. Too risky."

"We have to."

"What if there's some kind of break in connection? It's better to wait."

"Listen to me," says Arronax. "The world outside is mayhem, and it's ramping up."

"There are people after us," says Mally, thinking of Govender and those whom he has no doubt told about Arronax. "It's just a matter of time before they find us."

"Which people?" asks Zack.

"Bot Hunters."

"Because of me," says Vega.

"Not because of you," says Mally. "Because they're mouth-breathing meatbags who have less intelligence in their whole body than you have in your little finger."

"I killed a human," says Vega.

Keke stares. "What?"

"It was self-defence," says Mally. "Vega saved my life, but now they want her RTS-ed."

Zack blinks and shakes his head. Despite his inherent knowledge of where he originally comes from, a lot of this strange 2036 world is new to him.

"Return To Sender," says Morgan. "The Special Task force has been briefed to round up all the roguebots. The problem is, you can't tell if an android is corrupt just by looking at them, so now they're just arresting indiscriminately."

"If they focussed on the Bot Hunters instead, things would be better."

"Mally," says Morgan, gently, "I don't think you realise the gravity of the situation. The special police—"

"I do realise! I'm not a child! But if—"

"The V1R1S is spreading quicker than any pandemic in history. They're saying it's got an infection rate of one thousand. One thousand! Do you know what that means? For every one robot with the disorder they will infect another thousand." The DarkDoc's face is ashen, as if he, too, didn't understand the implications of the V1R1S until he spoke it out loud. It's all happened so quickly.

Arronnax moves towards the exterior glass wall, looks

down at the city they have just traversed. Fires smoke and shimmer. Apoca-pirates throw rocks at storefronts and grab jewellery they'll never need. Roguebots and alt-tech nazis clash in the streets with vektors and tasers and roscoes and hand-to-hand combat. She watches as a few city cowboys look up at the building and decide to enter.

"We all need to move to the safe room right now."

"You didn't tell us there was a safe room," says Morgan.

Sounds start emanating from the lower floors: it won't be long till the security has been compromised.

"It's not safe to move them," says Morgan, "but it's not as dangerous as staying in here."

Zack unclamps the break on Silver's gurney, and the DarkDoc takes Kate's. Arronax leads the way.

"I expected Seth to be here by now," says Zack in a low voice. "He needs to be here for it to work."

Bernard grunts in agreement.

"For what to work?" asks Keke.

"Nothing."

Keke whips around to face Zack. "It doesn't sound like nothing."

"I'll re-phrase it. It's nothing for you to worry about."

Keke side-eyes him. "I'm watching you, Zachary Girdler."

"Noted," says Zack.

"I'm not fucking around. I've got my eagle eye on you."

"Damn, I missed you," says Zack.

Their eyes connect for a moment; they keep moving forward.

The steel gurneys rattle down the wide white passage.

SKELETON TURNS TO ICE

89

Arronax receives an emergency email from an anonymous source at NASP. Thinking it's about the security breach at the hands of Govender, she opens it, and immediately regrets her decision. She tries to close it, delete it, but it's too late. Shaking, she switches off her interface. Whoever is hacking her is already boring his way in, and there's no getting him out. He'll find out who she is and what she's done and broadcast it, and it'll be the end of everything for her. Her whole skeleton turns to ice.

DRAGON DAGGER

90

White Mezzanine, 2036

Kate feels the weight of the knife in her hand. "I'm not going to kill you."

"It's the only way," says Silver.

"There must be another way."

"There's not!"

"It's impossible."

"You won't be killing me. You'll be saving me. If you don't do it, I'll be stuck here forever, and you know what? I'd rather die! I'd rather die a hundred times over than be in this place."

At last there's some colour in her cheeks; her eyes are feral.

"Please!" she says. "Please, Mom. I can't do it myself. You have to do it for me."

"You know I can't!" Kate throws the dagger on the bed. "How could I?"

"How could you? Think of me! Think of me in the real word, stuck in my useless body forever."

Kate holds her head as if her cool palms will stop her thoughts from exploding her brain.

This is crazy. This is so crazy. It's all a dream. It must be.

Kate's countdown timer clicks over to nine minutes.

"Nine minutes," says Kate.

Silver scrambles for the dragon dagger, puts it back into Kate's hand.

"We have to do it now. Right now."

"How can I?"

"Straight into my heart. It'll be the quickest."

"I can't!" shouts Kate.

"Stop being so selfish!"

Kate splutters. "What?"

"The reason you can't do it is because you're thinking about yourself! How it will make *you* feel. Not what it will do for me."

Kate stutters.

"Please, Mom. Please. I'm asking you to set me free."

Eight minutes.

Seven and a half minutes.

Kate swallows hard. "Lie on the bed."

Silver sobs in relief and climbs onto the stretcher, eyes stunned wide. Pills scatter to the floor. Silver clasps her hands together over her stomach. Her hair splays: silver thread on the white pillowcase.

"Thank you!" She sobs. "Thank you, Mom."

"Sh-sh-sh," says Kate. "Don't say anything else."

Before I change my mind.

Don't say anything else.

This isn't real life.

I'm not killing her. I'm setting her free.

Still the dagger feels too heavy in her hands.

Seven minutes.

"I'm ready," says Silver. "I love you."

Kate's eyes burn. She swallows again and lifts the dagger using both her hands.

It's not real.

It's a fairytale.

She is the huntsman after Snow White's heart.

"I love you," Kate says, and drives the knife into Silver's chest.

Kate feels the blade penetrating the rib-bone, then with an extra push it gives way. Silver shrills in pain, and Kate lets go of the dagger as if it's shocked her.

Fuck!

She instantly regrets what she's done; she must be insane. Certifiable. To do something as depraved as this. Silver keeps screaming, thrashing on the bed. Blood begins to wick into the white cotton of her gown.

"I'm sorry!" Kate's tears drip down onto the bed. She hadn't even realised she was crying.

What have I done? What the fuck have I done?

Silver's screaming transforms into a low moan, and her writhing slows. She's half-sobbing again, relieved, her eyes alight as if she can see the other side. Her small damaged starfish of a hand searches blindly for Kate's, and they hold onto each other while Silver's chest bleeds and her heart drifts away.

Is she dead?

Silver's image starts deconstructing. Blocks like giant pixels shift and dissolve. Right there on the bed in front of her, as she's holding Silver's hand, she fades away as if she's a computer-generated dandelion blown in the wind. And just like that, the room is empty and Silver is free.

CRIMSON CHEMICAL COPPER

91

Kate's shattered. She needs time to recover, but there is none.

Six minutes.

She calls up her interface but it doesn't work. She tries again.

"Escape," she says. "Escape." She's still there in the white room.

I'm going to be lost inside here forever.

She tries blinking 'force quit' but the button isn't there. Barbed tendrils of adrenaline reach up and unfurl inside her.

Don't panic, she tells herself. *You know what to do. You know how to force quit.*

Kate reaches for the knife so she can open her own veins, but it's gone—disappeared with Silver.

Fu-u-uck!

Desperate, she looks around the room. What did Silver use on her first attempt? Kate spots the mirror and tries to smash it, but it's self-healing mercury glass and just knits itself back together. She casts around, trying to swallow her panic, trying to stay calm so that she can think clearly.

Five minutes.

Then she sees the pills on the porcelain tiles, knocked off the bed in Silver's rush to climb on. Kate falls to her knees and begins to pick them up, starts shoving them in her mouth and looking for water before realising they will never work in time. And Silver said to not eat or drink anything here, anything that could tie her body to this place. She imagines Silver smashing the glass of water out of her hand. Kate spits the bitter blue pills out into her palm. She needs a quicker way, but they are all she has.

Kate thinks of Seth's snaffeine, of Keke's pexidine, knows how quickly and efficiently drugs can work if they're inhaled. She put the mound of pills on the white tiled floor and smashes them under her boot heel, grinds them as quickly as she can into a rocky powder, then snorts the blue talc off the thumb joint of her hand. The first hard sniff is like a sapphire bullet in her brain. The sparks shoot up her nose and detonate. Kate cries out, covers her nose with both hands—a reflex—and gasps in pain. Her eyes stream, her brain chokes.

Holy fuck, what is in *these things?*

Kate can hardly see what she's doing for the second round as the sparks obliterate her vision. She does the best she can to line up the next dose and sniffs again. Another bullet, another explosion. The jerk of pain sends her body reeling backwards.

"A-a-a-h," is all she can say as the drug burns into her brain. It's like eating a fresh birdseye chilli and having brain freeze at the same time, squared, cubed, times a hundred, and in flashing neon blue. But it's working. Kate can feel the synapses begin to shut off, the electrical impulses lose their juice. She has to get all of this in before she passes out. Her heart is slowing already.

Three minutes.

She lines up another shot, then another, then another, till all that's left of the powder is a fine dust on the floor tiles. The last dose is the trickiest, but the least painful, because her whole face is now completely numb. Kate struggles to keep her eyes open as the drugs pull her eyelids down, start dragging her whole body onto the floor, as if gravity is leaking into the room and pushing on every part of her, even her cheek-skin into her skull, even her eyeballs into their sockets.

It's working, she thinks, but then there's a strange fluid sensation at the back of her damaged sinuses and Kate thinks it's her body's way of fighting back, that it's all going to come back out again, and she can feel the pressure build and the next thing there is liquid gushing out of her nose and mouth. She expects it to be snot and saliva but when she forces open her eyes for the last time sees it's blood. It flows out of her and puddles on the tiles. Liquid crimson chemical copper. Then an invisible tidal wave flattens her and she lies spreadeagled on the floor, waiting for oblivion. She doesn't see the clock tick down to 00:00.

BLOOD HANDKERCHIEF

92

The Lipworth Foundation

Johannesburg, 2036

The door to Arronax's office stands ajar. Arronax hesitates outside. Has the power already been cut? Is it too late for Silver and Kate? She tentatively pushes open the door.

Seth is sitting inside the room. He looks up at her, relief washing down his face. The door to the adjoining safe room is closed and a small red light flashes.

Arronax is about to run to hug him but stops when she sees his state. Seth's body is perforated, his knee is swollen to twice its normal size, and he's holding a piece of cloth in his hand, stained red. A blood handkerchief.

"What… Are you okay?"

"Define 'okay'," he says, coughing.

"Why is the safe room closed?" she asks.

"I don't know, I tried my code but it's not working."

Arronax tries to unlock the safe room door with her retina but it doesn't work. She punches in a code manually but it stays locked and the red light keeps flashing.

"Is Kate here?"

Arronax doesn't have to answer, because from behind her hurry in Zack, Bernard, the DarkDoc, Keke, Mally and Vega, and they're pushing two gurneys between them. He shoots up, grimacing when he sees it's Kate and Silver on the beds.

Arronax notices how Seth looks at Keke. Relief that she's alive, but that's not all.

Mally hugs Seth.

"What the hell happened?"

"The power's still on?" asks Zack. No one answers; they don't need to. The lights are on. The power has not yet been cut. They still have some time: minutes, maybe seconds. The clock reads 13:58.

"Come on, Kate," says Keke, holding on to the bed rails. "Come back to us."

Kate's face is pale and without expression.

Silver starts gasping, and they all crowd around her.

"What is it?" asks Seth, his eyes mad. "What's happening to her?"

Morgan takes Seth by the shoulder and leads him to a chair. "You need to sit down. You look like you're about to pass out."

Seth shakes him off. "Just tell me what the fuck is going on. What did you do to them?"

Silver gasps for air as if she is drowning.

"What's happening?" Keke is desperate. "Can't you help her?"

"It's good. It means she's surfacing."

"She's choking to death!"

"She's not," says Arronax. "She's coming back to us."

Silver writhes and gulps. Her eyes roll back so far it looks like she has giant pearls for eyes.

Seth elbows his way to the side of Silver's bed, unties her wrists. He levers her limp torso against his chest, cradles her small body. He holds the back of her bandaged head, pushes his cheek up against hers, tries to infuse her with his warmth and what's left of his vitality. He kisses her cheek hard.

Silver starts blinking, and her eyes spin back to normal. One last gasp that seems to take all the oxygen out of the atmosphere and then she's there, back in the room with them, body and mind.

"Silver!" says Mally, and grabs her other hand.

Silver sits there, taking in the surroundings. She looks down at her chest, then back up at her family. She swallows hard and is about to say something when Kate starts gasping in exactly the same way, and they crowd around her, too. Kate's surfacing is more violent. She thrashes around as if she's fighting someone in a dream. She retches and shouts.

"Kate," says Morgan. "Everything's okay. Can you hear me? Silver's okay."

Kate retches again, and then her body starts vibrating with some kind of seizure. Bright blood trickles out of her nose.

"Shit!" shouts Keke. "What's happening to her?"

"I don't know," says the DarkDoc. "Kate? Kate? Can you hear me?" He tries to feel her pulse with his fingers but she is flailing too much.

"Mom!" shouts Mally.

"If she doesn't come out of it right now then it's too late," says Arronax.

The thin blood runs and gets onto everything. Her whole body shakes, every part of her. Seth takes her hand like he did with Silver and the seizure stops. And then it's worse because her limbs and mouth go slack and she looks dead. The only colour in her face is that bright red smear of blood. It's as if her body cools and shrinks right in front of them.

"Kate?" Unadulterated fear tears Seth's voice like a piece of paper. "Kate!"

Enormous seconds tick by.

"Mom," says Silver, in a little-girl voice.

There's a hint of movement on Kate's face, an almost invisible twitch of an eyebrow.

"It's over," says Arronax. "We're out of time."

The clock ticks over to 14:00.

Zack swears loudly and kicks a nearby chair. Bernard covers her face with her hands. Keke's eyes stream.

In the distance: wild whooping and crashing. Clattering.

"They're going to be able to get in here, now," says Arronax, eyes flashing with fear. It's only a safe room when the power is on. They know I'm here. They'll kill us all."

"Mom," Silver says again, with more power, and she reaches over and takes her mother's limp hand. As Silver touches Kate, it's as if she's given her an electric shock, because Kate jolts up and her eyes click open. Kate turns her head to see Silver and they look into each other's eyes. Their chests rise and fall with hard breaths, and then the lights go out.

TWEAK

93

"Silver?" says Kate, "are you okay?"

Silver nods. The two of them are helped out of their beds, and the others push the gurneys to the side of the room. Keke cleans the blood off Kate's face, and Mally brings them water to drink.

"Barricade the doors," says Arronax, and Morgan and Bernard do so, fumbling in the dark.

"It's not going to hold," says Morgan. "We need something heavier."

"We need to get into the safe room."

Arronax tries to unlock the safe room door again, and is again denied access.

Instead they lock the latch of the office door manually with the deadbolt, then they push a couch and a filing cabinet against the door. "They'll just batter it open, anyway," says Morgan. "They'll find their way in."

"I don't understand," says Mally. "Why would they want to come in here? Isn't there enough to plunder in the rest of the building?"

"It's because I'm in here," says Arronax.

Mally turns to her in the dark. "But why?"

"They blame me for the roguebot attack."

"Because Nautilus engineered them? Because you champion their rights?" asks Mally.

Arronax taps a spherical battery-powered touch lamp and brings it to the middle of the room, and it's like the moon is there with them. Their long shadows paint the walls.

Arronax's face is a mask. "Because I designed the V1R1S."

BLOODTHIRSTY BOT HUNTERS

94

Mally's affronted. "You did *not*."

Arronax looks at him with cold pools for eyes. "I'm afraid I did."

Kate can't think of anything to say. *Is this really happening? Is this the real world?*

"Arro," says Seth, deadly serious. "What the fuck are you talking about?"

Arronax takes a deep breath. Her skin is ceramic in the lunar light. "It's my fault. All of this. Everything. I designed the V1R1S."

"No, you didn't." Kate's voice is hoarse. "You wouldn't."

"That doesn't make any sense," says Seth, coughing into his handkerchief. "Why would you want your machines to malfunction?"

Kate notices Seth's blood and her stomach turns to stone.

"I didn't. I don't. I just made a mistake with … I didn't think the design through properly. Rather … the actual design is perfect, I know it is. It's the delivery system that—"

"I can't believe what you're saying."

"It was supposed to be an improvement! It was the smallest tweak in code. All it was supposed to do was to allow the robosapiens to say 'no'."

"You programmed artificial intelligence to refuse humans' instructions."

"They deserve the right to say 'no'!"

"Jesus, Arronax."

"It was meant to improve their existence."

Keke crosses her arms in front of her. "Have you seen the clips? That hotel butler who crushed that woman? That school bus that drove off the bridge with fifty kids in it?"

Arronax's hands fly up to her face. "I know."

"Do you?"

"I know!" Arronax shouts. "I know, okay? Do you think this is easy for me? None of it was meant to happen. The tweak was supposed to be an insignificant upgrade. But, somehow—"

Seth paces, limping, in the near-dark. "I can't fucking believe this."

Kate's again caught by the idea that this isn't really happening.

"Part of the problem was I couldn't access all the machines, I couldn't do a recall. Not without drawing attention to what I was trying to do. So … I had this idea. I was looking at my flu vax sticker and then it came to me. I made the code … contagious. It was the only way to spread it. I tested it and tested it till I was certain it was safe. But I think that it must have somehow, I don't know … mutated. Like a real virus does when faced with resistance. I can't explain it."

Seth sits down with a grimace, and rubs his eyes.

"Regardless of who is responsible for the uprising," says Zack, "we have more important things to discuss."

"More important?" Mally looks at him. "Are you serious? There is a horde of vicious Bot Hunters moments away from breaking down that door and killing us all, and you have something else you'd like to discuss."

Zack regards everyone in the room. "What if I told you there's a way to escape?"

Mally looks at the barricaded door. "Not very likely."

There is a huge bang from outside, then another one.

"Fuck," says Kate. Not particularly eloquent, but at the moment it's all she can manage.

Bernard and Morgan shore up the barricade with whatever pieces of furniture they can grab in the dark. The hammering continues. They'll break right through soon. The Bot Hunters outside are yelling and the sound makes Kate's heart pulse neon green.

"She should be here by now," says Bernard.

"Who?" asks Kate. She's so relieved to have made it back but this, here and now, feels just as much of a dream as her immersion did. A dark room, Arro confessing, bloodthirsty Bot Hunters baying at the door. She grabs Silver and holds her close. Bernard doesn't answer her.

"She'll be here," says Zack.

SHOULDER CROW

94

The horde finally manages to break a hole in the door. An arm comes through, crusted and grimy, and searches for the handle. It can't reach. Instead they continue to chip away at the aperture, through which flows a stream of angry cursing, and the smoky scent of civil war. Kate clutches Silver to her; imagines what the savages would do to her delicate daughter.

A hologram avatar appears in the middle of the room: an ivory crossbow with a diamond-tipped arrow on a white disc.

Zack and Bernard both look relieved. The light on the safe room door changes from red to green, and then it swings open. Solonne walks out, glowing in her trademark white robe.

"Solonne," Kate says. Could this scene be any more surreal? The robe is like a beacon of light in the dim room.

"What are you doing here?"

Arronax touches the top of her head, as if something has occurred to her for the first time. Her mouth hangs open.

"It's you. *You're* the anonymous founder of the Lipworth."

Kate considers all the white everywhere, from the tiles to the ceiling—she should have guessed Solonne had something to do with it. The limbo where Silver was trapped was white too.

How long had Solonne been in the safe room? How did she manage to get here unscathed? Then Kate remembers the SurroTribe, and how handy they are at guarding important people. She pictures hundreds of SurroSisters all over the city with their white uniforms and bows and arrows, like glowing sentinels, or angels. The green light on the safe room door fades and dies. There will be no more locking it now.

There's a howl from behind the main door, and the hole is quickly widening.

"We don't have much time," says Solonne to Zack. "Have you explained the situation?"

"Not yet. Kate's just come out of the Mezzanine. I haven't told her anything."

Not for lack of trying. Kate remembers the day she met Zack in the unisex bathroom at The Gordhan so long ago. *I have to tell you something*, he had said urgently to her, before he was whisked away by the cops. It's haunted her for twelve years; a grey-feathered shoulder crow. Kate is ready to listen.

The opening in the door is now large enough for a man to claw his way through. As he crams his arms and shoulders in, Bernard whips him on the back of the head with her steel baton, knocking him out and temporarily plugging the hole.

"You get out here, you robofucker!" shouts one of the mob from outside.

"Your machines killed my brother!" yells someone else.

"Come out here or we'll kill you all!"

Kate trembles as the dread billows and swirls around her like dirty wind. They'll break in here. Who will they murder first?

"Ow, Mom," says Silver, and Kate loosens her grip.

Arronax's face is a tight mask; her hair is pulsing purple.

"Don't even think about it," says Seth, coughing. Kate imagines his lungs bubbling with blood.

"I have to."

"Are you crazy? Do you know what they'll do to you?"

Arronax's body language is firm with resolve. "I'm going."

"That's insane," says Kate. "You'll be dead within a minute."

"If they have me they'll leave you alone."

"No, they won't," says Seth.

Keke and the kids watch with wide eyes.

"Even if they don't, it'll buy you some extra time."

"You're not going out there, Arro," says Seth. "No way."

Solonne clears her throat. "It's the right thing to do."

"It's crazy!" says Seth. "I won't let you!"

Arronax moves closer to Seth and lowers her voice. "You've never told me what to do. Don't start now."

"Please don't do it. They'll rip you to shreds."

"I'll get what I deserve."

The thudding on the door is louder now, as if the men outside have found something heavy to barge it with.

"No one deserves that. You made a mistake."

"A mistake that killed a hundred thousand people."

"You meant well."

"You know what they say about the road to hell, right?"

"All we need is five minutes," says Solonne. "Then we'll be safe."

Arronax nods. "It's the least I can do."

SOUL SHARD

96

"I'll go with you," says Vega. "Protect you."

"So you'll *both* die? No way!" says Mally.

"We won't die. My roscoe is fully loaded and my jujitsu is on fleek."

"It's too risky."

"Mally," says Solonne. "Do you trust me?"

Mally turns towards her. "Of course." Everyone in the room knows he wouldn't be alive if it weren't for Solonne.

"Then, please, listen to reason. Let Arro and Vega distract them while we escape."

"Escape?" says Keke, motioning at the battered door. "There's nowhere to escape to!"

"What if they're killed?"

"At least *we'll* be alive," Solonne says. "If they don't go out there ... it's over for all of us."

Morgan says in a low voice, "They're going to die either way."

The words hang in the air.

"I don't want to live without Vega." Mally blinks away hot tears. "She's everything."

"Think of your mother, and Seth, and Silver. Everyone in this room will die if you don't let them go."

Mally starts sobbing.

"Don't worry, Purest Human," says Vega. She unbuttons her top again, just like she did hours ago, for a completely different reason. Sex and death, magnetically entwined, forever pushing and pulling at one another.

Vega reveals her chest, and opens the pocket that lies over her heart. She clicks out a ruby DNA chip with her star-shaped Alpha Lyrae logo on it: her Soul Shard.

"Everything I am is in this chip."

"It's not *you*, though," cries Mally.

"It is," Vega says, touching her breastbone: warmed titanium under stamped silicone. "This body, this is the thing that's not me. I can get another one of these, but that chip is nothing but me. Do you understand?"

"No!" Mally shouts through his tears. "If you're going out there, I am too!"

There's a massive thud on the door that dislodges the shored-up furniture. Bernard and Zack rush to pack it back.

Zack gives Arronax a soft look. "If you're going, now is the time."

"You're not going!" Mally sobs.

"Mally. Mally. I need to tell you something," whispers Vega.

"It won't change anything," cries Mally. "Nothing you say will change how I feel about you."

"I have the V1R1S."

"What? No, you don't."

"I do. That man from NASP—"

Mally remembers Govender interfering with Vega's hardware. Remembers the flash disk he plugged into Vega's neck, the LED lighting up, and then the quick stashing of it in the inside pocket of his flashy new suit.

"No." Mally shakes his head. "Oh, no."

"This body is broken." Vega takes Mally's chin in her hand. "Look at it."

Mally blinks and studies Vega. Her head is still conked in from last night's attack, and the silicone skin is coming away from where Arronax sutured it back onto her silver skull. She has a frozen neck joint, and a pronounced limp from her broken ankle. He imagines the insidious virus teeming all over her insides, painting over her code with evil. Once it takes over completely, she'll kill him as if he means nothing to her.

Oh, his heart is breaking. Right there, right then, it's as if someone is squeezing it right inside his chest cavity. The pain blooms inside his chest like the smoke of an atom bomb. It takes every ounce of will he has to stay standing, instead of melting down to his knees.

It hurts so much.

"This body is broken, but my Shard is pure." Vega puts it in Mally's hand and closes his fingers over it.

Mally tries to rise above the ache. "I love you," he says, almost knocking her over with a bear hug. "I love you, Alpha Lyrae."

Vega steps away. "I know."

Mally looks as if he's about to say something, and Vega smiles. "I love you too, Purest Human."

"It's settled, then," says Arronax, smoothing her hair. It turns a serious shade of aubergine and makes her look even paler than before. Another huge bang on the door and the furniture is again dislodged.

Zack moves to kiss Arronax on the cheek, and as he does so, he slips a quill into her pocket. They exchange a look of understanding.

Seth hugs Arronax, grasps her hand. She offers Seth his Vektor back, but he refuses. He disables the bio-info in his name and adds her dynap code in its place. He shows her the trigger, and how to hold the Vektor so it doesn't kick back too hard. They look into each other's eyes as if there is more to say.

Arronax breaks away and hammers on the door with the heel of her hand. "I'm coming out!" she shouts. "Stand down! Stand down and I'll come out!"

Seth coughs up more blood. The horde outside quietens a little.

Mally puts the Shard in his pocket, and he kisses Vega goodbye. The tears are still running down his face. Kate catches Vega's eye and nods, and Vega nods back. They move the furniture away from the door to allow Arronax and Vega passage. Seth puts his arm around the still-sobbing Mally. They open the door just enough, and the two women slip out.

"Get into the safe room," says Solonne. "Quickly."

SHIELD

97

Arronax and Vega hold on to each other as they move out of the room and into the clutches of the mob. Arronax holds the Vektor in a way she hopes makes her look like she's used the weapon before.

"Why did you lie to Mally?" she whispers to Vega, "about being infected?"

The deceit had shocked Arronax. Not because she knows Vega doesn't have the V1R1S, but because she built, refined, and polished the design for 7thGen robosapiens, and she knows for a fact it's impossible for them to be dishonest.

"It was the only way he'd let me go."

The dirty pack grabs at the women and pulls them away from the door, to the middle of the crowd. There must be two dozen people there, all shouting at them. A man hawks and spits in Arronax's face. When she wipes the saliva away, her trembling hands betray her fear. The barbarians are armed with solar lamps and makeshift weapons and guns. Arronax and Vega turn around slowly within the circle, not wanting to turn their backs on any one of them for too long. When Arronax sees Govender, the NASP imposter, she trains the gun on him. He's out of place in his smart blue suit in the tide of ripped and grimy ragbag uniforms of the Bot Hunters.

Arronax stiffens with anxiety; her mouth is cotton.

"Ah, look," says one of them. "She's brought her robowhore with her."

A man with a Vektor takes aim, and Vega moves instinctively in front of Arronax to act as a shield.

"Wait," Govender says. "I've been dreaming of this moment for months. I want to enjoy this."

Arronax realizes Govender is the one who's been beaming her death threats.

"Fuck that," says one of the men. "They're mine." He takes aim again and the suit knocks the weapon out of his hand. "What the—" He rolls his hands into fists, ready to fight, and Govender pulls out a subrocket from the breast pocket of his shiny jacket and shoots the Bot Hunter in the head. Maroon brain matter sprays out of the back of his skull and he falls to the floor. This shocks a few people in the crowd, arouses others. Ready for blood, they rumble forward.

It's only been a minute. Not long enough for the others to escape.

Govender points his rocket at Arronax now, and searches her face. She returns his scowl with the glare of the Vektor. Her trigger finger twitches, but if she shoots him it might set off the rest of them.

Arronax needn't have worried; the men advance steadily without any encouragement from her. Her hair turns white.

It's a strange thing, when you know you're about to die. It's not like your life flashes before your eyes, not really. It's more like a total surrender of everything, from your fondest childhood memories to the designs you'll never complete, to the feeling of your lover's skin on yours. Regrets and joy swirl together into a strange bittersweet moment of absolute clarity, a crystal instant when you realise you'll never see the ocean again, never again sink your feet into the soft warm sand or hear the waves crash and roar, and you're strangely accepting of it because the knowledge pulses in your chest that in this lifetime you've loved more than you've lost.

"All right," Govender says to the hopped-up horde, "take them apart."

The Bot Hunters are an arm's length from them, now less, and Arronax starts shooting. She takes out four or five of the men before they wrench the gun out of her hands and she screams as they struggle. Their hungry paws grab at her body. A blue-eyed man with a rusted blade is ready to drive it into Arro's stomach.

Arronax roots around in her lab coat pocket for the quill, uncaps the injection pen, and, beneath her lab coat, jams it into her thigh. There is a hot current to her heart.

She hugs Vega close.

"Ready?" Arronax whispers, feeling the drug taking hold. Vega nods.

"Now."

Vega pops open her shoulder cap and Arronax presses the red self-destruct button. There's a flash of impossible white as Vega detonates, and the concentrated explosion takes out everybody in the room so quickly no one lives to hear the sound of the bomb.

GENESIS CHILD

98

They rush into the darkness of the safe room. Solonne closes the door behind them and stands with her back against it. Bernard lends her weight to it, too. She can't lock it without power, but the heavy steel door will offer some measure of protection.

"Get down," she says, and they do. Kate pushes Silver to the floor and covers her with her own body.

There's a loud flash and a boom.

The building shakes.

"The fuck was that?" says Seth, not wanting to know the answer.

Debris rains down around them. Kate lets Silver go. The

safe door swings open, allowing them a dim view of the main door that has been knocked off its hinges. Shrapnel from the exploded furniture crackles on the floor. The barbarians are dead, but Kate knows there'll be more on their way.

Seth and Mally look desolate.

"Let's run for it," says Keke.

"No," says Solonne. "There're a hundred more of them on their way in. There's no way we'll get out in time."

Kate breathes in the heavy black air. Smoke burns her eyes.

There's a scratching sound, and then a spark and the smell of phosphorous and chlorate as Solonne lights a match, and then a candle.

"You need to listen very carefully for the next minute," says Zack. He has everyone's attention. "There's only one way to get out of here, and we need to move fast."

Kate looks at the broken door and the dead bodies outside, coated in blood and ash.

"Kate, Silver, you're the ones who know how to do it."

"No I don't," says Kate. "I have no idea."

"You do, because you've just done it. You two escaped the Mezzanine, which is a lot more difficult than this will be. It was essential practice, and you succeeded."

"Experience Points," says Silver.

"Exactly," says Zack. "And now you're ready."

Keke touches her bandaged back and grimaces. "Ready for what?"

"For the next level," says Solonne.

Kate's brain whirrs. "I don't understand. This is real life, not an immersion. There is no next level. Unless you mean—"

Zack looks into her eyes and Kate finds she can't look away. Violet Velcro.

"Unless you mean *dying*," says Kate.

Zack doesn't break eye contact. "Think of it as levelling up."

Kate feels as if her head is imploding in a hundred shades of neon.

"Did you just say what I thought you said?"

"We don't have much time," says Solonne, flames in her cheeks. "We need to do it now. The others are close."

"That day at The Gordhan when I said I needed to tell you something. It wasn't the right time or place then because you weren't ready to hear it."

"Zack's entire existence is for you, about you," says Solonne. "You think it was a coincidence that he worked with Keke on that trial?" She gestures around the room.

"Do you think any of this is a coincidence?"

"The prophecy," says Keke.

Solonne nods. "Yes."

"That prophecy was about *Mally*," says Kate. "The Genesis Child will lead us to the ledge. Mally's the Genesis child."

"Are you sure about that?" asks the Matriarx.

"Of course I am. You told me so, yourself."

"You heard what you wanted to hear. You think of Mally as the stronger child, but Silver is the one. You've seen her super-abilities. Silver's always been the one."

Kate thinks of Silver's Atrium jack-in pod. 'GK' the engraving had said. Kate knows there's always been something different about Silver, knows deep down that what Solonne is saying is true. *Impossible to kill,* the guy at the Atrium had said. *Ghost. Genesis Kid.*

"But what does it mean?"

"What does it mean?" says Solonne. "It means that when Silver turns sixteen it'll be the end of everything."

"I'll be sixteen in a few hours," says Silver.

"Which is why I created the Mezzanine," says Solonne.

Kate splutters.

"I needed you to break Zack out of SkyRest, and I needed

you to both get meshed in order to understand what we're about to tell you. There was no way you'd agree to free Zack or get the neural lace without me forcing your hand by trapping Silver in the Mezzanine."

"Forcing my hand?" Kate says, fury burning a hole in her stomach. "I almost died at SkyRest. I was almost torn apart. I had brain surgery without anaesthetic. *I had to kill my daughter.* Do you have any idea—?"

"I'm sorry. I wish it had been easier for both of you."

"You're *sorry?*" says Kate.

"The V1R1S mutation," says Keke, looking at Solonne, her understanding beginning to dawn, "That was also you."

"I had help," Solonne says, looking at the DarkDoc, who has a shadow on his face Kate's never seen before. Bernard stands guard at the door.

"You fuckers," says Keke. "Solonne. Zack. Morgan. You were all in on it."

Kate's rage builds, her hands are fists.

Seth coughs and spits blood on the floor. "And you let Arro believe she had caused the rebellion when all she was trying to do was to make the world a better place. And you let her walk out of here to claim a redemption she didn't even need."

"Don't worry about Arronax," says Solonne. "We took care of her."

"You certainly did." The candlelight flickers in Seth's eyes.

Kate looks at Morgan and thinks of being in bed with him, how uninhibited she was. How sick she feels with the intimate betrayal. How could she have allowed this to happen to her again, to trust and be betrayed like this *again*? She thinks of Marmalade James and wants to scream and pull out her hair. She wants to punch them all. She wants get out of this room where tentacles of claustrophobia are reaching for her breath.

"You said you sent Silver *home*."

"I know it's difficult to hear, Kate," says Morgan, "but we did it for you."

WORLD'S WORST JEHOVAH'S WITNESS

99

Too many far-out concepts hover in the air around Kate; she can't get a handle on what is happening, what is really happening. Not what people want her to believe, not what is easy to believe, but the real truth of this moment. How does this all fit together? The betrayal is a stab of bitter on her tongue, a hint of cyanide, like chewing an apple seed. How fitting.

"So how do we get out of here?" asks Keke.

"They want us to kill ourselves," says Kate. "That's how we surfaced from the Mezzanine."

"Seems a little counterintuitive," says Seth, coughing. "We're trying to stay alive here, in case you've forgotten." Kate can tell he's finding it harder and harder to breathe.

"After all we've been through!" Kate paces. "Van der Heever, Mouton, Jackson, Lumin. Fighting to stay alive, fighting to keep the kids alive. After all of that, you want us to kill ourselves."

"Don't think of it as killing yourself," says Zack.

"Ha," says Seth. "I know where this is going. Here's a gun! But don't think of it as a gun. Here's a knife! But don't think of it as a knife. The power of positive thinking, right?"

Zack shakes his head. "All those people I helped—"

"Killed," says Keke. "All those people you killed."

"I saved them."

"Saved them? Is that what they're calling it nowadays?"

"What Ramphele didn't tell you is that all those people wanted to die."

"So … you're an angel of mercy now."

"They were all suffering. All I did was introduce them to the truth."

"And what's that?"

"That they could escape this reality for a better one. That they can enter the larger domain of reality above this world."

"Oh my God," says Keke. "Seriously? Escape this reality for a better one? You're a fucking evangelist? Are you going to tell us you're the world's worst Jehovah's Witness now?"

"Best Jehovah's Witness," says Kate.

"What?"

"Well, he'd be the world's best Jehovah's Witness, wouldn't he? By getting this far?"

"I know it's a difficult concept to get your head around," says Zack.

"Understatement," says Keke.

Kate puts a warm hand on her forehead, as if it will help her to understand. "You're saying ... Heaven exists?"

"No," says Zack. "Not unless your version of Heaven means stepping up into the real world."

"Fuck." Seth knuckle-scrubs his hair.

"I'm not asking you to kill yourself," says Zack.

"Really?" says Keke. "That's what it sounds like."

"What I mean is, it's not coming from me. The message."

"Who, then?" asks Kate. "Who sent you?"

Zack's eyes are alight. "You did."

THIS IS WHAT KOOL-AID TASTES LIKE

100

"Bullshit," says Kate. "I think I would have remembered that."

"It's not something you can remember here."

"Remember *here*?"

"We're not on the same plane of consciousness here. Think of it … think of the place you're going to … as the future."

"Holy fuck. We're time travelling now."

"Not quite."

"Well, that's a relief," snarks Keke.

"Put it this way," says Zack. "The future has already happened."

Kate sits down and gives her thigh a hard pinch. It hurts. "So …" she says, looking up at Zack, speaking slowly and clearly. "You're saying I sent you from the future."

"No, but that's probably the easiest way for you to understand it right now."

There's hollering in the distance. The new barbarians have entered the building. More apoca-pirates are bashing to get in.

"I'm trying to explain it to you in the simplest and quickest way possible, because if this is going to work, we need to do it right now. But I know you won't do it if you don't understand the stakes."

"Tell me, then. Tell me in the simplest way possible."

Zack and Kate's eyes connect. "I need you to have an open mind."

Seth's breathing is worse than ever. He smacks himself on the chest, trying to clear his airways, but it just makes him cough more. His handkerchief is now dripping red.

"Christ on a cracker. Just get on with it," says Keke.

Zack draws a breath. It's clear he has to build himself up to what he's about to say.

"Did you ever wonder how I was able to wipe myself off the security footage at the Carbon Factory?"

"Of course we did," says Keke. "Not just from the footage, but from people's minds too. I questioned every one of those jury members we did duty with and not one of them remembered you from the Lundy trial."

"Impossible," says Kate.

"Not impossible," says Zack. "We've been doing it forever."

"Doing what?"

"Re-programming thoughts. Tweaking memories. Smoothing over glitches."

"What the fuck are you talking about?"

"Are you sure you don't know?" asks Zack. "Because I think that, deep down, you do."

"I don't know anything," Kate says. "Tell me what's going on."

Zack clears his throat, steeples his fingers. "This is a simulation."

Kate blinks. She doesn't understand. "What's a simulation? This room? This day?"

"He means everything," says Keke. "Everything's a simulation. He means our lives have been a simulation."

"*Are* a simulation," says Zack.

"Shut up," says Kate.

"I know it's difficult to hear—really difficult to hear—but I promise you it's true."

Kate stares at him. She was beginning to believe some of the things he said, but now he's gone too far. He's delusional and dangerous and belongs back in the crim colony. Why the fuck had she risked her life to break him out?

"That's why there's a suicide contagion," Zack says. "That's why more and more people are ending their lives here. Not because people are suicidal but because they've learnt the truth—that you need to die in this sim to get back to the real world."

"Whoah," says Keke. "Go home, Girdler, you're drunk."

"It's expected, of course. That you'd be skeptical," he says.

Keke laughs. "The Net knows I like a good mind-fuck, Zachary Girdler, but you have gone too far."

Kate doesn't find it funny at all. "Okay, I can't," she says. "I give up. I can't do this anymore."

Seth coughs. "It's not impossible."

"What?" Kate spins to look at him.

"What he's saying. It's a well-endorsed theory. Scientifically speaking, the odds of this world being a simulation are much higher than it *not* being a simulation."

"Not you too," says Kate. "Mister Never-Drink-the-Kool-

Aid. I've got news for you. *This* is the Kool-Aid. This is exactly what the fucking Culty Kool-Aid tastes like."

"No," says Seth. "Kate. I know you don't want to hear this, but mathematically, it makes complete sense. There's very little probability of us *not* living in a simulation."

"Shut up," says Keke, blinking her wide eyes.

"But I can feel that I'm real," says Kate. "I know deep down that I'm real. Nothing you can say will change that."

Zack is gentle with her. "You feel real because that is how you've been programmed to feel. Like a robosapien is programmed to feel human, and they do, because they don't know any better. That's why it's so hard for you to grasp this. You were never meant to hear the truth. You were designed to function within the rules of the game, not to subvert them. By its very nature, it's a box you cannot think outside of."

Being shut in an invisible box is still being shut in a box.

"But the neural lace expands your consciousness," says Solonne. "You've never been able to see the whole truth before, but now you can, if you choose to."

"Quarks," mutters Seth.

"What now?" says Keke.

"Quarks. The rules that govern subatomic particles' behaviour are almost identical to computer codes that correct for errors in manipulating data in computers." When Kate stares at him, he says, "Basically, it looks like everyday particles are being run on computer codes. The universe *is* mathematics. That can only point to one thing: that it's been *designed*. You know the Fibonacci ratio, Kate. We spoke about it the day we found each other again."

"I remember," she says.

"It occurs in so many aspects of the cosmos, and that's just the beginning. The constants of nature—like the strength of fundamental forces—have values that look fine tuned. Even the smallest alterations would mean that atoms would become unstable. That planets would be catapulted out of their orbits. There's only one possible explanation. The universe—this universe, anyway—has been constructed."

Kate wants to reject what her brother is saying. It's just too far out, too conspiracy-theorist. The conspiracy to end all conspiracies.

"Look at the hyper-reality achieved in the games Silver plays at the Atrium. Our tech is still lagging, but the time will come when it'll be possible for us to create something similar to our universe—allowing us to play God—then it'll stand to reason that a civilisation one level above us with advanced computing power has done the same thing, and that their work is the reason you and I are living and breathing."

"You of all people," Kate says to Seth. Brilliant, cynical Seth. "How can you believe this?"

"It's not about belief, Kate. It's mathematics. I'm not the only one. Bostrom. Minsky. Musk. They all said the same

thing. You can't deny science. It's not just plausible, but …
inescapable. If you look closely—some might say, too
closely—on a molecular level, you'll see that you can only
zoom in so much before it gets blurry. Fuzzy."

"Like it's pixellated?" asks Keke.

"Exactly," says Seth. "Look closely enough, and
everything is fucking pixellated."

CYBERCOSMIC DUST

101

"You know all those times you've wondered if this is all there is?" asks Zack. "You know that feeling? Like, surely there must be more to life? Well, now you know why. Because intuitively, you've always known that there's more out there. Kate, you've always known."

Kate understands this is true—the black hole that has been with her forever. Gaping all through her life despite finding her lost twin, despite being reunited with her biological parents, despite giving birth to a child of her own and getting the gift of Mally. The dark vacuum has haunted her for as long as she can remember.

Seth rubs his face. "I feel it too."

"There are other clues," says Zack. "Clues you couldn't understand before now. Before you laced up."

"Like what?" asks Kate.

"Your synaesthesia. Your numbers and colours, the shapes and smells. It's residue from the real world."

Kate thinks of Silver's jack-in pod again, and remembers the slogan splashed in violet on the wall.

As we design, so, perhaps, we were designed.

Kate looks at Silver. "The game you play. You design simulations."

Silver nods.

"Simulations like this."

Silver nods again. "It's called co-creation. It's about beauty and purpose, like art. The players co-construct the worlds they play in."

"So this all makes sense to you."

"Yes," says Silver.

"Silver will lead you," says Solonne. "It's what she was born to do."

The chaos is closer now. Soon they'll be here and then it will all be over, anyway. Even if nothing Zack says is true, a quick, painless suicide in here will be better than being killed by the bloodthirsty barbarians. Who knows what they'll do to her, do to Silver?

The players co-construct the worlds they play in.

The new knowledge shines like a light in Kate's head. She's starting to understand. The beginning thoughts of new concepts stream into her head. Things start to become obvious, when before they were obscured by the everyday drama of her life. The idea of artifice nags at Kate. Hasn't she thought it a hundred times, herself? That her life seems to be on some kind of cruel fictive loop? The burnt orange *deja vu*.

The same story told in spiralling, parallel ways with slight variations: Evil doctor van Heerden; Evil cult leader Lumin. Kate and Seth being abducted as toddlers; Mally and Silver being abducted as small children. Kate breaking her arm—the same arm—over and over. Cutting a chip out of her head in 2021; cutting her head open to insert the mesh in 2034. Rescuing Silver from the Resurrectors; Rescuing Silver from the Mezzanine. Mally falling in love with his robotic puppy; Mally falling in love with Vega. Kate being betrayed by James; Kate being betrayed by Morgan. Kate cutting off James's thumb; Lumin cutting off Silver's little finger. Now, looking at Zack, the familiar stranger, she can't help thinking that she's lived this story before.

You've always known.

A breeze of hot sparks blows inside Kate's head. The fairytale retellings now also make sense. That's what her subconscious was trying to tell her when she was newly meshed and immersed in the Mezzanine. Whoever designed this sim was playing with the story arcs of classic fairytales. Hansel and Gretel was, of course, Kate and Seth being kidnapped as children. After that came The Pied Piper: The outwardly benevolent-looking Maistre Lumin and his rathunters leading the children away. Today's story is Snow White, or Sleeping Beauty: porcelain-skinned Silver under the spell of Solonne, catatonic, waiting to be brought back to life. Kate in the rose maze, Kate in the labyrinth. Abduction, hypnosis, poison, roses, thorns, rescuing, redemption, re-awakening. She knew this. Inherently, she knew this.

As we design, so, perhaps, we were designed.

"This simworld is ending," says Zack. "Soon it'll be nothing more than cybercosmic dust. It's always had this expiry date."

Solonne takes a step closer. "That's what Lumin didn't understand. He thought if he killed the Genesis Child he'd save the world, but this world is broken beyond repair. The fact that the expiry date is the same as Silver's sixteenth birthday is symbolic more than anything else. Nothing anyone does in this sim would change that. Of course, Lumin has a God Complex, and he doesn't listen to sense. He believed his own interpretation of the prophecy, and that he could influence the algorithms by killing Mally. He thought he was saving the world."

"You're in touch with Lumin?" asks Kate.

"I wouldn't say that."

"But he's around?"

"Loosely speaking, yes." Solonne's eyes say: *We haven't seen the last of him.* "He's caused me such headaches, that man."

"He almost derailed the mission when he got me arrested," says Zack. "Twelve brain-bleached years in SkyRest was *not* part of the plan."

"Lumin got you arrested?"

"In an indirect way, yes. Keke only made that deal with Ramphele to avoid arrest so that she could help find the twins and be with Marko when he way dying. Both of those situations were caused by the Resurrectors, led by Lumin."

"But why couldn't you just ... write yourself out of SkyRest?" asks Kate.

"We can smooth over glitches," says Zack. "Breaking out of a high security underground penal labour colony is not a glitch. I never expected to be convicted, but when I was, I thought I'd have time to work something out. Then they drugged me and wiped my memory before I could come up with a strategy to escape. I lost who I was when I was in there. Lost the plan. Lost everything."

"It all worked out, though," says Solonne. "Just like I knew it would. Sometimes we have to trust the process. It actually wrapped up quite neatly. Breaking you out of SkyRest was the perfect qualification challenge for Kate."

"Easy for you to say," says Zack. "You weren't the one getting your brains vacuumed out of your head."

"You needed some Suffering Points, anyway," says Solonne. "Yours were way down."

"Suffering Points are like karma," says Silver to Kate. "You need a certain number before you can level up."

I'm pretty sure we all qualify, now, thinks Kate, looking around at the people she loves. Seth coughing up blood, Keke with her back sliced open, Mally with his heartache, Silver still recovering from the Mezzanine.

"So, the expiry date of this simulation can't be changed," says Zack. "But the sim creator wants you levelled up before that happens."

POISON & LACE

102

Solonne retrieves a neat metallic case from her white pine-leather shoulder bag.

"This part is easy," says Zack. "Luckily. You've been through the worst."

A light blue breeze of relief.

Solonne opens the case to reveal a neat row of ten narrow gulleys in black foam. Three are empty, and the rest cushion seven injection pens. They're made of the most delicate glass and steel.

"Why the fancy tech?" says Seth. "If what you're saying is true then surely a quick bullet would do the job?"

"No." Zack takes the case from Solonne and snaps out the first of the pens. "Dying is not enough to level up. People think they can just kill themselves to escape this simulation—like they do in Eden 7.0—but this sim is a far more sophisticated system. It's not a game. Its technology is hundreds of years ahead of this reality. You can't just die. You need the tech, too. You need the neural lace."

"An injectable mesh?" says the DarkDoc, inspecting the quill Zack hands him.

"Not just mesh. It's the perfect combination of poison and lace. Think of escaping this sim as a portal that is only open for a couple of seconds. You only get to see that portal as you die, and you only get to go through it if you're meshed. It's a delicate thing."

Zack hands everyone a pen, apart from Solonne.

"You're not coming?" asks Bernard.

"No," says Solonne. "I've done the job I was meant to do."

Kate knows it's not quite as simple as that. There are eight of them in the room, and only seven quills.

"Who has the other three?"

"Arronax had one," says Zack. "Then we sent one to Marko, and one to your mother, but we have no way of knowing if they reached them, and if they'll use them in time."

Her mother! Kate pictures Anne in another dimension, healthy, unravaged, and out of her wheelchair.

The voices are close now.

"Hurry," Solonne urges.

Kate stands on an imaginary ledge. There's nothing underneath her but air the colour of Skiss Sky, wisps, cool trails of cirrus. Open sky everywhere, the crispest air to breathe. She takes giant lungfuls of it. Will she jump? Will she make her kids jump? After all she's been through to keep them alive, is she going to now leap into oblivion with them?

"Fuck," she says.

Keke looks at her with wide eyes. "You can say that again."

"What do we do?"

"We level up or die trying," says Seth.

"Kill ourselves?" says Kate. "Kill the twins?"

Her body feels like it's filled with acid.

"You can't," says Keke. "No way."

Zack steps forward with the case of quills. "It's the only way."

Kate moves to take one but hesitates. "I can't believe we're going to do this."

"Are we?" asks Mally. His eyes are still swollen.

"Holy fuck," says Keke. "Are you really going to do it? You believe this is real?"

"I don't know what I believe," says Kate. "All I know is that if we don't jump right now, someone will be in here to push us. And I'd rather jump."

"Me too," says Silver. "I'm not letting those men touch me."

"I'm dying, anyway," says Seth. "I can feel it. I won't make it through the night."

"You don't know that," says Keke.

"I do. My lungs are liquefying. I won't be able to breathe soon, and I don't want to be here for that. Sim or not, I'm claiming one of those quills."

"Me too," says Mally. "I've got nothing left to live for, anyway."

"Jesus," says Keke.

Kate turns to her. "Come with us."

Keke shakes her head. "I don't like this. I'd rather stay and fight."

"We're completely outnumbered," says Kate. "They're going to stream in here any second. I was almost … I was almost pulled apart by the creeps at SkyRest … I'm not letting it happen again. And I'm not going to let it happen to you, either."

Keke still seems undecided. She doesn't have the neural lace that Kate has, so she can't see outside the box, can't see the beginnings of the truth that Kate is glimpsing. How can Kate convince her? Keke's never been one to feel much fear, so Kate changes her angle.

"It'll be an adventure," she says. It's mostly a lie, because she doesn't even know if she believes Zack yet. "It could be one of the best fucking things that ever happens to us."

Or it could be plain suicide.

Keke taps her foot, crosses her arms as she thinks. There is clattering next door.

"It's a gamble, I know," says Kate. "It's fucking metaphysical Russian Roulette. But if there is a way out of here," she gestures at the twins, "I need to take that chance. And I don't want to go without you."

As Kate pictures the spinning barrel of a star-dusted revolver hovering in the air between them, a real gunshot rings out, then another, and her vision is scored by the hard, sharp zigzags of someone's serrated scream of horror. Shark teeth. A clatter and a crystalline crash as more windows are broken. It seems the savages have claimed another victim.

"Keke, please!"

The wound on Keke's back is bleeding again.

"Okay," Keke says. "Okay. I'll do it."

And Kate wonders, with a neon jab in her stomach, if

she's doing the right thing, convincing her best friend to poison herself.

RAPTURE PARTY

103

It's easy enough to inject your own quill, but in an unspoken agreement the family decide to inject each other. They hug, and Seth approaches Mally first, who sets his jaw and offers his right shoulder, and Seth, pale as ivory, administers the mesh. Mally's eyes roll back and Seth lowers him slowly to the floor. A sob catches in Kate's throat. Seth's eyes are also wet.

Kate looks into Silver's eyes.

"Are you sure you want to do this?"

"Yes," she says. "Yes, Mom."

Kate hugs her as tightly as she can, takes her face into her hands and kisses her cheek.

"Brave girl," she says. "You've always been such a brave girl." Kate's crying as she pushes the quill into Silver's arm and catches her as she wilts into her arms. She lays her delicate body next to Mally's.

Morgan gives Kate a flat wave and administers his own shot, as does Bernard. Zack checks each one of their wrists with his fingers to make sure their hearts have stalled.

Keke hugs Kate goodbye. "So, you got what you wanted."

"What?"

"A rapture party! It's perfect. Apart from the distinct lack of funeral cake."

Kate almost laughs. "How can you joke at a time like this?"

"What do you mean?" asks Keke. "Apocalypses are always the best times to joke."

Post-diabetic Keke doesn't flinch at having to inject herself, but Seth takes the pen from her and holds her tightly. She returns the embrace. They're all weeping.

Seth hesitates before shooting her up. "Keke."

"Seth. You don't have to say anything."

"I want to."

Footsteps outside. The smell of the horde reaches them

first: The scent of malevolence seethes into the room, sweat and blood and gunpowder.

"We don't have time," says Keke.

"I want you to know how I feel about you."

Keke's eyes soften. She covers his hand with her own shaking fingers and takes her quill back.

"We don't have time," she says, and drives it into her arm.

Keke's body to sinks into him, and Kate watches as he holds her, breathing her in for a moment longer, then lays her gently down.

Kate is still crying when she and Seth sit on the floor and squeeze each other's hands.

"Will it work?" Kate asks, looking at her dead children, anxiety like a bright bomb in her skull.

"I don't know," Seth's breath comes in gasps.

She takes a deep, shuddering breath. Her whole body is shaking from the inside out. "I guess there's only one way to find out."

Kate and Seth squeeze each others hands, whispering "I love you," and then tenderly inject one other.

Kate's shocked by the sharp sting of the quill. She can feel the poison painting the inside of her veins. It's exactly as she imagines a jellyfish sting to feel. A swarm, a smack. A bright blue current of venom shooting towards her heart. A rushing feeling in her head.

The barbarians hurtle in. Three, five, then ten of them, slick with fresh blood and stained by death and depravity. Kate sees them leer at Solonne in her white robe and feels sick for her. The rushing sound is taking over Kate's vision now, but she can still make out Zack injecting himself. Zack looks over at Solonne, who nods back, her face betraying her naked fear for just an instant.

Kate's eyeballs spin back and she expects to see darkness, realising then that she doesn't expect to wake up again, but instead there is white thunder, like she's standing in front of a giant waterfall. Kate and Seth fall backwards onto the floor together, still holding hands, and it feels as if they're falling through the floor. They take their last breath, and their souls swoop out of their bodies.

EPILOGUE

NIRVANA 1.0

It's not like waking up.

Not quite. It's more like when you've been daydreaming and then something happens to snap you out of it. You weren't sleeping, but now you're certainly awake. There's a green rush of clear consciousness (Mint Crackle).

Kate's standing in a field of seeding wildflowers. Symbolic, she's sure, of life and death and regeneration. She remembers the garden in her small apartment with James, the black-petalled rose maze at the Luminary, and the creeping wild weeds at the glass-paned Atrium. The word 'atrium' is another word for heart, and it makes sense—a glass heart—as other seemingly unconnected things also all start to make sense to her now: like her colours and shapes. As if she has a more developed perspective now that she's here, as if she's above, or beyond, her previous existence.

Kate's wearing her body-fitting orange catsuit again. It energises her, makes her feel as if she can do anything, like fly through the air. She touches her stomach, her hips, to make sure she's all there. The dragon dagger is back in its sheath on her utility belt.

"Mom," says Silver, and it is, at the same time, as if she has just appeared there and has been there all along. She looks so healthy in this dimension; Kate doesn't think Silver's ever looked this vital before. She has colour in her skin: sun-ripened peaches; vanilla ice cream flecked with cinnamon. She's dressed in white, and has a SurroSis-style crossbow and a quiver of diamond-tipped arrows on her back. Her shoulders and arms are strong and ribboned with muscles.

The others are there too, and it feels right. Keke and Morgan stand behind Kate, dressed like steampunk assassins. Mally's a sophisticated robot, sleek and strong in his titanium and silicone armour. He wears Vega's Soul Shard on his chest, over his heart.

Bernard has taken the form of a large wooly dog, and is huffing warm, wet air into the grasses. Saint Bernard, of course, named after the monk who helped distressed travellers along their treacherous journey across the highest part of the Alpine path and founded a hospice there. The marching partners of travel and death.

Has everything always been so obvious? It's like Kate can

see clearly—really clearly—for the first time.

Zack appears next to Bernard, and he has also taken an avatar. He looks like himself but taller, with a glowing bronze skin, and giant fire-feather wings.

Saint Zachariah.

Ouroboros appears as a fluttering gold leaf tattoo on his chest: a serpent eating its own tail. Eternal death; eternal return.

"Where is Seth?"

"We'll find him."

"My mom? Marko? Arronax?"

"We're not sure if they all made it, but we'll try to find them too."

Kate looks around. Outside of this lush natural field there is a white desert to the left, and a sparkling cityscape to the right.

"This is it?" asks Kate. "This is the real world?"

"Not quite," says Zack. "Not yet."

"What?"

"It's the first step."

"But you said the lace … would lead us out of the simulation?"

"And it did. Now you have to level up. You can't just get

straight in. You have to prove your worth."

"It's a game," says Silver.

"I'm not good at games."

"You have help." Zack gestures at the others, and then at Silver. "Including the best player we've ever seen."

"You didn't tell me this," says Kate.

"I knew you wouldn't have come. You'd be cyberdust, and I would have failed."

"What do I do now?"

"There's only one thing you can do. Win."

"Win? And if I can't? There's nothing to go back to."

"That's right," says Zack, feathers flaming. "So I recommend you win."

He begins walking ahead, in the direction of the shimmering city, leaving sparks and singed grasses rustling in his path. Bernard the dog pants and joins his side, parting the plants with her ample, wiry-haired flanks.

Kate's nerves and energy rise in a wave, up her body. "But how?" she asks. "How do I play?"

Zack turns. Burning feathers float to the ground. "You'll figure it out. After all, you invented it."

ACKNOWLEDGMENTS

Thank you to my committed and talented team
of beta readers: Jess David Lipworth; Mack Lundy;
Kim Smith; Brenda Helfrich; Robyn Ambler,
and Michael Lawrence.

Nerine Dorman, thank you for your mad editing skillz,
and Keith and Gill Thiele for your proofreading.

Nolakhe Gozongo for sacrificing time with
your family so that you can help me with my work and
look after my kids while I write. It's no small thing.
Thank you.

Deep gratitude, as ever, to my loyal readers.
I wouldn't be able to do this without you.
A special thanks to my supporters on Patreon:
Elize van Heerden and Christine Bernard.

I'm so fortunate to have you all on my team.

WHEN TOMORROW CALLS

• SERIES •

1. Why You Were Taken (2015)

2. How We Found You (2017)

3. What Have We Done (2017)

ALSO BY JT LAWRENCE

The Memory of Water (2011)

Sticky Fingers (2016)

The Underachieving Ovary (2016)

Grey Magic (2016)

ABOUT THE AUTHOR

JT Lawrence is an Amazon bestselling author, playwright & bookdealer. She lives in Parkhurst, Johannesburg, in a house with a red front door.

STAY IN TOUCH

If you'd like to be notified of giveaways & new releases, sign up for JT Lawrence's mailing list via Facebook or on her author platform at www.jt-lawrence.com

www.ingramcontent.com/pod-product-compliance
Lightning Source LLC
Chambersburg PA
CBHW030537020726
47494CB00005B/1405